Broken: Macy's Story

Janice Broyles

Late November

BROKEN: MACY'S STORY
BY JANICE BROYLES

Published by Late November Literary
Winston Salem, NC 27107

ISBN (Print): 978-1-7341008-4-6
ISBN (E-Book): 9781734100853
Copyright 2020 by Janice Broyles
Cover design by Sweet N' Spicy designs
Interior design by Late November Literary

Available in print or online. Visit latenovemberliterary.com or
janicebroyles.com

Library of Congress Cataloging-in-Publication data
Broyles, Janice.
Broken: Macy's Story / Janice Broyles 1st ed.

Printed in the Unites States of America

Dedicated to Arianna Claire.
Remember, we're never too far from His grace.

Chapter 1~

Broken Television

This didn't work out as planned.

I should have stopped drinking the schnapps yesterday when my stomach started flipping. My body gave me a warning, but I didn't listen. I only wanted to forget for a minute who I was. Or who I wasn't. I wasn't Hannah, and Jake wasn't mine. So, I kept drinking.

And today, I paid for it.

The heart monitor beeped beside my bed while the blood pressure cuff squeezed my arm. I heard my parents talking out in the hall in hushed whispers. There'd been a steady stream of church folk stopping by. Not to see me, but to be there for my parents. They're the ones who had to deal with a supposed rebellious—and now suicidal—daughter.

Which wasn't what happened. At least not on purpose. Technically, I did sit in Hannah's car with it running in the garage, sipping from a peach schnapps bottle that I stole from the 7-11. But it didn't register that I could die from carbon monoxide poisoning while trying to hide from my overbearing, micromanaging family. I merely pulled into the garage, pressed the button to lower the door, opened up the alcohol, turned up the music, and tried to drink myself into oblivion.

Now I was on watch, like a hand grenade with a trick clip. I might just implode. Or explode. Whatever a hand grenade does.

2 | Janice Broyles

The hospital room door opened, and my parents walked in, followed by the nurse.

"How you feeling?" Dad asked as he sat on the side of my bed. He patted my leg and gave a tight-lipped smile. The same smile he gave church members during awkward conversations.

"Fine. When can I leave?" I pushed myself up to a sitting position. "This room has a broken television."

"You don't need the television," Mom said. "This isn't a vacation. Instead of worrying about a broken television, why don't you worry about what's broken in your life?"

"No need to turn this into a sermon," I said under my breath.

The nurse placed my finger inside an oxygen reader. "As soon as the psychiatrist comes and takes a look at you and gives you the thumbs up, you can get out of here," she answered while writing on my chart. She glanced over at my mom, then added, "I'll see what I can do about that T.V."

"A psychiatrist?" I asked my parents. "I'm not psychotic. And if I am, it's only because my family makes me that way."

"The hospital wants to make sure that you are mentally stable. It's very straight-forward from what I'm told." Dad absently patted my leg, but at least he didn't give me that pretend smile. He used to be handsome, tall and built, a four-star quarterback both in high school and college. Then he got saved and got chunky. Maybe not chunky, but he definitely enjoyed the church picnics and after-service spaghetti dinners.

"Why'd you do it?" Mom asked, visibly upset. "You're not only ruining your reputation, you're ruining ours."

There were several reasons I started stealing alcohol, but none of which I was willing to share. First of all, as an eighteen year old, I couldn't purchase it outright and nobody I knew drank the stuff. It amazed me that, in church circles, alcohol was forbidden yet gossip and judgement flowed like a flooding river. But it was more than that. It had to do with a secret that would crush them. A secret that would show them what a horrible person I was. They might not like my actions as the 'rebellious daughter,' but they certainly would crumble if they truly saw my wickedness. And alcohol allowed me to forget all that. So, instead of answering Mom, I answered Dad. "Of course I'm mentally stable."

"There are things that concern us," Mom said, standing on the other side of me. She looked over at my father. "Are you going to tell her?" Mom still looked like the blonde beauty from her high school prom pictures. Her face had nary a wrinkle, her make-up was never out of place, and she was lithe and perfectly proportioned. How she birthed four children and still looked like that was a wonder. As in, I *wonder*ed how in the world I was her child. With my thick auburn curls that were way overgrown and my thick bottom and thighs, I resembled my Gram on Dad's side more than I did Mom.

"Tell me what?" I asked, trying not to cringe. "If Hannah is going to make me wear teal to the wedding, I'm done. It's the color of snot."

"Maybe now's not the time," Dad said to Mom. "Let's get her home, and we can discuss it there."

Mom stared at Dad in her I-am-not-happy-with-you expression.

"Remember what we talked about in the hall," she whispered.

"They haven't called back to verify…" Dad whispered back.

"You two realize that I'm sitting right here, and I can hear you."

"Macy," Mom started. "You know we have a lot going on right now. With Hannah's wedding approaching, we don't have time to…I mean, we can't deal with more complications."

"I get it," I said. "As I've stated…*repeatedly*…I wasn't trying to hurt myself. I was taking my frustrations out on a bottle of schnapps. Was it smart? No. But am I crazy? No."

"If Hannah hadn't have found you, you'd be dead," Mom said. "Think about that for a minute."

There was that. I pressed my lips together and swallowed the lump that had formed in my throat. I'd been told that Hannah found me unconscious, lying face-first in the passenger seat, in my own vomit. "It was an accident," I said quietly. "I wasn't thinking. For what it's worth, I'm sorry."

"No, you weren't thinking," Mom agreed, ignoring my apology. "This is supposed to be the happiest time of your sister's life, and you are determined to make everything about you."

"Meg, that's enough," Dad said.

"Someone needs to be real with her!" Mom said. Turning to me, she continued, "Sometimes tough love is required."

Dad tried to grab my hand, but I pulled it from his reach.

I used to cry every time Mom became upset with me. But it seemed like as I grew up she was never happy with me, and eventually the tears stopped. This past year I decided to stand up to her more often.

If I could move out, I would. But where would I go? The more accurate question was who would want me? Other than babysitting, I had never worked. And my parents said their money would only pay for a community college in town. That left my options limited.

It also made for a very tumultuous household. Both Mom and me were stubborn. "Are you talking about what happened with me and the car or what happened when Hannah found my sketchbook and passed it around to all her church friends? Because I don't remember Hannah experiencing this kind of 'tough love' when she ruined my life by violating my privacy and making fun of me in front of the entire *young adult* group."

Mom and Dad didn't say anything. They knew how difficult this last year was for me.

"Don't compare yourself with your sister," Dad finally said. "You've both been wrong lately. I don't know what's happening with either of you, but there's plenty of blame to go around."

"Especially when the sketchbook was full of drawings of Jake."

I felt myself blush, unable to look at either one of them. What they didn't know is that Jake—who just happened to be Hannah's fiancé—ended up being quite the willing participant. But no one could ever know that part. So instead I let them think I was a nerdy artist with a secret crush on the church's 23 year old youth pastor. "I draw a lot of people and scenes. In the world of art, they might think I have talent," I said.

"You know what? We would even consider helping you pay for art school if we trusted you. How can you transfer to an art school when you've dropped out of your first year of community college," Mom said. "Hannah's nearly done with her degree."

"She's graduating with an associate's degree in early childhood education," I said with sarcasm. "And it's taken her four years already. And out of the three online classes at the community college, I only dropped one. That hardly constitutes failure."

Mom massaged her temples. "I'm so tired of arguing with you."

The nurse came back in and took the remote, replacing its batteries. "And to think this is all that was wrong with it." She smiled while the three of us awkwardly waited for her to leave.

"Our family doesn't watch television." Mom looked at me.

"I'm eighteen years old. I can watch television if I want."

The nurse scowled at Mom before handing me the remote and leaving.

"If you can't abide by our rules, then maybe it's time you considered other options." Mom added, "Maybe it's time you moved out and tried to experience life on your own."

"Yes, please," I said.

"I've already searched some rehab facilities where you can get help. How's that sound?"

"Ha, ha. If you want to talk about me moving out to an apartment, I'm open to the discussion. But I'm not going to a rehab facility where drug addicts go." I wasn't surprised. Mom micromanaged everything. And I mean *everything*. Nothing escaped her notice.

"I don't know what else to do. I stopped trying to figure you out a long time ago."

Her words had the intended effect, like a bullet ripping through my chest. I held the remote in my hands and squeezed it, forcing myself not to show her how much it hurt.

"Macy," Dad said.

"Please, leave me alone."

"It's not that simple," Mom said. "We have some things to discuss. Since this is your mess, you need to know."

"I think you've done enough," Dad said to her, standing up.

"This is part of the problem," Mom said. "You coddle her. How will she learn that negative behavior has negative consequences?"

"Don't you think I know that?" I interjected. "I'm in a hospital, and my mental stability is being questioned. This isn't exactly frolicking in the daisies."

"Police stopped by and said that 7-11 turned in a surveillance tape of you stealing that bottle of liquor," Mom said. "Do you understand now how serious this is? You got caught shoplifting. And liquor of all things!"

"Which one's more of a sin?" I muttered. "Stealing or drinking? Or television?"

"I'm glad this is so funny to you," Mom glared at me, her hands on her hips.

"What do you want me to say? I've already said that I'm sorry."

"This is not the first time you were caught. The police said you'll probably have to serve probation. Possibly some community service. What are we going to tell our saints?" Mom shook her head then left my bed to glare out the room's window in apparent frustration.

I closed my eyes and exhaled. What a mess. The irony was that I had the money in my wallet. I only stole because Ahmad wouldn't sell it to me. I ran my hands through my hair until my fingers got stuck on the snarls. "Can I do community service at the church? That's what you did for Darren when he got in trouble."

"Darren wasn't my daughter," Dad said.

"Okay, well we know dozens of pastors. Can we call a few and see?"

"No, we won't do that," Mom said, still facing the window. "I'm not about to announce this to all the ministers' families that we know. It's *embarrassing*."

"That's enough for now," Dad said. "Emotions are high, and I don't want any more words spoken that will be regretted later."

"I think it's time," Mom said to both me and Dad. "If Macy wants to act like this, then she needs to be gone from under our roof."

"Fine with me," I said. "But I'm not going to a rehab place. For the thousandth time, I'm fine. I'm thinking of tattooing it to my forehead since you're not getting it."

The nurse opened the door. "There is someone out here waiting to see the patient."

One of Mom's friends waved from behind the nurse. "It's Nancy," Dad said to Mom.

Immediately Mom's frown shifted into her thousand watt smile. "Oh, she's here for me," she said, leaving the window. "I'm headed to worship practice," she said to Dad. "I'll be home before nine." She left without a word to me.

Dad stayed quiet for a moment, which was fine. I was trying to manage the bubbling emotions of anger, hurt, and rejection. Mom had never been affectionate with me, but sometimes she could be so condescending and mean-spirited that it was a like a kick in the stomach.

"She's concerned, that's all. Unfortunately, your mother doesn't handle additional stress very well."

I didn't say anything. There was no point. I couldn't change who my parents were.

Dad leaned down and kissed my forehead. "I love you, peanut. Always have. Always will."

"Love you too, Dad," I said. "At least Mom and I agree that I need to consider my options." I thought of Hannah and Jake and how hard it was for me to be around them.

"I want you home." He lifted my chin up to look at him. "But I also want you to be happy, and to find whatever it is you're looking for."

He left the room soon after. I grabbed my cell phone sitting on the bedside table to see if I had any messages. I knew not to text Jake. Hannah often checked his phone. But as I stared at the phone I willed him to text me that he changed his mind. That he hadn't chosen Hannah. That he had chosen me instead.

All those nights he snuck into my room. All those promises that when the time was right he'd pronounce his love for me and not my older sister.

Then, to my surprise, he asked Hannah to marry him.

And that was the first time I'd stolen alcohol. The first time I felt alcohol take the edge off the pain. But I never meant to end up here, my life in shambles, my sanity questioned.

I wiped at my eyes and decided that since I didn't have my sketchbook with me, there was only one thing to do to forget about my life. "At least the television isn't broken," I said to myself. Then I grabbed the remote control and turned it on.

Chapter 2~

Road Trip

I sat in the wheelchair and waited for someone to come wheel me out. Why I couldn't walk out of the hospital when my legs were perfectly fine, I had no idea, but the nurse told me to sit in the wheelchair and wait, so here I was.

After yesterday afternoon's conversation with my parents, I became more determined than ever to show them how normal I was. I wanted to move out more than anything, but not to some rehab place. When the psychiatrist came in to interview me, I said all the things necessary to show remorse for my actions and to show that what happened in the garage was an accident. I even ventured into admitting how community service would be good for me, and blah, blah, blah. Hey, the psychiatrist bought it. He signed the release papers. Hopefully, my parents would buy it.

Most of it was the truth. I realized now how stupid it was to steal the schnapps. I realized how stupid it was to shut the garage door. I realized how stupid it was to stay in Hannah's car while drinking. See? Progress.

What I might not have been entirely honest about was what

triggered me to do those succession of stupid things. To the psychiatrist, I chocked it up to stress over Hannah's wedding and possibly feeling a little jealous. Since the first time I got caught stealing was the night of Hannah's engagement party two months ago, it qualified as a good answer for both stupid moves on my part.

The truth I kept to myself. I understood that people don't want to hear the truth, especially if it messed up their plans. A ripple of painful truth could be manageable, but my truth was more like a tidal wave.

The door opened and an orderly stepped in. "Let's take you outside, young lady," he said, getting behind me and pushing the wheelchair out the door. He whistled down the hall and in the elevator and through the outside automatic doors. Dad had pulled up in our sleek black Navigator. He and Mom would have had a simultaneous heart attack if I drank and puked in their precious SUV.

Finally, I stood up and slid into the vehicle, grateful to be out of that wheelchair. "I understand why so many lame people in the Bible begged Jesus to let them walk," I joked to Dad.

He smiled his tight-lipped smile and headed out of the hospital parking lot.

"What?" I asked.

"Nothing," he said, then patted my knee. "Good to have you out of the hospital. I don't know what I would have done if Hannah had been too late."

"Yes, I thought we already covered this," I said, trying to keep my tone light. "Yay for Hannah. Hannah saves the day."

Dad didn't say anything, only kept driving.

"I'm assuming Mom couldn't miss her Thursday ladies' group?"

Dad sighed, "I thought it would be better for her to stay back." He made a right turn onto I-75.

"Why are we heading north? Visiting someone?"

"We're going to Gram and Gramps."

"Oh," I said. "Cool. Just us? Are they okay?"

"Of course. Everything's great." He paused, then continued, "We contacted the courts, and as long as you don't miss your court dates, you can hang out with them for a while. We're thinking that you can complete your community service up with them."

"With Gram and Gramps? In Manistee?"

"They are happy to have you and could really use your help at the motel."

My mouth fell open. "I'm staying with them?" For whatever reason, I was having a hard time connecting the dots. "In Manistee? Three hours from Royal Oak?"

"It's only for three to six months. We'll see what the court says. But at least until your sister's wedding. This is a great opportunity for you to spread your wings while helping out your grandparents."

Shock rendered me absolutely frozen. Other than my brain. That worked in a frenzy. So, I got caught stealing, now I had to do community service. Okay, I was good with that. But Manistee? Gram and Gramps owned a small motel in the middle of nowhere while pastoring a small church that sat right next door to the motel.

But until Hannah's wedding? That wasn't until Labor Day weekend. It was only the first of April!

"It's not that I don't love Gram and Gramps, but Manistee? Dad, that's in the middle of nowhere. There's nothing to do. Nowhere to go. And don't I get a say?"

"I'm sure the community service hours will keep you busy," Dad said.

I stared out the window, trying to come to terms with the decision. Sure, I loved my grandparents. They were the sweetest people on the planet. But that wasn't exactly what I had in mind when I thought of living on my own. "Can't I just save for a few months? I can get a job and earn some cash then get a place. Maybe find a roommate."

"A down payment on an apartment is at least $1500 dollars. And I know you think you're all grown and stuff, but come on. You're eighteen."

"You know, if you and Mom would have let me go off to college, then I could be on my own and out of your hair."

"We don't have that kind of money. Our finances are tight right now, especially with Hannah's wedding. I don't think us asking you to go to a community college is unreasonable."

I nearly asked how much the payment was on the Navigator. "Speaking of college, I've got two exams to finish up."

"Your community college classes are online. Gram and Gramps have WIFI at the church. Besides, I thought you said you already finished up the winter semester."

"Yes, but I have my final exit essays to do. And all my stuff is at home. My books. My laptop. My clothes...my pillow!"

"Your mother got it all packed for you. It's right in the back.

Even your comforter and pillows. Everything you'd need to feel at home. Think of it as an opportunity."

I turned around and noticed the back of the Navigator packed to the ceiling. "She literally packed everything."

"Mom didn't want you to miss the comforts of home."

"Can we just cut the spin?" I turned off the radio, which had been playing on low the entire drive. "For once, be real with me! You and Mom don't want me around. There. See? Not hard to say the words!"

"Can you blame us?" Dad snapped, not looking at me, but staring straight at the road. "We love you, Macy, but cut us some slack. We've got Hannah and preparations for the wedding. Then there's Luke and Adrianne, and their schooling. Plus we have a 300 plus congregation and are right in the middle of the building project! It was either Manistee or some treatment home. You said you wanted to move out. This is moving out."

"I do want to move out, but on my terms. This feels like you guys are using the opportunity to get rid of me. There's a difference."

"Do you understand our decision? I thought this would give you space too. Maybe a chance to make friends."

"At Gram and Gramp's church? You're joking, right? Is there anyone in their congregation younger than fifty?"

"I don't know. But there's a chance. Besides, you attend a church of 300 and haven't made any real connections there. You sit on a pew in the corner and doodle in your sketchbook. Don't think I don't notice."

"Maybe because everyone is Hannah's friend," I said. "And

Hannah has made it clear since day one of any of my memories that there is no sharing between us." Hannah made everything a competition. We both took vocal lessons. She'd outperform me. We both took piano lessons. She started playing for the church while I was still learning chords. She had Mom's slim figure and blonde hair and the ability to look absolutely perfect. Add charisma, charm, and a mega-watt smile that could make an entire room swoon, and you have my sister.

"Don't put this on Hannah. She's four years older than you. That's a big enough age difference for you to be your own separate person."

"Newsflash, Dad, I stopped trying to be like Hannah since my butt got too big to squeeze into any of her clothes."

"That right there is your problem," he said.

"What? My big butt? It's the least of my concerns."

Dad groaned. "I can't even have a serious conversation with you. I'm trying to tell you to stop comparing yourself to her and then putting yourself down. Maybe if you saw the value in yourself, then you'd think twice before shoplifting liquor."

"I didn't steal the schnapps because I don't see value in myself," I said. "I stole it because alcohol lets me forget." I thought of how unhappy I was at home. Going away and separating myself from Mom's micromanaging would be a good thing. My heart still felt hurt at the thought of my family not wanting me, but if I was honest with myself, getting away from Hannah and Jake would be the best thing for me. "You know what? Manistee is fine. I don't know why I'm arguing." I positioned myself to stare out the window. I didn't need to hear any more. My parents wanted me gone, and I wasn't going to beg to stay. Whatever.

My cell phone rang. I saw Adrianne's face peering at me, requesting facetime. I accepted the call and began to video chat. "Hey there, lima bean," I said, smiling at my eight year old sister with her big hazel eyes and frizzy straw-colored hair tamed with a headband. My little lima bean was the only one of the four children who could eat those dreadful beans. She'd eat them right out the can. Disgusting. Yet, impressive.

"Mom said you're going on vacation," she said with a deep frown. "That's not fair."

"A vacation?" I glared at Dad. "Is that what she said?"

Dad gave me a look that pleaded with me to play the game.

"Why do you get to go on vacation and not me?"

"I know. I wanted you to come with me, but I didn't have enough money," I said. Looking at my little sister's sad face had my heart breaking. "I'm going to miss you the most, lima bean."

"How long are you gone for?" she asked. "Hannah was yelling yesterday at Mom and Dad telling them that you better not step foot at her wedding. Why? Is she mad she can't go on vacation, too?"

I swallowed down the hurt. What did I care? I didn't even want to be in her stupid wedding. "Yeah, probably," I choked out.

"You didn't say good-bye or give me a bear hug." Adrianne pouted, "Are you going to Florida? Did you have to hurry to catch the plane?"

"No," I said, deciding on the truth. "I'm going to Gram and

Gramps for a while. They need help with the motel, so I'm going to go do that. Not much fun, I'm afraid. It's better that you're home."

"I want to see Gram and Gramps!" Adrianne whined, sticking out her bottom lip out. "And with you gone, who am I going to cuddle with?"

"Cuddle with Rex," I said, speaking of our pug mix.

"He snores."

"Yes, but he's a great cuddler. Not to mention, you can sleep in my bed while I'm gone."

"No, I can't. Mom and Dad are letting Jake stay in there."

"What?" I asked, as the words sank in. The phone slipped from my fingers and smacked the floor. My eyesight narrowed, and my pulse quickened.

Jake. Hannah's fiancé. In my room.

I vaguely heard Adrianne trying to get my attention, but it was like through a tunnel. Dad was saying something.

"Macy!" he yelled.

"Just pack me up, so he can move in?" I asked, spinning in the seat to face him.

Dad gripped the wheel and pursed his lips together. "Tell Adrianne you'll call her back. She's not supposed to be on Mom's phone anyways."

"You mean you don't want her telling me any more information," I said. Bending down, I retrieved the phone. Mom's face now showed up next to Adrianne's.

"That's enough," Mom said, turning off Facetime.

Anger moved through me like waves in the ocean. "You know what I find ironic?" I said, unable to even look at my father. "Is that you and Mom and everyone label me a liar, yet when you both tell lies, it's perfectly acceptable."

"I never told you to lie to your sister."

"She thinks I'm going on vacation, Dad. What's that? Is there a new term for deception?!?"

"Don't be sarcastic," he ordered.

"What do you expect? I'm getting kicked out of the house, and I don't even get to say good-bye! To Adrianne! To Luke! To Rex! Just snatch me from the hospital, and tell everyone that I'm going on vacation." Tears blinded my vision, so I wiped at them furiously. "Lima bean's going to miss me. You might not, but she is." I turned to face the window. "And now you've let Satan himself move in three doors from her room."

"Your room sits above the garage with its own entrance. It made sense for him to be there. He and Hannah are trying to save money for a down payment on a house. Your mother thought since we had the space available that it only made sense. We're not doing this to hurt you. But since you're not going to be there anyway… why let it go to waste?"

I dug my fingernails into the palms of my hands to keep myself calm. I couldn't think about Jake Steward sleeping in my room. On my bed.

He hadn't even bothered to check up on me these last couple days, but that wasn't the only reason I hated him. I hated him because he used me and lied to me, and in the end, he still chose Hannah.

"My sister got caught up in the drinking," Dad said. "Then it turned worse. I'm trying to prevent that from happening."

Dad rarely talked about his younger sister. The wound was still deep. Supposedly I had met her, but I couldn't recall it. She died from taking too many pain meds, but I was pretty sure there was more to the story. "I'm not anything like your sister."

"You're a lot more like her than you think. In a good way. She was amazingly talented, just like you. Her artwork was incredible. And she could sing. She'd light up the room just by walking in. She had so much potential."

"Yeah, well, something must have happened to send her to California."

"Yep," Dad agreed. "She met a boy. A young man with a penchant for trouble. She hopped on his motorcycle and was gone."

"I'll try to avoid men on motorcycles," I said sarcastically before staring out the window again.

The rest of the way up north was cringe-worthy awkward. Dad would try to engage me in conversation, but I wasn't in the mood to talk. For two-and-a-half hours, I stayed silent. Decisions were made, and I was not consulted. Not when it came to Jake, and not when it came to my own life. So, as far as I was concerned, I had nothing more to say.

Chapter 3~

Snow in April

I sat on the front porch steps of Gram and Gramps place and stared at the small mounds of snow still littered across the landscape.

Snow. In April.

One thought kept repeating in my head: *This wasn't what I had in mind.*

I would melt into a heaping pile of tears and shattered dreams, but Dad was still here. My performance in *not caring* still must go on. I reasoned with myself that I was technically an adult. Might as well start acting like one.

I heard his hushed voice. Talking with my grandparents. Probably warning them of my horrible delinquency. Possibly encouraging them to stick a clove of garlic under their pillow and extra-large wooden crosses around each neck. You know. In case my taste for alcohol turned into a thirst for blood.

Too annoyed to stick around, I pushed myself off the steps and started to investigate. Most of the ground was at least snowless, but it was extremely squishy and wet. Gram and Gramps had a dirt driveway, which was nothing more than a glorified mud puddle at the moment, so I stayed on the squishy grass until I got to the road. Directly across the street stood their small clapboard church, First Congregational, with a bell tower and everything.

When we were little, and Hannah had no one else to play with, we would swing from the bell's rope. The memory gave me a knot in my stomach, so I turned my attention to the Manistee Forest Motel that sat right next the church. I wasn't sure what came first: owning the motel or pastoring the church, but Gram and Gramps had managed both for as long as I'd known them.

There were three weekends when the motel reached no-vacancy: Memorial weekend, July 4th weekend, and Labor Day weekend. The holy trinity of Michigan vacationers. I remembered Gramps saying one time that the rest of the summer stayed moderately busy. At the moment I counted two cars in the motel parking lot. Then again, who'd want to visit a place that still had snow on the ground in April?

"Macy!" Gram called. "Come inside and have some cookies and milk."

Oh dear Lord. Comfort food. If I wasn't careful, I'd get bigger than I already was.

Remember, a minute on the lips is a pound on the hips. I could hear Mom saying the words. I would catch her checking her wrists to make sure her fingers easily touched, so I started doing that. It didn't take long for her to use that as ammunition against me. If she caught me going for a second helping, she'd scold, "Be careful, or your fingers won't touch."

"I'll be there in a few minutes," I called up to Gram before crossing the street.

Supposedly, I would be helping clean the motel rooms. I wanted to check and see how awful they might be. As I walked across the small parking lot, I was impressed with how immaculate the grounds were. This might have been an older motel, but everything looked well kept up.

I checked the gate to the pool. Still locked. Then again, the pool had been drained and was covered by blue plastic. *That'll be kind of cool*, I thought to myself as I headed to a corner motel room. *I don't have a pool back home.*

The motel room's door was locked.

Duh. Of course it would be. What'd I think? That Gram and Gramps kept everything unlocked?

"Excuse me?" a man said from behind me.

I turned around and kept my hand on the doorknob as if it was supposed to be there. I probably looked guilty. "I'm supposed to be here," I said. "My grandparents wanted me to check everything out."

"Good," he said in relief. "My daughter and I are in need of more washcloths and towels. Ms. Elmsworth said they were in the dryer, but it's been a couple hours. Do you think they're done by now?"

"Uh," I said. "Let me go and see."

I walked past him and studied each door. Which one was laundry? I couldn't remember!

Everything was on one floor, so I headed to the office, but it was locked too. I noticed the man had followed me. "I'll have to ask my grandmother. She's right across the street."

"Thank you," he said smiling.

He made me nervous. From his head to his shoes, he was filthy.

Not in an unclean sort of way, but in a mechanic kind of way. He had smudges of grease on his face, and his hands were covered in it too. He had on a blue-striped uniform that said Jay's Auto Palace. None of that made me nervous though. It was that underneath all that car residue, he was handsome with big brown eyes and full lips. "I'm eighteen," I blurted, before wanting to face palm. "I mean, you know..."

He raised his eyebrows. "Okay. About those towels..."

I nodded and ran to the road, completely mortified. As I ran across the street and up my grandparents' driveway, I repeated, "I'm eighteen? That's what you come up with?" I cringed again. "You're a hundred different kinds of special, aren't you?"

"Who are you talking to, Macy May?" Gram sat on the porch, smiling at me like I was a ray of sunshine. I would have smiled back but I was still recovering from mortification.

"Towels," I blurted out again. "The guy over there, who is a mechanic or something, not that he told me, but I was able to tell because of his clothes and he was dirty. Not that mechanics have to be dirty, but he just looked like a mechanic, you know?"

Gram blinked at me and kept smiling. "Derek needs towels? They should be dry now. Why don't you be a good girl and get them out of the dryer? Make sure to fold them neat."

"Where's the dryer?" I sighed. I wanted to refuse, but Dad always taught us to treat elders with dignity and respect. I might have had issues with my parents, but I wasn't about to talk back to Gram. Especially since she had cookies and milk waiting for me.

"On the other side of the office is the laundry door. It's locked, but all you have to do is put in the code."

"A code? As in there are no keys?"

"The laundry room and office are keyless entries. It was your grandfather's idea. We kept losing keys!"

"Okay, so what's the code?"

She leaned forward and motioned for me to come closer. "1, 2, 3, 4, 6." Then she sat back and laughed. "That was your grandfather's idea too. Just jump one of the numbers! No one will ever guess it! But our old brains remember!"

I ran back down the driveway and across the not-very-busy road to the backside of the office. Sure enough, there was a heavy steel door with a LAUNDRY sign attached to it. Right above the doorknob was a number panel. I pressed in the code and pushed open the door when the green light came on.

First of all, the laundry room could have been a sauna, it was that hot. Secondly, the lights were off, making it super creepy. I tried finding the light switch on the one wall, but couldn't find it. Inwardly groaning, I found a rock outside to prop open the door. Where were the windows?

I stepped inside, found a massive dryer, and opened it. Pulling out some towels and washcloths, I folded them quickly. The creepy vibes were still there. With a stack in my arms, I turned to leave. And spotted a small shadow outlining the door.

I screamed and fell back, throwing the stack of towels in the air.

The shadow screamed and went running from the doorway.

When my heart returned back to my chest, I picked up the laundry that fell on the floor. I had no idea how clean or dirty the floor was, but I refused to stay in the laundry room a moment longer. These were the towels I would deliver.

Kicking the rock out of the way, the door slammed shut behind me. I rounded the corner to the front of the motel and saw mechanic guy squatting and hugging a little girl. She had to have been the scampering shadow. Now I felt kind of bad for scaring her, even if she scared me first.

The little girl noticed me approaching and pointed her finger at me. "There she is," she said with a slight lisp.

"Sorry," I said to her and then to her father. "She surprised me."

"Lillian needs to learn not to run off without telling me. Right?" he asked, looking down at the girl.

"I was exploring," she said, but it sounded more like, *I was esporing.*

She couldn't have been more than five. With light brown hair pulled back into a messy pony tail and wisps of hair dangling in her face, she might have been adorable, but she looked like she needed a bath.

Suddenly, I missed Adrianne something fierce. "Here," I said, handing him the towels. "Now you can get clean."

He raised his eyebrows, as my words dawned on me.

Sighing, I shoved the towels at him. "I didn't mean...it sounded worse than I intended...Sorry," I said again before walking off.

Our black Navigator pulled into the motel's parking lot and stopped right in front of me. Dad rolled down the window. No smile this time. Actually, he looked like he'd been crying.

Good. I shouldn't be the only one in my family to shed tears over the total suckiness of this situation. "Taking off?" I asked, not hiding the accusation. "See ya' around." I kept walking toward the road.

"Wait! Peanut!"

I stopped when I heard Dad's door open.

"Don't be like this. Please."

I turned around to face him and noticed the little girl peeking her head out of a motel door, watching me. She gave a slight wave. "What did you expect?" I asked, placing my focus back on the dismal disaster at hand. "That taking me from home without letting me say good-bye would turn into a big '*Yay, I'm so excited for this opportunity,*' reaction? Well, I'm not excited. A decision about my life was made without my input. I'm sorry that spoils your mood."

"Would you rather be admitted to a rehab institution? Say the word, and I'll take you back. But I ran out of options, Macy."

"I stole a stupid bottle of liquor, Dad. I don't *need* rehab."

"You tried to commit—"

"Are you serious?" I cried. "How many times do I have to say that it was an accident?"

"The psychiatrist and your mother think that you're covering up your actions."

My mouth dropped open. Obviously my performance with the psychiatrist wasn't as successful as I'd thought. "So, you think that I'm lying?"

"I don't know!" he said, throwing up his hands. "Your mother demanded I do something. That you either go to a rehab facility and deal with your mental condition or that I find another way for you to get help."

"My mental condition?" I brought my hands to my head. "Wow. So, now I'm crazy. Crazy and a drunk."

"I don't believe that," Dad said. "I think our family is under stress. I think what happened with you and the sketchbook has pushed you to act out against your sister. I don't necessarily blame you. What Hannah did was deplorable. But I had to give your mother something. I thought that you wanted to move out, and this seemed like the perfect answer. I thought if you stayed here and stayed out of trouble that everyone would see what I already see. Just do the community service time up here. You can escape from the sketchbook fiasco. Hannah and Jake won't be bothering you. And I will visit you every chance I get. I'll bring Adrianne up next time. I promise."

I couldn't put into words how lonely I felt. How rejected. How ostracized. Even if what he said made sense.

"I'm going to be back in one or two weeks," he kept talking. "You'll have a court date. Maybe you won't be stuck with six months community service."

"Doesn't matter," I said. "Hannah doesn't want me at the wedding, remember?"

"She'll get over it," Dad said with steel in his voice. "You are my daughter, and you will be there." He brought me to him and hugged me hard.

I wanted to shove him away, but instead I melted into my Dad and cried. I cried over all the things I couldn't change. I cried over the hurt.

I cried over the broken pieces.

Chapter 4~

Nightmares and New Employees

I drowned the spicy chicken and vegetables with sour cream and shredded cheese, then folded the tortilla and bit into the fajita. "Mmm," I said with a mouth full.

"Gram never makes dishes like this when it's me and her, so this is a treat." Gramps was already plowing into a second one. With graying hair, long legs, and a bit of a belly, he reminded me of an older version of Dad.

"You act like I starve you," Gram teased. "You eat just fine," she said. "But tonight is a treat, and Macy's favorite meal is fajitas."

I nodded as I dived into my second one. *What can I say?* I could be the poster child for stress eating.

"Your father placed your belongings up the guest room upstairs for you," Gram said. "This morning, we cleared out most of it other than the bare minimum, so that you could make it all your own."

Piling more chicken onto a tortilla, I said, "Thanks. It'll be fine."

"We couldn't believe all the stuff you packed. Then again, a girl likes her clothes," Gramps said.

"I didn't pack it. Mom did," I said in between bites. "She

couldn't wait to get rid of me." I meant to say it light-heartedly, but once the words were out, they sank like a heavy weight.

Gram gave me a thin smile. Okay, well, now I knew where Dad got it from. "We don't care the reasons. We're happy to have our granddaughter with us." She patted my arm. Then changing the subject, she said, "We still have those chocolate chip cookies for dessert. How does that sound?"

"Yes, please," I said, resisting the urge to grab the plate of cookies and place them in front of my face.

After three cookies and a glass of milk, I leaned back in the chair and groaned. "I'm a glutton," I announced.

"You keep eating like that, maybe I can put a few more pounds on those bones," Gram said, getting up and clearing the dishes.

I snorted. "I've already got a nice layer of fat, Gram. I don't need a winter coat of it."

Gramps started chuckling. "You and your sense of humor. You're going to be a real treat around here."

I made myself get up and help with the dishes. What Dad said made sense. I would show everyone who doubted me what a good girl I could be. With Hannah and her butthead boyfriend not here stressing me out even more, hopefully I could resist doing stupid stuff. But I couldn't think about Jake moving into my bedroom. I couldn't let my brain go there.

"I've got this tonight," Gram said. "Go upstairs and get your room the way you want it."

"Make sure to sleep well tonight," Gramps said, as he left the kitchen. "You will need to report to the motel at 8 a.m. sharp."

I crinkled my nose and frowned. One thing about homeschooling is that I could wake up when I wanted. And since my online classes were mostly done, I had been staying up late to sketch and sleeping in until around noon. "How many hours a day do I have to work?" I asked.

"When the motel rooms are clean, you're done," Gramps said from the other room. "Pedro and Nancy would normally get done around four. Poor Pedro's been strapped these last few weeks trying to clean on his own since Nancy moved to the U.P."

"Pedro?"

"He works for us. We're trying to help him stay on the straight and narrow, so your grandfather gave him a job cleaning the motel. He's gotten into trouble with the law a few times, but you know Gramps. Always seeing the best in people." Gram paused. "I don't want to talk entirely negative about the young man. He shows up early and works hard. Every day. For the last six months."

"Great," I said, not knowing what else to say. "Why haven't you hired someone else to replace the lady who left?"

"We were getting around to it, but Pedro said he didn't mind working extended hours because he needs them. He wasn't too happy this morning when your grandfather told him you were taking Nancy's place."

"He can have my hours. I won't fight him for it," I said teasingly.

"Very funny, Macy May," Gram said. "You need those hours too."

"Yeah, I know," I said, embarrassed that my Gram knew about what I had done. "I don't know what Dad told you, but I didn't do what I did on purpose. Like...I wasn't trying to hurt myself."

"I know."

"You do?" I asked surprised. "Mom doesn't believe me. I don't think Dad does either."

"I think he does. He has a lot going on right now, and I think my son is feeling overwhelmed. Please be patient with him. He loves you so much."

"I love him too. I don't get why he dumped me up here, but I think it'll be good. At least I don't have Hannah and her jerk fiancé here making my life a living hell. No offence," I said, realizing I said a swear word. Well, to my family it was a swear word.

"As soon as we talked to him last night, and he explained the situation, we volunteered. We asked him if you would come and stay with us for a while and help at the motel. Your father was relieved that you had a safe place to go. He's worried about you around Hannah. You think he doesn't know what's going on, but he does."

No, I thought. *Dad doesn't know what's going on. At least not everything.* Instead I said, "Well, I'll head upstairs and unpack."

"Macy," Gram stopped me as I was leaving the kitchen. "Please know that we are thrilled to have you here. And whatever happened doesn't matter anymore. Here, you get a fresh start." She came over, her hands dripping with soapy water, and kissed me on the cheek. "You've always been my favorite, but don't tell. I'd have to deny it."

I grinned at her. "You tell that to all of us grandkids."

"Do I?" she asked, feigning confusion.

I took the steps upstairs and saw the light on in the bedroom on the left. There were two bedrooms and a bath up here. The other room was Gram 'project' room. It also had two futons for when company came. Gram and Gramps stayed downstairs in the master bedroom. I walked into the room with the light on and saw my pile of stuff. Two large suitcases, my backpack, laptop case, and comforter and pillow zipped up into their original plastic wrapping. Gram was right. The room had been completely cleared out other than a full bed in the middle of the room, a dresser beside it, and a chair in the corner. I swallowed down the homesickness and hurt.

This will be good, I told myself. *You're safe here. No one will bother you.*

Suddenly, exhaustion from the day hit me hard. *Would it be so bad if I went to bed at 7:30?* I slept lousy last night in the hospital, and I was too angry in the car ride up here to take a nap.

Without touching any of the suitcases, I grabbed the large plastic zip bag and pulled out my comforter and pillow. Gram had made up the bed, so I threw my comforter over the blankets and sheets already on the bed and straightened it out. There.

My cell phone buzzed. I hoped it was Adrianne again. I didn't know who else would call me. Then I saw Hannah's text.

It cost $245 dollars to clean the upholstery in my car!!! ☹ Mom says ur paying for it!!

I set the phone on the dresser, turned off the light, and climbing into bed, I pulled the comforter completely over my head. Decision made.

***

The bedroom door creaked open, and I became suddenly aware that someone else was in the room. Could it be Adrianne? No, she was spending the night at a friend's house.

My bed shifted as if someone sat on it.

"Macy?" he whispered.

I felt his hand on the comforter. My stomach trembled.

What was he doing here?

This had to be a dream, but it felt so real. My comforter moved, and I felt his hand rest upon my actual thigh. I became aware that I only wore my boy shorts and tank top to bed.

His hand slowly moved up.

This time I moved, no longer comfortable. I pushed his hand away and sat up. "You shouldn't be here," I whispered. "You need to leave."

"I know," he said, moving closer to where I sat. His face mere inches from mine. "Just one kiss."

I'd be lying if I said it wasn't affecting me. It was. My insides shook with pleasure. He came into my room. He'd been sneaking in here, and I basked in his attention, telling myself it would only be a matter of time before he announced our relationship to the world. But I also knew this was wrong. And I was still angry at him. "You need to leave," I said again.

"I can't. You know your sketchbook woke something up inside me," he said, leaning in and kissing me on the neck. "It's you I want.

Not her."

"But you called me a stalker," I whispered, as he kept kissing behind my ear lobe.

"I have to play pretend," he said. "I can't let anyone know my true feelings for you." He kissed me on the mouth, and I nearly melted right there.

It was everything I wanted. Him. Right here. On my bed.

"NO!" I cried out, shoving him as hard as I could.

I fell onto the hard floor of my grandparents' guest bedroom with a thud. I trembled.

I hated that dream.

I hated him.

I hated myself.

Now, I climbed back onto the bed and curled myself into a ball. Memories flooded my brain of our last time together. When I agreed to take it further. My body ached, betraying me. "No," I whispered to the darkened room at my grandparents' house. I couldn't let my mind go there. How could he still affect me like that?

Instead, I thought of Hannah. I thought of the betrayal she'd feel if she knew all of it. And I prayed to God she never found out. Not like God would ever answer any of my prayers. I allowed my sister's fiancé to sneak into my room at night. If that wasn't a one-way ticket to hellfire and damnation, I didn't know what was.

The first time, Jake came in on his own from our house's upstairs hallway. "Those sketches woke something up in me," he had said. "I didn't know you felt toward me the way I feel toward you." He surprised me, but I was so star struck that he wanted to be with me, that I let him kiss me that night. After that, it wasn't every night. Sometimes it wasn't even every week. But the anticipation only fueled the desire. Would tonight be the night he'd visit? When he would sneak in and see me, he would whisper promises in my ear, telling me how beautiful I was. That he thought of me when he was with her. And I desperately wanted to believe him.

For four months, Jake would visit me in the night. For four months, I left the outside door unlocked. Since my bedroom sat atop of the garage, I had an emergency escape. Perfect for Jake who wanted to go unnoticed. It was a much bigger bedroom than any of the others, but I got it instead of Hannah because Dad worried about Jake and Hannah being sneaky. Dad trusted me. Besides, in my eighteen years, I never had so much as a date.

That made me feel guilty more than thinking about Hannah. Dad could never find out about what happened. Ever.

After the trembling stopped, and my heartrate slowed to normal, I rolled onto my back to stare the ceiling. Gram and Gramps didn't drink, or I'd already be up and out of bed taking a swig of whatever they had available.

I found out last summer, after the whole sketchbook incident, how much alcohol took the edge off. It made me forget. Maybe not forget completely, but it dulled my feelings. It had been a youth campfire at the county park. I had been forced to go, even though the sketchbook ordeal had yet to die down.

I had left the campfire almost as soon as I arrived. Hannah and

Jake were all over each other, and the thought of watching that all evening sent me running in the opposite direction. Not too far from the youth group's campfire another party had been taking place. Young couples danced to country music while the fire blazed and the music pumped. I watched from behind a tree, mesmerized at how happy they looked. One of them noticed me and invited me to join them. She said they all attended Oakland University. She asked if I went to college. The lie came easily enough. Soon, someone had shoved a drink in my hand. I didn't even think about. I grinned and drank. It had been awful, but I chugged it down like a trooper.

And that's when I first felt it. The buzz.

I became flushed and warm and fuzzy. Suddenly I was drinking from another cup. Then I was chatting it up with everyone. Telling them about my pretend life at my pretend university. I laughed. I danced. And not once did I think about my older sister or her boyfriend who ignored me or treated me cruelly in public. Alcohol took me out of my sister's shadow.

And it had been exhilarating.

Now lying here three hours from home, the temptation to take the edge off was stronger than ever. But Dad had basically planted me in the middle of nowhere. Restless, I pushed back the covers and turned on the light. Opening the suitcases, I found where Mom had packed my undies and bras. Grabbing what I needed, along with another tank and shorts, I tip-toed to the bathroom.

A hot shower helped. It eased the knotted muscles along my neck and shoulders and eventually the dream evaporated from my mind.

I might not be able to control my dreams, but while I was awake, I visualized having a little compartment in my brain. There, I shoved all my memories of him. It worked most of the time. In that regard, being up north was a God-send. He wouldn't bother me up here, and I wouldn't have to see him with Hannah.

Feeling refreshed, I threw on my clean clothes and tried to comb through my thick hair. I pulled it back in a high ponytail. Considering my new job was a motel maid, I decided simple would be fine.

Once in the room, I checked my phone and saw it was 6:30 in the morning. I didn't feel like unpacking, so instead I found my sketchbooks and pencils, propped myself up in the available chair, and began to draw.

I enjoyed drawing nature, but I had a knack for drawing faces. I outlined the little girl's face on the paper, smiling to myself. In this scene I drew her peering out from the door while I had been talking to Dad. *What was her name—Lilly?* With her blue eyes and brown hair.

Completely lost in the sketch, I didn't hear Gram come up the stairs. When she knocked on my open bedroom door, I nearly jumped out of my skin. "Good morning," she said, cocking her head to the side. "I called your name at least a half dozen times. I thought you must sleep like the dead."

"Sorry, Gram," I said, reluctantly shutting the book. "When I get into my artwork, I sort of forget everything else."

She smiled—a genuine smile—and nodded. "I understand. What do you say to some breakfast? It's 8 o'clock already, but you need your fuel before going to work for your grandfather."

"Oh no! I'm late for my first day."

"Don't worry. I told your grandfather that you'd eat some breakfast then head over."

I followed her down the stairs, my mouth watering at the smell of coffee. Dad used to pour a little bit of coffee in a mug, then pour milk in the rest of the way. Then the two of us would sit at the table and drink our coffee together. I still drink it with milk and a little sugar, but the cup is mostly filled with coffee.

"So, what were you drawing?" Gram asked, as I filled a cup with coffee and milk and spoonful of sugar.

"I do sketches mostly. Sometimes of nature, but mostly of people."

She set a bowl of oatmeal and brown sugar in front of me. I hadn't had this since the last time I was up north about two years ago. I started shoveling the warm mush in my mouth. "Do you no longer say grace?"

I paused and mumbled, "Thank you, Lord, for this food," before continuing to eat.

"Are you going to tell me who or what you were sketching?"

I paused again. "My sketchbooks are kind of private. Well, they're supposed to be. Like a diary or journal, you know?"

"Of course, dear. Just make sure if you're going to sketch me to take at least 20 pounds off my thighs."

"Deal," I said, gulping down the rest of my coffee. "Got to go. Don't want to be fired the first day on the job."

Gram laughed. "Be careful out there. I heard the boss can be a real handful. Oh, don't forget a jacket. It's chilly this morning."

By the time I ran upstairs to dig out a jacket, then laced up my converse, I was already pushing 8:30. I jogged down the driveway, dodging the mud holes, and jogged across the street. I opened the door to the motel office and exclaimed, "I'm here!"

Gramps glanced up from the newspaper. "No need to shout. I'm not deaf yet. And you're late."

"Gram said I should eat breakfast," I said, realizing it was a pathetic excuse. "Sorry. I'll try not to be late again." I paused, "What do I do? Go to the rooms and vacuum and stuff."

"Yes. Pedro will show you." Gramps motioned to someone behind me.

I turned to see who it was and sort of froze in my spot. Pedro sat on the long couch in the office, staring at me with an annoyed expression. The first thing I noticed after that was the tattoos. There were a lot of them. He wore a muscle shirt, which was weird considering it was about 45 degrees out, but it gave a good view of the tattoos. Completely covering both arms and shoulders. He had some on his neck too. The shirt probably covered a host more. His head was completely shaved, and he had a variety of earrings in his ears and one in his eyebrow.

My grandparents wanted me alone with the guy?

I looked back at Gramps. "Can I talk to you?" I whispered. I stepped up to the counter. "This is who I'm supposed to work with?"

"Yes," Gramps said without whispering. "You have more in common than you think. You both got in trouble with the law, for starters, and you both need me to help you with community service. Now, there's work to be done, and time's a'wastin.'"

"Did you tell him? Grampa, that's private!"

"If it's so private, you shouldn't have done it." He waved his hand at me, as if to shoo me off.

I threw open the door and marched outside. Placing my hands on my hips, I inhaled deeply to try to calm my nerves and frustrations. What would Dad do if he knew that my grandparents had me working beside Mr. Ex-Con? And why would Gramps compare me to him? We were nothing alike. I stole some liquor. He probably killed someone with his bare hands.

BIG difference.

"If you're done with your tantrum, let's vamenos," Pedro said behind me.

He walked away, but I didn't feel like obeying. But how else would I earn those stupid community service hours? Groaning, I followed him to the back where the laundry room was. He pressed in the code, opened the door, and walked into the darkness. I paused, waiting outside.

I heard him pull on a light switch, and suddenly, I could see inside. "There it is," I said, staring at the string dangling from the ceiling attached to the light bulb. "I was looking for that yesterday."

"So then you did this?" he asked with a slight Mexican accent. Pedro pointed at several washcloths and a towel on the floor.

"Oh, oops." I stooped over and picked them up.

"They'll have to be washed again," he said, taking them from me and dropping them in an oversized laundry container.

"Sorry. I couldn't find the light switch yesterday." I stopped because he wasn't listening. He had walked behind the double set of washers and dryers and pulled out a push cart loaded with cleaning supplies.

"This is mine. Another one is back there. Stock it and let's get moving." He pushed the cart around the machines and out the door.

"What am I supposed to stock it with?" I called out. Great. I was in the laundry room again. At least this time the light was on. I moved behind the washers and dryers to where several shelves stood. They were filled with an assortment of cleaning products. The laundry room was actually larger than I presumed. There was also enough room for a long table against one of the walls for folding and another shelf stocked with folded linens. Seeing another cart tucked in the corner beside the shelves, I pulled it out and started picking a little bit of everything. On the bottom shelf sat a box of those yellow, cleaning gloves. Definitely want those. I bent over and grabbed two pair.

"Aren't you done yet?" he asked, directly behind me.

I jumped, smacking my head against the shelf above me. "Ow!" I yelled, pressing my hand to my head. "Don't do that! I hate it when people sneak up on me!"

"Yeah? Well, I hate it when people come to work late and make me wait for them!" he snapped, reaching past me to a vacuum and slamming it on my cart. "Did you grab a garbage bag?" he asked, not masking his annoyance, taking one from top shelf and opening it up to place in what was evidently the cart's garbage holder. He picked up a box of Band-Aids I had placed in my cart. "Really? Haven't you ever cleaned before? It's not like you need Band-Aids to scrub the toilet!"

I snatched them from his hand. "I might injure myself. It's always good to be prepared, and yes, I've cleaned! I'm not some moron."

"Are you sure about that?"

"You don't have to be a jerk! I've never been a motel housekeeper before, so EXCUSE ME!"

Angered and embarrassed, I pulled on my cart to turn it around, then pushed it out from around the washing equipment and out the door. What was this dude's problem? He obviously had some type of anger management issue. I thought Gram said he was nice. I was so keyed up, I started to push the cart across the parking lot to the farthest room.

"Where are you going?" he asked. "We start here."

"I can clean a room by myself. Thank you very much. I'm starting over here."

"Fine," he said, throwing up his arms. "And when you haven't done it right because you haven't been trained, you can stay here and reclean the rooms." He pushed the cart to the first motel room door. Knocking on it, he said, "Housekeeping!"

I hated this. Tonight I would ask Gram and Gramps to give me something else to do. I refused to work with this guy. Dad would probably have a fit anyway if he took one look at him. Just the same, I didn't want to be here late, so I pushed the cart back to the first room where Pedro was already inside. "Fine. What do I do, know-it-all?"

He was pulling covers and sheets off the one bed. "All bed linens come off."

"This one looks like no one touched it."

Pedro dumped the pile of linens in the canvas laundry bag on his cart. "When someone has stayed in the room, we cannot assume that a bed is clean. Comprende? ALL. BED. LINENS. OFF."

"What is your deal?" I snapped. "All I can say is my Gram is so *wrong* about you."

He didn't answer. Instead he put on yellow gloves, grabbed spray cleaner and a new sponge and went into the bathroom.

Okay. I went to the perfectly made bed and angrily yanked the covers off. Then the sheets. I had to crawl over the mattress to pull off the fitted sheet. By the time I was done, I was sweating. "What next?" I asked.

Pedro stepped out of the bathroom. "Put clean ones on and make the bed," he said it super slow.

I narrowed my eyes. He stared right back at me.

"Got a problem, gringa?"

"Yeah, I want to know if you forgot to take your anti-cranky pills."

"I don't know. You must have remembered to take your white-privileged, stuck-up white girl pills."

His words and animosity stung. Just another person who didn't like me. And I was done fighting. "You can clean this room by yourself," I said. "I think I've got the hang of it." I walked outside to my cart and nearly smacked into Gramps. "Hey," I said nervously.

Gramps didn't look amused. I'd never seen him get angry, but his grim expression sort of bordered on it. "I can hear you two clear across the parking lot."

I swallowed. "I'm going to start another room, so it shouldn't happen again."

"Good. Go ahead and get started. I need to talk to Pedro."

My heart dropped. I glanced inside the motel room and saw that Pedro had been putting on the sheets to the bed, but now stood still, staring at his hands. "It's fine, Gramps. Seriously. Please. We won't argue anymore."

He patted my arm and stepped past me into the room and shut the door.

"Oh, lovely," I sighed, opening up the next door. I pulled up the blankets and bed linens, completely agitated. "Serves him right," I muttered, but then I stopped myself. What was he guilty of? Yelling at me? Okay, so maybe he was a little intense, but I was a half hour late. And he assumed that I knew what I was doing, which I clearly had no clue. But I didn't want the guy fired. Especially because my plan revolved around Gram and Gramps placing me somewhere else.

Taking the cleaner and paper towel, I went into the bathroom. Then crinkled my nose. Disgusting. Absolutely disgusting. The person didn't even flush! "What is wrong with people?" I lifted my leg and used my shoe to press the lever. Then I sprayed like crazy. By the time I got done, the entire bathroom had been doused with cleaner.

"You don't need that much."

I jumped again, banging my head against the door. I pressed my lips and inhaled deeply, reminding myself not to raise my voice. "Could you please not sneak up on me?"

"Why are you so jumpy? I just came over here to see how you're doing."

"Nasty. That's all I've got to say."

"You haven't seen the half of it. Listen, I set your clipboard in your cart. There's a checklist where you mark everything that's been cleaned. Make sure to initial it. At the end of the day, the paper gets turned into the office." Pedro turned to leave.

"I hope you didn't get in trouble," I blurted. "With my Gramps."

"Why would I get in trouble?" he stopped at the outside door to ask. "*I* didn't do anything wrong. *I* wasn't the one who showed up late, and *I'm* not the one who has put us behind at least an hour."

"What about all of the mean things you were saying? It's not exactly professional."

His eyes narrowed this time. "You're the kind of girl that gets under people's skin, aren't you?"

"Maybe," I said, starting to feel irked again. "But at least I don't have a massive cranky chip on my shoulder."

Pedro shook his head and chuckled humorlessly. "It's no wonder your family dropped you off up here."

Like a flaming arrow to the heart. The rejection burned again. But I wouldn't let him see it. I turned and went back into the bathroom without another word. When I finished wiping up the floor, he had left the doorway. With him gone, I peeled off the yellow gloves, sat on the bare bed and wiped at the tears. Gramps totally should have fired him. The jerk.

But it didn't matter. The words were spoken. And the sad part was that Pedro got it exactly right.

Chapter 5~

Motel for Misfits

A full week passed, and I figured out a few things.

First, Gram and Gramps had a soft spot for Pedro. They, in not so many words, told me to suck it up and work with him. Gram reminded me not to be quick to judge. Gramps told me that if I knew his story, I'd feel really bad for the way I treated him. *Really?* How had I become the bad guy in the situation?

Second, I figured that if I arrived to the motel earlier than 7:30 in the morning that I could get my cart and get started before Pedro showed up. Gramps didn't seem to care, telling me to start on rooms with early check-out. By working early, I barely saw Pedro. I had my set of rooms, and he had his. I hated getting up early, but I disliked Pedro even more. So, 7:00 am won.

Third, people who stayed at motels were super gross. Did they live like this at home? Every day so far there had been something that made me gag. Every. Day. Even the rooms that weren't as bad, still grossed me out. Changing strangers' sheets was icky. Very, very icky.

Fourth, motel room cleaning happened every day. Seven days a week. Gramps had a woman come in on the weekends for an additional housekeeper. But did that give me the weekend off? Nope. Weekends were busiest. The problem was Gramps still expected me to work every Sunday until 10 a.m. Then I was supposed to run back to the house, shower and change for the 11 a.m. church service.

At least I was sleeping sounder. I hadn't had the nightmare since my first night in Manistee. And I didn't worry about someone sneaking into my bedroom in the middle of the night. So, even though I was super lonely, and in an almost constant state of irritation while working at the motel, I was glad about feeling safer.

"Macy May! Let's move!" Gramps called up. "Church starts in a half hour."

I wiped the fog off the bathroom mirror while rolling my eyes. What was with my family and making me attend church? I sprayed leave-in conditioner in my hair and combed through the wet mess.

"Macy May!" he called again.

Groaning, I opened the bathroom door an inch and yelled, "Yes, I know. Go on ahead of me. I'll be there on time."

I heard the downstairs door close and sighed. What I wanted was a nap. I'd been working like a dog this entire week, and my body wasn't used to it. Seriously. My body throbbed in places I didn't even know had muscles.

Running to the bedroom, I changed quickly, throwing on a black pencil skirt and dark green throw-over blouse. Taking a quick look in the mirror, I sighed. Oh well, I looked tired, but I could nap in church. I had it down to a science. I would pretend to look down at my sketchbook or song book or Bible or whatever was available and doze off. I slipped into my black flats, grabbed my sketchbook from the bed, and headed out the room and down the stairs.

As I walked down the driveway and across the street, I took a deep breath, smelling the clean air. Spring had arrived, and today showed it. Birds chirped, the breeze blew, and sun shone warmly. It almost put me in a good mood.

"There she is," Gram said from the top step. "I'm excited to get to introduce you to everyone."

As we walked inside the old church building, I realized that *everyone* was about twenty people. And none of them younger than 50.

By the time Gramps started the service by opening up the hymnal, I had been hugged by at least a dozen grandmothers. I sat near the back, then again, there were only seven long benches on each side. After Gramps finished leading us in "Glory to His name," I noticed Pedro slipping in across from me, two rows up. He took off his ball cap and set it on the bench beside him. He had on the same muscle-shirt and jeans that he worked in, completely out-of-place in this historical clapboard church. Maybe Gramps made him go to church as part of his community service.

Still, as another song begun, I couldn't help but watch as Pedro took out a hymnal and sang along. Had this been the same guy who had yet to say a nice word to me this whole week? Who had so many tattoos, I could barely see the natural skin on his arms? Before I knew what I was doing, my sketchbook was open and I was drawing.

His profile gave me no problems. Since his head was shaved, his hair had no nuisances to master. His nose straight, his mouth full, and his chin strong, I easily outlined them. But what fascinated me was his arms. From where I sat I couldn't make out the images of the tattoos. Eventually, I got stuck. I stared down at the sketch frustrated at its incompleteness.

"My granddaughter, Macy May Elmsworth, will be staying with us for some time, and we are delighted to have her," Gramps was saying.

My head snapped up, and I mimicked my Dad's tight-lipped smile.

"We've asked her to come and sing. Let's give her a round of applause."

Oh crap, I forgot. Gram and Gramps asked me a couple nights ago if I still sang and played the piano. "Not really," I had said. "Hannah does it all. Not me."

"We didn't ask if you've been singing or playing lately," Gramps said. "We asked if you could still sing and play. There's a difference."

"Talent doesn't just go away, and you have always been talented," Gram said, patting my hand.

"I guess I can," I said. "Why?"

"We'd like you to sing a song for our congregation," Gramps said. "They would love it. Now before you get all nervous and say no, remember that we have a small group of people, most of whom are older. They rarely get a treat like this."

Singing in front of a bunch of old people sounded unappealing. But it was my grandparents. What could I say other than "Sure?"

Now, in the church, with Pedro across from me, my brain went completely blank.

Everyone was clapping and encouraging me, other than Pedro, who had yet to look in my direction.

Fine, I thought. *What do I have to lose?* I walked up to the piano bench and opened up a hymnal. Back when we were younger, Hannah and I would sing a duet of The Old Rugged Cross. It had been my favorite. I turned to that page, knowing that I at least knew how to play it. Taking a deep breath, I studied the notes on the page briefly, counted the rhythm in my head, and began.

> *On a hill far away stood an old rugged cross*
> *The emblem of suffering and shame*
> *And I love that old cross, where the dearest and best*
> *For a world of lost sinners was slain.*
> *So I'll cherish, the old rugged cross*
> *Till my trophies at last I'll lay down.*
> *I will cling to the old rugged cross,*
> *And exchange it someday for a crown...*

As I sang, I felt the music deep inside and let my fingers play as if they'd been freed. I stumbled a few times, but I didn't care. It felt good to sing and play. I could hear Hannah singing the tenor in my head, and for a moment, I missed her. Not who she had become, but the sister she used to be. In those moments when there was no one else around, when we would sit at the piano and take turns playing and singing, I missed those moments more than I cared to admit.

I ended the song and had to blink back the tears. As I stood up, the small congregation clapped enthusiastically. Gramps came over to me and whispered, "That's my girl."

As I walked to my seat, I noticed Pedro watching me. I gave my Dad's signature tight-lipped smile and sat down.

When Gramps finished his sermon and said the closing prayer, Pedro quietly slipped out. A part of me was disappointed. I didn't know why. It's not that I liked him. I absolutely did not. At all.

Gram came up and put her arm around me. "You sing like an angel. I can't believe you don't sing more at your church."

"It's more Hannah's thing," I said with a shrug.

"You sure about that?" she asked, studying me. "Could it be that it might be easier to step into the background than to make yourself vulnerable in front of people?"

"No, I just don't really care if I sing or not. It's important to Hannah, so I'm not going to fight her about it." The conversation made me uncomfortable. I kept eyeing the door.

"Why does it have to be a fight?"

"Because it is," I said. "To her, it's a competition. And I've learned that when I compete against her, I lose." Taking a breath, I said, "I'm going to go back to the house and change."

"A bunch of us usually go to Big Boy's here in town for Sunday dinner. I thought you'd join us."

Dinner with a bunch of old folks? "If it's all right with you, I'd like to relax back at the house. I haven't even had time to unpack any of my stuff yet."

"Of course. We'll bring you back a burger."

I walked out of the building, determined to take a long nap, when I noticed the little girl from earlier in the week, playing by a large maple tree near the road. "Lillian?" I called, going over to her.

She turned around and grinned. "Look," she said, pointing up. "A bird's nest. I'm trying to get it down."

I glanced up and saw the nest and heard the chirping of baby birds in it. "Cool, but we can't get it down."

"Why not? That's why I have this big stick." She held up the stick as far as she could, but it wasn't close enough. "Here, you try it."

"But if we take the nest down, the momma bird won't be able to find her babies, and she'll be sad."

"Really?" she asked with rounded eyes. It came out like *Rewwee*.

"Yes. That's why the baby birds are crying right now. They're telling their mom that they're hungry."

"Where's their mom?"

"She probably went to get food."

"What if she's sick," Lillian said. "What if she doesn't come back?"

A semi-truck zoomed by on the road, a little too close for comfort. "Come on, Lillian. We're too close to the road. Let's go find your Dad."

She took my hand, and I walked her back to the motel. "Daddy's sleeping," she said. "I'm not to disturb him."

"Oh," I said. "Did he say to go outside?" I had a hard time believing any parent would let a little kid roam around outside unattended.

"No, I'm supposed to be a good girl and watch cartoons, but it's so boring."

I had to hide my grin at her dramatic emphasis, *it's so bowing.* "I understand, but Lillian, what if you got lost? You would make him really worried."

Just then a motel door flew open, and Derek—in nothing but a pair of shorts—came running outside. "LILLIAN!" he yelled.

"Right here!" She called, waving at him. He marched over to us, anger across his countenance. "Uh-oh," she whispered. "I'm in trouble."

"Lillian Diane Blackstone! What have I told you about leaving without permission?"

"Not to," she said. "But, Daddy, I found a bird's nest! With little birds!"

He ran his hand through his thick hair and pressed his lips together. "You're going to be the death of me," he told her.

"Will you go to the hospital too?" she asked, her eyes suddenly tearing up.

"No," he said, his countenance changing. "No, hon, that's not what I meant. I meant that when you leave and don't tell me where you're going, I get really scared." He picked her up and hugged her. "But I'm not sick. I'm right here."

I stood there, completely awkward, knowing I should probably walk away but not wanting to be rude about it. "Well, I'm glad she's okay, so I'm going to go back to the house and make something to eat."

"Can I go?" Lillian asked, releasing her Dad, and taking my hand again.

"With me?" I asked, the idea of a nap fleeting away. "I'm kind of boring."

"No, you're not," she laughed. "You know all about birds."

Great. There was no way I could say no to this little girl. I looked over at her Dad. "Is this okay? Can she come over for a little bit?"

"Yeah," he said, actually looking relieved. "That'd be great. I had to pick up hours last night, so I'm running on about four hours sleep."

"As a mechanic? I didn't think they worked late."

"That's my day job. When I can find a sitter, I work part-time as a security guard for two of the business buildings downtown."

"Oh," I said, not wanting him to get any ideas of me being a potential babysitter. I was already enduring slave labor. Still, I found myself stuck and didn't know how to get out of it. "Well, we'll be fine across the street. No worries."

"I'm not worried just be careful because she does like to wander off. Thanks." To Lillian, he said, "But you, don't ever do that again, or no more popsicles."

She already pulled on my hand. "Come on, come on," she said. "I want to see your house."

"It's nothing special," I said. "Don't get your hopes up." I led her to the road, and taking extra care to look both ways, helped her cross the street.

"It's not a motel room!" she said. "That means it's specialer than mine!"

I glanced down at her, feeling dumb. "Are you living at the motel?" I thought of Derek working two jobs in Manistee. Why would they be staying at the motel? Surely, he could afford a place.

"Yes, silly," she giggled. "Why do you think I'm there?"

We reached the porch, and her eyes grew big. "This is beautiful."

Gram loved her wrap-around porch. "Are you hungry? I could make you a sandwich and we could eat it out here."

"YES! Like we're rich, fancy ladies, eating on our big porch." She ran up the steps and sat on a rocker. She lifted her chin and said, "We should drink tea and cakes. Like princesses."

I found myself genuinely smiling. "That sounds lovely," I said in a British accent.

We giggled together. Then Lillian pointed at the road. "Hey, look! It's our room cleaner!"

I looked over my shoulder to see Pedro running across the road and up our driveway. What was he doing? And why did he have to look so angry all the time?

"Is your grandfather still here?" he asked, once he approached.

"Hi," Lillian said, waving at him. He waved at her but kept his attention on me.

"No, they went to Big Boy. They shouldn't be gone too long."

"Did he say anything about pay? Normally, I get paid on Sundays."

"Want me to give him a call?" I already had out my phone and punched in his number. Lillian started talking to Pedro about princesses and tea. "Hey, Gramps?" I said, as soon as I heard his voice. "Pedro's here, and he wanted to know about getting paid." I listened, then hung up. "He said he'll drop it off at your place after dinner."

Pedro did not act pleased. "I guess we'll have to wait." He turned to leave.

"Well, it's Sunday anyway," I said. "Banks aren't open. So you'll still get your check with enough time to cash it."

"Ever heard of check-cashing places?" he asked. "Probably not. You've probably never needed money in a hurry."

"No need to be mean."

"Never mind," Pedro said, shaking his head. "Someone like you would never understand. Now if you excuse me, I have mouths to feed."

Mouths to feed? "Wait!" I called out. When he stopped, I said, "Wait right there. I'll be right back."

I ran inside and up the stairs to my bedroom. Grabbing my purse, I unearthed a twenty dollar bill Dad had given me before he left. Running back down the stairs and outside, I saw that Pedro hadn't waited and was already walking down the road.

"Lillian, stay right here. I'll be right back." I ran down the driveway. "WAIT!"

Pedro didn't stop.

"WAIT!" I called again, nearly gaining on him.

He spun around. "What is your problem?"

I shoved the twenty dollar bill at him. "Here. I just wanted to give you this."

He shoved it back without looking at it. "I don't want it."

"You said you needed the money. Just consider it a loan. After you cash your check, you can pay me back."

Pedro's face stayed hardened, but eventually he sighed and took the money. "I will pay you back tomorrow."

"Yes," I said, acting serious. "Don't forget."

He looked from the money to my face and gave a half-smile. "No need to get self-righteous."

"Oh my word, did you almost give me a compliment? I thought I almost heard it."

"No," he said, then left me standing there.

"Absolutely no sense of humor," I said under my breath. I watched him walk away for probably longer than I should have before I realized that Lillian was still—hopefully—on the porch waiting for me.

I ran back and saw her playing, acting like a princess and giving orders to her phantom servants. When she saw me, she pointed inside the house. "Make my lunch, by order of the queen."

"You're the queen? I thought we were princesses."

"I changed my mind. You are my servant, and you have to do whatever I say."

"Well, I'm not too sure about that," I teased. "But I can make you lunch. Want to come inside?"

"YES!" she jumped off the rocker and grabbed my hand. I smiled, thinking of Adrianne and how much she would have enjoyed playing with Lillian.

An hour later, Lillian and I sat outside, our stomachs full of grilled cheese sandwiches and grapes. She chatted nearly nonstop, while I sketched her on the front porch. She would peek over my shoulder and giggle. "Is that me?"

"Yep."

Gram and Gramps pulled up right as Derek crossed the street to the house.

"What have we here?" Gram asked, thoroughly pleased at seeing Lillian. She handed me a take-out box with a burger and fries in it.

"I am the princess of this castle," Lillian said.

"She keeps going back and forth from princess to queen," I quipped, closing my sketchbook and sitting on it. I didn't want to draw attention to it.

"Have you ate any cookies yet?" Gram asked, going inside.

Lillian looked at me, her mouth open. "You've been hiding the treasure!"

"Yes. Yes, I have."

Lillian, without waiting for an invitation, followed Gram inside and to the kitchen.

"Is everything going good?" Derek asked Gramps and me. "She's not being a handful, is she?"

"We just arrived ourselves," Gramps said. "But she's in good hands with our Macy May."

"We had a great time," I said. "She's a lot of fun."

The screen door opened with a bang as Lillian came out with two big cookies in her hands. "I got cookies!" she said to her dad.

"I can see that," he said. "You ready to get going?"

Her face fell. "No, I just got here."

"You've been playing with Macy for two hours."

"That's not very long."

"I know, but you can always visit again. Besides, mommy likes to see you."

Lillian sat on the steps and crossed her arms, both cookies still in her hands. "She can't see me."

"She can hear you," Derek said. "And it makes her happy. Come on." He reached over and picked her up.

I glanced over at Gramps, wondering if he knew what Derek was talking about. Was Lillian's mother blind? I remembered Lillian said something about living at the motel, and it dawned on me that something was going on beyond father and daughter at motel. "You can come play again. I promise." I looked down at the take-out box. "Would you like a burger?" I asked Derek. "I already ate with Lillian, and I don't want it to go to waste."

"Are you sure?" he asked.

"Positive." I handed it to him.

As Derek thanked me and left with his daughter, I asked Gramps, "What's going on with her mother?"

Gramps watched them leave and answered, "They got in a motorcycle accident. Derek and his wife. He came away with minor fractures, but she hit her head against an electrical pole. Something like that. She's been in a coma for about two months. They don't have insurance, so he sold everything they owned besides his car to pay for medical expenses. He keeps hoping that she'll wake up. But even if she did, it wouldn't be good. She'd have to be in a nursing home facility or somewhere that could take care of her."

"That's awful," I said, my heart hurting for all of them, but especially Lillian.

"Yeah. The guilt's ate him up. He told me he can't pull the plug. It's as if he's killing her all over again." Gramps rested his hand on my shoulder. "It's good that you show kindness to Lillian. She doesn't understand what's going on other than her momma's sleeping."

"That's why they're in the motel," I said, as it started to make sense. "He sold their home."

"They didn't own a home. They were renting, and he was evicted because he couldn't pay it. When he and his daughter came to the motel, he was paying for one night with a jar of change. I've been letting him stay ever since."

"For free?"

"Yep. It's my way of helping."

I swallowed hard, feeling sad over the events in their lives. "That's nice, Gramps."

"Well, I'm a nice guy," he said. "Now, I've got to run to my office and pick up Pedro's check."

"About that," I said. "I thought you said he was doing community service, too. Why is he getting paid?"

"Half the hours go toward community service, half the hours he gets paid. He has mouths to feed, you know."

"So, you're helping him, too?"

"Yep."

"And you're helping me."

"Yep. Just call me Saint Gramps."

"It's almost like it's a motel for misfits," I said, being silly, but he had already walked to his car.

But I sat on the porch for the rest of the evening, thinking about everything Gramps had told me. Then I pulled out my sketchbook from under me and started drawing. It was just the therapy I needed.

Chapter 6~

It's Complicated

"Here."

I looked up from changing sheets on a bed and saw Pedro in the doorway, holding a twenty dollar bill. "Oh, don't worry about it," I said, thinking about what Gramps told me the night before. If Pedro had mouths to feed, then maybe I should be a little nicer.

Pedro sighed, stepped into the room, took my hand, and placed the twenty in it. "I told you I'd pay it back."

I nodded. *Fine, pay back the stupid money.* Could this guy be any more stubborn? As he was leaving, I asked, "So, do you have children?"

He turned slowly. "How old do you think I am?"

"I don't know. Maybe in your twenties. But you said you had mouths to feed, so I assumed—"

"What is with you and your assumptions?"

"Sorry," I said, throwing my hands up. "Don't shoot."

He narrowed his eyes. "What's that supposed to mean?"

Dropping the clean sheet onto the bed, I marched over to him. "It's a joke. It means you're really defensive." I tried to smile, but he wasn't having it.

"Just do your job and let me do mind."

As he made a move to leave, I grabbed his arm. Why? I had no idea. It was impulsive. He stopped and glared at me. "Listen, can't we start over?" I asked.

"You want to start over?" he asked. "You think I'm dangerous, remember? You begged your grandparents not to work with me, remember?"

"That was last week," I said. "Before I knew you."

"You don't know me."

"Okay, fine. Stop being so contrary. I'm trying to make peace."

"You clean your rooms, and I'll clean mine. That's all the peace you're going to get."

As he left the room, a car zoomed into the parking lot, squealing right in front of us. Derek got out and ran over to me. "Macy! Thank God, you're here! I need a major favor."

"Um, sure, if I can." I watched as Pedro left us to keep cleaning.

"Lillian's kindergarten is on week-long break, and that includes her latchkey program. I completely forgot about it. I've got no one else to watch her. Please. You're the only one I could think of. I've got to be at work, and I don't know what to do."

"I'm cleaning the rooms pretty much all day."

"Great, she'll help."

I glanced inside the motel room I had started working on. It would be difficult to take care of Lillian while cleaning.

"Please, Macy," he said, as if reading my thoughts. "I've got no one."

"Sure," I said. "We'll figure it out."

Derek gave a relieved sigh. "Thank you. It'll be all this week." He opened up Lillian's door and unbuckled her car seat. "The auto shop closes at six. So, I'll be here after that." To Lillian, he said, "Be a good girl for Macy."

She ran up to me and gave me a hug. "I get to be with you!"

"Yay!" I said, trying to act enthusiastic. I didn't mind watching Lillian, but I had no idea how I was going to clean and watch a wandering girl at the same time. She'd already disclosed yesterday how cartoons bored her.

But Derek hadn't wasted anytime, and had taken off, squealing out of the parking lot.

"What are we going to do today?" she asked. "Play princesses?"

"I've got to work at the motel. So, we'll have to play servants."

She crinkled her nose. "Okay, I guess." Then marched into the motel room I was currently working on. "What can I do?"

I looked around, then thinking quickly, grabbed a dust rag. "Here. Your job is to dust everything. Dust it really good. If you do a good job today, I'll pay you."

"Money?"

"Yep."

"Deal." We shook on it.

Even though Lillian couldn't be any more adorable, the day became challenging. She wanted to help with everything. That meant explaining and demonstrating. Then we had to stop to have lunch. Normally I worked right through it, eating a protein bar or sandwich as

I cleaned. But with Lillian she wanted to go to the house to eat, so I took her to the house to make her lunch there. Gram ha   d left to run some errands, so I couldn't leave Lillian there. By the time 4 o'clock came around, Lillian had already become bored and was running around the motel, which meant I had to chase her. And I still had half of my rooms left to clean.

When Gram pulled in the driveway, I took Lillian over to her. "Hey, Gram, do you mind if Lillian hangs out with you? Maybe she could help with dinner?"

"Have you had her all day?" she asked.

"Yeah," I said, not hiding the exhaustion. "I've still got half of my rooms left to do."

Gran held out her hand. "Come on, Miss Lillian, let's cook up a nice supper for Macy. What do you say?"

Lillian clung to my leg. "I want to stay with you. You're my best friend."

"As soon as I'm done cleaning, I'll be right here. Then we can play princesses again."

All Gran had to do was offer cookies and milk. Lillian went to her, and I went running back to the motel. Once at my cart, I pushed it to the next room, but the door was already propped open. Pedro was vacuuming. "Hey!" I yelled, waving at him.

He turned off the vacuum and raised his eyebrows.

"Isn't this my rotation today?"

Pedro shrugged. "I'll take this one and room 112. You had your hands full." My face must not have hid my shock because he asked,

"What?"

"Thank you," I said.

"What you did for Derek was nice. He's in a bad way right now. With his wife and all."

"Yeah," I said. We stood awkwardly for too long. "Okay, well, I'll go finish rooms 113 and 114. Thanks again."

He had already turned on the vacuum.

With Pedro's help, I finished just after five. As I pushed my cart back into the laundry room, my cell phone buzzed. Normally Adrianne would call every evening, but it was too early for her. Then I saw Hannah's text:

Mom needs your account #. We're taking the money out. And did u take my gold sandals? Not cool.

I practically growled and furiously texted back:

No, I didn't take your stupid gold sandals. And I'm not giving you my account #. That's my savings for college! ☹ I'll give Dad the money when he visits.

I shoved the phone in my pocket and pushed the cart to behind the washers and dryers. "Stupid!" I said to myself. "Totally stupid, Macy! Now you've got to give that wench over $200 dollars! I hate her!" I stopped when I saw Pedro refilling his cart.

"What's stupid?" he asked, not stopping his inventory.

"Me," I said.

"Who do you hate?"

"My sister. Everyone." I needed to refill my cart, but I was too exhausted. Before leaving, I muttered, "They all hate me, too. It's a mutual feeling."

"I doubt that."

"My family dumped me up here because they didn't want me down with them. What was it you said last week? Oh, yeah, that I got under people's skin." I walked to the door. "See ya. Thanks for your help today." My anger and hurt pulsed through me. I wanted to confront Hannah. I knew her insurance would cover the damage. Dad said so himself. Yeah, I puked in her car, and I was ashamed about it, but she acted like I destroyed it.

"Wait!" I heard Pedro call out. When I turned around, he said, "I shouldn't have said that. About your family not wanting you. I don't know what's going on with your sister or with your family, but I'm sure they miss you."

I shook my head and tried to hold my emotions in. I didn't want him to see me cry. "My own mother has only called me once. In nine days. And it was because Dad wanted to talk to me about the court date. Only Adrianne, my little sister, calls me on a daily basis. I haven't heard from my twelve year old brother, and I only hear from Hannah because she wants my money. They're the perfect little family now that the trouble maker's gone."

"Troublemaker?" Pedro chuckled. "No offense, but you look like the opposite of a troublemaker."

"Looks can be deceiving," I said, not wanting to get into the story. I waved good-bye and then walked away quickly. I might have been appreciative that Pedro helped with the rooms, but I didn't want to talk about my family any more.

***

I lay on my bed, trying to sketch, but feeling too exhausted to move the pencil. After dinner, when Derek came to pick up Lillian, I decided on a bath instead of a shower to help calm my frustrations from earlier. The bath relaxed me so much I fell asleep in the tub, waking up because the water had turned cold. And I was still tired.

I closed the sketch book and rested my head on my pillow. Right as I started to doze off, someone knocked on the door. "Yeah?"

"It's Gramps. Can I come in?"

"Sure." I didn't move from the pillow.

He opened the door. "Sorry to disturb you, but your father's been trying to get ahold of you. Says you're not answering your phone."

"I turned it off. I was tired of receiving Hannah's threats."

Gramps went over to the chair and sat down. "I see you've yet to unpack."

My suitcases were opened on the floor, clothes everywhere. "I've started."

He chuckled, then stopped and coughed as if trying to change the subject. "So, I have papers to sign for your community service, but now your father says that these hours might not count yet because you've yet to go to court."

I sat up so fast, I startled Gramps. "What?"

"You've got to go to court first. After they assign you the actual community service hours, then you can start working toward completing them. I guess we're not supposed to bank the hours, so to speak."

"So, I'm here, busting my tail, just because?"

Gramps' expression fell. "I'm sorry, Macy May. But I do have a little bit of good news." He took a folded piece of paper out of his pocket and handed it to me. It was a check for $486 dollars. "You worked 54 hours so far, which by the way is too many for you to work, so I'll have to fix that. Anyway, housekeepers start out at $9 dollars an hour. You haven't filled out any tax forms yet because I didn't think you were getting paid. But until the court date, you will earn a pay check. I'll have you fill out tax forms tomorrow. I don't want the IRS breathing down my neck."

I stared at the check, trying to sort through my emotions. It was my first paycheck ever, and it was a big one. Almost $500 dollars! But I couldn't escape the one thought that wouldn't back down. "They couldn't even wait until the court date to get rid of me," I said, feeling the tears form. I hated that it still bothered me. Or that I cared.

"Oh, Macy dear, things are always more complicated than a simple conflict. There are things that you are not privy to that has a lot to do with the way your father handles things."

Gramps' words dried up my tears. "What am I not privy to?" I asked, repeating his words.

"That's only something your father can share with you. But I know he loves you dearly. I know that he's worried about you. I know that he's aware of Hannah's treatment of you. He thought that if you were up here with us and away from Hannah that you could maybe relax and find yourself. The decision, at least on his part, was made out of love for you."

"Doesn't feel that way."

Gramps stood up and patted my head. "For what it's worth, Gram and I are glad to have you. We wouldn't mind if you decided to stay here for a long while. Even if you are a troublemaker." He winked at me before leaving the room. Then he popped his head back in, "Oh, one more thing. We're decreasing your hours for the time being. 40 hours a week max. So plan on your Saturdays and Sundays off."

After he left, I felt restless as if my insides were going in a 100 different directions. I heard the T.V. downstairs and knew Gram was watching some Hallmark show. It was the only channel she watched. Sometimes I would go downstairs and watch with her, but not tonight. I would sketch but didn't feel like sitting still.

Grabbing my converse, I slipped into them and tied them up. Then I threw a sweatshirt over my head and pulled on a pair of yoga pants since I only had a t-shirt and shorts on. Once down the steps, I peeked in the living room where Gram sat. "I'm going to go for a walk."

"But it's dark now."

"I won't go far, and I'll stick to the road."

"We don't have a lot of street lights around here."

"I'll be fine." I walked away before she could give me a definitive no.

I barely made it past the driveway before I realized that Gram was right. It was dark outside. Across the street two lampposts lit up the motel parking lot, but that was it. Looking down one stretch of road and then the other direction, I saw nothing but darkness.

Not quite ready to go back in the house, I crossed the street to the church. Lights were off, but Gramps had given me a key. Mostly for all the times he'd have me running over here to get something for him.

I fumbled with the lock for a few minutes—thanks to not being able to see—before finally unlocking and opening the door. Gram always left a dim foyer light on, but I still felt the chills shoot up my arms. Something about an empty dark church reminded me of a horror movie. Not that I'd ever watched any. With my parents' strict no T.V. policy in our house, the only movies we could watch were rated PG. Finding the light switch, I turned on another set of lights and felt better.

There was something about old churches that smelled like old wood and Pine sol. I stood in the foyer for several minutes gathering up the nerve to do what I came over here to do. Oh yes, I wasn't fooling myself. I knew exactly what my fingers were itching to do.

Taking a deep breath, I opened up the swing door to the sanctuary, and flipped on a couple sets of lights until I figure out which ones lit the platform area. I walked to the piano, remembering all the times I'd play while Hannah sang. By the time I turned eleven, she had turned fifteen, and she no longer wanted to sing duets with me. For the last couple years, I would have to sneak time to play the piano at our house. Mom complained that it was too loud, and Hannah would always snap that my chords were too clunky. Every now and then, when they were gone, Adrianne would get me to play. She would sing beside me as loud as she could. Unfortunately for the poor girl, she was completely tone deaf, which meant Mom wouldn't have her sing in front at church. I wasn't sure why the musical gene skipped my little sister. Lucas was only 12, but he was already gifted at the guitar.

I sat on the piano bench and ran my fingers over the keys. The piano was easily the most beautiful instrument. The notes that blended together to form melodies could touch anyone's soul. I began playing softly, a few progressions that I had put together when I was younger. Then a song came to me, one of my own, and I began to play. One turned into another as I let the music surround me, sheltering me from the outside world, from the pain of heartache, from the betrayal of not being wanted.

Eventually, I felt depleted. I ended the song, then ran my hand over the piano again. "Thanks, friend," I whispered. "You're the best therapy. Right there next to sketching."

I walked down the aisle, turned off the sanctuary lights, and shut its door to the vestibule. When I opened the outside doors to leave, I noticed Derek sitting on the steps, smoking a cigarette. "Hey," I said, shutting the door and locking it. "Everything all right?"

He shrugged and brought the cigarette to his lips.

"Was I too loud?"

"No, not at all." He turned and glanced up at me. He still had his dirty mechanic's uniform on.

"Is everything okay?" I asked again. "Is Lillian fine?"

"Yeah, yeah, nothing's wrong."

I heard the catch in his voice. I sat on the step next to him and watched him while he smoked. I didn't know what to say.

"You play the piano?" he said it more like a statement than a question, not looking at me.

"Yes. My parents started lessons for me when I turned four."

He nodded. "I can tell. You're really good."

I felt the surge of warmth inside from the compliment but shoved it down. Now wasn't the time to feed my pride. "Thanks. My sister's better."

"I doubt that. What songs were you playing?"

"My own. There's not really words to them, just my…feelings. Weird, but it works for me."

He chuckled humorlessly. "I'd love to do something like that for Lillian. Maybe one day her daddy can afford music lessons."

Once again, I didn't know what to say. "How's your wife doing?" I finally asked.

Derek didn't answer at first. It was hard to see his face in the dark, but it sounded like he was choked up. He wiped at his eyes and pushed himself up. "I should probably go check on Lillian."

"Okay," I said. I watched him walk back over to the motel. For the first time, I didn't feel alone in my pain. And it made me feel even worse.

Chapter 7~

Surprise!

"Rooms 107 and 108 finally checked out," Pedro said the next morning. "You take one, and I'll take one."

I nodded while I finished filling my cart.

"You might want to add a few additional items. Those guys were partiers. The rooms are probably nasty."

About seven or eight guys rented our two largest rooms and had put out the 'Do Not Disturb' signs as soon as they checked in four days ago. Even though they were gone most of the days kayaking the Manistee River, their nights were pretty active. "Got it," I said, throwing a couple extra gloves and garbage bags onto the cart.

"You doing better?" Pedro asked.

I stopped and looked over at him. Just a couple days ago, he acted like he hated me. It seemed weird, although relieving, that he was talking to me now. "I'm fine."

He nodded, then pushed his cart around the washing equipment. "I'd get started on that room before Lillian comes over. You probably don't want her in that mess."

I followed him out and headed to the room to get started. As I opened the door, I could already smell the pot and stale beer. I pushed open the door and braced myself. The room had been trashed, but it wasn't as bad as I thought it would be. The mattresses with the bottom sheets were still on the beds, but the rest of the bed linens were dumped on the floor. The small trash cans were overflowing with pizza boxes as make-shift trash holders. The small kitchenette that this room had was basically used as a trash container as well. The small counter and sink were loaded with empty bottles and food bags, used paper plates and Solo cups.

"Not as bad as I thought," Pedro said, popping his head in the room. "At least the mattresses are where they should be."

"That's what I was thinking," I said, already grabbing the garbage bags from the cart.

Pedro left to clean the accompanying room. I began dumping everything in the trash bags. There were a few unopened bags of chips, but I didn't care. In the trash they went. As I threw away the empty cups that littered around the television, I paused at the hundred dollar bill. A note had been folded around it: *Sorry about the mess. Here's a little something for the extra trouble.* But it wasn't the money that had caught my attention. It was the small, unopened bottle of Jack Daniels that accompanied the money and note.

My pulse quickened as I picked up the bottle and rested it in my hand. I should probably get rid of it, but I didn't want to. I wasn't stupid. I knew how much Jack Daniels cost. But did I want the temptation? Since coming up here, I might have been heartsick and a little lonely, but I hadn't had the nightmare since the first night. I didn't fall asleep worrying if my door was going to squeak open in the night. Plus, Hannah wasn't here to bully me.

But I couldn't bring myself to throw it away.

"Good morning," Derek said from the door, making me jump.

"Hey," I said, turning around with my full hand behind my back. My heart pounded so loud I wondered if he could hear it.

"What a mess," he said, checking out the room.

"Yeah. Big-time partiers."

"I know. I could hear them through the night. Even with the air conditioning fan on." He stopped looking around to focus on me. I tried to act as nonchalant as possible. "Lillian is still sleeping. I didn't have the heart to wake her up. Can I leave her in bed?"

"Sure. I'll check in on her in a little bit then get her some breakfast. Gram told her yesterday that she'll make her chocolate chip pancakes."

Derek laughed. "That's nice of Ms. Elmsworth. You all are spoiling her. She talks nonstop about you."

I smiled, the bottle of liquor burning in my hand. No doubt my guilty conscience was causing the flames. "She's wonderful," I said. "I enjoy having her around."

"I'll be back earlier than normal. On Thursdays, I take her up to see her mom."

"I bet she likes that."

"No, not really," he said. "She doesn't understand why her mom won't wake up. But the doctors say that hearing Lillian's voice could potentially help. I don't know…"

"I'm sorry," I said.

"About last night," Derek started. "Thanks for not making a big deal about my emotional state. I go through rough patches."

"Understandable."

"You're a good soul," he said. "Just like your grandparents." Derek left me standing in the dirty motel room with a full bottle of alcohol in my hands.

No, I'm not, I thought to myself as I stared at the liquor bottle. I contemplated giving it to Derek. He might need it more than I do. Instead I stuffed the money in my pocket and the whiskey underneath the cleaning supplies. I wasn't sure what I would do with it, but I wasn't ready to give it up just yet.

*** *

By 10 a.m. the party room had been finished, Lillian and I were stuffed full of chocolate chip pancakes. Lillian now followed me room-to-room, insisting that she was helping. Even though I had to go back over everything she had technically cleaned, I found myself enjoying the little girl's company.

She would rattle off about Disney princesses, or she would beg me to turn on music so she could dance. "Let's boogie!" she'd yell, then start jumping on the beds.

When early afternoon came around, I noticed Pedro in the parking lot with two boys. One looked about my brother's age, the other couldn't have been much older than Lillian. Both of them resembled Pedro. Minus the tattoos and piercings. The older one couldn't have been his son because Pedro said he was nineteen. Possibly brothers?

Pedro came over to me, but the boys stayed put. As he approached, I noticed how pale he had become and how nervous he acted. He kept wringing his hands and darting his eyes.

"Is everything all right?" I asked.

"I hate to do this to you, but I've got to go."

My stomach fell. There were still several rooms left, not counting Pedro's. "Oh."

"Please. Do this for me, and I'll owe you one. Here," he shoved a hundred dollar bill in my hands. "Take this. It came from the party room."

"No," I said, giving it back to him. "I got one too. This is yours."

He might have argued, but whatever had agitated him seemed to take center stage. "So, we cool?"

"I'll manage. Go."

Pedro looked from me to Lillian. "I won't forget this."

He ran over to the boys, and they followed him to the motel's office. Pedro grabbed a bike along the wall, while the other boys got on theirs. The three of them pedaled down the road hurriedly.

Pedro pedaled a bike to work? How had I missed that?

"We sure have a lot of cleaning to do," Lillian said, giving a gratuitous sigh. "It's hard being a servant. When is our Prince Charming going to come?"

"I don't know," I said, watching Pedro becoming smaller the further he biked. "All I know is that I'm going to be here a long time."

I pushed the cart to the next room and opened the door.

Lillian took my hand. "You and me together."

"Yep," I said, smiling down at her.

But she didn't smile back. "I told daddy to kiss mom because that's how princesses wake up. But it's not working."

There might have been rooms to clean, but none of that mattered as I stared into the eyes of this sweet little girl. I knelt down to become eye-level with her. "Maybe she'll wake up still. We have to keep praying and be patient and see."

Her eyes filled with tears, and she shook her head. "A man in a black suit came to mom's room. He seemed nice and asked to pray for her, but daddy yelled at him and told him to take his god and shove it and made him leave. I don't like seeing daddy angry." Big tears rolled down Lillian's cheeks. "So, don't say the word 'pray' around him or he'll go tell you to shove it too. And I don't want you to leave."

I pulled the little girl to me and hugged her. "I'm not leaving," I said, not knowing why I was saying that when I would be leaving at some point. But this girl needed comfort, and I didn't know what else to say to give it to her.

For the next three rooms, Lillian seemed content enough to watch T.V. while I cleaned. She'd become melancholy, but I couldn't stop or I'd be cleaning until dark. Luckily, Derek showed up early to take her to visit her mother. "Come on, I'll stop by the E-Z Mart and buy you a slushee," he said.

Lillian perked up enough to run to the car. But not before giving me a hug. "I'll be a servant with you tomorrow."

"Deal," I said, hugging her back. "Enjoy that slushee."

As she climbed in the car, Derek asked, "Everything go okay?

You're not too far behind, are you?"

I had to bite my tongue to keep the truth from stumbling out. "Everything's fine. You two have a nice time."

He paused, as if contemplating his next words. "This is probably the last time she'll see her mom alive."

"There's nothing more they can do?"

"They've done everything they can for a family with no insurance. But I already owe nearly a hundred thousand dollars. That's with the local charities helping. The longer she's on a ventilator, the more I fall down the never-ending pit of financial despair. It would be different if they offered any hope..." he stopped. "Don't mean to unload on you. Thanks for watching Lillian."

Derek walked to the car, made sure Lillian was buckled in, then went around to the driver's side door.

"Wait!" I said, going over to him.

He raised his eyebrows.

What was I going to say? What could I say? I wanted to hug him, but then again, I wasn't comfortable hugging any guy. Not after Hannah's jerkface fiancé ruined my trust with men younger than forty. "It royally sucks, Derek. And I'm so sorry." I went to give him a hug, but felt awkward and let my hands drop to my side. I kept my emotions together although I was sure he could see how close to tears I was.

"Yeah, it royally sucks." He reached over and squeezed my shoulder.

"Here." I took the hundred dollar bill from my pocket and handed it to him. "It's not much, but it'll help a little bit."

"You're already watching Lillian for free. I'm not taking your money too."

I shoved the money into the pocket of his shirt. "You're not taking the money. I'm giving it to you. Go, and do something nice with Lillian. Please. I can't do much, so let me do this for you." I moved away from him, so that the conversation would end.

Eventually, he slid into the car and drove out of the motel parking lot.

For the rest of the afternoon, I threw myself into cleaning. My arms felt like noodles, but I pushed past it. My thighs and butt muscles were sore, but I couldn't stop. As I vacuumed I thought of a woman I never laid eyes on, dying in a hospital bed, and her young daughter afraid to pray. *Then again, why should she?* I thought as I tucked in clean sheets. *What kind of God puts an innocent woman on a ventilator to begin with? What kind of God lets a little girl lose her mother?*

I vacuumed with a vengeance, angry because I realized how many questions I had. Angry that people like Hannah and Jake get to be popular and successful while actual good people, like Derek and his wife and their daughter, suffer.

Locking up the cleaned room, I pushed the cart to the next door and nearly plowed into my father.

"Hey there, peanut," he said, grinning from ear to ear.

My brain was having a hard time computing that my father was actually standing in front of me. "Dad?"

"Are you going to give me a hug, or do I have to stand here awkwardly with my arms open?"

I moved the cart aside and threw my arms around him. I should have been angry at him. But instead, especially with all the volatile emotions rolling through me, I was just really glad to see him.

"I missed you so much, I jumped into the car and came right up. So did everyone else."

"Everyone?" I released him and eyed him warily.

"Well, Hannah stayed back because of her college classes still going on, but everyone else is here. Adrianne is going insane missing you. I made her stay back at Gram and Gramps to unload."

"Cool! I can't wait to give her a big hug. Let me finish up here, and I'll head over there."

"You're not done yet? Gramps said that you should be done by four. It's already five."

"Yeah, I'm really backed up. We had these big partiers leave this morning, and their rooms were horrible."

"It looks like you're by yourself." He turned to examine the rooms around us.

"The guy who works with me had an emergency, so I'm covering for him."

"Macy, you shouldn't work more than 8 hours a day."

"I know. It was an emergency."

"Tell your Gramps. Does he know?"

"I don't think so, but it's fine. Really. Pedro has helped me out a few times too."

"MACY!"

Dad and I turned to see Adrianne crossing the street and running over. Luke ran too, quickly closing in the gap. Mom trailed behind them both. "Adrianne!" I said, running to her, grinning like a fool.

She jumped in my arms and hugged me fiercely. "Daddy surprised us today and said we get to see you!"

I set her down. "You surprised me! That's for sure!"

"Hey, big sis," Luke said, holding out his fist. He had never been a big hugger.

I hit his fist with mine. "Luke! So happy to see you!"

Mom approached. "There she is. I want to hug you, but I'll wait until you're cleaned up." She laughed like it was funny. Then again, she had on her designer jeans, six-inch heels, and Claiborne jacket.

"I probably wouldn't hug me right now either." I glanced down at the faded jeans with dirt streaks and the oversized sweatshirt that I had thrown on this morning.

"But this looks good," Mom said, glancing around the motel. "Working hard, staying out of trouble."

"Yep," I said, telling myself not to get defensive. It still stung thinking about how she practically packed up my entire life and had Dad dump me up here. "Gramps works me so hard I barely have time to shower, eat, and sleep."

"I'm going to talk to him about that," Dad said. "There are parameters around the community service."

"Right, but currently I'm not doing community service. Gramps is paying me until I receive a court order for it." I made sure to say the words with a little bite to them. I wanted my parents to know that Gramps had told me.

"Still," Dad said, not even acting guilty for the news that community service hadn't started yet. "You shouldn't be cleaning the whole place."

"Oh, she'll be fine," Mom said. "Hard work builds character. And think of all the money you'll earn!"

"Can I help clean?" Adrianne asked. "I want to earn money too."

"Absolutely not," Mom said, acting disgusted. "You are a little lady and must act like one. Come on, let's go get settled."

Her words hit me with the weight of a sledgehammer.

"I can help," Luke said. "I don't mind."

But I didn't answer. Finally, Dad said, "I'm going to help. Why don't you go back and see if Gram or Gramps need you to set the table for dinner."

Luke left with a wave.

I pushed my cart to the next room. "I'm fine here, Dad. Go back to the house."

Dad reached for my arm. "She didn't mean it like that."

"Then how'd she mean it?" I opened the door, took one look at the unused room, and shut the door. At least I didn't have to worry about that one.

"She didn't want Adrianne to get dirty. Housekeeping can be a dirty job. That's all."

"Yep, it can be."

"Stop. I didn't come all this way to fight."

I pushed the cart to the next room. "Dad, I've got to finish these rooms. Check in began at four, which means that Gramps can't let out these rooms until their cleaned."

"All right, which rooms still need cleaning? I'm at your command."

"I'll be fine—"

"Macy May Elmsworth, which rooms? I used to work here too, remember?" Dad rolled up the sleeves to his designer shirt.

"I've got three rooms left. Why don't you start on 114? If you could go and pull up the used sheets and dump them here in the linens' bag, that'd be great." I handed him my master key.

"Do I still knock and say, 'Housekeeping?' We used to have to do that."

"No, these last couple rooms don't have anyone in them anymore. But you can do it for old times' sake." I gave him a smile.

"I'm on it." He knocked on 114, and in a high-pitched voice, called out, "Housekeeping!"

We both laughed, then got to work.

Dad pulled up the used linens from all three of the rooms, then headed back to 114 to start vacuuming. I appreciated his help, but I would have rather been alone. I was already on edge. How a person could be glad to see her family only to want them gone was a mystery. Well, not all of them, just Mom.

I cleaned the mirrors with glass cleaner, thinking about my mother. She had never been an affectionate parent. At least not with me. For as long as I could remember, I seemed to have this ability to exasperate her. That's how I got into art work. She put me in time out so much, that I began to doodle to pass the time. Part of the reason

Hannah started to see everything as a competition with me was because Mom would push her to play the piano better or to sing better. Then she'd have me sit out of a singing session. "Let Hannah practice. You don't have to hog all the attention."

With the mirror cleaned, I stared at my reflection, a deep frown on my face. My hair had been thrown up into a messy bun, I had a layer of sweat and grime on my face, and my sweatshirt was filthy. I looked nothing like a classy lady. The kind of lady Mom referred to when she warned Adrianne not to clean the motel rooms.

I moved through the chore of cleaning robotically, allowing Dad to vacuum the last room while I put fresh linens on beds and covered them with the bedspreads. The bathrooms weren't too bad, so I half-heartedly cleaned them, making sure they at least looked like a fresh bathroom. By the time the rooms were finished, even Dad was sweating.

"This is tough work."

"You get the hang of it, after a while. Pedro is a lot faster than me. But I've only been doing it about two weeks."

Dad pushed the cart back into the laundry room. When he came back outside, he said, "Well, I'm proud of you. You are really helping your grandparents out. Did they tell you how they lost two housekeepers on the same day?"

"No. Gram told me about Nancy moving, but that's it."

"Nancy had cleaned for your Gramps since he bought the place. Real nice lady."

"What happened? Who's the other one?"

"She and her daughter worked here Monday through Saturday.

Until Nancy got real sick. Laurette had to quit to help take care of her. They ended up moving to the U.P. to be near more family. Gram and Gramps have been strapped for help for over a month."

"Is that why I'm here? To help them?"

"Partially. It was more like an opportunity. You would need community service hours, and they needed help. Plus with the wedding, you know…"

"Yeah, I know. Let's go get some dinner. I'm starving."

"Wait, one more thing." Dad pulled at my arm.

"What?" My stomach growled, and I was stressed and upset. Food could help all of those issues.

"Jake's not in your room. Just thought you should know."

"Really?"

"Yes. I thought about it when I drove home two weeks ago, and I decided that it was insulting to you. That is your room. You are only away for a little while. So, I put my foot down. Your mother wasn't happy, and Hannah was furious, but they came to see it my way." Dad's expression clouded over briefly. His jaw set in a firm line, and he frowned as if not happy.

"Thanks, Dad," I said quietly. I thought about Dad telling Jake that he couldn't stay there. I imagined Hannah's fury, and mother's livid tirade, and I smiled. Dad stood up for me? "That means a lot."

His grim expression lifted. "You are my peanut. No matter what anyone says. And I care about your happiness and well-being. Not that your mother doesn't. She's just…really preoccupied with the wedding."

I decided not to push it, so I kept my sarcastic comment to

myself. "Whatever you say. Let's go get some food!"

Dad and I crossed the street and walked to the house. I dragged with fatigue and could seriously stuff my face and then crash. When we opened the door, Mom took one look at me and pointed upstairs. "Shower."

"Can I eat first?"

"Of course you can," Gram said. "Dinner's ready, and I don't want the lasagna to get cold."

"At least wash up," Mom said in exasperation. Why did she have to act like that all the time? "Think of all the germs you're bringing to the table."

I sighed and ran up the stairs and into the bathroom and slammed the door. *What was her problem?* I thought as I glared in the mirror. Okay, so I looked filthy, but still! My stomach seemed to be roaring at this point, but Mom would glare at me the whole dinner if I ignored her wishes. So, I irritatedly ran the shower water then stripped down and jumped in.

The water would have felt nice, but I was too upset. I scrubbed with a vengeance, rinsed the shampoo out of my hair, and turned off the shower. There. Fastest shower in the history of the world.

But now I had to run to my room with nothing but a towel. I peeked outside the door and saw Adrianne waiting at the top of the stairs. "Hurry!" she said. "The lasagna smells so delicious!"

"I know, I know!" I said. "But I didn't want to bring *germs* to the table."

Adrianne might have only been eight, but even she rolled her eyes.

I ran into my room and stopped in my tracks. All of my stuff had been taken out of the suitcases and put away. The suitcases were gone. The bed had been made with all the rest of my decorative pillows from downstate. My comfy beanie chair sat in the corner where the other chair had been. Even two of my posters hung on the walls. Anyone else would chock it up to thoughtfulness, but I felt like I had been slapped. It was as if Mom was saying that I'd better get comfortable. That I'd be here for the long haul.

And it shouldn't bother me. I liked it here. Gram and Gramps treated me like a human being. I had met Derek and Lillian. And Pedro. Not to mention Hannah and buttface were no longer bullying me or ruining my existence. *But still.* "This is *my* stuff," I said out loud.

"Do you like it?" Adrianne asked. "When Mom saw you hadn't unpacked, she decided to help you out. She was like, 'How can that girl live in such a mess,' or something like that."

I noticed my two sketchbooks open and on the bed. One was the sketch I started to draw of Pedro. It looked unfinished because I couldn't figure out how to draw all the tattoos on his arms. The other sketchbook was opened to a doodle of the motel I did when I first arrived.

My hunger forgotten, my veins pumped anger with every heartbeat. She had violated my privacy…*again.* All the negative emotions from the sketchbook fiasco with Jake came bubbling up to the surface like molten lava, burning its way through the landscape of my emotions.

"You're angry, aren't you?" Adrianne said, still standing beside me.

"I need to get dressed," I said evenly. "I'll be downstairs in a few minutes." I pushed her out and shut the door.

Then I slipped to floor, with only a towel around me, and sobbed.

Chapter 8~

Escape

The family sat around the table with empty plates. All waiting for me.

I slipped into the available chair and mumbled, "Sorry."

"So much better," Mom said with a wink. "I knew my daughter was under all that dirt."

I swallowed hard, purposefully keeping my face blank. This is how it was between us. Mom would say underhanded criticisms, and I would say the words she wished to here.

"So, how do you like your room?" Mom asked. "I couldn't believe you had yet to unpack. It was a disaster in there."

I said nothing. It was best for me to keep my mouth shut.

After an awkward moment, Gramps said grace, and everyone started passing around the food dishes. Somehow I managed to pile a salad in the bowl and a slice of lasagna on my plate. Normally, I would have plowed in and inhaled Gram's delicious cooking, but not tonight.

I ate robotically. I hadn't eaten since lunch, and that was a soggy sandwich on the go. I should have been excited to see Adrianne and Lucas, but it was hard to enjoy anything with Mom's scrutinizing eye watching me just waiting to see if I would make a mistake so she could pounce on it.

"Macy?"

I glanced up. "What?" I asked, not sure who addressed me.

"I was telling your grandfather how that young man walked out on the job today," Dad said. I noticed he had showered and changed too.

"What happened?" Gramps demanded.

"He didn't walk out on the job. There was an emergency. Two young boys showed up, and then Pedro begged me to help him. He said he'd pay me back. He even tried to give me his hundred dollar tip from the party room. But I wouldn't take his."

"You got a hundred dollars?" Lucas asked.

"Yes, we both did, and we deserved it. The rooms were horrible."

Gramps had become quiet. "He didn't give you any more information?"

"No," I said. "But he acted really worried."

"You should have come and told us," Gram said. "I don't like to see you working so hard so late. Especially with watching Lillian. It's too much on your plate."

"Who's Lillian?" Mom asked.

"A little girl I babysit," I said. Now that her name came up, I wondered how she and Derek were doing.

Mom's eyes widened. "Not even here two weeks, and you're babysitting?"

I shrugged. "Derek needed help."

"Derek?" she asked. "Who's Derek? And why do you know him on a first-name basis?"

"He's Lillian's dad," I said.

"Does he know about your record?"

"Meg! Really?" Dad asked. "Can you let up for God's sake?"

"A parent should know who is watching their child. Wouldn't you want to know?" she asked in huff, shoving her plate aside.

"You've got to stop this skeleton crew," Dad said to Gramps, purposefully turning away from Mom. "You never have enough people working at the motel. What do you do when someone wants to check in every evening? Still have the phone set up to call you over here?"

Gramps frowned. "There's nothing wrong with the way I handle the business. After dinner, I go over there for a few hours. On the weekends, I have some help come in. End of discussion."

Dad didn't press the issue, but I could tell he wasn't done talking about it.

"I don't mind helping," Lucas said. "Especially if I can get a hundred bucks. I've been wanting that new guitar."

"That new guitar costs a thousand dollars," Mom said. "It'll be a while before you'll be buying that. Speaking of money, Macy, don't forget to give me the three hundred dollars for Hannah's car clean-up."

Everyone at the table went still. I noticed Dad shoot Mom an angry glance. "Not at the dinner table," he said in a low voice. "Can't we just enjoy a family meal?"

"It's fine," I said, even though I felt anything but fine. "I have the money. Although it's $240 dollars, and not a penny more." I set down my napkin. My lasagna had a few bites taken out of it, but I was done. "Thank you for dinner, Gram."

Gram looked down at my plate, then up at me. Smiling her thin smile, she nodded.

"Excuse me," I said, getting up. "Gram, were you able to cash my check today? I'll need some of that money."

"Yes. It's in an envelope on the counter."

"Macy, come back to the table," Dad called. "We can do all that later."

I went into the kitchen, found the envelope with my name on it, and counted out the money. Luckily I had a few one dollar bills that I could give her the exact amount. Going back into the dining room, I noticed that no one was talking. Most likely they wondered what the crazy Macy May might do. I slammed the money on the table next to Mom.

"There's no need for an emotional outburst," she said evenly. "You are always so volatile."

"That's enough," Gramps said, but I didn't know if he was talking to Mom or to me.

I walked out of the dining room.

"Wait!" Adrianne called out. "Where you going? I want to go!"

"I'll be back," I said without looking at any of them. But I had no plans in coming back any time soon. There was a bottle of Jack Daniels hidden in my cart that had my name on it.

***

I turned on my phone's flashlight because I didn't want anyone to see the light on in the laundry room. I punched in the code and easily found my way to the cart. I had left everything in my cart, even the dirty linens. Normally, I would put them in the washer before leaving. I found the bottle right where I had placed it. Holding it in my hands, I stared at it.

Without another thought I ripped open the seal, lifted it to my lips, and swallowed a mouthful.

Then I coughed and wretched as it burned its way down. *What is this?* I thought as I kept coughing. It didn't take long for my face to start feeling flush. I didn't like the stuff, it tasted like acid. Flavored liquor had a much better taste. Still, I started to feel the desired effect, so I brought the bottle to my lips once more. I coughed and sputtered again. But I needed it to make me numb.

"You probably should quit there," someone said behind me. "You'll regret it if you don't."

I spun around so fast the bottle spilled down my mouth, chin, and chest. I jumped back and gasped, nearly throwing the bottle at Pedro's head. "STOP sneaking up on me!"

"It's kind of hard not to when the lights are off." He approached me and took the bottle, screwing on the lid. "I'd put this away. You're probably already going to be sick. You don't mess with Jack Daniels on the first try."

I tried to reach for it, but Pedro was quick or my reflexes were slow. "It's not yours. And it's not my first try."

"Why are you drinking it?" he asked seriously. When I didn't answer, he asked again, "Why is a girl like you hiding in the dark in a laundry room trying to get drunk off Jack?"

"You wouldn't understand. Why are you here? Sneaking up on girls in dark laundry rooms?"

"Because I stopped by your grandfather's house to talk to him about what happened today, and to see how you were doing. I left you with a lot of work."

I snorted. "Understatement."

"Your father, at least I think it was your father, lit into me about work ethic and not taking advantage of coworkers."

I snorted again. "That's funny." My belly had already begun to feel warm, and my tongue felt a little looser. "He's trying to protect me from coworkers when a youth pastor can walk right into my bedroom!" I started to laugh. "It's so ridiculous."

"How much did you drink before I got here?"

"I took two drinks. Sheesh."

"You're a lightweight," he said. I could see his grin in the darkness.

"Yeah, well, I'm a pastor's kid. It's not like drinking is a past time."

Pedro paused. "I saw your cell phone light when I got on my bike to leave. That's why I came over here. I wanted to thank you again. That's all. Sorry about sneaking up on you." He turned to leave.

All of a sudden I didn't want to be alone in the dark. I followed Pedro outside and watched him open up the bottle and pour the whiskey onto the grass. "You're going to waste it? At least let me give it to Derek.

The poor guy probably needs it more than all of us."

"You wouldn't give it to him. I can see it in your eyes."

"It's dark. You can't see my eyes."

"Yes, I can. And I know the look of someone who could get carried away with alcohol."

"Thank you, Dr. Who-Gives-A-Flip. Send me a bill." I snorted again at my joke. Okay, I needed to stop with the snorting.

Pedro walked up to me, so close I had to take a step back. "I can see you, Macy," he said quietly. "I can see the you that you try to keep hidden. The girl who will babysit even when she's overwhelmed already with her workload. The girl who gives twenty bucks to a guy who hasn't said one nice word to her. That's who you are. Don't let Jack Daniels or anything else turn you into something you're not." He turned abruptly and went to his bike.

My heart pounded in my chest. "You don't get to leave," I blurted. I clenched my fists to keep the nerves at bay and walked over to him. "You don't get to say something like that and leave."

"I have to go."

"No. You can explain—"

"I *have* to leave," he interrupted me. "You…stink."

I stopped at his words. So, I must have imagined the moment between the two of us. I took a step back, blinking back the tears, and swearing at him in my head for pouring out the alcohol. "I just took a shower…you…you…jerk!"

"You smell like whiskey," he said. "You must have poured a bunch on you. And I can't be around alcohol. That's why I'm leaving.

I'm trying to be strong."

"Oh," I said. I actually sighed in relief. "Okay, I don't hate you again."

Pedro chuckled.

We both turned to the sound of my name being called.

"Oh God, no. They can't see me like this."

"Listen, we have a lost and found container that is full of clothes from people who left it here. We launder it all and put it in the container to take to Goodwill. Go, grab a different shirt. I'll wait for you. Hurry."

"Wait for me for what?"

"Hurry," he hissed. "It's right beside the last dryer."

I went back into the laundry room, and using my cell phone light, found the tub full of folded clothes. Finding a shirt and a sweatshirt, I peeled off my own shirts and pulled both of the left behind shirts over my head. I kicked my alcohol-smelling shirts underneath a table. I'd get them tomorrow.

I heard my name again.

Running outside, I shut the door behind me. "Thanks."

"Get on," he said, indicating the handlebars.

"Are you serious?"

"Do you want to go back to your family, or do you want to go with me?"

Alone with a guy? My stomach flipped and released butterflies simultaneously. But I trusted Pedro. He hadn't touched me yet. "Yes, I want to go with you," I said, sitting uncomfortably on the handlebars. "I want to be anywhere my mother isn't."

He pushed off and began pedaling. I had to grip the handlebars and lift my legs to not fall, but eventually we found a rhythm.

A flashlight beamed at us. "Macy May?" Dad called.

"Yes, I'm fine, Dad! Just going for a bike ride. I'll be back in a few!" To Pedro, I said, "He is really going to hate you after this."

"It wouldn't be the first time I was hated," he said.

As he biked down the road, the darkness had descended for the night. "How can you know where you're going?" I asked, feeling nervous at the prospect of hitting something unseen.

"I know this road like the back of my hand," he said. "Just up ahead, is First Avenue. We'll take a left, and then there'll be lots of lights."

"Oh. I never realized that."

"Yeah, we're not that far from downtown. Maybe four miles."

"Is that where we're going?"

"You'll see."

For several minutes, I tried to enjoy the freedom of being away from my mother. My butt was majorly cramping, and I felt a little queasy from the alcohol. But this was a first. Bike riding with a boy. Well, technically Pedro was a man, but it was still a first.

Then I noticed his labored breathing and immediately felt self-conscious. "I'm sorry if I'm too heavy."

"Oh, shut up," he teased. "I ride with both of my brothers on here. We're going up a slight incline, that's all."

We passed under an overhead light and a scattering of houses. Soon, we rode past a small gas station. Then we descended down a hill.

"My favorite part," he said as he whooped into the night air. I followed suite as our speed kicked up.

Then he made a fast left and jumped the curb. I squealed while he laughed. He pedaled past downtown businesses and groups of people. I couldn't believe how alive the downtown was. "I've been shut up in my room for too long," I said, pointing to a pizza place. "Ooh, I want to try there."

"You hungry?"

"Yes, I am," I said, surprised at the answer. "I didn't eat at the house because I lost my appetite with Mom's incessant nagging."

Pedro turned the bike around and told me to get off. Once I did, I shook out my legs. "They're going numb," I grinned.

"You can ride behind me," he said. "If you can balance on the pegs."

"But first, pizza."

Pedro insisted on paying, and once we had the pizza in hand, neither one of us talked. We ate like we were homeless.

After three slices, I gulped down the rest of my iced tea. "Thank you," I said. "I feel so much better."

"No longer buzzing?"

"I don't think so. And I didn't puke. That's good. I tend to be a drink-and-puke kind of girl."

Pedro sat back. "Now you tell me?"

"Ha, ha." I threw my crumpled up napkin at him.

"So, tell me something about you that I don't know." He leaned forward again and stared at me intensely.

"What do you already know?" I asked, feeling uncomfortable. I could barely look him in the eyes!

"I know that you can sing and play the piano. And you're really good at it."

I knew I was blushing at the comment! My cheeks felt warm, and it wasn't because of any alcohol I drank. "I can draw," I said, trying not to think of Mom going through my sketchbooks again. "Sketches mostly, but I think they're pretty good."

"I'd like to see them sometime."

I cringed. "Probably not. They're sort of personal. Like journaling. But with pictures."

"Makes sense. Maybe one time you could draw something not for the journal, but for me."

"Maybe." I wanted to change the subject. "What about you? I pretty much know nothing, other than you are a housekeeper, and you evidently don't drink. Oh, and you have two brothers."

"Filipe and Pablo. Twelve and seven."

I nodded. "What else?"

Pedro shifted uncomfortably. "There's not much else. Just trying to keep my nose clean."

"Look at the two of us," I said sadly. "Both unwilling to reveal our secrets."

"Maybe that's why we'll make good friends. We can respect privacy."

"It's better than being enemies. Tried that, didn't like it."

"True." Pedro stood up. "Come on, we need to keep going."

"Where?"

"There's a place I want to take you. It helps me, maybe it'll help you too."

As we walked outside, and I climbed back onto the handlebars, I realized how much I desired to learn more about Pedro. I wanted to ask about what happened that he got community service, and I wanted to ask about his tattoos. I wanted to study them, so I could sketch them.

The more I thought about it, the more I believed that secrets wouldn't make us better friends. That if we kept the secrets, they would always be this wall between us.

And even though I hadn't decided on my feelings yet when it came to Pedro, I wondered if it was time I let my wall down to someone. Someone who would understand me in a way that my family couldn't.

Chapter 9~

Lighthouse

I stood on the shore of Lake Michigan and breathed deeply. The crisp air and the lapping waves were a drug to my weary soul. So I breathed it in. Again and again.

The full moon hung over us and a million stars seemed to litter the sky. I looked up and soaked in its energy. Its beauty. "I never realized how close my grandparents were to Lake Michigan. Not too observant on my part."

"How often do you come up here?"

"Maybe once or twice a year. Mostly around holidays." I scanned the darkened horizon and saw a few boats' lights scattered in the distance. "There are boats out there?"

"Of course there are."

"That must be nice to just hop on a boat and sail away."

"Are you ready yet?" Pedro asked. He sat beside me on the beach, waiting for me to be done. Not that I was doing anything other than breathing and soaking in the night majesty around me.

"I could stay here forever."

"That's great, but that's not why we're here."

Breathing in one more deep breath, I said, "Okay, let's carry on."

Pedro jumped up and took my hand. "This way."

I had to resist pulling my hand away from him. *Pedro's not Jake*, I told myself. Besides, Pedro's hand felt warm and safe, and I kind of liked holding it. He led me to a walkway that would take us out to the lighthouse. A big sign said "Warning. Proceed at Your Own Risk."

"Is this safe?"

"Should be. It narrows closer to the lighthouse, and it can get a little slick. But at least the snow and ice are melted."

As we walked out on the narrow concrete path that led to the lighthouse the chill in the air turned even colder. "Brr…"

"Yeah, I'm glad you threw on a sweatshirt from that bin. Do you want my jacket?"

"No, then you'll be cold."

Despite the temperature, walking out to the lighthouse was an adventure. Further out above the water, the waves were bigger, crashing against the rocks, lining along the sides of the walkway. "I'd hate to fall in," I joked.

"Yeah, don't do that. I'm not the best swimmer. We'd both probably drown."

I nervously laughed. "Not funny."

Pedro had yet to let go of my hand. We walked with him still slightly leading for quite a distance. I turned to see the shoreline was farther away than I realized. But looking up, I paused. "Wow," I breathed.

"I know." Pedro looked up too. "Out here it's just me and the water and the sky. But we're not there yet. Just wait. It gets better."

Eventually we made it to lighthouse that loomed above us. I had only nearly slipped twice. Not too shabby. "This is cool, but I can't really get a look at it in the dark."

"We're not here to look at the lighthouse. We're here to climb it. There's a metal ladder right to the side. I'll let you go first."

"Wait...what?"

"Live dangerously," he said, and I could see the playfulness in his eyes. He hadn't had a scowl on his face this entire evening. How could I say no to that?

"I hope I don't regret this," I said. "Where is the ladder?"

"Over here. You have to keep one leg on the concrete here, and then reach the ladder with your other leg. Be careful. The ladder gets a little slick from when the waves are high."

I scowled at him. "Are you trying to get me killed?"

For a moment his expression darkened. "No. If you don't want to do it, we can go back."

"I was kidding," I said quickly. "I want to do it. I think."

"Well, then get on with it. I'll stay here to help in case you slip. But you won't, so don't worry."

"Of course not. I'm totally not worried," I muttered to myself as I reached my right leg and hand over to the metal bars that led up the lighthouse landing. I grabbed the ladder wrung with my hand, then when my foot felt secure, I brought my left leg and arm over to the ladder and climbed up before my nerves took over.

"See?" Pedro said. "You're a natural."

I waited for him to come up the steps, while rubbing my arms.

The lake water must still be frigid because it had to be at least 20 degrees cooler out here than at my grandparents' house.

Pedro saw me and unzipped his leather jacket. "Here. Put this on."

"No, you'll freeze."

"You're teeth are chattering, Macy. I'll be fine. I'm the one who biked over here, remember? I'm still hot from that. Besides, I've got a sweatshirt on. I'll be fine."

I took the jacket and put it on, immediately feeling warmer. I zipped it up and tried not to think about how it smelled: a mix of his cologne and possibly tobacco.

"Over here," he said, leading me to the edge of the landing that looked out at the expanse of the water and sky. There was no railing, completely exposing us to the rocks and water below. "Sit," he said, sitting on the ledge, his legs dangling over. "I can sit here all night long. Sometimes, I'll even bring my sleeping bag and crash."

"Aren't you nervous about rolling off this ledge and into the water?"

"No. I'm not afraid. If it's my time to go, it's my time to go." He shrugged like it was no big deal.

I sat beside him and stared out at the water that practically surrounded us. I let my feet dangle too. "This is one of the riskiest things I've ever done. I'm such a rebel."

Pedro laughed. "You live a very sheltered life, my friend."

"That I do."

We stayed quiet, both in our own thoughts. Pedro was right. I could stare at the moon and stars over the water all night long. "I wish I had my sketchbook."

"When you get back, draw this for me," Pedro said quietly. "That way I can keep it with me wherever I'm at."

I studied him, trying to memorize his features. Suddenly I turned away. "You won't think it's creepy if I draw you in them?"

"Why would it be creepy?"

"Never mind." I had already said too much. I nearly told him about how I'd already tried to sketch him, but I couldn't bring myself to do it. I didn't want to ruin this moment.

"What happened?" he asked, still quiet. "What made a girl like you from your family come up to this pit of a town to do community service?"

I looked over at him again. "I thought we were good with keeping secrets."

"I'm just trying to understand you."

"If I tell you, then you have to tell me."

Pedro took a deep breath. "You probably won't be my friend after I tell you. It's better if you don't know."

"Same here."

"I doubt that. You could never do what I did. We're different in that regard."

We watched the view again. I tried to act calm on the outside, even though my insides were running wild. Something about Pedro was different than everyone I ever surrounded myself with. He had a sadness deep inside much like I had. Suddenly, I wanted to tell him, at least part of it, if for no other reason so that he wouldn't feel so alone. "I got busted stealing alcohol. Twice. This second time, the store is pressing charges."

"There are ways to get alcohol without stealing."

"Yeah, well, I'm a sheltered pastor's kid. I didn't know how else to get it. It didn't help that this last time around, I puked in my sister's car. And nearly died. There's that too. See? I'm a mess."

"How'd you nearly die?"

I cringed. "It's stupid and embarrassing."

"I won't judge. Too much."

"I took her car, without her permission, because I had to get out of the house. Anyway, once I had the schnapps, I pulled back into the garage, but I wasn't ready to get out of the car because my song was on. So, I pressed the button on the top of Hannah's visor that lowered the garage door."

"With the car still running?"

"Yep. I wasn't thinking. I just wanted to drink and pretend that my life wasn't my life."

Pedro shook his head. "You could have died."

"Trust me, my parents remind me often."

After a minute, Pedro said, "I'm really glad you didn't die."

"Thanks," I said. "You're the first one to actually say that. My parents remind me that I could have died. My Dad would have probably been upset, but I almost think that Mom would have been relieved."

"Why do you say that?"

"She doesn't like me. No really!" I added when I saw him shake his head. "I don't know what it is, and I can't explain it, but she is always exasperated around me, and she'll criticize me in a really hurtful way, yet say it with a smile. And when I was younger, she told me to stop playing the piano, and to stop singing, that I was hogging the limelight. Which wasn't true, but it still made me feel bad. And then my sketches…yeah, she humiliated me. But I don't want to talk about that."

"No, tell me. I want to hear."

"Why? Why do you want to hear all of this horrible stuff?"

"I like hearing you talk. I'm alone a lot, so it's nice to have someone to talk with. And I'm a good listener." He paused, "So, how did your Mom humiliate you?"

I covered my face. I didn't want to tell him, did I? He might have been a good listener, but telling him about what happened with the sketchbook would lead to talking about Jake. And I couldn't let my brain go there. I shook my head and stared out at the moon's reflection across the water. "Some things are better left locked away."

"I won't push," he said.

"So, what about you? Your story isn't as depressing as mine, is it?"

"Let's say that your mother is a real peach compared to mine."

"Then I'm so sorry."

"Your Mom doesn't leave you with your brothers for months on end. And I doubt your mother is addicted to meth. And I'm pretty sure that your mom doesn't bring bad men home who like to abuse women and hurt boys."

I turned toward Pedro and took his hand, finally understanding the deep sadness he walks around with. "Your fingers are cold."

"I'll be all right."

We made eye contact, and for the first time, I felt like we were really seeing each other. Broken pieces and all. "Is that why you had to leave today?" I asked quietly. "Was it about your mom?"

"She's been gone for months. Left with some guy. I promised my brothers I wouldn't let human services take them from me. I'm all they got. It's been hard because my hours at the motel pay for rent, electricity, and groceries. Your grandfather was a God-send. He's the only one who would hire me."

"Is that enough? Do you make enough?"

"For most of it. I have to admit we eat a lot of food from boxes and cans, but we're surviving."

"I'm sure there's some type of assistance—"

"No," he said firmly, not making eye contact. "I don't want help. Besides, Mom's on the food assistance program, but she's got the identification card. So, I can't get any help even if I wanted it."

I didn't say anything, mostly because I was horrified at Pedro's predicament and disgusted that while I acted like a spoiled brat, fussing about my mother not liking me, he worried about how he was going to feed his brothers.

"She came back," he said, after a few minutes. "That's why I had to leave today. My brothers found her crashed on our steps, her face all bruised up."

"Well, that's good she's back, right? At least you know she's safe."

Pedro grimaced. "This is going to sound really bad but no. It's not good. With her, come bad men. Right now she's alone, but once she's cleaned up, she'll hang out at her usual places until she meets another one. And then I'll be worried. All the time. At least she could leave us alone. My brothers are safe when I'm protecting them. But she shows up, and they're young and love her, and want me to take care of her too."

"Let me help."

"I'm not asking for help."

"I know, but I feel bad. I want to do something."

"You're doing it." Pedro looked over at me. "You're here."

Not knowing what else to say, I blurted, "You're cold."

"Yeah," he said, rubbing the sleeves on his arms. "You stole my jacket."

"No, I didn't!" I said in defense until I saw his grin.

"We should get going. I don't want your parents and grandparents to think I kidnapped you."

He pushed himself up then helped me to stand by taking my hand. He lingered for a moment before I gently pulled my hand away. "Your hand is ice. Let's get out of here."

We walked around the lighthouse to the ladder. I peered down only to look straight back up. "I don't think I can do this."

"Of course you can. I'll go first, then be right there to help you find the ledge." He started climbing down before I could protest.

After the third wrung I couldn't see him. There might have been only six or seven rungs, but I started to feel the tendrils of panic take hold. "Pedro?!"

"Yep. Give me a sec." I heard his shoe scrape on the concrete ledge of the walkway. "Okay, come down slowly."

"Oh dear God, don't let me die," I muttered, as I began to climb down. When I reached my foot out and could no longer feel the steel bar of the ladder, I gasped in fear, grabbing and clinging to the rungs with my arms.

"You're going to have to take your left foot and reach over here to the ledge. Then give me your left hand and I'll pull you to me."

"How'd you ever get me to do this?"

"I'm right here. The ledge is right next to the ladder. You've got this."

I took a couple deep breaths and while still holding the ladder, I reached my left foot over. Sure enough, there was the concrete ledge.

"Give me your left hand."

I could feel Pedro by my leg. I reached out my left arm. In one swift move, he pulled me to him as I let go. And I was on the concrete ledge of the walkway. In Pedro's arms. This time there was no lingering. He released me quickly.

"That was crazy," I gushed. Now that I was semi-secure on the walkway, going back to the beach, I found my adrenaline pumping. "Thank you."

"Anytime you need to get away, you can come out here and think. I'll share it with you."

When we got to the bike, I wasn't quite ready for the night to end. I really enjoyed hanging out with Pedro, and honestly, I wasn't ready to see Mom. "Want to get an ice cream? My treat."

"I'm freezing."

I unzipped the jacket and handed it back to him.

"You can still wear it. I'm just too chilled for ice cream. Besides," Pedro took out his flip phone. "It's almost eleven."

"Is it, really?" I said in surprise. "My Dad is probably having a mini-stroke."

"I hope not." He patted the handlebars. "Ready?"

"This time, I'm riding from the back. If the bike pegs will hold me."

Pedro groaned. "What is with you and putting yourself down?"

"I don't know. I didn't realize I did that."

"Well, you do. So, stop it."

As I positioned my one foot on the peg and lifted myself up onto the other one on the other side of the tire, I had to clutch his sweatshirt to balance myself.

"You'll have to lean on me a little."

I almost asked if he'd be okay with my weight against him, but I held my tongue. "Next time, put one of those child carriers in the back. That should work," I teased.

Pedro began pedaling away from the beach and to the downtown area. I really had to hold on, and the pegs to the bike were really wobbly. I ended up leaning on him more than I anticipated. And liking it a lot more than I wanted to.

Chapter 10~

Keeping Secrets

Most of the lights had been shut off in the house, but the front door was unlocked. I opened the door as quietly as I could and shut it gently. Hearing the T.V. in the family room, I peeked my head in and saw Gram and Mom sitting on the couch watching a show.

I knew I had to greet them, and I probably shouldn't say anything sarcastic about Mom watching the devilish T.V. "Hey," I said, leaning against a wall.

Both turned to look at me. Gram smiled thinly while Mom frowned. Lovely.

"Where've you been?" Mom demanded. "And what in the world are you wearing? That sweatshirt nearly goes to your knees."

A sarcastic, bitter reply almost came out, but I didn't want to fight right now. Especially with Gram sitting there. "I went on a bike ride with Pedro. He took me to see Lake Michigan."

"Is that his sweatshirt?" Mom's eyes narrowed.

I almost told the truth about it being in the lost and found, but that might lead to more questions, so I simply nodded. "It got cold."

"Is Pedro the man you're drawing in your sketchbook?" Mom

asked.

The question came out as innocent-enough, but I knew Mom. I knew what she implied. "I draw a lot of people in my sketches," I said through gritted teeth. "If you insist on going through my private things, at least spend the time perusing all of it." Looking over at Gram, I said, "Good night, Gram. Love you." Then I glared at Mom, making sure she understand that the message was only for Gram before turning and walking away.

Could a person love and hate someone at the same time? Of course I loved Mom, right? Then why did I dislike her so much? Now that she was here, it hadn't escaped my notice that I was happy to see everyone *but* her. It was like I hadn't missed her at all.

I heard low voices back in Gramps study. I decided that I needed to say good-night to Dad, so I walked back there. The door had been shut. Weird. Gramps never shut the study's door. That's when I heard Gramps say, "She deserves to know. Especially if Meg is going to behave badly because of it."

"I told you I would take care of it," Dad said.

I pressed my ear to the door, knowing they were talking about me.

"This has gone on long enough!" Gramps said forcefully.

"Lower your voice," Dad pleaded. "It's complicated, and you know it is. I have Meg and the other children to think about too."

"While you lose Macy? Because that's what's happening! The more you push her away the farther from your reach she'll be. She'll resent you, Paul. If she doesn't already."

"What about Meg? She's my wife. The mother of my children. You're asking me to choose between the two."

"No, I'm not!" Gramps said. "Meg is. She is asking you to choose between her and Macy. And son, you're making the wrong choice."

I stepped back away from the door as the words sent shock waves throughout my system. What was Gramps saying? Why did Dad have to choose between Mom and me? She must want me to stay here permanently. She must want me to not live at the house anymore.

The realization should have made me emotional. Before, not even two weeks prior, I would have cried and felt hurt. Now, I only felt calm...and a little relieved. Maybe staying with Gram and Gramps would be good. It might have hurt at first, and I agreed with Gramps, Dad seemed to be choosing everyone else over me. But at least here, I was free to be myself. And Gram and Gramps allowed me privacy. Maybe what I thought was a horrible idea, was a really good idea.

The door opened so fast that I jumped as high as a burglar holding a bag of loot. "Dear Jesus!" I cried, holding a hand on my heart. "Warn a girl!"

"Where've you been?" Dad asked. "I was just getting ready to come find you."

"I went for a bike ride with Pedro."

"Yeah, I saw that. I wasn't too happy. Where'd you go?"

"He took me to see Lake Michigan."

"Is that his sweatshirt?"

"Are yours and Mom's brain connected? She asked me the same

question."

"Because you're wearing a man's sweatshirt, Macy."

Gramps stared down at the sweatshirt, his brow furrowed. He recognized it. I could see it in his eyes as he looked at me.

"Pedro didn't want me to be cold. I think he grabbed it from the motel's lost and found." To Gramps, I added, "I'll wash it and put it back."

"I thought it looked familiar. I think that one might have been mine." He gave Dad a pointed look before leaving us standing there.

Looking inside I saw that the couch had been made up. "You sleeping in here? What about Mom?"

"She's upstairs in the guest room with the kids. I think Adrianne might have climbed in your bed. FYI."

"Okay," I paused. "I overheard some of what you and Gramps were talking about."

Dad didn't say anything, but I could have sworn fear shot across his countenance. But the hall light was off, so maybe it was more a look of annoyance.

When he didn't say anything, and before I lost my nerve, I said, "I think I want to stay here anyway. Everyone seems to know that Mom doesn't want me around. After tonight's dinner, I'm starting to think that I don't really want to be around her." I stopped myself, wondering if I went too far.

Instead of getting angry, Dad pressed his lips together and acted like he might cry. "This wasn't supposed to happen," he said, his voice catching. "She promised—" Dad seemed to stop himself too.

"I'm making it easy on you," I said. "Now you don't have to choose between us. If Gram and Gramps will have me, I'll stay here. Mom and Hannah should be relieved. Good night." I left him before either of us could say any more.

After climbing the stairs and entering my room, I saw Adrianne had left a bedside light on. They must have brought that up, along with the bedside table. I watched my little sister sleep, her chest rise and fall, and felt the familiar tug of loneliness. Up here with Gram and Gramps, I wouldn't have my lima bean to hang out with. But it had to be this way because I couldn't be around the rest of my family. Even being around Mom for a day had me chasing a liquor bottle. I didn't understand the disconnect between us, but it was there. And even though I felt lonely up here in Manistee, I also felt at home. Dad might have decided against Jake living under the same roof, but he would still be around. Still sneaking in. Still whispering promises he didn't intend to keep.

No longer wanting to dwell on Jake, I grabbed some pajamas, went to the bathroom to brush my teeth and clean up, then after changing, I climbed into bed with Adrianne and wrapped my arms around her. "Love you, lima bean," I whispered.

She rolled over, draping her arm around my waist. "Where were you?" she murmured, still sleepy.

"Shh," I said, holding her until she fell back asleep.

I closed my eyes and revisited the lighthouse with the surrounding water and the limitless night sky. I could see Pedro's outline beside me. My fingers itched to sketch. Since I hadn't turned off the bedside light yet, I slipped out of the bed and quietly retrieved one of my sketchbooks from its hiding place. After Mom had found them here, I realized I could no longer have them out in the open, so I hid them underneath a stack of blankets Gram kept in the closet. I kept sneaking glances at Adrianne to make sure I hadn't woken her up.

Once comfortable in my cushy chair by the bed, I started outlining. Since his arms had been covered up, the tattoos were no longer a distraction. I smiled as I traced his profile. My memory and my hand seemed connected as I filled in the shadows with a soft gray. The sky behind him took some time as I merged varying shades of dark blue from the horizon into the darkness that had been descending when we had first arrived.

My hand paused as I heard Mom's footsteps shuffle up the stairs. Shoot. My door was open. Sure enough, I sensed her standing there before I looked up.

She leaned against the door frame. Neither one of us spoke. I carefully shut the sketchbook, refusing for her to invade my privacy again.

"Couldn't sleep?" she finally asked.

I didn't respond because there was an obvious answer.

"Your Dad's really worried about you," she said. "We all are, but he's taking it the hardest."

"There's nothing to worry about," I said. "And I'm not going back with you anyway. I'm staying here." I pretended to ignore her sigh of relief. "I'm good here. I don't have to worry about grown men sneaking into my room at night."

We stared at each other, both of us trying to keep our voices down with Adrianne sleeping. Mom had caught Jake sneaking out of my room one morning. She of course had lain the blame entirely at my feet, telling Jake that she would keep it a secret if he was to never see me again. It had scared him enough. "You act like the victim, and everyone thinks I'm a horrible mother, but we both the know truth."

"It's not a lie. I never invited him into my room. He showed up."

"And did you turn him away?" she asked.

I didn't answer because she had a point there.

"If you're so innocent, why haven't you told your father or your grandfather or anyone else? If what you say is true, and Jake took advantage of you, then why aren't you telling anyone?"

I knew the answer, and so did she. No one would believe me. Jake was a youth minister, and I was the teenage girl with the big crush. And why would such a good-looking man like Jake want anything to do with his fiance's socially-awkward sister?

"Ever since you were a little girl you've been jealous of Hannah. I'd thought you'd outgrow it, but never in a million years did I think you would try to ruin her happiness because of it."

"No," I whispered. "I wasn't jealous of her at first. The only thing I ever desired that she had was for you to love me as much as you loved her." My eyes welled up with tears, and I hated myself for it. I didn't want my own mother to see how much her actions hurt me. I wiped at them and blinked back the tears. "But when I saw that nothing I could do would change that, I moved on." I opened up the sketch book with my coal pencil posed and acted like I was intensely staring at the picture. The conversation was over, and she needed to leave.

This would be the time when most mothers would say, "Oh no, dear, that's not true. I love you so much," but not my mother. After a minute or so had passed, I heard the other bedroom door opening and shutting. I looked up to see that she no longer leaned against my door frame.

I let out the breath I'd been holding and closed my eyes. I had partly lied when I said that I had moved on. Because a part of me still longed for her to love me, for her to tell me what it was about me that she's never liked so that I could fix it. A part of me was still jealous of the closeness she shared with Hannah and even Lucas and Adrianne.

"I love you, Macy," Adrianne said from the bed. "You're my favorite sister."

I shut the sketchbook for the second time. "I love you, too. You're supposed to be sleeping."

"How could I with you and Mom talking?"

Setting the book down, I shut the bedroom door and slid into the bed with her. "Sorry. We were trying to whisper."

I turned off the bedside light, then snuggled into my sister. "Good night, lima bean."

"Do you love her?" Adrianne asked in the darkness.

"Of course I do," I said, but my words lacked conviction.

"Why is she mean to you but not to Hannah?"

"I don't know."

"Mom and Daddy have been fighting a lot," she confided. "Dad doesn't sleep in their room anymore."

"Shh," I said. "Everything is fine. Don't worry."

Adrianne pushed my arms off of her and sat up. "Don't say that," she demanded. "Everyone keeps telling me that everything is fine. No, it's not. I'm almost nine, you know. I'm not a baby. I know that things are not fine. You aren't living with us any more, Dad and Mom are fighting, Hannah informed all of us that you are not to step foot at the wedding, which got Dad and Mom and Hannah fighting again…" she paused to gather a breath.

"Okay," I whispered, sitting up. I pressed a finger to my lips. "We can talk, but you have to talk quieter."

Adrianne nodded.

"Mom and Hannah are upset with me because I took Hannah's car to the store, stole some alcohol, then drank some and puked it up in the passenger seat." I left out the part about Jake, hoping Adrianne didn't ask any questions about him.

"Ew," Adrianne crinkled her nose.

"Yes, I know. It's gross. I shouldn't have done it. That's why Hannah doesn't want me at the wedding."

"Can't you say you're sorry?"

"I tried. So, anyway, that's why I live up here now. At least for a little while. Hopefully Mom and Hannah will forgive me."

"Why are Mom and Dad fighting?"

"I don't know," I said honestly. "Maybe it's because Dad didn't want me to move out but Mom did. But I'm not sure because Dad's the one who brought me up here. That's it. That's all I know."

"You shouldn't drink alcohol," Adrianne said. "Dad says it's bad."

"Yep, I know. I don't drink it anymore." I thought about the Jack Daniels from earlier.

"Then tell Mom and Dad so you can come home! I want you there. It's not the same. Even Rex misses you."

I pulled Adrianne to me and hugged her close. "I miss you so much," I said truthfully. "Things are complicated right now, but please know that I miss you and love you. You're my favorite sister too."

Sometime after two in the morning, I fell asleep, but it was fitful. I kept waking up with a start, thinking he stood at the foot of my bed. Eventually, I was so spooked that I snuck downstairs and lay on the couch in the living room with the lights on. I reminded myself that it wasn't like this when my family wasn't here. As I began to fall asleep downstairs, I hoped that they would leave soon. I needed my peace back.

Chapter 11~

Confession

"You look tired." Pedro waited for me outside the laundry room door.

"I am tired," I said, yawning. "My little sister insisted on sleeping in my bed, and my Gram's couch is lumpy."

"How long will you have to sleep on the couch?"

"They leave today." I left out a *thank God*.

"How about if you take a day off? Maybe take a nap or something."

"Ha, ha, very funny."

"No, I'm serious. You know how I told you my mom showed up yesterday? Well, she needs to earn some money, and she needs something to do or else she drinks the day away."

My brain was too foggy to compute. "I'm sorry, I'm not understanding. Am I fired?"

"No, I'm just asking for a favor."

"We'd have to talk to Gramps."

"Yeah, I sort of already did that. He said she could take your spot cleaning because I guess your parents don't want you doing that anymore. But I wasn't willing to go that far, not without talking to you."

I rubbed my head. "So, what am I going to do? I need community service hours."

"Not yet. You have to go to court first and get assigned the hours."

"You have this all figured out, don't you?" I said sarcastically. I was getting a little annoyed that Pedro was so ready to get rid of me. "If you don't want me cleaning with you, fine. Just say so. You don't need some stupid excuse." I stormed past him.

"Wait," he said, grabbing my arm. "It's not like that, Macy. I promise."

I didn't say anything, only kept walking to the motel's office. I pushed open the door and glowered at my grandfather. He looked me up and down and raised his eyebrows in surprise. "Did you just roll out of bed and stumble over here? You look like you're half-dead."

"No. I rolled off the couch and stumbled over here."

"You still have on the same big sweatshirt from yesterday."

"So? All I did was sleep in it. And why are you giving away my job?"

"I'm not. I told Pedro he'd have to talk to you."

"How am I going to do my community service?"

Gramps pressed his lips together. "Your father didn't tell you, did he?"

"Tell me what?!" I said, raising my voice. "I'm too tired for you to talk in riddles."

"You're going home."

I blinked at the words, as if trying to process them.

"I'm…what?"

"He wants you home. Says you have to go to court in a week, and he's going to set up community service at the church. Your Dad misses you, and he said that he felt horrible for dropping you off up here right from the hospital. He said he wasn't thinking straight." Gramps paused. "He should be the one to tell you all of this. He should be up by now."

"I told him last night that I was staying here."

"You don't get to make that call, hon."

"Why not? You don't want me either?"

"You know that's not true. You're always welcome. But your father is your father. He makes the decisions. I'm trying to honor his role in your life."

"That's great that Dad thinks he can make that decision, but he can't. I'm eighteen, turning nineteen soon. I'm an adult, and I'm staying."

The motel door opened. "There you are!" Lillian squealed, running to me and throwing her arms around my waist.

"Hey there, Lillian," I said with a smile plastered on.

"Why you crying?" she asked, suddenly sad. "You don't want to be a servant today, do you?"

I laughed, my heart warming at this little girl's sincerity. "You got that right."

"Everything okay?" Derek asked, stepping inside the office. Even he looked at me with concern in his eyes.

"Macy might be leaving to go back home this morning," Gramps said.

"What?" Derek asked at the same time Lillian gasped.

I glared at Gramps. "Like a bull through a china shop," I grumbled at him.

"They need to know. Derek will have to find someone else."

"I don't have anyone else," he said. "I've got to be at work in ten minutes."

"Shirley can watch her today after Macy leaves. At least for today."

Lillian began to cry. "You promised!" she said. "You promised you wouldn't leave me!"

I sucked in a breath, trying to hold my emotions together. "I'm not leaving you," I said. I looked over at Derek. "Don't worry. I'm not going anywhere."

Derek's panicked expression eased a bit. "Are you sure?"

"Macy," Gramps warned. "I know you're technically an adult, but you need to honor your father. You might want to talk to him first."

"I'm not going anywhere," I repeated. "I told Derek that I would watch Lillian. At the very least Dad will let me stay up here until my court date."

Gramps finally nodded. "True. See if he'll let me take you downstate then."

Lillian hadn't stopped crying. "So, you're still leaving?"

"I'm going to try really hard to stay."

"Please, do," Derek said quietly. "She's taken a liking to you, and right now…just please try to find a way."

I could see the pent-up emotion on Derek's countenance.

"How'd it go last night?"

I whispered.

He shook his head and looked away.

"Derek, you know that if there is anything me and Shirley can do, we'll do it." Gramps had walked around the counter and placed his hand on Derek's shoulder.

Derek was trying hard to keep it together, but I could see his chin and lips twitching in an effort not to cry. "You've already done more than I could every repay, Mr. Elmsworth," he said.

"Would you like me to pray for you?" Gramps asked. "I know you're not a religious man, but all of us could use prayer."

"I've got to go to work," Derek said quickly. He kissed Lillian's forehead. "Be a good girl." Then he left.

"I think you're right," Gramps said. "I think you need to stay. Lillian needs you. Go, talk to your father and tell him I'll bring you downstate when the time comes."

"What about the housekeeping?"

"Let Pedro's mother help today. We'll figure it out later."

I took in a deep breath and told myself to not make an issue out of it. "Want to go across the street? My grandma was making breakfast for everyone when I left."

Her face still forlorn, Lillian didn't say anything only walked out of the office without me.

"Gramps, you shouldn't have said anything about me leaving."

"There are too many secrets around here. I get confused with which ones I'm not supposed to be telling," he said gruffly. "Go eat some breakfast and don't forget to bring me a plate. I want extra bacon."

I shook my head and walked outside. Lillian had already walked to the curb by the street. "Lillian!" I yelled, running over to her. "Don't cross the street without an adult, okay?"

She crossed her arms angrily. "I don't have to listen to you. You're leaving me! Everyone leaves me!" She started to cry again.

"Hey," I said, wiping her face. "What did I tell you? That I was going to stay, right?"

Lillian sniffled and gave a slight nod.

"That's what I'm going to do."

Right as I stood up, I saw a Hispanic woman pedaling a boys bike and stopping outside the motel office. She had long, dark hair braided and looked a little malnourished, but she had a handsome face with strong features. I could see the resemblance to Pedro.

"Let's go," I said, holding Lillian's hand and jogging across the street.

Once in the house, I felt tempted to go upstairs and sleep for a hundred hours, but I knew that wasn't an option. So, I led Lillian to the dining room where Lucas and Adrianne were sitting, both drinking orange juice. Dad sat across from them, typing something on his tablet. All three looked over at us at the same time.

"Who's that?" Adrianne asked, smiling. I knew she had already deemed Lillian an instant friend. She had that way with other kids.

"This is Lillian. She's my buddy. We're going to have breakfast together."

"A special visitor?" Gram said, carrying in a plate stacked with pancakes. "Wonderful. She can take your grandfather's chair."

"By the way, he wants me to bring over a plate of food."

"Of course he does," she winked at me. "Why don't you come help your Gram with the rest of breakfast?"

"Sure," I said, even though I didn't mean it. "Sit over there," I told Lillian. But she was already pulling a chair next to Adrianne.

Inside the kitchen, Gram handed me two plates. One filled with scrambled eggs and one filled with bacon. "I'm not one to get into others' business," she said, not letting me leave. "But Macy May, you need to stay. Your transformation with them in the house has been troublesome. Whatever is going on kept me up all last night. Something is tormenting you. I can't place my finger on what it is, but I don't like it."

I bit my lip. Who knew Gram could be so astute? "I want to stay here," I whispered. "I need to. For Lillian. I promised her I would. And even though I acted like I didn't want to move up here at first, now that I've been here two weeks, I can't imagine going back and living in the same house with Mom and Hannah. Here, I can be me."

"Of course you can," Gram said with a smile. She kissed my cheek, then patted it.

"Let me help," Mom said, breezing into the kitchen like fresh air on a spring day. Everything was once again in perfect place, from her make-up to her hair to her high heels and jeans.

Mom raised one eyebrow at my appearance, but refrained from saying anything. She took the two plates from me and went into the dining room. Gram and I followed.

I sat beside Lillian, filling her plate with a little bit of everything. "Do you want butter on your pancakes?" I asked.

But she wasn't listening. Instead, her eyes were on Mom. "You're pretty," she said with her slight lisp.

"Well, thank you," Mom said with her thousand-watt smile. "And who might you be?"

"Lillian."

"This is the girl Macy's watching while her Dad works," Adrianne said. "Right, Lillian?"

"Yep," the little girl said.

"How'd that happen?" Mom asked me.

"It's just for this week. It's their spring break and Derek didn't have anyone else."

"Are they friends of yours?" Mom asked Gram while picking at her fruit and yogurt. Mom would never eat pancakes, eggs, and bacon.

I had already sat down and was dipping my pancakes in syrup before shoveling it in my mouth.

"Yes," Gram said. "They are staying at the motel until Derek gets back on his feet."

"Who's going to watch her if you leave?" Mom asked me but glanced at Dad.

"I am," I said, taking a bit of bacon. "I'm staying here."

The table became quiet.

"We miss you and want you home," Dad said, reaching for my hand.

"I want you to come home," Adrianne said, her bottom lip pouting.

"She has to stay with me," Lillian said matter-of-factly. "She promised. I need her."

My heart warmed at Adrianne's and Lillian's words. It was nice to feel wanted. I knew I had to play this right. Mom had no problem with me staying, but Dad was different. "Gramps said I could stay until the court date. He even said he'd take me downstate."

"You're only eighteen," Dad said.

"Which means I'm an adult."

"She's right," Mom said. "She's an adult, Paul. And I think it's a great idea for her to be here, helping your mother and father. Lord knows, they need help over at the motel."

I couldn't believe it. Mom and I agreed on something. Granted, she had dumped my entire wardrobe up here and didn't even say good-bye to begin with, but hey, at least we both admitted that we wanted to be away from each other.

"That's true," Gram added. "He never has enough help. He keeps thinking he's in his forties and can run the place like he used to. Macy May has been a big help."

"Well, I feel like Adrianne and I are the only ones voting for Macy to come home. What about you, Lucas?"

He looked up from his tablet and shrugged. "I don't care." Then he looked at me and said sheepishly. "No offense, Macy."

"None taken." I turned to Dad and raised my eyebrows.

"Fine," he said. "As long as you realize it's your choice to stay up here. I'm willing to take you back."

"Yep, it's my choice to stay up here."

"See?" Mom said. "It all worked out."

Dad didn't acknowledge Mom. I noticed his jaw clench. Was Adrianne right? Were Mom and Dad fighting? Was this the secret Gramps had been talking about a couple nights ago? I stared down at my now empty plate and wondered if it was because of me. *Of course it is*, I told myself. *They weren't fighting before you got into trouble.*

I suddenly felt really warm. My face seemed on fire. I fanned at myself and poured a glass of water. Luckily everyone was busy eating or talking to notice me. I knew what was going on within me. It was guilt. My acting out had affected the whole family. That explained why Mom had been so mean and hostile lately. She probably blamed me for the friction between her and Dad. And she had a point.

My parents might drive me crazy, but I didn't want them to take it out on each other. Swallowing down my ego and the excuse that I had a reason for doing what I did, I interrupted the conversation at the table. "Mom? Dad?"

They looked over at me.

I had to swallow the pride again. This was harder to do than I thought. Boy, my face felt warm! I guzzled some water.

"What?" Dad asked. "You okay? You change your mind?"

"I, um, I only wanted to say…" I couldn't look at Mom. This was hard enough saying to Dad. "I'm sorry."

Everyone quieted. Mom and Dad didn't say anything.

Oh, God, I needed to clarify. I took another guzzle of water. Do this for their marriage, I told myself. "I'm sorry for stealing and acting stupid. I don't want you two to argue over me. Please."

"Well," Mom said with a smile. "It took some time, but I'm glad you finally owned up to your responsibility in this."

And there it was. Mom's underhanded compliment wrapped in unspoken criticism.

I nearly opened my mouth to take back my words, but my gaze landed on Gram. She gave a slight turn to her head as if telling me not to do it. I closed my mouth and poured more water.

"All's forgiven," Dad said, squeezing my hand. "And I'm glad you're liking it up here. It seems Gram and Gramps are taking good care of you."

I downed another glass of water.

"Macy, you look flushed," Gram said. "Are you all right?"

"Just feeling really warm," I said. "Maybe I should clean up and change."

"That's a good idea," Mom said.

Dad frowned toward me in apparent concern. He leaned over and felt my head. "You're feeling warm. Probably caught a bug last night, hanging out with that guy."

"I doubt it," I said. "All we did was bike to Lake Michigan and stare at the water. Oh, and eat pizza."

"Nothing to worry about," Gram said. "Go change and then get some rest. Lillian will be fine with me."

But Lillian wasn't paying attention to Gram. Her attention was on me. Her eyes were big and full of emotion. "Are you going to go the hospital?"

"No, sweetie. I'm only going to clean up and maybe take a nap upstairs. You can stay down here and play with Adrianne and then the two of you can help Gram make some cookies."

I excused myself and ran up the stairs. Locking myself in the bathroom, I leaned against the sink and tried to even out my breathing. Because along with waves of heat, I was also fighting waves of nausea. I stared at myself in the mirror and hoped to God that it was only a bug and nothing more.

Chapter 12~

The Problem with Mothers

I woke up to quiet. Too quiet.

I rolled over onto my back and listened. I couldn't hear anyone talking downstairs. No moving around. No shutting screen doors.

My stomach growled. I glanced over at the clock and saw that it was past one in the afternoon. Sitting up, I stretched then pushed myself off the bed. I changed into clean jeans and black sweater and rebraided my hair. "Good enough for me," I said as I left the room.

Once downstairs I saw Lillian sleeping on the couch. Hunting the rooms, I found Gram in Gramps' office, folding up blankets.

"There she is," Gram said. "Feel better?"

"Yeah, I do. I must have been overly-exhausted or something."

"Probably. Plus, it's always stressful when there are a lot of people in the house. At least for me anyway."

"Did they leave?"

"Yes. They wanted to say good-bye, but they didn't want to wake you. Your father asked for you to call him when you woke up. He's worried about you."

"How long has Lillian been asleep?"

"About an hour. After they left, I put on some cartoons and told her to rest while the cookies were baking. She was out in under a minute. Then again, she and Adrianne were running around the yard for a couple hours, so she was pretty wore out."

"Are the cookies ready? I'm starving."

"They're on the counter."

After taking three cookies and checking on Lillian, I went outside to sit on the porch. Gram followed me and sat beside me. "Would you like one?" I asked, handing her a cookie.

"No, I make them for you."

"So, you don't normally bake cookies every day when I'm not here?"

"No, I do not." Gram said with a chuckle. "We don't have that fast metabolism anymore. By the way, I wanted to talk to you…"

I looked down, already aware of what she might say. "I know I didn't behave the best. I'm sorry, Gram! Sometimes, my mother brings out the worst in me."

"That's not what I want to talk to you about, but I think you handled yourself very well. It was difficult for me and your grandfather to hold our tongue. We try to be respectful of your father and his choices, but the things she says," Gram shook her head.

"You sense it too? That she doesn't like me?"

Gram turned to me and studied me for a moment, then she said, "Sometimes parents feel they need to be tough on their children. It's not that she doesn't like you, sweetie. She's only trying to protect you from more bad decisions, and she's also trying to protect everyone else.

Unfortunately, sometimes your mother has no tact, and can say some pretty critical things. Don't take it to heart." She grabbed my arm and squeezed affectionately. "You are a good girl. Once Hannah's wedding is over, hopefully things will die down."

"I doubt it. She's been critical of me my whole life." I stared out at the trees lining their yard, bursting with buds. I inhaled deeply, enjoying the quiet. Not that I would admit it out loud, but I was relieved that mother had left. Instead I said, "What did you want to talk to me about?"

"Oh!" Gram said. "Where is my memory? Anyway, I had an idea that might count as community service hours. Outside of the motel."

"I'm already working too much as it is."

"We'd have to adjust some things, but this would give you more money in a paycheck."

"How so?"

"I'd like you to teach Sunday School."

"Say what?" I leaned back, hoping I didn't hear her correctly.

Gram grinned. "That's right. *Sunday School.* Derek needs someone to watch Lillian on Sunday mornings, and she would be bored with the regular service. Pedro likes to come on Sundays, and he has said that he would come more often if he could bring his brothers."

"Umm…" *Think, Macy. Think.* "I don't think someone with my past should be teaching kids."

"Your past?" Gram scoffed. "Macy May, you drank some schnapps and puked. If that is the extent of your past, then you have lived quite the sheltered life."

"There was something else that happened," I started.

"About a boy? Do you think you're the only church girl who's made a few mistakes about a boy?"

Okay, Gram was destroying all my arguments. "I don't know how to teach."

"Rubbish," Gram said with a wave of her hand. "You've been in Sunday School classes your whole life. Plus, you are a smart young lady. You'll figure it out."

"I might not be staying here much longer."

"Then get the program started, and if you have to leave, I'll take over."

I sighed, "Gram, I'm not too sure. I never liked Sunday School."

"Listen, you'll be great at it. It can be fun with the right teacher. I'm sure of it. And I've watched you with kids. They adore you. Lillian does, Adrianne does, Pedro's brothers would too. You and the children can stay in the sanctuary for the songs and worship, then at offering, you all can slip downstairs to our Bible study rooms." Gram's eyes teared up. "Those rooms are so nice, and they haven't been used in almost ten years. I would love for the downstairs to be used again. There is a kitchenette and the large open area for crafts or games. Oh, I get excited just thinking about it."

Once again, I stared at my Gram knowing that I could not say no. Knowing that I could not tell her how I was questioning my own faith at the moment. "I guess I can give it a shot."

"Wonderful. We have some curriculum in our office for when I used to teach it. It gives lessons for each week, along with craft ideas and games. Hold on, I'll go get it."

As Gram entered the house, Lillian walked out. She rubbed at her eyes and crawled into my lap. "Hey there," I said quietly, wrapping my arms around her. "Did you have a good nap?"

She nodded, resting her head on my shoulder. "Are you feeling better?"

"Yes, my nap helped a lot," I said. "So, did you have fun with my little sister?"

Lillian shrugged.

"What does that mean?" I teased.

"I got yelled at," she said.

"Really? By who?"

"The pretty lady."

"What happened?"

"We were playing hide and seek, me and my new friend Adrianne, and I got lost."

I looked down at her in surprise. "How'd you get lost?"

"I was hiding behind the wood pile, and I saw a butterfly, so I chased it."

"Lillian! You know you're not supposed to wander away. You could get hurt."

She leaned into me again and closed her eyes. "Don't yell at me too."

I sighed, my heart racing at the thought of losing Lillian. Especially with everything Derek was already going through. "Promise me you won't wander off again. Ever."

"I promise."

"Good. I'm sorry my mother yelled at you, but she was probably worried. I would have been." *If I had been awake,* I thought, feeling guilty.

"She became madder and madder," Lillian said quietly. "And told that man that you shouldn't watch me anymore."

Great. How could that woman embarrass and shame me when she wasn't even here anymore? "You know what I want to do?" I said, mentally shaking myself. "I want to play a game. Want me to teach you how to play UNO? It's fun."

"Yes!" she exclaimed, jumping off my lap.

Gram stepped out onto the porch again, holding activity books in her hand. "I'll set these in your room," she said. To Lillian, she asked, "Are you going to play UNO?"

"Yes!"

"That's my favorite game, too. May I play?"

Lillian nodded.

"There was an issue at the motel," Gram said. "I'll start the game with Lillian, but your grandfather wants you to see if Pedro needs any help."

"Oh," I looked at Lillian, not wanting to leave her alone with anyone. Then I asked Gram, "Did you know about Lillian getting lost earlier today?"

"No, when did that happen?"

"I was playing hide and seek," Lillian answered.

"We will stay inside," Gram assured me. "Besides, you won't be gone too long."

I nodded and said to Lillian, "Start playing the game, and I'll be back in a few minutes."

After reassuring her that yes, I was coming back, I headed across the street. Spotting Pedro's cart outside one of the rooms, I walked in that direction. "Hey," I said, peeking inside the room. Pedro was finishing the beds. "Gram sent me over here. Said there was a problem."

Pedro didn't answer. Just kept working on making the one bed.

I stepped inside and without asking, grabbed the clean comforter and began finishing the other bed.

"You don't have to help," Pedro said without looking up. "I'll take care of it."

"I don't mind helping," I said, continuing to work. "Are you going to tell me what's going on? Or are you going to keep being angry?"

"I'm going to keep being angry," he said.

"Okay." I finished the bed, trying not to get riled up. I told myself that it had nothing to do with me because I hadn't been over here. "How is your mom doing? Is she giving you a headache?"

"She left," he said, throwing dirty linens in the canvas bag.

I followed him out of the room. "What rooms are left?" I decided not to ask him to talk about his mother.

"I've got this, Macy. I'm not asking for your help."

"What is with you and asking for help? I don't mind helping."

Pedro paused and took in a few breaths. "You've already covered for me before. I still owe you. So, don't worry about today."

"You don't owe me anything."

"Yes, I do. And I don't like owing people. It's gotten me into trouble before."

"Like I said, you don't owe me anything. It's what friends do for friends. If I say I'm going to help you, there's no expectation." I stepped closer and took his hand. When he turned to me, I felt the warmth inside that made me all tingly. Suddenly, I dropped his hand. "Anyway, if you need my help. I'm here."

"I've worked late hours here before, Macy. I'll be fine. But thank you for being my…friend."

"I'm going to get my cart," I said, ignoring him. "I'm going to clean some rooms because customers need to check in. So, what rooms still need to be done?"

Pedro finished wiping down the sink. "I think my mother left your cart on the other side of this building. It'll have her room list on it."

I went to leave, then paused. "What happened?"

"She didn't like it. Part of the problem is that drugs have made her really weak, and this is a pretty demanding job. She blamed it on her bad back. I don't know what to do," he admitted. "She needs to keep busy. And she needs the money."

"And Gramps needs help. He still needs to hire another person or two." I thought of all the hours he spent working in the motel office. "That's it! What about if she worked in the office? Gramps is practically there all the time. I'm sure he'd go for it."

Pedro nodded. "That's a good idea. If Mr. Elmsworth says yes."

"I'm sure he will. Okay, I'll go get started." I headed toward the direction of my cart.

"Macy?"

I paused and turned around. "Yeah?"

"Thanks," he said with a small smile.

"No problem. That's what friends are for."

I found the cart, abandoned behind the first row of rooms. Pushing it around the corner, I parked it next to room 124.

I frowned. This was Derek's room. I'd yet to clean his and Lillian's hotel unit. I wasn't sure why I was so hesitant, but I thought about asking Pedro to switch with me. There was something intimate about them living in the room and I didn't want to violate that privacy. Oh well, it needed to be done.

I unlocked the room, another one of the larger units complete with kitchenette, and was relieved at how picked up it was. Lillian's toys were flung here and there, and there was two laundry hampers full of dirty laundry, but nothing disgusting. As I cleaned, I kept eyeing the two hampers. No doubt Derek had to take the laundry to the laundry mat. The two looked to be separated. One for his clothes, and one for Lillian's. I wiped up the sink and counter, still thinking about their laundry. Finally, I gave up talking myself out of it. I dropped the rag and went over to the hampers. I could only pick up one at a time, so I grabbed one and carried it out of the room and across the parking lot to the motel office. Walking around the office to the back room, I opened the laundry room door, and using an available washer, dumped the contents of the Lillian's hamper into it.

Once the washer had been started, I headed back to their room and hurriedly vacuumed. I made the beds, stopping to study the photograph on the bedside table. It was a framed picture of Derek and Lillian with a pretty woman between them. She had a pixie cut with a twinkle in her eye, her chin jutted out as if ready for her next adventure.

"Where's Lillian?" Derek asked.

I jumped, dropping the frame. "Oh hey," I said, clumsily picking it up and setting it back where it had been. "She's with Gram. We were going to play UNO, but Pedro needed help, so…" I couldn't look him in the face. "Okay, so you should be set. Let me know if you need anything."

"Where's Lillian's hamper?"

"I, um, put in the washer. Just trying to help. Okay, so, yeah, um, I'll see you." I left him in a hurry.

"Macy?"

"Yeah," I said, turning to face him. This was where he told me to leave his stuff alone. "I know. I shouldn't have touched your picture. I was just curious, that's all."

"I don't care that you touched the picture."

"Oh, okay."

"I only wanted to thank you for washing Lillian's clothes. It saves me some money."

"That's what I thought," I said. "As soon as hers are done, I can throw yours in."

"I can wash my own clothes, but thanks."

"Well, then feel free to go into the laundry room. I know Gramps wouldn't mind."

"Maybe I should check with him to make sure. I don't want to take advantage of his kindness. He's done a lot already."

We both kept standing there, neither moving. "She's pretty," I said. "Full of life."

Derek nodded. "That picture was taken about a month before the accident."

"How old is she? She looks young."

"25."

"Wow."

"We met straight out of high school. I came up north that summer to visit some friends. She worked at a bar here in town. My buddies and I went into the bar, and there she was. We actually argued over who would hit on her." He gave a half-hearted laugh.

"You won the bet?"

"No," he said, laughing more. "But my friend who won the bet lost interest as the night went on. I saw my window, so I took it."

"Nice," I said, nodding in approval. "And the rest is history?"

Derek shrugged. "I fell in love, and spent the entire summer up here. She had left home for freedom and was rooming with a couple other girls. After a month at Western, I saw her. That's where she went to school. She looked so different. A proper girl with proper friends." He smiled at the memory. "Let's just say we picked right up where we left off. We quit college and decided to move up north where we met. That was seven years ago." He paused, then added, "Now I'm a 26 year old man living in a motel with a five year old daughter while my wife dies. Not exactly how I planned my life."

My heart lurched as I watched him struggle to keep his emotions in check. Without thinking, I took his hand, just like I had done with Pedro, an hour earlier. Only this time, I didn't pull away. "Your life's not over," I said. "I'm sorry about the accident and what happened with your wife, but you're still standing here. My Dad would say that means you still have purpose running through your veins."

"Thanks," he whispered. "I needed to hear that." He let go of my hand. "I should go get Lillian."

As I finished the room, I thought about that young, beautiful woman in the picture. I wish there was something I could do to help. Feeling powerless, I pushed the cart to the next room. And nearly plowed into Pedro's mother. "Where is Pedro?" she asked with a thick accent.

"Last time I saw him he was just finishing room 109."

"Is he your boyfriend?" she asked.

"Pedro? No, we're just friends."

"No," she said shortly. "Him." She pointed toward Derek who had already crossed the street.

"Oh. No," I said, waving my hand and shaking my head. "Definitely not. He's…you know…old. I mean, not old, but older than me. And he's married."

But she wasn't listening. Her gaze hadn't left Derek's direction. "Where's his wife?"

"In the hospital."

When she finally looked in my direction, she said, "I came back to help, but if you are helping, I will go."

"I've got this. Thank you," I said with a thin-lipped smile. Great,

I inherited the thin-smile gene. "But, I was talking with Pedro, and we thought maybe you could work in the office. That way it'd be easier on you."

She crinkled her nose. "I don't know. I'll think about it." Then she left me with the cart.

I shook my head and unlocked the next motel room door. No wonder Pedro was so stressed. Both of our mothers were a piece of work.

Chapter 13~

And the Verdict is...

Gramps pulled up beside my family's house. It was a typical two-story ranch with a two car garage and a small apartment above the garage that we used as an additional bedroom. It used to be my home. Now I felt like an outsider. The undesired and unwelcomed feeling of not being wanted poked at my heart. Not that I would show it.

"Ready?" Gramps asked.

"I guess so," I said. "Thanks for going with me. I know it's hard for you to leave the motel."

"Your Grandmother covers for me all the time. Plus, Lillian is back at school, so there isn't that additional responsibility. Come on, let's go say hello to the circus." He winked at me, then opened his door and stepped out.

I stepped out of the car, and straightened my black-and-pink striped dress. I had just worn it to Gram and Gramps church the last Sunday, and I received so many compliments, I decided to wear it and maybe win-over the judge. But as I wobbled in my black heels, I regretted not slipping on my flats instead.

"Stop fidgeting," Gramps said gently. "You look very nice. You look older with your hair twisted up like that."

"Maybe I should take it down," I said panicked. "I don't want them to think I'm older than eighteen."

Gramps chuckled. "Stop worrying. Worrying won't fix anything." We walked up the sidewalk to the door. Gramps opened it without knocking. "Hello, we're here."

"MACY!" Adrianne ran out of the living room with Rex at her heels. She threw her arms around me while Rex barked and licked my leg. "I've been waiting for you!"

I squeezed her tight, then leaned over to greet the dog.

"There's my girl," Dad said, coming out from the kitchen. "Look at you. Very pretty." He hugged me.

"Yeah, I'm not in a dirty sweatshirt, and I actually did my hair." I laughed nervously but stopped as Hannah descended the stairs and Jake followed.

What was he doing here? My heart banged in my chest, and my stomach churned. I quickly looked away.

"Lucas wanted me to say hello," Dad said. "He's in my office taking one of his online assessments to complete his school year."

I barely listened. "Are we ready to go?" I asked Dad.

"In just a few minutes. Your mother is still getting ready."

"Hannah," Adrianne said. "Macy's here!"

"Oh, look at that," she said with a bite behind her words. "And you're all cleaned up too. No puke all over your face." With the same breath, she smiled at Gramps and said, "Hi, Grandpa! Good to see you. You remember my fiancé, Jake, don't you?"

"Of course," Gramps said, shaking Jake's hand. "How're the wedding plans coming?"

"So stressful," Hannah said, interrupting Jake. "I'd elope, but I want to wear my dress."

"I'd never let you elope," Mom said, as she came down the stairs. "I want to see you walk down that aisle."

I wouldn't look up from staring at my shoes. I had to press my lips together to keep from mouthing off. It wasn't that I was afraid of Hannah. Whatever. I'd give her a piece of my mind in a New York minute. No, it had everything to do with Jake standing directly across from us, leaning against the stairwell. I allowed myself one glance before looking back at my shoes. He looked good. Really good. Images of our times together flashed in my mind, and my face warmed from a warring mix of guilt, anger, and shame. It didn't help matters that when I glanced up, he was staring right at me.

"Macy, you look very nice," Mom said, giving me a brief hug. "When I saw you last week, you were wearing a gigantic sweatshirt to your knees. This is much better."

I smiled tightly. "I'm aiming to impress."

Dad's cell phone rang. Before answering, he said, "Go ahead and wait outside. I'll be out in a minute." Then he turned from us and took the call.

Adrianne gave me another hug. "I have to stay here with Hannah."

"That's okay. You wouldn't want to go with me anyway. We'll meet up for lunch." I opened up my purse. "But I have something for you. I was going to give it to you last week before you all left."

"You took a nap because you were tired," Adrianne said.

"Yeah, because someone was hogging my bed." I winked at her and handed her the unfolded drawing.

"Is that me?" she asked.

"Sure is." While Adrianne slept in my bed, I sketched the scene, complete with my comforter and her stuffed bear.

"I'm going to hang it on my wall!" Adrianne showed Gramps the picture.

"Wow," he said, taking it in his hands. To me, he asked, "You did all this?"

I shrugged.

"If you think that's good," Hannah said. "You should see the entire book of sketches that Macy drew of my fiancé."

My head snapped up and my eyes narrowed. "Oh, shut it, Hannah."

Hannah stepped forward. "I'm sorry. Did you not tell Gramps about how you stalked Jake?"

"That's enough," Gramps said. "Hannah, I don't like your ugly spirit. You haven't said one nice thing to Macy since she got here."

"Maybe because she took my car without permission and puked in it while trying to commit suicide!"

Adrianne started crying. "Stop it! Stop yelling at Macy!" She threw her arms around me.

"Hannah, calm down," Mom said. "Your grandfather is right. You're acting ugly right now."

Hannah looked from Mom to Gramps to me, then shook her head. Before she could leave, Dad came back into the hallway. "The verdict's in..." he started, grinning at me. "And Macy is cleared of all charges!"

"What?" Hannah, Mom, and I all asked the question at the same time.

"Ahmad dropped the charges. The court just called and said that he didn't want to prosecute."

Relief washed through me. *Thank you, God*, I said in my head. *I'll try not to ever be that stupid again.*

"Do you know what that means?" Dad asked. "It means you can come home! You don't have to do community service. You, my daughter, are free and clear!" He hugged me, picking me up off the ground.

Adrianne's tears had dried up and she now danced across the floor. Gramps said a prayer of thanksgiving. But my eyes were on Mom and Hannah. Both shared a displeased look that held some secret conversation.

It didn't hurt as much as it used to, especially when I began to think of this new little life I created in just a couple weeks' time up in Manistee. I thought of Lillian and Derek and Pedro and Gram and Gramps. And that's when I knew for sure that I couldn't live here again. At least until Hannah married and moved out. Even then I wasn't sure this home would ever be mine.

But somehow I'd have to break it to Dad and Adrianne.

"Let's do an early lunch to celebrate!" Dad said, opening the front door.

"What's everyone yelling for?" Lucas said from the end of the hallway. "I'm trying to take a test."

"Sorry," I told him. "They cleared me of all charges."

"Cool," he said. "But keep it down a little."

Most everyone had already exited outside. Adrianne held my hand, waiting for me.

And Jake lingered. We made eye contact, and I could tell he wanted to say something. Oh well, there was nothing I wanted to hear from Mr. Jerkface. Even if he did look really, *really* good. Eventually he said, "The youth group misses you. A lot."

I pulled Adrianne out the door, completely ignoring him. But my insides trembled just hearing his voice. Outside Dad and Gramps were talking by Gramps car while Mom and Hannah were whispering by Dad's SUV. I decided to go stand next to Dad and Gramps. They were the safer bet. Suddenly, I felt Jake come up behind me and gently squeeze my shoulder.

"I'll tell the youth group you said hello," he said while slipping a piece of paper into my available hand. Then he walked toward Hannah.

His touch sent goosebumps down my spine. I hated that he could still do that to me. I closed my fist around the paper and led Adrianne to Dad and Gramps. "The two of us will ride with Gramps," I said cheerfully, while the paper burned a hole through my hand.

I opened the passenger door and slid inside. Adrianne ambled into the back seat. Dad and Gramps continued to talk about logistics.

"We left her stuff back in Manistee," Gramps said.

"No problem. We can make a trip up there."

But I couldn't concentrate on them with Jake's note in my hand. Adrianne chatted in the back, so I took the chance and opened the paper. Considering the length, he must have scribbled the note before I got there.

Why did you block my number? I have been going insane not being able to talk to you. I'm sorry for ending it. I wasn't thinking straight. You have no idea how this is killing me. Give me a signal, and I'll choose you. Over and over again.

Gramps opened his door, startling me. I crumpled up the paper and stuffed it in my purse, then sat on my hands, so he wouldn't see me trembling. I'd be lying if I didn't admit that a part of me trembled from pleasure, knowing that he missed me. But the largest part of me trembled from anger. He was engaged to my sister, and yet still pursuing me? He made his choice, and it wasn't me.

"I have to stop at an ATM," Gramps said, pulling the vehicle out onto the road. "I feel silly that we didn't pack all your things."

"We thought I had to do community service," I said. "And I wanted to do it up in Manistee. I still want to go back up to Manistee. Nothing has changed in that regard." Far away from Jake. Far, far away.

"What?" Adrianne asked. "You've got to come back."

"Your family misses you," Gramps said.

"Not all of them."

"I miss you the most," Adrianne said. "And Hannah's just been mad lately because Jake asked for a break."

"Poor Hannah," Gramps said. "Well, they looked fine today. He's probably getting cold feet."

"What's cold feet?"

While Gramps and Adrianne talked, my brain swirled with the new information. Jake actually tried to break up? Why? He and Hannah were perfect for each other. He must have thought I was upset over the fact that he told me he couldn't visit at night anymore.

And I had been.

I stared out the window and once again felt the guilt and shame resurface. I had been upset. So much so that I stole a bottle of liquor and tried to drink past the pain. I had tried to come between Jake and Hannah. I had tried to make him fall in love with me, even if it meant unlocking the door to my bedroom every night. For once in my life, I wanted to win against Hannah, even if I had to use my body to do it.

Gramps pulled into 7-11 and shut off the car. "I've got to run in and use the ATM. I'll be back." He glanced over at me. "Why are you crying? Are those happy tears?"

I wiped at my eyes, but the tears didn't stop. I felt so overwhelmingly guilty that my stomach threatened to lose its contents. But I couldn't tell Gramps any of that, so I merely nodded.

"Come on, Adrianne, let's buy Macy a slurpee. That'll stop the tears."

When they left, I took out the crumpled note and read the words. A month ago, these would have been the words I longed to hear. I threw the note back into my purse, as the guilt turned into annoyance. Annoyed at Jake. Annoyed at Hannah. Mostly annoyed with myself.

If this were a fairytale, I'd be the villain. I'd be the jealous sister, trying to steal away Hannah's boyfriend. It couldn't be that way anymore.

I couldn't be the villain in my own story!

I watched as Gramps and Adrianne paid at the counter, and that's when I realized what 7-11 we were at. The one where I stole the schnapps! And there was Ahmad behind the register. Deciding this was at least one area where I could make amends, I exited the car and headed inside.

"We got you a slurpee!" Adrianne said, handing me one.

"Thank you," I told her, as Ahmad and I made eye contact. "I'll be in the car in a minute." I watched her and Gramps head to the car. Taking a deep breath, I walked up to the counter. Luckily, only one other person was in the store, and he was by the coolers. "Hey there, Ahmad."

"Hey. I've missed you," he said sadly.

"Yeah, I've missed my slurpees, but I was embarrassed, and then my Dad dropped me off up north."

"Is that where you've been?"

"Up north? Yes. The Manistee area. I was getting a head start on my community service hours, but now I don't have to, thanks to you not prosecuting me."

He shook his head and grimaced. "No way. I cannot do that to you. I kept saying that over and over, but she would not listen."

I didn't quite connect what he was saying, but I didn't press. "I'm so sorry! I should have never stole the schnapps," I said. "I'd like to pay for it, if I could."

"No, you are still under age, and your father already paid for it."

"Oh, okay. Listen, I need to say thank you. I don't deserve your kindness, but I certainly appreciate it."

Of course you deserve it."

His words stunned me. "I do?"

"You are such a sweet girl. Nearly every day you come in here, and you say 'Good morning' or 'Good evening' and you always chat with me about the store and my family. I cannot let one mistake on your part hurt your reputation. I told your mother that, but she was so insistent. This morning, I was like, 'No! I cannot do this!'"

"It's been more than one mistake though...wait, what did you say? What about my mother?"

"I would have never pressed the charges, Macy. Please believe me. She got into my head, telling me that it would benefit you and you'd learn your lesson. I haven't been comfortable about it these last couple weeks. But she can be really pushy."

My world began to spin.

"Macy?"

I held onto the counter and closed my eyes and tried to regulate my breathing, but I couldn't. Because if what Ahmad said was true, and I had no reason to doubt him, my own mother wanted me prosecuted and charged. "Just to clarify, you're talking about my Mom, right? Blonde hair? Never a hair out of place? Always wears fancy jeans and scarves?"

"I know who Meg is. You used to come in here with her all the time, and yes, that's who I'm talking about. I was surprised because she kept saying that you needed to learn your lesson, and that she and your father expected me to prosecute to the fullest extent of the law."

I left the store. Once outside, I took off the stupid high heels. I couldn't be this furious and try to balance at the same time.

Gramps rolled down his window and gave me a quizzical expression.

I swallowed down the bile and told myself to calm down. "Deep breath in," I whispered. "Deep breath out." I went to the car and slid inside, using every ounce of willpower to keep my emotions under control. But I was squeezing the high heels like my regulated breathing depended on them.

Gramps stared at me. "Did I miss something?"

"Please drive," I whispered, barely able to talk.

"Don't you like your slurpee?" Adrianne asked.

But I couldn't answer.

The entire car ride, Gramps and Adrianne stayed quiet. Eventually, Gramps rested his hand over my trembling fists. "Whatever happened," he said quietly. "You can't bottle it up."

I shook my head. It hurt too much to think about, let alone talk about it. All I could say was, "I want to go back home now."

"Okay, we'll figure something out, and bring your things down—"

"No," I interrupted. "This is not my home anymore. I want to go up north. The one place I can be where she won't hurt me." I wiped at my eyes, then clenched my fist again.

"You're not living here?" Adrianne whined. "But I want you to."

"Macy's grown up now, sweet pea," Gramps said. "She's got to spread her wings, just like you will one day." To me, he asked, "What brought this on?"

"We can talk later. But I didn't pack anything to come down with because I knew where I wanted to be."

Gramps pulled into T.G.I. Fridays, usually my favorite place to eat. Now my stomach rolled even thinking about eating. Actually, I'd be able to eat no problem if I knew my back-stabbing, betraying mother wasn't in there.

"I'll be there in a minute," I said, as Gramps and Adrianne opened their doors. "I've got to get myself together."

Gramps acted like he wanted to say something but instead nodded.

"Hold me a spot by you," I said to Adrianne, making myself smile.

She nodded and left, holding Gramps hand as they crossed the parking lot. Gramps had parked on the far left side of the restaurant just like he always had. "As long as my legs are still kicking, I'm going to walk," he'd say.

Now I closed my eyes and let out a breath, rewinding Ahmad's words in my head. All I kept coming back to was that Mom had wanted me prosecuted and convicted. It stung all the more thinking about it again. Somehow something broke between my mother and me, and I hadn't the slightest clue what had happened or how to fix it. But what mother pushes for her daughter to go through the trauma of a conviction?

Gramps door opened, and he slid in the car.

"I'll be there in a minute," I said, as I opened my eyes to my grandfather.

Only it was Jake. Staring right at me. "You have no idea how much I've missed you."

I pushed myself back against the door, shock ripping through me. I shook my head. "No, you shouldn't be in here." I turned to get out.

The door locks clicked into position.

"Stop it."

"Please talk to me."

I manually tried to unlock the door, but my hands shook too much.

"Macy, please…"

"NO!" I shouted. All the emotions flooded out of me. "I'm not going to be the villain!"

"I love you," he said, touching my arm.

I ignored the electric current that lit up my insides at his touch. Instead I shoved at his hand. Finally, unlocking the door, I fumbled at the handle until it opened. "Don't ever talk to me again," I said, nearly falling out of the car.

"Macy, wait," he pleaded.

But I had already shut the door. I would have broken down and cried right there, but I couldn't. Because I was standing face-to-face with my mother.

Chapter 14~

Mommy Dearest

"Your grandfather said that you were upset after 7-11, so I came to check on you," Mom's words dripped with condescension. "But I guess you're lying to him now too."

My emotions had already exploded on Jake, and they weren't about to be put on a leash. "First of all, I'm not lying to Gramps. I didn't know Jake would be stalking me. Second of all, the only reason you're out here is to see if I found out your dirty little secret. Does Dad know you were pushing Ahmad to prosecute me?"

"Of course, he does. We're doing what's best for you. But no matter how hard we try, you continually screw things up!"

"You're not doing what's best for me. You're trying to put me in my place! Just like you've always done!"

"Don't talk to me that way! I am still your mother whether you like it or not!"

The door opened to Gramps car, and Jake slid out. "Meg, it's no big deal. I parked right there," he said, pointing to a spot behind us. "I dropped Hannah off already because I had to run to the post office. When I came back, I saw Mr. Elmsworth and Adrianne step out of the car, but Macy looked upset. I only wanted to make sure she was all right. I mean, she used to be a part of my youth group. I'll always care for her and her soul."

Mom smiled at Jake and nodded in complete understanding. "Of course. I'm sorry if you feel I judged you. It's only Macy's actions that I question. After her sketchbook incident and all."

I wanted to argue and yell and scream, but Jake had already begun to walk toward the restaurant.

"You leave him alone," Mom said with steel in her voice. "Don't you dare lure him back to you."

"I didn't. He's the one who wrote me a note!" I fumbled with my purse to retrieve it.

"Sure. Just like he stumbled upon your room one night."

My fingers froze as I made eye contact.

"You did everything you could to rip them apart, and it almost worked. Then you sabotaged yourself and nearly died. Do you know what that would have done to the family? So yes, I saw an opportunity to help my family heal. That's why I pushed Ahmad to prosecute. I thought that maybe if you were somewhere else that everyone could figure things out. How does that make me a bad mom?"

Gramps and Dad came out of the restaurant and hurried toward us.

"I am not the villain," I whispered.

Dad stood between us. "What in the world is going on?"

Mom stared me down while tears flooded my eyes. She despised me. I saw it. And she thought I was evil.

"Meg? Macy?"

"Gramps, can we please leave?" my voice shook.

"Somebody tell me what's going on," Dad pleaded. "And Macy, your home is here. Your charges are cleared. This is where you belong."

"No, it's not," I said, furiously wiping at my eyes. "I want to be far away from here. That'll make you happy," I said to Mom. "Right? Get Macy out of your hair? Save the family?"

"Don't twist my words."

"I think Macy should come back with me for a while," Gramps said. "I try not to get involved, but she gets so upset when she's around you all. It breaks my heart. We'll keep her with us. She's doing a great job at the motel. Plus she started teaching Sunday School this past Sunday. We can't lose her now."

It wasn't going to be that simple. Dad said to Gramps, "Take her to our house. We're getting to the bottom of this."

"She's angry," Mom said. "Her emotional outbursts are becoming more vocal and more embarrassing. If she wants to be away from us, maybe that's what's best."

"STOP IT!" Dad bellowed at Mom. Even with my window up, his words reverberated in the car. "Stop trying to push her out of our lives!"

"Stop favoring her!" Mom yelled back. "You're the reason she's rebellious. You have given her everything while ignoring your other children."

"Don't give me that garbage," Dad said, still yelling. "Our kids are just fine. The fact is you mistreat Macy, and you always have!"

Mom and Dad were causing a major scene. I watched as people stopped going into area businesses and instead eyed my parents. Someone actually took out her phone and looked to be recording them. Gramps' face was red from embarrassment, but neither of my parents were paying him or anyone else any attention.

What a mess. And I, once again, felt tremendously guilty for causing it. No matter how angry and hurt I was about Mom and her actions, I didn't want my parents fighting. Especially about me. I sighed and opened the door. "Dad," I said, pulling on his arm.

"What?" he snapped until he saw it was me. That's when I noticed Adrianne coming out of the restaurant with Hannah and Jake.

"We're in a public parking lot," I said. "Neither of you should lose your cool. What if members of the congregation found out?"

Both of them turned their attention on me. I couldn't look at Mom. The betrayal I felt seemed irreparable, but I wasn't about to add their divorce to my lengthy list of sins. So, I would suck it up and play the part. I was, after all, their daughter. My family knew how to pull off a façade better than anyone. To Dad, I said, "I'm sorry I acted emotional, but please don't fight with Mom on my account. The fact is that I shouldn't have done the things I did. They were wrong. Hannah has every right to be upset with me, and you and Mom almost lost me because I wasn't thinking. That's why it's good for me to get away. Just like you thought it was good for me to get away three weeks ago."

"I never thought that. Your mother pushed me just like she always does--"

"But it worked. I'm not bothering Hannah and Jake anymore.

And they're not bothering me. That's good, right?" I said, trying to keep the façade going, especially since Adrianne, Hannah, and Jake now stood with the rest of us. "I'm working. I'm earning my keep. I'm helping at the church. So, let me go back."

"If that's what you want, peanut. I just want you to be happy, and I feel I've messed up and can't fix whatever it is that I broke."

"Nothing's broken," I lied, feeling like all the broken pieces of my heart lay scattered across the T.G.I.F. parking lot. "I'm only asking that I have time away. It's turned out to be a good thing."

He nodded, then wrapped me in his arms. I had to force myself not to lose it. I wanted to fall into a heaping mess right there. I wanted to tell him everything. I wanted Dad to tell me it would be all right and to make me feel safe. But I couldn't do any of those things. I needed to be strong. So, my insides shook, but on the outside, I remained composed. "Love you, peanut."

"Love you too."

"Are you leaving?" Adrianne whined. "You just got here!" She threw her arms around me. "I don't want you to go."

"I know, lima bean, but I've got a job now."

"You love Lillian more than me."

"Of course not. But her Mommy is really sick, and I help watch her. How about if this summer, you come up and stay with Gram and Gramps for a couple weeks?"

She turned to Mom. "Can I? Can I?"

"*May I,*" Mom corrected, then answered, "I don't see why not, as long as your online schooling is completed and you pass the exit tests."

I glanced over at Hannah and Jake and observed her annoyed expression. She probably thought this blow-up was entirely my fault.

I opened the car door again, but before I stepped inside, I added one more lie, "And Dad, please stop fighting with Mom. It's neither one of your faults that I'm messed up."

I noticed Dad and Mom nervously glance at each other, as if they knew something but weren't saying. Looking over at Gramps I saw that he wasn't looking at me but at Dad. I remembered what he said the one night in my room about something being complicated. I might have pressed the issue, but exhaustion saturated me. From the volatile emotions to my conversation with Jake to having to play pretend so that Mom and Dad could stop fighting, I felt spent.

***

When I opened my eyes, I was briefly disoriented. I sat up and saw Gramps driving up Interstate-10. Raising my seat back to the upright position, I asked, "How long was I out?"

"About two hours," he said without taking his eyes off the road. "You basically cried yourself to sleep, and have stayed that way for the entire trip."

"Sorry," I mumbled, feeling rumpled and more exhausted.

"You don't have to apologize."

I stared out the window, leaning my head against it. "I'm so glad to be going back," I admitted.

"I can understand why."

"At first it hurt that Dad would drop me off with you guys. Like he was kicking me out or something. But now, I'm so grateful that I have an escape."

"May I ask you a question?"

"Sure."

"What happened at the 7-11? That seemed to be a trigger for you."

"That's the 7-11 I stole from," I said.

"Oh." Gramps paused, then asked, "Did the owner say something mean?"

"No, not at all. He was very kind." I saw that Gramps had furrowed his brows together in confusion. Taking a deep breath, I continued, "Ahmad told me that he never wanted to press charges against me, but that it was my mother who kept pushing him to do it. She told him that I needed to learn my lesson, and that this would help me learn it. I guess Ahmad decided to not listen to her at the last minute. He said he couldn't do that to me." I thought it might hurt worse to say the words, but I felt numb to it.

Gramps was silent for an extended period of time. Too long.

"Gramps?"

"Do you believe him?" he finally asked. "Do you think that man is telling the truth?"

"I don't see why he would lie, and it makes sense. Ahmad has always been kind to me. I would go there all the time for slurpees and gum. And I wouldn't put it past Mom either. When I brought it up in the parking lot, she didn't deny it."

"I've told him and told him," Gramps muttered. "Tell a lie, reap a lie."

"I don't think Dad had anything to do with it."

"Why were you the one apologizing?" Gramps ignored my statement, acting more and more irritated.

"Because they started yelling, and everyone was looking at them. I didn't want rumors to get back to their congregation."

"Why not? Why shouldn't they see that the Elmsworths are not perfect?"

"I was only trying to calm them down. And I do feel bad, Gramps. Dad and Mom are sleeping in separate rooms. Hannah hates me, and I deserve it. And Mom loves Hannah, and Dad loves Mom, so it seemed right that I should apologize. If I would have never stolen the schnapps, none of this would have happened."

"This has been happening long before you stole alcohol. At least your parents fighting. They have worked real hard to keep it from you kids, but trust me, they have been struggling for years. Ever since your father told her he wanted to give up the church."

"Give up the...church? Dad would never want to do that!"

"Yes, he would. Do you remember when I was in the hospital? You were young, maybe 8 or 9."

"I remember visiting, and Dad stayed with you for a couple weeks to help with the motel."

"I had to recover from a minor heart attack. It ended up scaring your Dad, and he didn't want me and your Gram up in Manistee by ourselves. The longer he stayed, the more we talked about me handing the motel over to him and eventually the church too. When he left for home, the decision had been made. Until he talked to Meg."

"She hates up north."

"Exactly. She's not a big fan of us either. For different reasons that I'm not supposed to talk about. Anyway, she absolutely refused. Said that he had to choose between her or us, and even threatened to fight for full custody so that he'd never see his kids. Well, he wasn't going anywhere without you four kids. But it hasn't been the same, and I think she knows it."

"Poor Dad," I murmured. "So, for the last ten years, he's been pastoring a church that his heart isn't in?"

"Yes. He told me that Meg said if everything went right with Jake and Hannah's wedding, they could start to groom them to take over. She won't move up here, but she told your Dad that maybe they could buy a condo in Florida."

"But he wants to be up north?"

"From what he's told me, but I'm his father. He might be saying it to appease me."

"Are you twisting his arm?"

"Not at all." Gramps shot me a look, acting insulted. "I feel good. I like pastoring. And I like the motel. I like helping people. But would it be nice to have my son spend some time with me? Of course it would."

"Our family is a mess," I said, changing the subject. "We could be a reality T.V. show."

"When you build a foundation upon unstable ground, it's bound to crack and collapse."

"That sounded like a sermon," I teased.

"From the Gospel of Matthew."

"Yes, I know. I've sat on the pew my whole life." I paused before asking, "How was our family built upon unstable ground?"

Gramps shook his head.

"Gramps…come on…"

"It's only my opinion, that's all."

I could tell there was more he wasn't saying. I decided to keep pushing. "Do you know why Mom doesn't like me?"

Gramps said nothing, just kept staring out at the road.

"If there's a reason, shouldn't I know? That way I can fix it."

"Meg loves you…in her own way. She's a tough cookie, that's all. Maybe she's trying to motivate you to be successful in life."

"By keeping me in the shadow of Hannah? When you asked me to play the piano and sing, that was the first time in years, I did it publicly. I used to love playing the piano, but Mom would never let me practice around her. Which ended up being all the time."

"You have a natural gift for it."

"So, I started drawing more because I needed an outlet. I itched to do something creative with my hands. But she'd yell at me to put my sketchbooks away. That I was wasting time."

"Listen, Macy May," Gramps said, as he made the turn off the main road and onto the one that led into Manistee. "Life is messy. I'm sorry your mother hasn't been perfect, and yes, it would seem that she has been tough on you. But nothing is coincidental. I firmly believe that if you stop pointing a finger at her and stop thinking about all the negative things that have happened, that you have the potential to truly make a difference in your own life and in the lives of many people. Just look at what a blessing you've been to us and to Derek and to even Pedro. Just this past Sunday, you held our first Sunday School class. It's the first class we've held in the past several years."

"It was Lillian," I said unimpressed with myself. "And all we did was play Go Fish. I would hardly call that Sunday School."

"Yes, but when Pedro saw that you were starting it up, he told me he would start bringing his brothers. And in a couple weeks, Mitch and Deborah Hill will have their grandkids for the summer, and there's three of them. They were thrilled when we told them that you were starting up Sunday School."

I leaned my head against the window and resisted groaning. "I'm only doing the Sunday School thing because I'm watching Lillian. I'm not cut out to study lessons and do crafts and all that...stuff."

"Well, we're glad you're doing it. Who knows? Maybe it'll grow on you."

"I doubt it."

We pulled up onto Gram and Gramps driveway.

"Everything's still standing," Gramps said. "Then again, with your Gram at the helm, of course it would be."

"Thanks, Gramps, for going with me. I could have driven down myself, but I was glad for the moral support."

"Well, you're one of my favorite granddaughters." He winked at me. "Don't tell."

As we got out of the car, I stretched and said, "Mind if I borrow the car? Just to the beach. It's really peaceful there."

"Sure, but before you leave, go check on Pedro. He cleaned all by himself today."

I went inside, ran up the stairs, and changed into jeans, my extra thick hoodie, and my sneakers. Then I sprinted down the stairs, grabbed Gramps' keys, and headed out the door and over to the motel.

First I peeked in on Gram, sitting at motel's front desk, watching a talk show. "Hi, Gram, we're back."

"Oh, come here and give me a hug, you free bird," she said. "Your father called me and told me they dropped the charges."

I squeezed her neck. "Yep," I said, leaving out everything else that happened. "No community service after all."

"So, what did you decide? Are you going back downstate to stay?"

"Nope. You're stuck with me."

"Good. I can keep baking desserts."

I glanced around. "How'd Pedro's mother do on her first day in the front office?"

"Well," Gram said frowning. "She came late, stayed until lunch, and I haven't seen her since."

"Oh man," I said, feeling bad for Gram and Pedro.

"I know. Pedro has apologized at least three times, not that he needs to."

"I'm going to go check on him and see if he needs any help."

"That's my girl," Gram said, kissing my cheek.

I left the front office and found Pedro easily enough. He sat on the ground outside the laundry room door. "Hey," I said. "I came to see if you needed any help."

"No," he said. "I'm finished."

"Already?" I asked. "It's only 5:30."

"I work fast when no one is around. And when I'm angry."

"Want to talk about it?"

"No."

I nearly walked away, but instead, I extended my hand. "Take my hand."

He looked up at me. "Why?"

"I'm trying to help you up."

"I'm fine, Macy."

"Listen, I'm taking Gramps' car to the beach, and I'm going to chill at the lighthouse. That's why I'm wearing my thickest, warmest hoodie. Want to come with?"

This time he slowly smiled. "Yeah, I do."

"Good. Then take my hand and let me help you up."

Chapter 15~

The Truth Hurts

The evening spring sun shone on me, and I extended my arms out, throwing my head back as if I was superman needing a recharge. "I feel invincible," I said to the wind that kissed my face.

"You're not going to try and steal my secret spot, are you?" Pedro teased. Already his mood, like mine, was a million times brighter.

"I totally am," I said, taking my seat beside him at the lighthouse's edge. "Besides, it's hardly secret. Look at all those people on the walkway."

"Yeah, but we're the only two up here," he said, looking out at Lake Michigan.

We stayed quiet for some time. Pedro leaned back, closing his eyes, while I immersed myself in the view. Out here, everything I went through earlier today seemed so far away. Out here, there was only peace. I felt relief that Dad did not fight to get me to stay. I didn't think I could ever stay under the same roof with my mother again.

"What're you thinking about?" Pedro murmured.

I turned to him and saw him watching me. "That I'm glad to be home."

"Did it go that bad?"

"The charges were dropped."

Pedro raised his eyebrows. "Congrats. Why don't you sound happy about it?"

"Because I found out that the only reason the business owner tried to prosecute was at the insistence of my mother."

"Ouch."

"Tell me about it."

"Why would she do that?"

"She wanted to teach me a lesson. Personally, I think she wanted me out of the house. Hannah and I were fighting, and it was really toxic."

"And she sided with Hannah?"

"My mother has always sided with Hannah."

"In one of the psychology classes I took, I remember some kind of mental condition where a parent is abusive to one child, but loving to all the rest."

"When did you take a psychology class?"

"Don't act all surprised," he said with a grin. "In high school. I used to like getting away from my mom. But we're not talking about me. We're talking about you."

"Mom's never been abusive. I don't think she's ever spanked me. Not that I can remember."

"There are other forms of abuse."

"I know," I said. "But is it abuse if she just doesn't like me? She's never done anything outright. Besides, it's not only her. It's Hannah and Jake."

"Your sister and fiancé? What'd they do?"

"Hannah can't say one civil word to me, and Jake…" I stopped and thought about his note.

Pedro sat up. "What about Jake?"

"Oh nothing. He's annoying too."

"If it's nothing, why can't you look at me?"

I turned my face to his, then looked away. "They actually have a right to be upset at me," I said. "Well, Hannah does. Jake is just a jerk."

"I doubt it's that bad."

"It is. Let's talk about you."

"I don't want to talk about me. We're still talking about you." He scooted closer and took my hand. "Macy, something is bothering you. More than just your mother."

I shook my head. "I don't want to talk about it." I removed my hand from his. "Just like you don't want to talk about your past."

"My past is nothing like yours," he said. "And my past landed me in a juvenile detention center, and I even did some jail time."

I tried not to act surprised, but my face probably gave it away.

"That's why I don't talk about it," he said. "Because it changes things."

"You were in prison?"

"Jail is different than prison, but it still isolates you. No one wants to hang with a felon. Shoot, you took one look at me and wanted nothing to do with me."

"That's not fair. I didn't know you."

"Exactly. It's not fair to be judged, but it happens. Just like you're judging me now but trying to hide it."

"No, I'm not," I lied. "Maybe a little. But it's more curiosity."

"I get it. But I don't want to be judged. I'm not that same person."

I didn't say anything for a moment because I couldn't stop my brain from thinking about Pedro in prison. And here I was sitting on the ledge of a lighthouse with a convicted felon.

"I'll wait for you at the beach." Pedro stood up. "Actually, I'm really tired. It's been a long day. I'll just walk home."

"Wait!" I cried, pushing myself up. "Don't leave me. I wasn't judging. I just wasn't expecting it."

"It's fine," he said with a shrug. "I'm only fooling myself to think we can be…friends."

"Why can't we?" I asked. "I like you. You get me. With you, I can be me, and you're cool with it."

"What are you talking about? You don't trust me. You have all these secrets, and I'm the charity case that you're trying to help."

"You have secrets too! And you don't tell me because you don't want me to judge, and I don't tell you because I don't want you to judge!" I walked closer to him until we were toe-to-toe. Sighing, I released the words I had been holding in for months. "Jake cheated on my sister. With me."

Pedro's right eyebrow slightly raised. Other than that, his expression stayed the same.

"He would sneak into my room at night," I said the words fast before I chickened out. "And I let him. I wanted him. I wanted him to want me and to love me. During the day I would be mad with jealousy, watching him with her, but at night, he came to me. A good person wouldn't do that, right?"

"He doesn't seem like a good person."

"No, not him, me. I'm not a good person."

"Did you invite him?"

"Not at first. He just showed up. Sat on the edge of my bed. Then he told me everything I wanted to hear. And, like a stupid girl, I fell for it."

"Wait," Pedro said. "He came into your room? Uninvited? How old is this guy?"

"He's 23. He was 22, but that's beside the point."

"Whoa. How old are you again?"

"Eighteen."

"You were eighteen, and he was 22?" Pedro's voice kept raising.

"Yes, that's not a big age difference. Anyway, a good sister wouldn't do that."

"No, you're missing the point," Pedro said, exasperated. "A grown man came into your room and took advantage of you."

"It didn't happen like that. After I got used to the idea, I wanted him to come visit me."

"After you got used to the idea? Did you tell him no at first?"

"Why are you repeating my sentences? And maybe, I don't remember," I said.

"Macy, think about it!" he said, grabbing my arms. "Let's say you have an eighteen year old daughter. Let's say Lillian."

"She's not my daughter."

"Go with it. She's eighteen, and you find out that some guy who is in his twenties, is sneaking into her room at night, while you're sleeping. Would that bother you?"

"Of course it would, but if the girl is sketching pictures of him, and even worse, if later she starts writing him notes about how much she can't wait to see him, then I would find her guilty too."

Pedro shook his head. "Tell you what. Go, ask your dad. Call it a hypothetical question. See who he'd side with."

"That's different. And there's no way I'm talking to my dad about this. Hypothetical or not."

"He'd call the cops, Macy. And you know it. If some dude snuck into my daughter's room, I'd come after him with a glock in one hand and a club in the other."

"Okay, okay, forget I mentioned it. See? This is why it's a secret." I went and sat back down, but I couldn't stop thinking about what Pedro said. I always saw myself as guilty, but what about Jake? The first night he came to see me was not an invitation. No, that night I ran to my room in tears because Hannah had made my life miserable at youth service again. That was the night I ripped up several pages of sketches I had drawn of Jake. The same night I decided I would no longer crush on such a horrible person. But then he came into my room and sat on the edge of my bed. He said the words that I had fantasized to hear: *he wanted me.*

Without saying anything, Pedro sat beside me and took my hand again.

"Mom caught him that first night because he had come in through the door that leads into our upstairs hallway. He told her that I invited him, and that he told me he couldn't do that to Hannah."

Pedro scoffed and shook his head. I could tell he wanted to say something, but he pressed his lips together as if to hold it in.

"From then on, Hannah teased me mercilessly. She would fawn all over him, especially around me. Jake would sometimes tease me too. He would tell me at night that he had to keep up the act, so that no one would suspect. That's when I started keeping my outside door unlocked."

"Outside door?"

"Yeah, my room's like a small apartment over the garage. Dad let me have it because half the room was my art studio. But there's an outside door with fire escape stairs."

"Is this what led to the schnapps and car incident?"

I nodded. Without looking at Pedro, I added, "After I finally gave in, and...you know...."

"There was only the once?"

I nodded again. "I kept putting it off. I was a good girl, remember? Or at least, at that point in my life, I thought I was. Jake and I never did *that*. He kept pressuring me, but I'd always chicken out. I thought that if I didn't do that, then he wasn't really cheating on Hannah, and I was still a good girl."

"Let me guess. After that, he dumped you."

I cringed at the words.

"Sorry, I didn't mean it to sound that harsh."

"That's what happened. Sort of. He told me that God had been dealing with him, and that he couldn't do this to Hannah. He made it sound like I had seduced him or something. He even said he had to break the hold Satan had on him, like I was Satan or something. Anyway, that's when I started stealing alcohol. It sort of numbs everything."

Pedro stood back up and started pacing the small ledge of the lighthouse. "I want to punch him," he kept saying.

"Yeah," I said. "I do too."

"Good! So, you see how this predator stalked you and took advantage of you?"

I didn't say anything because I was more upset at myself. Just talking about it reminded me of how stupidly I behaved. "Well, I'm smarter now. And I'm not going to be the villain." I opened up my purse that hung diagonally across my shoulder and hip and pulled out the crumpled paper. I handed it to Pedro. "Jake had the nerve to give this to me today."

Pedro smoothed out the paper and read it, his frown deepening. "Please, tell me that you didn't fall for it."

"Of course I didn't. Even after Adrianne told me that he has been trying to break up with Hannah. I told him to never talk to me again. He's never touching me again, that's for sure."

Pedro raised his eyes from the note to me and gave a small smile. "For what it's worth, I think you are a good person."

"I'm not too sure about that, but I'm trying to be better."

"Macy…" he stopped.

"What?" I urged.

"It's just…you deserve a guy who'll treat you like a queen."

Our gaze held, and my heart warmed. "I've been told for so long that I'm jealous and a liar and the bad guy, that I don't know what to believe," I said quietly, opening my heart even more.

"Whoever told you all that is the liar. The Macy I know helps everyone, even if it means working more hours or being inconvenienced. You've been a big help to me and to Derek and Lillian and to your grandparents. I mean Sunday services have been so much better since you've been there to sing."

"I need my mind to believe it because I feel like one really big fraud. If my grandparents knew what happened, I doubt they'd let me sing."

Pedro shook his head. "You're wrong. Mr. and Mrs. Elmsworth are the kindest, most humble people I've ever met. And the most forgiving. He's the only one who gave me a job. Not only that, but he helped me keep my brothers, so that social services didn't come sniffing our way. Not many people would take a chance like that on a convicted felon. And even more than all that, they helped me to believe that I can start over. Start fresh. You know, grace."

My cell phone rang in my purse. Sighing, I took it out and saw it was Gram. "I can't believe I get coverage out here…Hello?"

"Hi sweetie. Dinner's nearly finished. Will you be back?"

My stomach grumbled. "Yes, I definitely will." I hung up. "Are you hungry? Want some dinner?"

Pedro's eyes widened. "Really? You want me to come over for dinner?"

"Um yes," I said. "Don't be silly. Want to pick up your brothers?"

"I wouldn't want to overwhelm Ms. Elmsworth. My brothers are bottomless pits."

"She'd love to have them, but I can call and check if you want." I called Gram back. "Gram? Can Pedro and his brothers come over for dinner?" After Gram's answer, I ended the call. "No problem," I said. "Come on, let's go pick up your brothers."

"Hey," Pedro grabbed my hand as I was making my way to the steps. "Thanks."

"I should be saying 'thank you.' You let me get a lot off my chest."

"I'm glad you told me," he said. "Not that it changed anything, but now I know you trust me."

"I do," I said honestly. "I wish you'd trust me with your secrets."

"I will. I do. I mean, I'll tell you, but I know that it'll change things between us."

"No, it won't," I said.

"Yes, it will," he said sadly, dropping my hand. "But you deserve to know."

***

"Just park here," Pedro said, unbuckling his seat belt.

I slowed the car and looked around. "But I don't see any houses."

"That two-track goes back into our property, but I'd rather you not see where I live. Just stay here. I'll be back in a minute."

I went to protest, only to close my mouth. I reminded myself to respect Pedro's wishes. Maybe if I did so, he'd let me into his life...and tell me about his past.

Once out of the car, he started jogging up a small two-track path. We were already in the middle of the woods, on a tiny dirt path that led about a half mile into the trees. I tried to peer through the dense forest to see if I could spot a cabin. Slowly, I crept the car up until I could see down the path Pedro had taken. I could barely make out a trailer. From where I sat, it looked rough...really rough. The awning had busted one side and nearly touched the ground, and what must have been a yellow color on the outside had turned gray. But the clearing around it looked clean and well kept up with the boys' bikes resting against the house.

I slowly reversed to the same spot the car had been and waited. Eventually, Pedro and his two brothers ran to the car and got in. "Hi," I said to the two boys in the backseat. "I'm Macy." As I pulled up and into their two-track to turn the car around, I noticed Pedro's happy demeanor from earlier had changed. "Everything all right?"

"My mother never came home," he said.

"Do you want to look for her?"

"No," he said decisively. "My brothers and I are going to have some dinner."

"What's for dinner?" the little boy, Pablo asked.

Pedro said something to him in Spanish.

The boy said, "Lo siento. Sorry."

"Don't be sorry," I said. "I'm not sure, but my grandmother is a great cook. And she makes the best cookies."

I looked at the rearview mirror and saw the boys grinning at each other.

Pedro said something in Spanish again, to which the boys agreed. "What'd you say?"

"To mind their manners and to say please and thank you."

"That's cool that you speak both Spanish and English."

"Yeah, I try to only speak Spanish to the boys because I want them to remember their identities. You know, maybe being bilingual will help them later in life. Plus my mother and I used to speak in Spanish to each other because a lot of the guys she brought home never knew the language."

"It's like our secret code," Filipe said.

"Very cool. I wish I could talk in your secret code, but since I was homeschooled, I never had to take Spanish classes."

They began to teach me a few phrases and sentences as we made our way to Gram and Gramps. "So, if I want to ask 'What's for dinner,' I say 'Que hay para cenar?'"

The three of them started laughing.

"Did I say it wrong?"

"A little," Pedro said. Then he said the question slowly.

I repeated it until I pulled into the driveway. I kept repeating it until we walked through the door. As soon as Gram came out of the kitchen, I stated the question in Spanish, then looked over at the guys and gave a thumbs up. Pedro shook his head slightly. "Was I at least close?"

He shrugged, then turned to Gram. "Thank you for having us over for dinner."

The boys said, "Thank you," as well.

"We're happy to have you. Go, wash your hands, and then we'll eat. The boys can go to this downstairs bathroom, Pedro, you and Macy can use the one at the top of the stairs."

I led Pedro up the stairs. "You can go first," he said.

"I'll be out in a minute." I shut the door, used the restroom, then washed my hands. I noticed my hair was sticking out all over from being wind-blown. I quickly brushed it, deciding to leave it down. I told myself it had nothing to do with Pedro, but it sort of did.

"Your turn," I said, opening the bathroom door. I noticed him at the doorway to my room, peering in. "It's a little messy," I said. "I was in a hurry this morning. We had to leave by eight in order to get downstate in time.

"Is that one of your sketchbooks?" he asked, pointing to the bed.

I went over to it and flipped it open. "It's weird that I don't hide the books when my mother's not here."

"May I see one?"

I found the one I had started to draw of Pedro sitting in church. "Please don't laugh," I said, then showed him.

Pedro took the book and whispered, "Wow."

"This was easier because you had on a shirt with sleeves. I tried one other time, but I couldn't capture your tattoos perfectly, so I gave up."

Pedro turned the page, and then another, and I let him. "These are incredible," he finally said, stopping at the one I sketched of him at the lighthouse with the stars surrounding him. He touched the picture, tracing the lines with his hand. "I don't know what to say," he whispered.

"You said you wouldn't find it creepy, remember?" I started to feel self-conscious, and went to take the book.

Pedro pulled it back. "Creepy? Macy, these are amazing. I want them."

"I'll draw you another. Those are mine."

"Promise?"

"Yes, of course, I promise."

"Will you draw one of me and my brothers?"

"Yes."

He handed me the book, his handing brushing mine and lingering. He acted like he wanted to say something.

"What? You do that a lot, you know. Act like you're going to say something, then don't say it."

"I wish you could see yourself the way other people see you. That's all. You have more talent in your little finger than most people."

I set the book on the bed. Not knowing what else to say, I said, "I'll meet you downstairs."

The boys were already at the table, practically gaping at the spaghetti, garlic bread, and salad that waited for us. Then again, so was I. My stomach grumbled. "I am starving," I said, giving Gram a hug before sitting down. "Thank you. This smells wonderful."

"When your grandfather called and said you were coming back, I got started on dessert."

"What's for dessert?" Filipe asked.

"Caramel fudge brownies with vanilla ice cream."

"Yum," Gramps said, rubbing his hands together.

"Not for you," Gram said to Gramps, smiling at Pedro as he sat down.

"A little piece?"

"Maybe. All right," Gram said. "Who says grace?"

"How about Macy?" Pedro said.

I made a face at him, then bowed my head. I began to recite the prayer Gram used, "Thank you, Lord, for the food we are about to eat. Thank you for our guests and for the friendship they bring...and thank you for Gram and Gramps for opening up their home to me and so many others. Amen."

"Amen," everyone said.

The boys devoured the spaghetti and bread. Pedro and I exchanged glances and grinned.

"Sorry," Pedro said to Gram and Gramps. "They eat a lot of instant mac-and-cheese at our place."

"And peanut butter sandwiches," Pablo added with a mouth full.

Pedro said something to the boy in Spanish. Pablo grabbed a napkin and wiped at his mouth.

"How did your mother do today in the office?" Gramps asked Pedro.

Pedro's smile vanished. "Um, she left early, sir. You don't have to give her a job. I thought that if she stayed busy with work, she'd avoid falling into some of the same traps. But, yeah, that didn't happen."

"Don't give up on her," Gram said, patting his hand. "Let her keep showing up, and we'll work with her."

Pedro nodded and asked, "Are you going to hire for housekeeping? Now that Macy doesn't have to work, I could use some full-time help."

"Hey, I haven't quit," I said, acting offended.

"I only thought that—"

"Well, you thought wrong," I said. "I like working with you."

The table fell quiet. Pedro quietly said, "I like working with you too."

Suddenly Filipe whistled and said, "Oooooooo, Pedro's got a girlfriend!"

Pedro threw his napkin at his brother playfully as Gram and Gramps laughed. My face must have turned a hundred different shades of red.

Someone knocked at the front door, and Gramps went to stand.

"Let me get it," I said, wanting to leave the room to gain some composure. I left quickly before he could protest.

I opened the door to find Derek standing there with Lillian. His eyes were completely bloodshot, and he wobbled, seeming to have a problem standing straight.

"Macy!" Lillian cried, hugging my legs. "Daddy's scaring me."

"Just...Just take her...please..." he turned and stumbled down the steps.

"Gram," I called out.

"I'm right here," she said, behind me. "Lillian? Want some

spaghetti? Pedro and his brothers are here."

"No!" she yelled, clinging to my legs. "I want Macy! Macy, don't leave me!"

Gramps and Pedro had already went outside to help Derek.

"Okay, I'm here." I knelt down and hugged her. "You're safe."

Then she started to sob. "Daddy shook me. Really hard."

I kept hugging her, my heart aching for the both of them. "Your daddy loves you," I said, kissing her head. "He shouldn't have shaken you, but at least he brought you over here to see me, right?"

She nodded into my shoulder. "He was drinking soda from a bottle, and I went to take a drink. He always lets me take a drink, but he shouted at me to leave it alone. He yelled at me really loud," she said through another round of tears. "Then when I started crying, he shook me and yelled, 'SHUT UP, LILLIAN!'" She paused, then asked, "Does Daddy hate me now?"

"No," I said, pulling her from me to look at her. "He's had a bad day, and it sounds like he wasn't drinking soda. He was drinking a grown-up soda that kids can't have."

"Why can't I drink it?"

"Because it's alcohol, and it would give you a horrible belly ache and make you get sick."

Gramps came back into the house. His expression was crestfallen. "Macy, Lillian will stay here tonight."

I nodded. "We get to have a slumber party!" I said as cheerful as I could.

Lillian gave a little smile. Then she turned to Gramps, "Is Daddy okay? Tell him I'm sorry I tried to drink his grown up soda."

"I'm going to stay with him just to make sure," Gramps said and gave her a wink. "And I'll give him your message."

"Go to the dining room, and see if there's any spaghetti left," I told her. "I'll be there in a minute."

She clung to my neck for a few seconds more, then reluctantly went to the dining room.

"Did his wife—?" I couldn't bring myself to say the words.

"Yes," Gramps whispered. "Derek's wife passed away this afternoon."

Chapter 16~

No Rest for the Weary

I finished making the bed, only to seriously consider lying down on it. The last two days had been highly-charged and emotional. Mostly because Derek had left and hadn't come back.

Gramps said yesterday evening that it was okay, that he knew where Derek was. And Derek had called last night to talk to Lillian and to tell her that he had to take care of some things for her mommy. But my heart broke for Lillian who kept wondering if her father left because she drank from his grown-up soda bottle.

None of us told her the truth, but it hung in the air like a thick fog, making it hard to move around.

Last night, after Lillian had fallen asleep, I pressed Gramps. "Where is he?"

"He's supposed to be back soon."

"Gramps…" I said.

"Macy, do not push me for information. Part of being clergy is keeping things confidential."

"Yes, that's true. But right now, and I can't believe I'm actually saying this, I'm a part of the ministry. Right?"

"It doesn't work that way."

"Who's watching Lillian? I am. Who was up most of last night because that little girl kept having nightmares? I was. Who had to change the sheets because Lillian had an accident? I did. If I am an extension of your ministry, which I'd like to think I am, then I should know. At least the basics."

Gramps stared at me for a moment before sighing, "Fine. You're right. You should know some of it. He had to go back to his father. To see if he could help with funeral expenses. Then he had to go to her family." He stopped and paused, clearly emotional.

"They don't know yet?"

"None of it."

I covered my mouth as the realization hit me. Her family had no idea that their daughter had been sick? "How could he not tell them?"

"Derek and his wife haven't talked to their families since they ran away together. The families don't even know about Lillian. That's why she's here for right now."

The news hit me like a sledgehammer. "What happened? Do they not even know their daughter has been on a ventilator? And why wouldn't their families want to know about Lillian? She's such a beautiful little girl."

"From what Derek shared with me, his father is a gambler and a drinker. He had a heavy hand with Derek, so Derek saved up enough money to try to go to college to get out of the dump they lived in. He had to work three jobs to stay in school. His wife, on the other hand, came from a highly influential and rich family. You get where this is going? He was the bad boy from the other side of the tracks. Her family forbid it, so the two ran away together and never looked back."

I remembered Derek telling me about how they moved up north where they had first met. Had they been running away?

That question had been going through mind all morning. Now as I yawned, I pushed the cart to the next room in a sleepy daze. I took another drink of my coffee. "Wake up," I ordered myself. "These rooms aren't going to clean themselves." My cell phone buzzed. I saw that it was Dad, but I didn't take the call. I was too tired to talk. I shut the phone off and entered the next room.

I turned the T.V. on full volume to keep me focused and awake. While vacuuming, I noticed Pedro peeking his head through the doorway. I turned off the machine, lowered the T.V.'s volume, and asked, "What are you doing, goofball?"

"You scare so easily," he said, grinning. "And I make you jump all the time. So I'm trying to let you know I'm here before, you know, you have a heart attack."

"Thank you for the consideration," I said, yawning again.

"Lillian didn't sleep better last night?"

"She refuses to sleep in any room other than where I'm at. I think she's gotten used to always having an adult sleeping in the room with her. I've tried sneaking off to crash on the couch, which sort of works, but she wakes up crying. Not to mention she's been having accidents." I shrugged my shoulders. "I'll be fine. I'm more concerned about her and Derek."

Pedro approached me, his normally hard face softened. He reached up and gently tucked some stray hair behind my ear. "You are such a good person, Macy Elmsworth," he said. "Definitely not a villain."

His words impacted me, and I found myself blinking back emotion. "You think so?"

"I told you that I see you. *Really* see you. And you would do anything for anyone. I mean, I treated you like garbage, and yet, when I needed help, you said yes. You didn't even have to think about it."

Our gaze lingered, and even though we were standing in an old motel room, everything faded as if there was only the two of us. Pedro hesitated briefly before leaning in and kissing me.

I didn't push him away or step back. In that moment, I realized I wasn't afraid of Pedro or his past. That he might have seen the good in me, but I also saw the good in him. So, when he went to release me, I tugged on his shirt and pulled him back to me again.

Afterward, he rested his forehead on mine and smiled shyly. "I've wanted to do that for a while."

"I'm glad you did."

"I don't really remember what I came in here for," he said, stepping away.

I grinned. "Checking up on me? Making sure I hadn't fallen asleep?"

"I think I just wanted to see you..."

My heart thudded loudly. He probably heard it.

After we stood there, grinning at each other like a couple of school kids, he went to leave the room. "I'm going to go check on my mother. She actually showed for work again today."

I nodded and waved good-bye, then brought my hand to my lips and smiled. Even though I didn't say it out loud, I had been wanting to do that for a while too. I had no idea what it meant, other than admitting to myself that I was attracted to him and it looked like he was attracted to me too.

But it was more than that. Much more. My heart hurt, but in a really good way. Maybe because I didn't have to hide this. I didn't have to be deceitful. Maybe it was because it felt completely natural unlike the other situation I had been in. With Pedro, it just felt…right.

The rest of the afternoon went by fast as I replayed the kiss over and over again in my mind. The bus dropped Lillian off, and she tagged along while I finished. I tried to leave her with Gram yesterday afternoon, but she refused to be anywhere but with me. And she only went to school the last two days because I pinky-promised to be here when she came home.

"What do you think's for dinner?" I asked her, as I pushed the cart back in its spot in the laundry room. I noticed Pedro's had already been dropped off. I felt the sting of disappointment that I wouldn't see him this evening.

"Hamburgers and French fries," Lillian said. "Gram told me. Will Daddy be there?"

"I'm not sure if he'll be back yet, but if not, I'm sure he'll call you like he did last night."

We crossed the street and walked up the driveway. Lillian ran over to Gram who was planting some annuals. I turned my phone back on, knowing Adrianne would be calling soon. My phone started buzzing with missed calls. And they were all from Dad.

As soon as we stepped inside, Gram said, "Your father's been trying to get a hold of you. Says it's urgent."

"Yeah, I guess so," I said. "He's called five times." I hit the dial button and waited for Dad to pick up.

"It's about time," he said exasperated.

"Sorry. I was busy working. What's up?"

"It's about Hannah."

"Okay, what's so important that you blow up my phone?"

"Jake's gone."

I had just entered the dining room and had nearly taken my seat. Now I turned and headed toward the downstairs bathroom. Once I shut the door and locked it, I said, "What are you talking about? Where did he go?"

"We don't know. Hannah's beside herself. Said that last night he told her he wanted to take a break for a while, but that she talked him out of it. Apparently, she didn't because when she went over to his apartment, all his personal stuff was gone."

I sank to the floor, repeating to myself that it had nothing to do me. *I'm not the villain.* I told Jake no. I was no longer the bad guy in this story.

"Macy?" Dad asked. "Hannah told us that Jake mentioned you. Your mother said it's time you tell me. Do you know what that's about?"

I closed my eyes and took in a shaky breath. I couldn't bring myself to say the words.

"Does this have to do with the sketchbook incident?"

Someone knocked on the door behind me. "Macy?" Lillian asked. "Are you done washing your hands?"

"I can't talk about this right now," I said. "I've got to go."

"Please talk to me. I want to help both my daughters, but I need to know what's going on."

I ended the call and turned off my phone. I couldn't talk to my Dad. I couldn't tell him the truth. I wasn't ready to be the villain again.

Chapter 17~

Time Will Tell

Dinner remained subdued. Gram and Gramps must have talked to Dad because they didn't push conversation but would glance at me every now and then and act like they wanted to say something. Lillian even stayed quiet, picking at her food and acting melancholy.

I busied myself with dinner clean-up, then helped Lillian take a bath and get ready for bed, but once she was in my bed and the lights were off, I found my grandparents sitting beside each other on the couch waiting for me.

"Sit," Gramps said.

I sat across from them but couldn't look them in the eye.

"Macy," Gramps started. "Your father told us what happened with Hannah."

I swallowed the lump in my throat, still keeping my eyes focused on the carpet.

"We want you to know that you don't have to tell us anything."

Now I levelled my gaze with theirs. "I don't?"

"No," Gramps said. "But we need to know if Jake would have any reason to come up here?"

I felt the air deplete from my lungs. I could barely gather a breath. *Oh my God, would Jake come up here?*

"Macy, breathe," Gram said concerned.

"This can't be happening," I said more to myself. I rubbed my thighs and my arms, feeling as if my skin was crawling with horror. "He can't come up here. I'm safe up here."

"I don't want to push you," Gramps said, no longer masking his concern. "But your father and mother and Hannah have reason to believe that Jake is headed up this way. If there is anything we should know, we would appreciate the information."

"We won't judge, hon," Gram added. "You know that about us. But is there a reason why he would want to come up here? Is it you?"

I pushed myself up and started to pace the floor. Why would he come up here? I wanted nothing to do with him! Suddenly, I had to leave. I needed to go to the one person I had confided in. "May I borrow the car?"

Both Gramps and Gram blinked as if not expecting the question.

"I promise I'll be back in a little bit. I just…I want to go talk to a friend…Please, I promise, I will be back soon."

"What friend?" Gram asked.

"Pedro." I paused. "He…He gets me."

"Do you know where he lives?" Gramps asked.

"Yes, I think I can find it."

"It's back a ways off the road."

"Right. If I can't find it I'll come right back."

Gramps and Gram exchanged a look. "We're worried about you," Gramps admitted. "And we're not done with this conversation. If you promise to be back within an hour or so, we'll trust you with the car."

"I promise." I crossed my heart, then went over to them and kissed them both.

I practically ran out of the house, shaking so hard it took a couple tries to start the car. I kept looking over my shoulder and kept pressing the lock button to the car to prevent Jake from slipping inside. I reversed the vehicle, nearly hitting a tree, but fixed the turn just in time. Once in drive, I pressed the gas and sped down the road.

Tears blinded me, and I nearly missed the two-track that led through the woods. I wiped at my eyes and focused on staying on the small trail, but feeling completely terrified of the dusky woods. Goose bumps erupted on my arms as my eyes darted from right to left. Somehow I managed to find the turn-off that led to Pedro's trailer.

Once there, I stumbled out of the car, and ran up to the door, pounding on it and watching behind me at the same time.

Pedro opened it, and I flew into his arms, bursting into tears. "He's coming for me," I cried. "I don't know what to do! He's coming for me!"

"Whoa," Pedro said before finally putting his arms around me. "I don't know what's going on, but take a deep breath."

"He's coming up here," I whispered, still shaking. "I thought I was safe up here, but I'm not."

"Give me a sec," Pedro said, releasing me.

I nodded but wrapped my arms around myself. Filipe and Pablo sat on couch that looked like it came right out of the 1970s. Their mother

206 | Janice Broyles

sat with them. And all three were watching me with a mix of curiosity and bewilderment. "Hi," I murmured, forcing myself to push past my emotions. "I didn't mean to barge in like this."

"Who's coming to get you?" Filipe asked.

"Never mind," Pedro said to his brother. Then he said, "Come on, sit at the table. Dinner's ready."

It was then I noticed the small table right beside the kitchen with three mismatched chairs around it. Pedro had placed two hotdogs on pieces of bread and a serving of corn at each spot. I watched him as he poured milk into plastic cups. The boys turned off the boxed television and came over to the table. "Is there any for me?" their mother asked.

"Of course," Pedro said, although his tone was less than inviting. "Take my spot here. Go ahead and get started. Save me some," he warned his brothers.

"Go ahead and eat," I said, feeling guilty that I was pulling him away from his only real meal of the day.

"They'll save some for me," he said. His family had already began to eat. But I didn't see any more food left for Pedro. "I'll be fine," he said and took my hand. "There are two more hot dogs in the pan and plenty of bread." He led me down the narrow hall to a small bedroom on the right. It had a futon laid out as a bed, a thin dresser cluttered with a variety of paraphernalia, and a laundry basket of clothes sitting on an old chair.

"Is this—"

"My room? Yes. I'd have picked up a little more, but I wasn't expecting company." He reached out and touched my face. "I know it's not much. That's why I didn't want you to see it."

"No, your home is warm and cozy. I...I'm feeling kind of silly to barge in like I did."

"I'm glad to see you. So, what's up? Who's coming?"

"Jake."

Pedro's expression darkened. "The man who came into your room uninvited and took something that didn't belong to him?"

"I thought I told you that I left my door un—" One look at Pedro, and I said, "Yes, that's the same guy."

"Why is he coming up here?"

"He broke it off with Hannah."

"He's not over you."

"I think it has something to do with that letter he gave me."

"Seeing you reminded him of what he wanted."

"But I don't want him. I told him that."

"Men like that don't care what you want, Macy. He came into your room without an invitation and preyed upon you for months. He's a taker, not a giver. He might come in a shiny preacher-package, but I've known men like him."

"What do I do?" I asked, feeling shaken again.

"Did you tell your grandparents?"

"No, they know something's up because they're the ones who told me, but I can't tell them."

"Why not? They need to know."

"Because..." I paused, then said what had been bothering me all evening. "Because they've been the only family who has loved me and helped me and believed in me unconditionally. It'll be over when they find out who I am." I wiped at my eyes, embarrassed over the tears.

"Two things, Macy. First of all, their love isn't going to stop once you tell them. If anything, they're going to be just as upset as I was about Jake…not about you. Second thing is this: they already know who you are. One mistake doesn't change that."

"It was a BIG mistake."

"Tell them," he said gently. "They need to know. Then you won't have it hanging over your head. You'll be free from it."

"What am I going to do if he comes up here?"

"You tell him to leave. You call the cops. You put a restraining order on the guy. There's a lot you can do." Pedro added, "I better not see him, that's all I have to say. I can't risk getting in trouble again, but if I laid eyes on him…"

"No," I pleaded. "I don't want you in trouble, especially over him." I wrapped my arms around Pedro and rested my head on his shoulder. "Thank you."

With Pedro's arms around me, I felt safe. We held each other for several minutes. Then I heard his stomach growl. "You're hungry," I said, stepping back. "I'll get going so that you can eat."

"I'm all right," he said, but his stomach rumbled again. He laughed, "Okay, okay, I'm a little hungry."

"Eat," I said, opening the bedroom door. "If your brothers haven't eaten it all."

"They better not."

As we made our way to the living room and kitchen area, Pedro's mother was slipping into a pair of high-heeled boots.

"What're you doing?" he asked.

"I was going to see if your girlfriend could drop me off in town," she said, then looked at me.

"Um," I glanced over at Pedro, who was already placing two hot dogs from the pan onto two slices of bread. "I guess I could."

His mother stepped outside.

"She's going to ask you for money," he said already eating the second hot dog.

I closed the gap between us and kissed him on the cheek. "Thanks for talking me through it."

"Listen," he said, touching my elbow. "Whatever my mother says take with a grain of salt."

"Got it."

Even though I felt worlds better after talking with Pedro, I still felt skittish as I made my way in the darkness to the car. Pedro's mother might have been a little weird, but I didn't mind the company. "All right," I said, giving her a tight-lipped smile and starting the car. "Let's get out of these creepy woods."

She shrugged and said, "The worst thing out here is a bear or two."

I maneuvered the car around the clearing before straightening it out on the two-trail. Pedro stood in the open doorway, waving at me. I waved back. "He's a good guy," I said to the woman who had just lit up a cigarette in my grandparents' car.

She snorted. "Pedro? Is that what he's calling himself these days?

Sure, whatever you say."

I rolled down the window to circulate the air. "What do you mean? Does he have another name?"

"Turn right," she said at the road. "Take me to Tillie's. It's just off First Street."

I decided not to press the issue. Besides, what about this woman demonstrated that she could be trusted?

For the rest of the drive, she chain-smoked and I held the steering wheel white-knuckled, thinking about Jake and having to tell my grandparents. Several minutes later, I pulled up in front of Tillie's and unlocked the door. "Stay safe," I said.

She opened the door, then acted like she forgot something. "Oh man, I forgot my wallet back at the trailer. Do you have any cash I can borrow?"

"Pedro warned me that you'd ask for cash," I said, as I dug through my wallet. "I've got eighteen bucks." I took out the cash and handed it to her.

"You think you've got me figured out, huh?" she asked, taking the money. "You don't know anything. You don't even know your boyfriend's real name or why we have to hide out in that trashy trailer!" She got out and slammed the door, marching into the bar like she owned the world.

I shook my head, reminding myself not to listen to her. How many times had she walked out on her family? Too many. Besides, I had my own volcano on the brink of explosion. I drove home and talked through how I would tell my grandparents. After Pedro's encouragement, I wasn't nearly as scared at the outcome. Still, once I pulled in the driveway, I sprinted through the yard and up the steps and slammed the door behind me, locking it immediately.

Gram and Gramps no longer sat in the living room. I set the keys down on the hallway table and followed the voices to the small kitchen table near the back door. Derek sat there, a plate of leftovers in front of him. He ate while Gramps talked. They both noticed me at the same time.

"How're you holding up?" I asked, trying not to stare. Derek's eyes were bloodshot, and he hadn't shaved in days. His greasy hair and rumpled clothes looked like he'd slept in them.

"I've been better," he said, his voice gravelly like he had cried a thousand tears and had little voice left.

"I'm sorry for your loss."

Derek didn't answer, only stared down at his food.

"We'll keep Lillian here for a little while longer," Gramps said, patting Derek's arm. "But she should see you. She misses you and wonders if it's her fault."

"She doesn't know, does she?" he asked.

"No, she thinks you're upset about the soda incident," I answered.

There was a slight glimmer of a smile before it disappeared. "I hurt my little girl," he whispered fiercely, clenching his jaw and fists like it was nearly impossible to stop the emotion.

"It was an accident," I said. "Nobody's perfect, but she still misses you, and she doesn't understand."

"She's all I have left."

Gramps pushed his chair back. "Should we make up the couch? You're more than welcome to stay. I don't know that I want you alone."

"No, I'm fine. I need to shower and get ready for work. The bills don't stop because of grief."

"Let me get Shirley. She'll want to see you out."

"Thank you, but don't bother her," Derek said, walking out of the kitchen to the front door.

"I'll never hear the end of it. Please," Gramps said. "Macy will keep you company."

Gramps went in the other direction to where their room was. Derek headed for the door. "Tell them thank you," he said, "But I need to shower and crash." He grabbed the door knob, turned his head to the right, and paused.

I followed his gaze to Gram's old, upright piano against the wall.

"Does that work?" he said, his voice choked up again.

"It needs to be tuned. We don't really play it."

"Play for me." He turned all the way around, and I saw the tears leaking from his red, angry, bloodshot eyes. "Play what you did before. Please."

I glanced upstairs and hoped I didn't wake Lillian, but Derek looked so horrible, there was no way I could say no. Going over to the piano, I sat on the bench and patted the space beside me. "Come, sit with me."

Derek slowly nodded, walking the steps to the bench, then sitting on the edge of it. I had to breathe through my mouth, he smelled so strongly of alcohol. Instead, I closed my eyes and felt the keys. I gently fingered the chords and began the melody. I played through, singing a few lyrics that I had recently wrote and was willing to share.

I felt his hand over mine. My eyes shot open, and I pulled my hand to my chest.

"Sorry," he said, getting up. "I only wanted to see if I could remember the keys." He moved to the door, opened it and left without another word.

I saw Gram and Gramps in the hallway. "I hope I didn't bother you."

"That was beautiful," Gram said. "Did you compose that?"

"Yeah," I shrugged. "But it's not finished or anything. It's more like I play my feelings at the time, and they sort of turn into a melody."

"Very talented," she said. "And it looked like it really moved Derek."

"About earlier," Gramps said. "If you're not comfortable talking about whatever happened, we will respect that. I'm not sure your father's going to give up as easily, but at least you don't have to tell us."

"I need to tell you," I said, thinking of Pedro's words. "I want to be free from it."

"Can we sit down?" Gram asked. She and Gramps moved to the living room where they sat beside each other.

I, on the other hand, couldn't sit. I started before I lost my nerve. "When Jake first came to our church, I had a really big crush on him. All the girls did. But I started fantasizing about him. A lot. That didn't stop when he and Hannah started dating and got serious. If anything, my jealousy fueled my fantasies even more. I would sketch his profile, or his eyes, or his lips, it didn't matter. Any part of him, even parts I hadn't seen before." I took a big breath. "I didn't mean for it to be creepy, but I was young and I had no friends. The only thing I had as an outlet was my music and my art. Mom took away my music, so all I had to express myself were sketchbooks."

"Seems pretty harmless," Gram said.

"And it would have been. It wouldn't have amounted to anything because I had stopped them on my own, but Mom found them and showed all the sketchbooks to Hannah. At least I think that's what happened. Hannah wouldn't ever go in my room. Mom does."

"She what?" Gramps asked.

"Showed the sketchbooks to Hannah," Gram repeated.

"Why would she do that?" Gramps asked.

"I don't know," I said honestly. "It's bothered me for a long time because I don't know why Mom would hurt me like that. I could see if she showed Dad privately, and then they talked to me…privately. But there was nothing private about it. Hannah then showed them to Jake. You can only imagine my embarrassment, especially when Hannah started teasing me. And she wouldn't stop. She told the entire youth group. Even Jake started to tease me."

Gramps had a scowl on his face. "No wonder you don't want to go back. Meg and Hannah should be ashamed of themselves. Family always sticks together."

"Well, that's not all the story." I suddenly became very hot and very thirsty. But I pushed through it, as if Pedro stood beside me cheering me on. I pressed my hands to my face, knowing that it was it. My grandparents might kick me out. "After Jake saw the sketchbooks, he started to visit me…at night."

"Visit you how?" Gram asked, but Gramps' expression seemed to show his understanding. His eyes widened and his scowl turned to stone.

"He told me he wanted me, not Hannah. And even though I was so angry at him, I was thrilled that this man wanted me and not my sister."

"How old is he?" Gramps boomed.

"Lower your voice," Gram scolded him.

"When he first showed up to my room, he was twenty-two," I answered. "I was eighteen. Nothing illegal."

Neither one of them said anything for several minutes.

The guilt and shame were eating away at me. "I'm so sorry," I whispered, unable to stop the tears. "Hannah has a right to hate me. And Mom was right about me all along. That's why it's good that I'm up here. I have a chance to start over without all of this weighing me down. I'm not the bad guy when I'm here."

"So?" Gramps asked. "He knocked on the door, and you answered? Or you sent a secretive note or text? I'm not following how he got to your room in the first place."

"I didn't invite him," I said. "Not at first. He just showed up."

Gramps and Gram went completely still.

"After he saw the sketchbooks, he must have took that as an invitation. Once he was in the room though, I didn't necessarily want him to leave."

"And your father doesn't know?" Gramps voice had turned to steel.

"No, but Mom does. She caught Jake leaving the first night he visited me. She thought I lured him there and told me not to tell Dad because it would break his heart."

"So, your mother knows that a grown man snuck into your room, and she told you that it was basically your fault and to keep it a secret?" Gramps had not lowered his voice. He stood up and stormed down the hall. "I'm calling your father."

"Gramps, please!" I pleaded. "He'll never forgive me!"

"Forgive you? You didn't do anything wrong!"

"I LET HIM IN!" I yelled, raking my fingers through my hair in frustration. "I kept my door unlocked for months! It's my fault. I could have said no. I *should* have said no. But I didn't. I'm the villain."

"You were a young lady that a grown man took advantage of," Gramps said through clenched teeth. "And your father deserves to know." He slammed the door to his office, and I started to sob.

This was it. The moment I dreaded. The moment my father would stop talking to me. The moment he'd see that everything Mom said about me had been true.

"Macy," Gram said gently. "Look at me."

"It's all my fault," I said. "If I hadn't obsessed about him, or if I would have told him no, but I didn't. I wanted him."

"Is that why you stole the alcohol and drank it in Hannah's car?"

"Yes. I was so confused. He'd treat me like garbage in public, only to sneak into my room at night. I didn't know what to do. Then with Mom and Hannah hating me, I...I needed an escape. And then one day, he was done. He ended it after..." I paused, humiliated.

"After what?"

"After I gave him what he wanted," I was barely audible. "It was only the one time, and after it happened, he ended it. I didn't know what to do because I thought I gave him what he wanted. So, I stole the schnapps and got drunk because it took away the pain." I looked up at Gram to see tears travelling down her face. "I'm sorry that I'm not the person you thought I was. But I'm trying to be."

Gram shook her head fiercely. "I am crying not because I'm disappointed in you, but because my granddaughter has had to live with this heartache and shame for all this time, and I had no idea. I am crying because a conniving man preyed upon you and took something that wasn't his to take, and somehow you feel it's your fault." She hugged my tightly. Then she began to pray. Gram not only prayed for me, but for Derek and Lillian and Pedro and even Hannah.

As she prayed for peace and healing, I cried into her shoulder, and even though I had questions about everything I'd ever been taught, I hoped the prayers worked.

Chapter 18~

Tell It Like It Is

The hot water beat down on me until my skin turned pruney, and even then I refused to turn it off. The nightmare had come back, which surprised me. Not because I hadn't expected it but because I hadn't realized I slept. Most of the night, I lay on the couch, staring into the darkness, fretting over every possible scenario with Dad. He told Gramps he'd leave first thing in the morning, which meant there was no escaping the truth now.

And it was about to cause a tidal wave.

A part of me wanted to believe what others had told me. That I was the victim of a man who took advantage of my volatile emotions and vulnerability. But I remember the first night he visited. Sure, I had freaked out, but I had also been thrilled. After our first kiss, I remember wanting more. Since he hadn't been ready to go public, I satisfied myself with our nightly visits. And as far as going all the way? I said yes. It had only been two months ago. Had he pushed me to finally let him have his way? I knew the answer was yes, but I also knew I wanted to be a woman, and I thought if I gave him what he wanted, that we could stop hiding in the dark.

So, I said yes. Knowing it would hurt my sister. Knowing I could never go back.

Gram had mentioned before she went to bed that if Jake was so innocent, why was I so scared?

As I stood in the shower, I finally admitted to myself the answer. "I'm scared of *the truth*," I said to the wall. I didn't want Jake in my life anymore, but I didn't trust myself to resist him. I didn't trust myself to do the right thing. If he snuck into my room again…If he kissed me again…If he did those things to me…could I push him away?

Then again, I had resisted him in the car. That was a good sign. Maybe the more I was away from him, the stronger I became.

Just the same, I hoped to never see him again.

Someone knocked on the door. "I got to go potty," Lillian said.

Sighing, I turned off the water and dried off, wrapping a towel around my head, then throwing on a pair of sweats and a t-shirt. Gramps told me not to go to work this morning, but to wait for Dad. At least there was a small bright side: I could stay in my sweats. I opened the door. "All yours, little missy."

Lillian was hopping then scooted inside the bathroom. "Whew! It's hot in here. Look at all this fog."

"It's steam from the shower." I shut the door to give her privacy. "I'll be downstairs getting you breakfast," I said before heading down the stairs.

I walked into the kitchen and poured some coffee.

As I drank, Gram asked, "Did you sleep okay?"

"Not at all. Let's just say that I'm missing my bed," I said, leaving out the nightmare and anxiety part.

"We have other places to sleep than just the couch."

"I know, but it's just easier to grab a blanket and crash on the first available surface."

Lillian came into the kitchen and hugged my legs. "I don't want to go to school."

"That's because you don't have breakfast in your tummy," I said, pouring a bowl of cereal.

Someone knocked on the front door. Gram went to open it while I watched Lillian sit at the table and eat.

Derek walked into the kitchen and gave me a slight wave. I noticed he hadn't shaved, and his eyes were still a little blood shot, but he at least looked clean. Lillian eventually noticed her dad standing there and jumped up in excitement. "DADDY!"

He knelt down and hugged her fiercely. "Hey there, baby girl."

"Where were you?" she cried.

"I had to go visit some people. I'm sorry I worried you."

"Don't leave me again."

"Didn't you have fun with Macy?"

"Yes, but I missed you."

"Well, I'm back. I have to go to work now, but we'll be together after school. Okay?"

"You'll pick me up at latchkey?"

"For sure. Take the bus this morning 'cause Daddy's running late, but after school, I'll pick you up just like I always do. Then maybe we'll stop and get a slushee. But you have to be good."

"We can buy a slushee for Macy too!"

Derek glanced up at me. "We owe her a lot more than a slushee, but that's a good place to start."

"I will never say no to a Coca-Cola slushee," I said. "But we need to get you on the bus."

"And I've got to get to work," Derek said. To me, he said, "Will you let Mr. Elmsworth know that I thought about it, and yes, we can have the memorial service in the church?"

"Of course," I said.

"We'll take care of everything," Gram said gently.

"Um, and her parents will be here this evening," he whispered. "So, if Lillian can eat dinner over here?"

Gram and I exchanged a quick look. I knew it rubbed her the wrong way that Derek kept Lillian from her grandparents.

"It's just better this way," he said, as if understanding our exchange.

"For who?" Gram said just as gently.

"Come on," I said to Lillian. "Let's go catch that bus!"

She gave her Dad a quick hug, and the both of us ran out the door and down the driveway. The bus pulled up before we could catch our breath. Lillian threw her arms around me. "I promise I'll get you a slushee."

"Sounds good," I said, waving to her.

As the bus left, Derek came out and stood next to me. "What do you think?" he asked. "Do you think I'm wrong too?"

"About what?" I asked, but one look from Derek, and I knew that he had caught on in the house. "I don't know your situation."

"But…"

I sighed, "But I feel bad for your wife's parents too, especially because they haven't talked to their daughter in years. They're grieving now in lots of different ways. Maybe if they met Lillian, it would help them heal. And you too."

"They gave her an ultimatum," he said. "Me or them. If I had been smart, I'd have ended it right there. I would have left her with her parents. She'd still be alive."

"But there wouldn't be Lillian. We can't change our pasts. I've learned that. I would do anything to change certain things, but I can't. All I can do is move forward and hope to God I don't screw up my life anymore."

Pedro came around the motel's office across the street and smiled in my direction. I smiled back. Our gaze lingered a little longer.

"You two a thing?"

"What?" I asked, realizing that Derek had been observing the stupid grin on my face. "Um, we're friends. I think. I don't know."

Derek shook his head. "Wow. Things can be so weirdly weird."

"Weirdly weird?"

"You have a penchant for bad boys."

"No, I don't."

"Sure, you do. Wasn't it a bad boy who put you up here in Manistee? And now Pedro?"

"Actually, it was a youth pastor who pushed me up here. And Pedro's not a bad guy."

"Do you even know…? Never mind. Sorry, I said anything.

Everything's still raw, and you remind me a lot of my wife. She was a minister's kid too. And she fell in love with the baddest of boys."

"You're not bad, Derek."

"You don't know that," he said, walking away from me toward the street. "Lillian's mellowed me out a little, but I've got quite the sordid past."

"Yeah, okay, thanks for the heads up."

"Seriously, I'd be careful, if I were you. The good girls who fall for the bad boys? It never turns out well. At least it didn't for my wife."

I almost replied, but I stopped myself. Derek was grieving, and I had my own drama. Before going back inside, I watched as Pedro pushed his cart to one of the rooms. What was he hiding? It's not like I would care. But both Pedro's mother and Derek seemed to think otherwise.

Sure, Pedro looked like a bad boy. From his tattoos to his piercings to his constant angry expression, he could be intimidating. But he wasn't. With all the messiness of my life, he helped me make sense of it.

Glancing both directions, I jogged across the street. I might have been exhausted, but I wasn't about to sit around and wait for my dad to show up. I went into the laundry room, pulled out my cart, and started my usual routine.

Now that we were into May, and the weather had decided to actually stay in spring mode, the motel had picked up. Every room but two had been used last night, and the weekend we were already booked through until Monday morning. I had nearly finished my first room when I noticed Gramps approaching.

"Hey there, kiddo," he said. "You didn't have to work today."

"Who else would help Pedro?" I placed the vacuum back on the cart. "Besides, I'm sure Dad won't be here for at least a couple hours."

"That's why I'm here actually. He called and said he's delayed because the zoning inspector is showing up today for approval on the church's building project."

"So, you didn't tell him?" I knew that if Gramps had explained to Dad what happened that he would have dropped everything.

"I decided it's your story to tell. All I told him was that you had some information about what happened, and he should come up so that you could tell him in person."

"I don't look forward to that conversation," I said, thinking about how it went the night before.

"About last night," Gramps said. "I'm sorry I yelled at you. My anger wasn't directed at you, but I still should have handled it better."

"I don't want to let you down," I admitted. "I messed up back home."

"You haven't let me down," he said. "Did you mess up? Yes, you made a few poor choices, but everything that happened is a direct correlation to decisions by your parents. And then there's Jake." Gramps said his name through gritted teeth. "The fact is that he is a grown man, and I'm not sure that he would go to jail for what happened between you two, but at the very least, it's sinful and unethical, and morally abhorrent. And I want to punch his face in."

I had a hard time not smiling. Until my cell phone buzzed, and I saw the text from Hannah. Any smile vanished from my face.

Thx for ruining my life. Hope ur happy. ☹

"What?" Gramps asked.

"Some people aren't as ready to forgive me," I muttered.

He took my phone and read the text. Sighing, he handed it to me. "Then fix it."

"Not so easy. She hates me."

"When you first got here, Pedro despised you. Now he looks at you all googly-eyed."

"What does that have to do with anything?"

"People change. Their feelings fluctuate. If you spent time trying to repair your relationship with Hannah with as much time as you tried to make amends with Pedro, you and your sister wouldn't be at odds."

"It's different," I said.

"Not that much. Look at the situation from her perspective. Her fiancé was cheating on her with…you. And even though the situation is deplorable, and I hold him largely at fault, she might not see it that way."

"So, I do have a reason to feel guilty."

"As your grandfather, I don't like the situation for either of my granddaughters. I'm only asking that you think about making amends with your sister."

"I don't think it'll do any good, but I'll think about it."

As Gramps walked away, I stared down at my phone. Shaking my head, I sighed and texted, *Sorry about all of this.* Then I deleted the words and shoved the phone back into my pocket. The words felt hollow.

I pushed my cart to the next room and worked through the morning. As I cleaned I thought about the different ways I could apologize to my sister. I thought about sending flowers, but that seemed cheesy. I thought about actually calling her and saying sorry over the phone, but I'd only be asking for a screamfest. Honestly, hiding up in Manistee seemed like the safest bet until emotions calmed down. But I knew that was nothing more than a cop-out.

When I reached Derek's room, I saw Pedro had already started it. "Hey, need help in here?"

"Nah, he just got back, and Lillian has been with you, so it's not bad." Pedro stopped wiping the mirror and asked, "How're you holding up? I'm surprised to see you this morning."

"I'm doing better since I talked to you." I smiled at him. "Thanks for your help. I came home and told my grandparents."

"You did? How'd it go?"

"A little traumatizing, and my dad's coming up for me to tell him, but my grandparents still love me, and they haven't kicked me out, so there's that."

"Any sign of that guy?"

"Jake? No. I thought about it last night. He doesn't know where in Manistee to look, so he'd have to be pretty determined. So, I decided to not be afraid of something that probably won't happen."

Pedro didn't seem as convinced. "Just be careful. If this guy still has a thing for you, it wouldn't take long to find the church next to the motel. I'm sure he's listened to conversations and has picked out some clues."

"Are you trying to frighten me?" I asked, feeling the goose bumps sprout along my arms.

"No, I'm sorry." He came over to me and took my hands. "Everything will be fine. We're in the middle of nowhere. Trust me, I've been hiding in plain sight."

I tilted my head. "From what?"

"The police," Pedro shrugged. "Social services."

Thinking of what his mother said, I asked, "Is your real name Pedro?"

He sighed and shook his head. "My mother, right?"

"Yep, she said that wasn't even your name. I tried not to listen to her like you said, but when she said that, I became curious."

"Listen, I know you don't have any reason to trust me, but I'm asking you to please trust me."

"Okay…"

"I can't tell you right now," he said. "The less you know, the safer I am. And the safer my brothers are."

"What are you talking about?" I asked, pulling away from his hands. "I'm not going to do anything to you."

"You're not, but someone else can and will. The more people know about secrets, the greater chance of the secrets being exposed."

"So, you think I'll tell?"

"No…Yes…Possibly." He must have noticed my offence because he added, "If the police were to interrogate you, I wouldn't want you to lie. Besides, they are really good at pulling out the truth. That's what I mean."

"Why would the police interrogate me?"

Pedro rubbed his hand over his face. He looked torn with what to do or say next.

The phone in the hotel room began to ring, completely ending what might have been said. Pedro went to it.

"Why are you answering?"

"A lot of times your grandfather calls the room instead of walking over." Pedro picked up the phone. "Good afternoon. This is Pedro from housekeeping."

While Pedro listened to the other end, my heart was crumbling. So, Pedro did have secrets. And they were dangerous enough that I couldn't know. But what bothered me more than any of that was the simple fact that I didn't even know his real name. "Derek was right," I whispered to myself. "Bad boys aren't the ones who get hurt."

I turned and walked out of the room, not wanting Pedro to see my hurt feelings. As I made my way to the next room, Pedro called out to me. I stopped but didn't turn around. "Do you know where Derek is?" he asked.

"Derek?" I asked, trying to wrap my brain around another topic of conversation. "Work."

"That was Jay's Shop. He's not there. Hasn't been in all morning. And I guess some older couple stopped there looking for him."

"He's probably at a quiet spot and dealing with his grief. I'm not worried about it. I don't think he'd leave Lillian." Oh God, I hoped not! "This is too much," I said more to myself. "Everything from everyone. Just let me clean."

Pedro touched my arm. "Macy."

"No, don't say my name," I said, trying to keep my emotions in check. "You don't get to say my name when I don't even know yours." I entered the next room and started cleaning with a vengeance.

Suddenly Pedro was right there in front of me. He grabbed my shirt and pulled me to him. "You swear on your grandparents' lives that you will tell no one?"

"I swear it," I whispered. "You can trust me."

He closed his eyes and breathed out, then he leaned over and whispered in my ear, "Ricky Lorenzo Acosta Fernandez." He released me. "If you want to find out my secrets, just type my name into Google."

I stopped him from leaving. "Why'd you tell me?"

Pedro—Ricky—Whatever his name was clenched his jaw and acted torn again.

"Oh for God's sake, just answer the question!"

"Because even though I know we don't have a chance, I can't help hoping that we might."

Warmth spread through me, even with Derek's voice in my head warning me not to fall for him. "Hopefully," I said.

His gaze lingered on my mouth, but he stepped away. "Find out who I am first."

I went to reach for him, but he had already walked out of the room. *Ricky*...what had it been? *Ricky Lorenzo Acosta Fernandez?* I finished the room, repeating his full name over and over in my head. If I was being honest with myself, I liked the name. And how bad could his past be? It's not like he could have killed anyone. He probably stole a car or something. Maybe he broke into a house. Whatever it was, I vowed that I would be strong enough to not let his past take away our hope.

My last room couldn't finish quick enough. I itched to find out who Pedro really was. Once the room was locked, I pushed my cart to the laundry room and dumped the dirty linens into two large-capacity washers. I could see that Pedro had saved me two. As I worked on laundry, I noticed Pedro out of the corner of my eye. He leaned against the door, watching me, a deep frown on his face.

"Hey," I said, turning around to face him. "I thought you had taken off."

He shook his head. "I was waiting to talk to you."

"Oh, okay." I closed the distance between us. "What's up?"

"I've been thinking. Most of the afternoon actually. And um, well, I was wondering if you wanted to go on a date?"

"Really? Like a sit-down restaurant? Maybe putt-putt golf? Or a movie?" I grinned. "I've actually never been on a date."

"Yeah," he said, no longer frowning. "I've been super nervous about asking you, but I thought after today…well, if you're still here tomorrow, and I haven't scared you off, then maybe we'll go on an official date."

Someone coughed outside the door. "Hope I'm not interrupting."

I jumped back at the sound of my Dad's voice. "Dad!?"

Pedro acted unruffled. "Sir," he said. "Good to see you again."

Dad glared at him, not saying a word. I had to give it to Pedro, he stared right back at him.

"What are you doing here?" I asked. "Gramps said that you were coming up tomorrow or something."

"The meeting with zoning ended early, so I decided to try to make it by dinner," he said, his eyes not leaving Pedro. "What's going on here, Macy?"

"Pedro was just asking me on a date," I said, choosing to tell the truth. Plus, I wanted Pedro to know that I didn't want to hide my feelings for him. And that I wasn't afraid. "And I said yes."

Now Dad looked at me. "You what?"

"I said yes."

"Will you excuse us?" Dad said to Pedro.

"Bye, Macy," Pedro said, giving me a sad smile before leaving.

"Why did you treat him like that?" I asked Dad, once Pedro rounded the corner. It hit me that I had treated him much the same way when I first arrived. "Looks are deceiving."

"You can't go on a date with him," Dad said. "He's a criminal."

"So? Technically, I am too."

"Macy, I mean it. Between you and your sister, I'm going to have a heart attack." He paused, then said, "Have you seen all those tattoos? And how many piercings can one guy have?"

"I happen to like the tattoos. They're creative and they're a part of who he is."

"Don't even think of getting one."

I stopped myself from saying something I would regret. But it bothered me that Dad was so quick to judge Pedro.

"Come on, let's go to the house. You have something to tell me about Jake? Your grandfather seemed to think it needed to be said face-to-face."

Maybe it was the high-emotions of the moment, or maybe it was because Pedro had reminded me about the power of truth, but I felt a sudden surge of energy. Dad drove up north to hear the truth. Might as well tell it like it is, then clean up the damage afterwards. "I'm just going to be out with it," I said. I closed my eyes though, not wanting to see my father's expression.

"You had an affair with Jake?" Dad asked. "That's what Hannah said. Please tell me it's not true—"

I heard the sadness and hurt in his voice. I kept my eyes closed. "I'm only going to say it once, so please listen. A couple months ago, a little while after Hannah and Jake found out about my sketchbooks, Jake snuck up into my room. No, I did not invite him. He just came in, and he told me that he wanted me. He said all the words I wanted to hear. After that, I let him in—"

"Wait a second. Did he come in without an invitation or with one? You just said you let him in?"

"The first time, he wasn't invited. I kept telling him that we shouldn't, but he was really good at convincing me."

"He came into your room? I can't believe it."

"For a few months, he would sneak into my room at night. After the first night, I left the outside door unlocked. Not every night, but a lot of them. Then a couple weeks ago, his constant pushing finally worked, and I agreed…" I paused there and opened my eyes. Okay, so this part was hard. And I shouldn't have looked at my Dad who was staring at me with mix of horror, fury, and disbelief. Yeah, it was quite a combination. I closed my eyes tight again. "I agreed to...his advances. After that night, he was done. Told me that he couldn't be with me, that it was wrong, all that jazz. But I was really broken and upset about it because I thought that by giving him what he wanted that we could stop sneaking around. That's why I stole the schnapps and why I did what I did. I was really hurt and confused." When I opened my eyes, my insides turned cold with dread. Dad wasn't taking it well.

"You...and Jake...together...?" Dad's eyes filled with tears. "Under my roof?"

"Just the once," I said. I left out all the other stuff we did in my room. I didn't think my father wanted a play-by-play.

"With Jake? Your sister's fiancé?"

"Yes," I said, finally admitting my guilt. Only I didn't feel free. I felt really horrible.

"And this whole time, I couldn't understand why Hannah seemed so angry at you. I couldn't figure out why your mother wanted you out of the house, but now it's all clear."

My Dad wasn't acting like my grandparents or Pedro. My Dad wasn't telling me that I was innocent and that an adult man took advantage of me. No, my father was seeing me through the eyes of his other daughter. "I'm the villain."

"Why'd you do it? What has your sister done to deserve that?"

"First of all, let's get one thing straight. I did *not* invite him to my room. Ever. He showed up. And he would have never showed up if

Mom and Hannah hadn't shown him my sketchbooks. Oh, I was the joke, wasn't I? Only that showed Jake how big of a school-girl crush I had on him. And then why did I let him keep coming back? I don't know. Maybe it was because when he was in my room I felt wanted."

"You were jealous," he said. "You always were."

Pedro came from around the corner. He had a fiery glint in his eyes. "Are you serious?" he said to Dad. "She just told you that a grown man came into her room uninvited, and you're going to blame her?"

"This is NONE OF YOUR BUSINESS!" Dad exploded.

"Yes, it is," Pedro said, without backing down. "Because I care about your daughter, and I don't want her mistakenly thinking that this crazy, psychotic situation at your house is her fault."

"You better walk away, boy," Dad said through gritted teeth. "You don't talk to me that way."

"Don't tell me what to do."

Both of them glared at each other, ready to pounce.

"Pedro, it's okay," I said.

"No, it's not." He turned to me. "I don't get how your family can pin this on you."

"I shouldn't have done it."

Pedro shook his head. "And your mother shouldn't have stolen your sketchbook, and she certainly shouldn't have shown Hannah and her boyfriend. And they shouldn't have publicly bullied you. And they shouldn't have pushed you into a corner where you reached for the first person who gave you any attention. How your father doesn't see that—"

Dad suddenly grabbed Pedro by his muscle shirt and threw him back. "Get away from my daughter!" he bellowed.

"That's enough!" Gramps said, coming around the corner.

Seriously? Who else was coming to the party?

"Why are you throwing my employee on the ground?" Gramps asked Dad. To Pedro, he said, "Thank you for calling me." To me, he asked, "Are you all right?"

I didn't know how to answer.

"Tell him to leave," Dad said. "He's butting his nose into our business, and I won't have it."

"He's trying to protect your daughter," Gramps said evenly. "Something you should have been doing."

"What's that supposed to mean?"

"You know exactly what that means. You have absolutely no right getting upset at Macy when you keep secrets from her."

"Don't you even think about it," Dad said to Gramps. "Don't you bring that up. Not here. Not now."

"Why not? I am amazed at how you do not see your culpability in all of this. Macy has felt like an outcast for most of her life. And there's a reason for that. A reason you have refused to see."

"Stop it," Dad ordered. "You are not turning this around and making this about me! I just found out that my teenage daughter was sleeping with a man under my roof. The same man that was supposed to marry my other daughter! Let me deal with one problem at a time!"

"What's gotten into you?" Gramps said, stepping in front of Dad. "Why are you acting like this? At the very least, lower your voice.

This is my place of business. If you can't respect yourself or your daughter enough to calm down, then do it for me. This is the start of one of my busiest weekends."

Everything happened so fast that my mind and heart were reeling in shock and guilt and hurt. "Dad?" I asked, going over to him and taking his hand. "Please forgive me?"

But he wouldn't look at me. He only closed his eyes briefly before saying, "I need to process some things. I'll be back in a little bit."

Then my father left me standing there, watching him walk away.

"What is going on with him?" Gramps asked. "He would never become that angry."

"I broke his heart," I said.

Pedro had pushed himself off the ground and made his way over to me. "Macy, I'm sorry. I didn't want to start anything with your father, but I couldn't believe that he wasn't even listening to you."

"Just...Just leave me alone for a while," I said.

"Macy, you shouldn't be alone right now," Gramps said.

"I'll be fine. I have to process this, as well." I started to walk away. Before I knew what I was doing, I was running past the office, across the street, and up the driveway. I burst into the house, grabbed Gramps' keys and yelled out, "Gram, I'm taking the car. Be back in a few."

I couldn't start the car fast enough. My hands shook, my stomach trembled, and my eye twitched. I backed out nearly hitting the garbage can, before peeling out of the driveway and heading toward town. The late afternoon sun still blazed and the spring weather had turned warm. Perfect for alone time at the lighthouse.

As I pulled up to a stoplight, I noticed the convenience store. I thought about alcohol for the briefest of moments, then shoved it out of my mind. Whatever. I had enough problems to deal with, the last thing I wanted was to turn out like Pedro's mother.

Once at the beach, my cell phone began ringing. "What does it take for a girl to be left alone?" I asked, looking to see who called. I didn't recognize the phone number, but it had a local area code. Sighing, I answered, "Hello?"

"Yes, this is Meadowbrook Elementary. We're looking for Derek Blackstone? This number was on the emergency contact list."

"I'm not with him," I said, feeling the tendrils of worry reaching further inside of me. "Did you try his cell number or work number?"

"We've tried all of it. He's not at work, and his cell phone goes right to voicemail. After-school latchkey closes at seven, and it's already ten after. Someone needs to pick up Lillian."

"Of course," I said, resting my head on the wheel. I had my own issues, and now I had to take on Derek's? But that wasn't Lillian's fault. I knew what I had to do. "Where is Meadowbrook?"

I peeled out of the beach's parking lot, my heart hurting for the little girl. As I followed the woman's directions, I found my own problems had to take a back seat. I couldn't get the question out of head. *Where is Derek?*

Chapter 19~

Not an Invitation

Lillian sat quietly in the back seat. Even she knew something was wrong. I covered for Derek and said I forgot that he asked me to pick her up, but she hadn't bought it. "My Dad's never been late."

"How about a slushee?" I said, pulling into 7-11. "I could use one right now."

"Okay," she said with little enthusiasm.

I tried to be cheerful in the store, but once in the car again, Lillian asked, "Can I go see my mom?"

"When your Dad gets home, we'll ask him."

"I just want to say hi and give her a hug. You haven't taken me to her. Ever."

"That's because your Dad likes to take you," I said, leaning back and squeezing her hand.

"You LIE," she cried. "Daddy hates taking me. He said so."

"I think he meant that he hates taking you to see her because she's sick. That's all."

"I want my mom!" Big tears rolled down her cheeks. She leaned against the door and cried.

"I know you do," I said, still holding her hand. "And I'm sorry I can't take you." With my free hand, I texted Derek. *Where r u????????*

Just then, my cell phone buzzed. But it wasn't Derek, it was my Dad. *I'm sorry about earlier. Can we talk?*

Now's not a good time, I texted back. I started up the car. My alone time would have to wait. "Let's go see what's for dinner."

"Will Daddy be there?"

"I don't know," I said. "He had to work late." For a brief moment, I thought about grabbing Derek by the shoulders and shaking some sense into him. But I reminded myself he was grieving. At least Lillian had us. Then I started thinking of Derek not telling her grandparents about her, and felt myself getting irked again. How could he keep this adorable little girl away from her grandparents? I gripped the wheel and reminded myself—once again—that he was grieving. If I got a chance, I would try to talk to him. Maybe he'd listen to me.

We arrived at Gram and Gramps, and I found myself tensing up. Dad's SUV sat in the driveway.

As soon as I walked inside, Gram came out of the kitchen and hugged me. "Don't stress about your father," she whispered in my ear. "He's upset about a lot of things that have nothing to do with you."

I released her and nodded, not wanting to talk about it. Honestly, I was more worried about Derek. "Lillian, go wash your hands," I said.

"It smells good," she said.

"That's because it's pot roast and potatoes," Gram said, leaning down and smiling at the little girl. "And for dessert, I made pineapple upside down cake because that's my son's favorite."

"Is your son here?" Lillian asked.

"Yes, I am," Dad said, coming out of the kitchen. "How are you, little lady?" he asked, extending his hand.

Lillian shook it and giggled. "I remember you! You're Macy's daddy!"

"Yes, I am," Dad said again, glancing up at me. His eyes were filled with regret and sorrow.

"Hurry," I said to Lillian. "Wash your hands, so we can eat."

As she scampered into the bathroom, Dad leaned over and hugged me. I stiffened. "I'm so sorry about how I acted," he whispered. "Can we try again?"

"Not now," I said, stepping back. "Lillian is my first concern." To Gram, I said, "Have you heard from Derek? He didn't show to pick her up."

"Really?" Gram asked, immediately concerned. "I have no idea. How'd you know to go get her?"

"The school called me. Derek wrote my number down as an emergency contact."

Gram raised her eyebrows. "Your grandfather's in his study. I should tell him."

When Gram walked away, Dad and I still stood there.

"I should go wash up too," I said, moving to leave.

"Wait," Dad said.

"Not now," I snapped.

"This is important," he said. "You are important."

"We don't have anything to say to each other. It is what it is."

"I have something to say." Dad took a breath and continued, "I apologize for acting like a complete numbskull. I handled everything poorly, and I'm sorry."

"You have a right to be upset," I said, feeling the pain all over again. "But I can't change what happened. And even though some of the blame falls on my shoulders, not all of it does."

"I know. I don't blame you. What I said earlier was wrong. Completely wrong. I had your mother and Hannah in my head, and then when I saw you and that kid, I sort of lost it."

"Pedro's not a kid. He's nineteen. And he's treated me better than most of my immediate family."

"He's a kid to me. That's all I meant."

Lillian came out of the bathroom. "I'm done!" she exclaimed.

"Okay, my turn!" I said to her. "Go, save me a seat." I headed to the bathroom and shut the door before Dad could say anything more. I stared at my dirty reflection, thanks to a full-day's work at the motel, and saw the dark circles under my eyes and messy bun on the top of my head. The tears came, but I kept staring. I stared at the girl who made a complete mess of things. And I didn't look away. I thought of what Gramps had said earlier: *If you spent time trying to repair your relationship with Hannah with as much time as you tried to make amends with Pedro, you and your sister wouldn't be at odds.*

Making a decision, I nodded at my reflection. "You can fix this," I said to the girl staring back at me. I used the facilities and washed my hands and face. I dialed Hannah's number, hoping she wouldn't pick up.

"What do you want?" she said without a greeting.

"Hey," I said nervously. I paused. Why had I called again?

"What do *you* want?" she asked again, getting more upset.

"Listen, Hannah, I never apologized for…everything, and I'm sorry. You didn't deserve what happened, and I regret it."

There was silence for several seconds. Eventually, she said, "Don't ever call me again. We have nothing more to say to each other."

I heard the click of a dead line and exhaled. Okay, so that went horribly. But how'd I expect her to react?

I left the bathroom and made my way to the dining room. "I'm ready," I said to everyone. "Gram, the roast smells great."

"Doesn't it?" Dad asked. "It's my favorite." He smiled at his mother.

"I'm just glad you got to make it up for dinner," she said pleased. "Why doesn't Macy say grace tonight?"

I blinked in surprised. "I've been saying grace a lot lately, but sure, why not?" Lillian folded her hands, mimicking everyone else. I closed my eyes and began, "Thank you, Lord, for this food we are about to eat and for the family we are to eat with. Protect us near and far and bring us all back together again…" I paused, then with my eyes closed, added, "And if you're truly listening and you truly care, please take care of Pedro…and Derek and Lillian…and please mend everything I broke." I whispered, "Amen," and discreetly wiped at my eyes.

"Amen," everyone said. But no one moved to eat.

"Peanut," Dad said, his voice choked up.

The tears wouldn't stop. I sat at the table, wiping at my eyes, until finally I buried my face in a napkin. I felt my Dad's arms around me. "I'm sorry, Dad," I sobbed. "I'm sorry I messed up our family. I'm sorry I hurt Hannah."

"Macy, don't cry," Lillian said.

"And I'm sorry that I made you doubt my love for you," Dad said. "I'm sorry that I refused to see how broken my family was. I'm sorry I blamed you and not Jake. There's so much I'm sorry for."

"Me too," I said.

"Let's just agree that we're sorry," Dad said, removing the napkin from my face. "We'll deal with everything together."

I nodded, still sniffling.

"That was the best prayer I've heard in a long time," Gramps said. "I should let you lead in service."

"No way," I said, giving a slight laugh. Feeling a million times better. "You've already twisted my arm to sing and teach Sunday school. Don't push your luck."

The adults laughed. Lillian still watched me with concern on her face.

"I'm okay," I whispered to her. She got up and hugged me.

"How about we eat?" Gram said, serving Lillian's plate, then passing to the others.

Even with Derek missing and the mess of my own life, I ate and talked with everyone, enjoying this little bubble of time where I felt cleansed and my burden a little lighter.

***

As I finished helping Gram with the last of the dishes, someone knocked on the front door.

"Derek," I said, dropping the kitchen towel and running to the door. Even with everything going on, I was still worried about him. I opened the door and smiled, but it wasn't Derek I was smiling at, but an older couple—possibly in their sixties—who looked well-put-together but acted like they were struggling to keep their emotions inside. The woman, with her blonde cropped hair, had red rims around her eyes, and the gentleman, with his tucked-in, collared shirt and khaki pants had dark circles around his. I knew immediately who they were.

"Hello," I said, not quite opening the door all the way. Derek said he hadn't told them about their granddaughter yet. "Can I help you?"

"We're looking for our son-in-law, Derek Blackstone? We were told that he stays in the motel across the street, but there is no one in the office," the woman said. "One of the customers said to come over here."

"My grandparents own it," I said.

"I'm heading over there right now," Gramps said, opening the door all the way. "Macy, you should have invited them in." To them, he said, "Please, come in."

"Thank you, but no," the man said. "We need to find Derek."

"Derek?" Lillian said. "Where's Daddy?"

I pressed my lips together and closed my eyes. Oh man. Not good.

No one said anything for what seemed like an eternity.

When I opened my eyes, the couple were staring at Lillian, as if trying to figure out the puzzle piece.

"Do they know where Daddy is?" Lillian asked me.

"I think they're trying to find him."

"Where is he?" she started to get emotional. "Why didn't he pick me up? He promised me a slushee."

"But I bought you one," I said. "And he'll be here. He just had to finish up some business."

"Why..." the woman's voice shook. "Why does that little girl look just like my daughter?"

"I don't know," I said. "Who are you?"

"We're Tom and Nancy Garrett. Lindsey's parents," the woman became more and more upset. "Who are you?"

"I'm Macy," I said, extending my hand to shake theirs. "I'm Lillian's babysitter."

"Is this... *our granddaughter?*"

Gramps and I exchanged glances. I wasn't about to lie about this. Especially because I was becoming more and more worried about Derek. "This is Derek's daughter. Was Lindsey his wife?"

They didn't answer. Both of them looked at Lillian clearly emotional. Nancy covered her mouth as if that would keep the sobs back.

"Why is everyone crying today?" Lillian asked.

Tom knelt down and studied Lillian, smiling at her. "You have your mommy's eyes," he said, getting choked up.

"No, I have my eyes, not mommy's."

"Please, come inside," Gramps said. "My wife put some coffee on to go with our dessert. We'd love for you to join us." Gramps turned to Dad who had been standing behind us. "Son, could you go and man the office for a couple hours? Reservations will be coming in, but I should stay here."

"Of course," Dad said. To me, he added, "When you get a chance, come over and chat with your old man."

I nodded, then he excused himself. Mr. and Mrs. Garrett stepped inside. Gram greeted them while I led Lillian to the television. "Movie night!" I exclaimed, trying to keep it cheery. "What movie do we want?"

"Frozen!" Lillian yelled excitedly. "Tonight, I'm Elsa, and you're Anna!"

"You always get to be Elsa," I teased.

Lillian hopped around the living room singing, "Let It Go." I was relieved that she could bounce back from all the heavy emotion of today. My relief at the dinner table had been short-lived, and I was now full-on worried about Derek.

The rest of the evening progressed with Gram and Gramps in the dining room, talking with the Garrett's and with me and Lillian watching Frozen. She had snuggled up on me, and we cuddled, but I kept sneaking glances out the picture window, looking for Derek's headlights. Near the end of the movie, Lillian fell asleep. She wasn't in pajamas yet, nor had she brushed her teeth and bathed, but I picked her up and climbed up the stairs, laying her on the bed. Turning off the light, I left the door open a crack just as she liked. I paused at the top of the stairs, pondering what to do. Should I go talk to Dad over at the motel? Should I go find Derek? Should I check what they were saying in the dining room? Instead I sat at the top of the stairs and rested my head against my knees.

I was tired, exhausted, and mentally overwhelmed. Seriously, could life get any more complicated? Then again, I didn't want to know.

My cell phone buzzed.

"No more complications," I whispered to myself as I checked the number. I didn't recognize it. I told myself not to answer it, but it might be Derek. "Hello?"

"Hey, I wanted to see how you were doing. And to apologize. I shouldn't have confronted your father."

"Pedro?" I asked, relief filling me. I found myself grinning. "Oh my word, it's so good to hear your voice."

"You know, I don't think I've ever called you. I had to get your number from your grandfather earlier this evening."

"Well, I'm glad to hear from you. Sorry, I took off so suddenly. I had a lot to process."

"Did you go to the lighthouse?"

"No, but that's where I was headed."

"Really? I left that spot alone all evening because I wanted to give you your space."

"I would still be there, but I never actually arrived."

"Why?"

"Because I got a call from Lillian's school. Derek must have put my number down as an emergency contact. He never came to pick her up."

"Are you serious?"

"As a heart attack. Then to make things more complicated, Derek's wife's parents show up on our doorstep. They take one look at Lillian and know she's their long-lost granddaughter."

"Wow. Did Derek ever show up?"

"Not yet." I yawned and rubbed my face. "But I'm glad to hear your voice. You help keep me calm."

Pedro chuckled. "I aim to please. So, I'm assuming you didn't Google my name."

I slapped my forehead. "I completely forgot! With all this craziness, I haven't even got to a computer."

"That's probably a good thing."

"Why don't you tell me? I'd much rather hear it from you anyway."

"I don't know. Maybe another time. You sound like you already have a lot going on."

"Hey, I always have time for you," I said. "Besides, I really do feel bad about taking off today."

"I understand."

"Still…If you want to talk, I wouldn't mind."

"I don't necessarily want to talk about my past, but I would like to see you," he said. I could hear the shy hesitation in his voice.

"I want to see you too," I admitted. "We wouldn't be able to go far because Lillian's here, and I have to wait for Derek. If you don't mind hanging with me on the front porch, maybe you could come over. Be careful of my father though. He's still here."

"I'll be there in a few," he said before hanging up.

Not quite ready to go downstairs, I snuck into my room, grabbed my sketchbook and pencils, and went back to the top of the stairs. I continued working on an intricate drawing I had begun a couple of nights ago. It was of Derek and Lillian amidst long grass on a rolling hill in a meadow. It might sound cheesy, but that's how I envisioned them happy. I outlined Derek's arms releasing Lillian, needing them to be absolutely perfect. His face had no worry lines, no five o'clock shadow, no dark circles under his eyes. Instead, I drew him looking up at his daughter, laughing. Lillian was already suspended in the air, arms extended, her beautiful smile lighting up her face. I even drew her pigtail trailing behind her like a balloon-string.

None of that I had trouble with. What I had been struggling with was the faint shadow of the woman whose face I had only studied in a family portrait in their motel room. I even unlocked their room to sneak another couple peaks at the picture. I had placed her just off to the right of the page, as if getting ready to walk into the forest. The sun's rays poked through the trees like an invitation. I liked that part. Her gown was perfect, light and faintly moving from an imaginary breeze. Her hand and arm extended just right as if reaching for her family one last time. But it was her turned head and facial features that I doubted myself on. I had sketched her looking back at her family, but I couldn't figure out what expression she should have. Sad, because she's leaving them? Happy, because she's going to a better place? I had erased her facial expression at least a dozen times.

Suddenly, the front door banged open, and Derek stumbled inside. "Where are THEY?!" he yelled. "Get them out of here!" He stormed through the house.

Dad ran into the house, completely out of breath. "I tried to stop him!" he yelled.

I dropped my sketchbook and pencils and set them off to the side before racing downstairs. Derek had already started yelling at the Garrett's.

"No!" he yelled at them. "Get out!"

"Derek, please," Mr. Garrett said. "We are not here to start anything. We only want to help with her funeral."

"No!" Derek yelled again. "Get out!"

"This is my house," Gramps said sternly. "Let's talk about this like adults."

"What's there to talk about?" Derek turned on Gramps. "They disowned their own daughter! They don't get to be here!"

"We will never forgive ourselves for that," Mrs. Garrett said, already starting to cry. "But how could you keep our grandchild from us? You two didn't even let us know!"

Derek stepped back like he'd been slapped. "You…"

"They know," I said quietly. "I'm sorry, I tried—"

"You're sorry?" Derek asked, turning on me. "You told them? And now you're sorry?"

"I didn't tell them," I said. "Lillian did."

"HOW DID THAT HAPPEN?!?" he bellowed at me. "I thought I could trust you! I asked you to protect her! You're supposed to keep her safe!"

"Don't speak to Macy that way," Gram stepped forward, her

voice stone. "Now you calm down, or you can leave. I will not have you attacking my granddaughter. Macy has been there for you when no one has been. She has watched your child without asking for a cent. You don't get to come in here and yell at her when she's been more a parent to that little girl these last couple weeks than you've been."

Derek glared at me with absolute contempt, but I also noticed him swaying as if he could barely stand.

"I'm sorry," I whispered. "They just showed up on the doorstep."

"You don't have to apologize," Gram said. "Derek does. You may be grieving," she said, still in her scary, steely voice, "but you don't berate the people who have helped you from day one."

Derek stumbled back. "Where's my daughter?" He went to leave the room.

"Derek, please," Mr. Garrett tried again. "Let's talk about this. We realize we were wrong. We can't take back how we treated our daughter, but please give us another chance with Lillian. That little girl is all we have left of Lindsey."

"NO!" Derek yelled so loud, everyone flinched. "You…You…" he pointed at both of the Garrett's. "You told her to choose. Then you told her that if she chose me that you never wanted to see her again. Well," he said, panting. "You got your wish. You never get to see your daughter again. And she died thinking her parents hated her!"

Both the Garrett's were in tears as Derek fumbled through the hall and up the stairs.

"Let her sleep," I called out.

Dad stepped in. "Let your daughter sleep. Don't involve her—"

But Derek shoved Dad out of the way.

"Call the cops," Dad said to Gramps.

"No," I said. "He's grieving. Please, don't involve the cops."

Derek had already climbed the stairs and had a sleeping Lillian in his arms.

"Daddy?" she asked. "You didn't get me a slushee." Then she rested her head on his shoulder.

Derek went to run down the stairs, but he tripped over his own feet. Suddenly he and Lillian were falling down the stairs.

Chapter 20~

Strong and Brave

Everyone gasped.

Lillian's head smacked the wall, and Derek partly landed on her. She began to shriek and held her head.

"Oh my God," Derek said, picking himself up and trying to help his daughter.

Gramps shoved him aside while I picked up Lillian and carried her to the kitchen. Gram and Mrs. Garrett followed. "I've got you," I whispered, but she still shrieked.

"I'm a nurse," Mrs. Garrett said. "Is there blood?"

I set Lillian on the counter. "Not much. Here, take a look." I moved aside.

Lillian wouldn't have it. She screamed and kicked. "MACY!"

"Okay, I'm right here," I said, holding her again. "We only have to see if you have a big boo-boo."

Lillian wrapped her arms tight around me while Mrs. Garrett tried to check the back of her head. "She has a goose egg forming," she said. "And a slight cut, but there's not much blood."

"Should we take her to ER?" I asked.

"She should be okay. Let me check her eyes, make sure neither is dilated." Lillian squirmed while Mrs. Garrett examined her eyes. "It doesn't appear to be a concussion."

Gram had already grabbed an ice pack and placed it on Lillian's head. Lillian wiggled away from it.

"Lillian," I said. "We have to put an ice pack on your boo-boo. You don't want your goose egg to get too big, do you?"

She started to cry. "I don't want a goose's egg!"

So, I held Lillian in my arms, trying to get her to keep the ice pack in place. Eventually her tears subsided, and she rested against my shoulder. "Where's Daddy?" she murmured. "Does he have a goose's egg?"

"He probably has a little boo-boo, but he's okay. He feels really bad about falling down the stairs."

"He scared me," she sniffed.

"Come on," I said. "Want me to put you back in bed? We can draw pictures until we get sleepy."

She nodded into my shoulder. I noticed Mrs. Garrett watching us, her chin and lower lip trembling. No doubt she was going through her own battle, but right now, Lillian was my concern. "I don't think she has a concussion," Mrs. Garrett repeated. "She should be okay to lie back down. Do you have any children's pain medicine?"

"No," Gram said. "I can run to the store and get some."

"Maybe I'll go with you," Mrs. Garrett said. "If you don't mind? I'd like to be doing something useful."

I carried Lillian to the stairs, noticing the men were not in the house anymore. Climbing the stairs carefully, I began to sing a lullaby. Once in the room, I set Lillian down and took out a notebook that I let her draw in. But she didn't touch the notebook.

"I want my mommy," she said, big tears welling up in her eyes.

"I know," I said, taking her small hand.

"When will she wake up?"

I couldn't look Lillian in the eyes. I couldn't lie to the little girl anymore, but I couldn't bring the words together. Instead, I thought of a story that I had always loved as a little girl. "I'm going to tell you a really cool story. How's that sound?"

"About mommy?"

"About an awesome woman, probably a lot like your mom."

"Was she a princess like Anna and Elsa?"

"No, she was a queen."

"A wicked queen?"

"No, she was good, but she had to make a really scary decision. A decision that could turn out very bad. Her name was Esther."

"Queen Esther," Lillian murmured, already listening to the story.

"She was a poor girl who lost her mommy and daddy."

"Why?"

"Because they died. So, she lived with a relative. I think he was like an older cousin or uncle or something. Anyway, his name was Mordechai."

"Was he evil?"

"No," I laughed. "He was nice. And he loved Esther like a daughter. So, one day the king was searching for a bride. He sent his servants to search all the land, and one of them saw Esther. She was so beautiful, but she didn't want to go to the king. She was really shy. Mordechai talked her into it. And sure enough, the king fell in love with Esther and made her his queen."

"Did they live happily ever after?"

"Well, not at first. The king had a friend, and that friend was not nice."

"He was evil?"

"Yes," I laughed again. "Very evil. He wanted everyone to bow before him and treat him like the king. But Mordechai, Esther's relative, he wouldn't do it. That made Haman, the king's friend, very angry. He vowed that he was going to hurt Mordechai and all his people."

"Even Esther?"

"Haman didn't know that Queen Esther and Mordechai were family. He tricked the king into signing a law that would kill Mordechai and all of his people in the land."

"That's mean!"

"I know. Mordechai sent a secret message to Esther and told her that she needed to do something, but Esther was scared. If the king found out, she could get punished too."

"Would she die?"

"That's what she thought, but Mordechai told her that if she wasn't strong and brave that all of their people would die. So, Esther made a decision to tell the king the truth. She had to pray and believe that the king would believe her over his best friend."

"Who did the king believe?"

"He believed Esther, and Haman got punished instead of Esther's people."

"Did they live happily ever after?"

"Yes, I think so."

Lillian was quiet for a minute. "I like that story."

"I do too. My mom use to tell that story to me and my sister. She'd say that if Esther could be strong and brave, then so could we." I left out that it was one of the few positive memories I had of my mother. "Sometimes I have to remind myself to be strong and brave, so that I'm not afraid."

"I love you," Lillian whispered as she rubbed her eyes.

"I love you, too," I whispered back. "Do you want to draw, or are you ready to go back to sleep?"

"Don't let anyone come in the room, okay?"

"Okay," I promised. "Stay strong…"

"…and brave," Lillian said before closing her eyes.

I stayed beside her, softly singing another lullaby. I vowed to talk some sense into Derek as soon as he sobered up. He might be grieving, but enough was enough.

Soon, Lillian was sleeping soundly, so I tip-toed out of the room, mostly closing the door. I spotted my sketchbook still on the floor from earlier. Picking it up, I studied the nearly completed piece. I thought of Lillian's look of longing when she said she wanted her mommy and knew exactly what features to sketch for Lindsey. I sat at the top of the steps again and meticulously worked on Lindsey's ghostly expression. Sorrowful eyes, a slight frown, a stray tear.

The front door opened, as Gramps, Mr. Garrett, and Dad walked in. All three of them acted solemn and concerned.

"Where's Derek?" I asked.

"He took off running toward the motel and back behind it," Dad answered. "We tried looking for him, but we need flashlights and some walkie-talkies."

"We're going right back out," Gramps said. "How's Lillian?"

"Trying to sleep. Gram and Mrs. Garrett went to the store to buy some children's pain medicine."

"You wouldn't have any idea where Derek would run, do you? He left his car. Took off on foot." Gramps scratched his head.

"No," I said honestly. Then an idea came to me. "I might know how to bring him back though."

"How?" Dad asked.

"Well, if he didn't go far, he might be drawn back if I play the piano. One time I was playing in the church, and when I came outside, he was on the front steps listening. Then the other night, he asked me to play for him again."

"Great idea," Gramps said. "Let's head to the church. We'll open up a few of the side windows, then keep searching."

"Wait. What about Lillian? Gram isn't back yet." When the men didn't have an answer, I said, "How about if I open up the windows and play the piano here? When Gram comes back, I'll head over to the church."

"If I was Derek," Dad said, "I would come back to check on my daughter, but I'd be embarrassed about it."

"Good point," Gramps said. "He trusts you, Macy. We'll leave. You start playing that piano."

I took the steps to the main floor, rested my sketchbook on the piano, opened up a few windows, and sat down to play. Dad came over to me and kissed my forehead, "You were quick-thinking with that little girl. I'm proud of you."

"She's scared," I said. "And she misses her mom. It must be hard for a little girl to lose her mother."

"I wish there was something I could do. I feel helpless."

I got the feeling that Dad wasn't necessarily talking about Derek and Lillian anymore. "Tell the truth. That's what I've learned from all of this. Keeping secrets never turns out well."

"Ready, Tom?" Gramps asked, as he came up from the basement. Mr. Garrett followed him, his hands full of flashlights. "I found two flashlights for each of us."

"Yes," Dad said, leaving me and taking two flashlights from Gramps.

The three men left me in the house, alone with Lillian. I wasn't sure where Derek was, but maybe he'd hear the piano and be soothed. Honestly, I thought we were grasping at straws. Derek had looked slightly deranged and highly drunk. I wasn't sure I wanted to lure him back to the house by playing the piano. Just the same, as I sat on the bench and stared at the keys, I couldn't help myself. The ivories called to me. I had played the piano more in these last several weeks than I ever had within the last few years back home.

Just as I began to play, someone knocked on the door. It couldn't have been Derek. Then I remembered that Pedro was stopping over. "Thank God," I murmured. It'd be nice having him in the house with me.

I swung open the door, took one look at the visitor, and my knees nearly buckled. "Jake."

"Hi, Macy. I've missed you," he said with his lopsided grin, which used to send butterflies fluttering in my stomach. But not anymore. Absolutely not affected by that grin. Or his blue eyes. Or his broad shoulders.

"What are you doing here?" I snapped, not inviting him in. "My grandmother is going to be back any minute, and my Dad is here too. So, you need to leave."

"Macy," he said again, this time more seductively. He stepped closer. I could smell his cologne. "I did what you wanted. I ended it with Hannah. I should have done it long ago because there's only one girl for me. You."

Those were the words I pined for. The awkward girl get the hunky youth pastor? I'd be lying if I said his words weren't affecting me.

"No," I said, trying not to be pulled into his intoxicating game.

"I came all the way up here for you. I ended it with Hannah. I'm sorry I ever ended it with you, Macy. I got scared because after that night, I knew I was falling hard. But then you were gone. And it was like the air that I needed to breathe was gone too."

Okay, this was bad. I thought I was over him. Then I thought of Hannah. Of Pedro. Of my family. Of Lillian. Of Derek. And I stepped back. "No."

"What?" Jake acted confused.

"I said, 'No.' And I mean it. We're done."

"You can't be serious? After everything I went through to come here? After breaking up with Hannah, I also stepped down from the youth pastor position. For you. For us."

"First of all, there is no 'us.' Secondly, you shouldn't have been a youth pastor to begin with."

"Excuse me?"

"Any guy who sneaks into a girl's room in the middle of the night shouldn't be in a position of leadership."

Jake acted slapped. "You didn't say no," he said. "I came to your room because I knew you wanted me as much as I wanted you. That sketchbook of yours was practically pornographic!"

"Really?" I shook my head and gave a humorless laugh. "Get real, Jake. I was sixteen when I met you, and eighteen when you discovered my drawings. They were pictures from a curious teenager who had a school-girl crush on her youth pastor. And they were not pornographic. Yes, I was jealous of Hannah when you two started dating, but nothing would have ever happened if you would have left me alone. I would have grown up and moved on. But no. You took advantage of me."

Jake's expression had turned cold. His well-acted seduction routine had passed. "Seems you have a selective-memory. From what I remember you enjoyed everything we did in your bedroom."

Now that I said no, it was as if the fog had been lifted, and I was seeing crystal clear. "Don't you get it? I shouldn't have ever let you into my room. It was wrong, and I'm sorry. Hannah's my sister, and she was engaged to you. My jealousy consumed me, and I'm going to have to pay for that. My relationship with Hannah will probably never be the same. But I don't have to keep making the wrong decision. I can stop. I can choose to do the right thing. And the right thing is being as far away from you as possible."

I tried to slam the door in Jake's face, but his foot stopped the door. "We're not done here," he said, grabbing my arm. "You don't get to say no. Not after everything I went through to get here."

"Let me go," I said, trying to pull my arm from his grasp.

Suddenly, Jake was yanked back onto the porch. "She said to let her go." Pedro cold-cocked Jake right in the face, then sent him over the porch railing to the front yard.

While Jake moaned out on the lawn, my gaze stayed on Pedro, and my heart felt like it had grown ten times its size. Pedro came over to me. "You okay?" he asked.

I nodded. "Yes."

We didn't say anything more because Gram's car pulled up into the driveway.

"You broke my nose," Jake whimpered.

"If you don't shut up and get out of here, I'll break more than just your nose," Pedro said menacingly.

"Don't do that," I whispered. "I don't want you to do anything risky because of me."

"Too late," Pedro said.

Pedro and I watched Jake stumble to his car, holding his

bloodied nose, and get inside. He threw the car into reverse, squealed it out of the driveway, nearly hitting a tree.

"That's the same tree I almost hit," I said, as Jake finally drove out of my life for good.

Pedro took my hand. "I wanted to really hurt him," he said. "But I held back. I told myself not to let my anger consume me."

"I'm proud of you," I said.

"It's because of you."

"Me?"

"Yeah. With you, I feel hopeful. Like maybe life will turn out okay."

"Of course it will."

Pedro studied our entwined fingers. "You still didn't Google my real name, did you?"

"Actually, I forgot again. I told you it's been crazy today. From Dad's overreaction to Derek's weird behavior to Lillian's injury to Jake showing up....yeah, it's been nuts."

"Well, I stopped over to tell you everything."

"Tell you what, sit down and I'll be right back."

"Where are you going?"

"To get cookies," I said like it was an obvious answer.

Pedro's eyes lit up. "Yes, please."

I walked inside and leaned against the door. I closed my eyes and took in a shaky breath. What would have happened if Pedro hadn't showed up when he did? Would Jake have forced himself in the house?

I went to the kitchen and set some cookies on a plate, then

poured some lemonade in a glass. I carried both outside.

"Here. Let's eat some cookies and talk about anything other than my crazy life."

Pedro and I shared several cookies, and for the first time that evening, I felt relaxed.

"My grandmother can cook too," Pedro said, popping the last of a cookie into his mouth. "I miss her, but being around Mrs. Elmsworth helps."

"Where is your grandmother now?"

"Still is Mexico. I'm from Toluca. Most of my family is still there."

"Maybe you can go visit her someday."

"I hope to. I want to bring my brothers. We have a lot of family they've never met."

Now that Pedro had opened up some, I wanted him to keep going. "How long have you been in the states?"

"Since I was about nine. My mother fell for an American who promised her the world."

"I take it things didn't turn out too well."

"He promised her a new life in America, and all she had to do was smuggle his drugs." Pedro studied his hands. "There was a moment when she considered having me stay with my grandmother, but I wouldn't have it. I couldn't bear the thought of being away from my mother."

"You were just a child."

"I wonder a lot how life would have been if I'd stayed back in

Toluca. But, oh well, can't change anything."

"If you would have stayed in Mexico, you wouldn't be able to be with your brothers."

Pedro took my hand in his. "I went to juvie when I was young. Trying to protect my mother."

The words hung in the air.

"I didn't mean to kill the man," Pedro said, without looking at me. "It was a different guy. It was always a different guy. But this one, he was mean. I was thirteen, and I was tired of having him terrorize my family. He was beating up on mom for the thousandth time, and Filipe started crying, so the monster threw him across the room. That was it. Something snapped. I followed him outside the apartment because I was going to confront him. I don't know. I was just a kid. He stopped at the top of the stairs and turned around to look at me. He'd known I was there. Then he grinned. This evil, twisted grin. He said, 'When I get back I'm coming for you.' I was scared and angry--"

"What did you do?" I tried imagining a young Pedro having to face down a drunken predator because his mother wouldn't.

"I lunged at him. I knew I wasn't strong enough to fight him, but I thought maybe if I caught him off guard, he'd lose his balance, fall down the stairs, and wake up sober. He did lose his balance, and he fell down the cement stairs pretty hard. But he never woke up."

I thought of Derek and Lillian falling down the stairs tonight. "I don't get it. Falling down stairs can be painful, but how can it kill someone?"

"Some of the concrete was broken up at the bottom of the stairs, and his head hit it hard enough that it knocked him out. I guess. That's what I've been told. I was also told that he had a heart condition, and that the fall might not have killed him. That's why I got out of juvie early."

"It was an accident," I reminded him. Pedro's eyes found mine. I saw such sorrow in his that I nearly put my arms around him. But I didn't. "There's more?"

"I told you when you knew the truth, you wouldn't want to be my friend."

"Stop saying that. You haven't scared me off yet."

"Once out of juvie, I did a lot of stupid stuff. Mom would convince me that I needed to help her out. That basically meant smuggling or stealing or whatever. Mostly, I got involved in stealing cars. Mom met a guy who had connections. There was a lot of money in that, and I was too young to realize the severity of the crime. Our car-stealing ring got busted, and they threw me under the bus. Only this time, I was almost eighteen, and they decided to try me as an adult."

"And you went to prison."

"Yep," he said sadly. "For six months. The worst six months of my life. But I did sober up, and I found my faith, which has kept me. I thank God for that."

"That still doesn't explain why you changed your name."

"The guy who threw me under the bus thinks I stole about 20 grand. If he finds me, I'm dead."

Okay, now I was a little scared. "Did you steal the money?"

"No. But I'm pretty sure my mother did."

"And she doesn't have any of it to give back," I said in horror.

"I was barely out of prison before she took off for months on some big binge. Then she came back to us, all scared and demanded we leave at once. She said they were looking for me and the money. So, I got scared too. I knew what those guys were capable of. We took off. One of mom's old boyfriends lives up in this area, and she decided that he would be safe until things clear."

"And you can't tell the police? Wouldn't they help?"

"I'd have to rat on my mom. They'd kill her. Not the police, but the guys she stole from."

"And if you're found?"

"I keep praying that God will make things work out. I'm truly trying to change. I don't want to live the dirty life. That's why I like working at the motel. It's good, honest work. It keeps my nose clean." Pedro sighed. "I just don't know what to do about my mom. Life would be a lot easier if I left, but what about my brothers?"

I rested my head on his shoulder, wanting to fix all his problems, but not knowing how.

"I didn't scare you away?" he said, wrapping his arm around my shoulders.

"Not at all," I said. "And with all the craziness that's going on with my family, and now with Derek, being with you calms me down."

We stayed on the steps of the porch, leaning into each other, for as long as we could, as if neither one of us wanted the moment to end.

I know I didn't.

Chapter 21~

In Memory Of...

Two days past before Derek showed up. But he was more like a ghost, occasionally checking in on Lillian and then completely avoiding everyone else.

While my grandparents navigated the Garrett's, Dad took over the motel office. Even though he was constantly on the phone with mom or the younger kids, he seemed to enjoy the office duties. He had even started being a little nicer to Pedro.

"How long are you staying?" I joked.

"As long as I'm needed. Your mother understands." He gave me a kiss before heading across the street.

All of this gave me two days' time with Pedro. Two days where we worked and laughed and hung out at the lighthouse. Two days where I wasn't worried about Jake. Two days of calm.

Now, I awoke to someone lightly tapping my cheek. I blinked and squinted at the morning light, trying to remember where I was. My sleep had been deep. Then I saw Lillian's face inches from mine, and I jumped back in surprise.

"You're awake!" she squealed, climbing up onto the futon with me.

After last night's shower, I went into the room across from mine and crashed on the futon. There had been too much going on downstairs, so I couldn't crash on the couch. The reason I had never slept in here since Lillian had taken over my bed is because it still smelled like my mother's perfume, but luckily I had been too tired to dwell on that.

As Lillian snuggled up next to me, I asked, "How's the goose egg?"

"I told it to go away," she said. "I don't want a goose's egg on my head."

I laughed softly. "It's only a bump. That's all. It's not a real goose's egg."

"It's still there."

"Does it hurt?"

"A little."

"Gram bought some medicine, remember? I'll give you some this morning. It should help."

"Macy, what's wrong with my daddy?"

"He's sad, hon, that's all. He misses your mommy, just like you do."

"You should tell him the Queen Esther story."

"Maybe I will."

I kissed Lillian's head, inhaling the strawberry shampoo scent. But I also smelled the faint aroma of pee. "Lillian, did you have an accident again?"

"But I changed my underwear because I'm a big girl."

Sighing, I sat up. "That's good, but you'll still have to take another bath before getting dressed. Come on, let's go run the bath water."

I helped Lillian start the bath water and grabbed some clean clothes for her while she cleaned up. I tried to hurry because I could tell by the sunlight that I had overslept. As Lillian bathed, I went into my room, stripped the sheets and blankets, and then ran downstairs to dump them in the washer. As I dumped the detergent in and started the washer, I inhaled deeply. The whole downstairs smelled delicious. "Gram, do you ever sleep?" I called out.

Leaving the laundry room, I walked into the kitchen. Every inch of counter space was being used. There were three crockpots plugged in, and desserts galore. "Um, Gram? Is there a party I don't know about?" I turned and saw Gram sitting at the small kitchen table, her head on resting on her arms, sleeping. I walked over to her and gently placed my palm on her shoulder. She didn't stir. I studied her face, the lines around her eyes and chin, and my heart swelled with love and gratitude. My grandmother gave and gave, never asking for anything in return. When I thought of the woman I wanted to be, it was my grandmother who came to mind.

I thought about helping her to her bed to rest, but she seemed so peaceful that I didn't want to disturb her. Suddenly, Lillian called out from upstairs, "MACY! I'm done!" and Gram stirred.

"Oh my," she said, yawning. "I didn't mean to doze. There's so much to do."

"You're tired. Go, lay down. I can take care of this. Is the church having some sort of Saturday lunch?"

"It's the memorial service," she said. "Did we not tell you? I'm sorry, sweetie. Everything has been so chaotic. It must have slipped our minds. But a lot of these dishes are from members of the church. I didn't do all this cooking, I promise."

"What time is the service?"

"Noon. She was cremated, so there's no burial. After the memorial, we'll have the luncheon downstairs at the church."

"Is Lillian going? Does she have something nice to wear?"

"I think Derek was hoping that you'd stay here with her."

"What?" I asked. "That little girl needs to go to her mother's memorial."

"I agree, but we're trying to honor Derek's wishes."

"No," I snapped, becoming angrier by the second. "Enough of this." I turned and headed toward the stairs. I would get dressed, then I would go and tell Derek exactly what I thought.

"Remember, sweetie," Gram called from the kitchen. "It's better to heal wounds with honey than with vinegar."

"Who said anything about healing wounds?" I muttered under my breath as I threw on a pair of jeans and a t-shirt. I slipped into my converse, then knocked on the bathroom door. "You dressed?"

Lillian opened the door, all smiles. The bathroom was an absolute mess, but I couldn't act angry as she grinned up at me.

"I've got to head over to the motel. I'll be back in a little bit."

Lillian bounded down the stairs. "It's Saturday, so I don't have to go to school?"

"That's right. Gram, I'll be back shortly to help."

"I'm all right," she said, shooing me away. "I'm tired, but I'll survive. Tonight, I'll sleep really well."

I left the house and ran across the lawn and street, bounding over to the motel. Thankfully, the new hire—an older woman in her fifties who chain-smoked and cussed like a sailor—had trained easily. She worked with Pedro on weekends. She waved at me as she came out of a room. Lorette? Was that her name?

"Busy morning, huh?" I asked, knowing good-and-well just how busy this weekend was on Gramps' books.

"Yeah, but so far, the rooms haven't been terrible."

I made it to Derek's room and pounded on the door. After a pause, I pounded again. "I know you're in there, Derek Blackstone, so you might as well open this door." When he still didn't answer, I said, "Don't make me use my key!"

The door flew open. He reeked of alcohol, and his disheveled appearance and growing 5 o'clock shadow announced that he hadn't changed in a couple days or bothered to clean up. "Leave me alone," he muttered, going to slam the door.

Fury lit through my veins, and I slammed my body against the door, pushing my way in. "This room stinks," I said. "And so do you."

"Is that why you came over? To criticize me? Thanks, but I get enough of that already."

I shook my head and clenched my fists, trying hard not to punch him in the face. I had to remind myself that he was grieving. Still, I grabbed him by the shoulders and pushed him into a chair. He went to get up, contesting. "Sit down!" I ordered. He glanced up at me, surprise in those bloodshot eyes of his. "Enough of this! This self-destructive pattern has to end!"

Derek looked away, but at least he didn't argue with me.

Sighing, I continued, "I get that you're grieving, and what's happened to you and Lillian is awful, but Derek, you've got to pull yourself together. If you can't do it for yourself, do it for your little girl. Just this morning she asked what was wrong with her daddy?"

Derek shifted uncomfortably. Good. I wanted him to think about his actions. To realize he was hurting more than just himself. "You two are a family. A good family. It might only be the two of you right now, but two is better than none."

"I feel powerless," he admitted quietly. "I couldn't save my wife, and now I've got her parents sniffing around. They're going to try to take Lillian. They're already asking questions."

"Then fight for her!" I yelled. Derek finally turned to me, meeting my gaze. For several moments we stared at each other, but at least he didn't look away. "Fight for your daughter. The way your wife would want you to fight."

There it was. I saw the flicker of emotion. He closed his eyes, resting his head in his hands. "I'm not the man Lindsey thought I was. She should have stayed with her parents."

"Stop it," I said. I wasn't sure where this toughness came from, but I saw some of myself in Derek. That same self-sabotage. "You can't change the past. She left her parents for you. Don't let that decision mean nothing." He glanced up at me again. "Stop with the excuses and be the man your daughter needs."

Slowly he nodded. "You're right."

"Of course I am," I said, believing it. "Now, come on, let's get you ready for the memorial service."

"I'm not going."

"Yes, you are." I walked into the bathroom and turned on the shower. I came back out to see Derek in the same spot. "Get up. You need to take a shower and get ready."

"I'm not going."

I sighed again in exasperation. "Yes. You. Are." I marched over to him and stared him down.

"I don't do the church thing. Never have. Never will. I only told your grandparents that the service can be at the church because it was the easiest."

"No one's asking you to convert," I argued. "It's a place to congregate and memorialize your wife. Lillian needs to say good-bye, and so do you."

"No." He gave me a steely look. "Don't involve Lillian. I'm serious."

"So, you're going to rob your daughter of honoring her mother?"

"You're not manipulating me. I have my reasons."

I stepped back and studied him. He was obviously just as stubborn as I was. Then I had an idea. "Babysitters charge a minimum of $10 dollars an hour. This week alone I have watched her every day, all day. If I add up all those hours, along with all the other weeks I watched her, you would owe me a couple thousand dollars."

Now I had his attention, but his grim expression and deep-set frown told me he didn't appreciate my tactics. "Are you bribing me?"

"I'm saying that I have watched your daughter because I care about you and her. And I haven't asked for a cent. But I'm asking for this. I'm asking for you to get dressed and walk through those church doors and to take your daughter with you."

"Why are you doing this?"

"Because…" I paused. Why *was* I doing this? "Because I care… and I worry…and this is all I know how to do to help. It's not much, but maybe if you and Lillian go to the memorial service, you'll get the closure that you need. Together."

"I can't face the Garrett's again," he said, more to himself. "I can't see their grief again."

"They're grieving, yes, but for more than just their daughter's death. Earlier this week, she was beside herself because she allowed her daughter to walk out. I think they blame themselves as much as you blame yourself. Though it's nobody's fault."

"Yes, it is," Derek said. "I was driving the motorcycle. And somehow, in some sick, twisted way, I'm here and she's gone."

"We can't blame ourselves for accidents. None of us would ever have peace. Trust me, I know. At least with you, you did everything you could for Lindsey. What happened was truly a tragedy."

"I shouldn't have let her leave her parents' house. If I would have been patient, we could have finished our schooling, maybe her parents would have come around. But no, I told her I wanted to leave right then. I was reckless, and she loved me. And now she's dead."

"Some would argue what is life without love?" I sat on the bed beside him.

Derek let out a shaky breath, then bent over, resting his head on my knees. "I'm a mess," he admitted.

"Come on," I said quietly. "Let's get you into the shower."

He sat back up, and with a look of resignation, nodded. I stood up and held out my hand. Derek stared at it for a moment before reaching for it.

I tugged gently. "That shower's calling your name," I teased.

Derek stood up. "Yeah, yeah, yeah." He walked past me into the bathroom while I rummaged through Lillian's drawer, trying to find something suitable for her. "Hey Macy?"

I looked up. "Yes?"

"What do I say to my little girl?"

"I'm sure you'll think of the right thing," I encouraged. "And no matter what, she's going to wrap her arms around you and love you because no one can replace a girl's dad."

He gave a slight smile before shutting the bathroom door.

I grabbed an outfit, slammed the drawer, and shut the door behind me. Then I took a massive breath.

"You okay?" Pedro asked.

I opened my eyes, looked over at him, and saw the concern on his expression. The butterflies took off in my stomach. "I'll survive. There's a lot going on."

"I know. I'm glad we were able to get away to the lighthouse last night."

We shared a smile and let it linger for a moment.

"Are you going to the memorial?" Pedro asked.

"Yes. I've got to go help with Lillian. What about you?"

"If I get a minute, I'll sneak in the back. Not everyone gets weekends off," he joked.

"Once everything returns to normal, I'll come help out. But I've got to get Lillian ready. I'll see you later?"

Pedro took my hand, pulled me to him, and kissed me. "Just had to sneak a kiss."

"You can kiss me all you want," I said against his lips.

Derek's motel room door opened. Pedro and I stepped apart. "Sorry," Derek said, acting uncomfortable. "I only wanted to see if the Garrett's car was here. I wasn't expecting you…two…outside my door."

"Trying to avoid them?" I asked. "They are a little uptight, aren't they?"

"Yep," he said, without making eye contact, and closed the door again.

I said good-bye to Pedro and headed back to the house.

When I made it back to Gram and Gramps', I found Lillian at the small kitchen table with my dad. They both were facetiming with Adrianne. "Are you coming back soon?" Adrianne asked. "Tell Macy that Rex really misses her."

"Are you sure it's only Rex that misses her?" Dad teased. "And I'll be home soon. Gram and Gramps have several projects they need my help on, and Macy needs my help too. But it shouldn't be too much longer."

"You can come up here," Lillian said to Adrianne. "And we can play again."

"Okay, but no wandering away. I don't want us to get in trouble again."

"I promise," Lillian said.

"Hey there." I poked my head between Dad and Lillian. "How're you doing, Lima Bean?"

Adrianne's smile turned to a frown. "Horrible! You left me, then Dad left, and Hannah's never here! It's so boring with just Lucas. All he cares about is his stupid guitar and computer games."

"It's almost summer," I told her. "Finish up your online tests, then you can hang out up here."

"I only have two more left."

"Well, get cracking!" I blew a kiss at the phone, and Adrianne put her lips to the screen and virtual-kissed me in return.

Dad said his good-byes and so did Lillian. It was then I noticed Dad had a bag of frozen peas, resting on his knuckles. "What happened here?" I asked him, indicating his hand.

Dad chuckled sadly, ending the call. "I found out that Jake was still in town. I'm afraid your old man's not what he used to be."

"What did you do?" I lifted the frozen peas and studied his slightly swollen knuckles. I hadn't thought about Jake for two whole days, and it had been blissful. Pedro made me forget him completely. But I guess Dad hadn't forgotten.

"I haven't been able to sleep since you told me that he showed up on the doorstep. He's hurt both of my daughters, but what he did to you especially was enough to have me hunt him down this morning. I told myself that I was just checking to make sure he'd left town. It wasn't that hard. His father's a premium member of Hilton hotels. I looked up the closest Hilton, drove over there, and spotted Jake's car. I went to the front desk, told them I was a pastor wanting to drop off a basket of snacks for the traveling evangelist, and lo and behold, they gave me the room number! As soon as he opened the door, wham! I punched him right in the face. Although it was more the jaw which is why my hand is still throbbing."

I maybe squeaked a response. I didn't know if I should be shocked, thrilled, or worried. At that moment, all three vied at being the ruling emotion. "Dad, what were you thinking? You're a pastor. Pastors don't hit youth pastors at hotels!"

"I'm a pastor, not a saint. And before I'm a pastor, I'm a father. How can I lead a congregation if I can't take care of my own family?"

"But he'll tell his father, and his father's on our church board!"

"Good."

"He could tell the church!"

"Good."

"They could vote to dismiss you!"

Dad sighed. "Good."

I saw it then in my father's eyes. Discouragement or sadness or a mix of both. I turned to Lillian who was finishing up a glass of milk. "Miss Lillian, I need you to take this outfit upstairs and change into it. Your Daddy's coming to get you, and he is so excited."

"Is he okay?"

"Yep. He had a good sleep, and he took a shower, and he can't wait to see you."

Lillian jumped down and took the clothes from my hands.

Once I heard her little footsteps upstairs, I sat in the chair next to Dad. "What's going on? I feel like there's something you're not telling me. And Gramps has been eluding to some sort of family secret for a while now."

Dad acted uncomfortable, suddenly squirming in his chair and not making eye contact. "I have been contemplating—and praying—about some issues for a long time."

"Like giving up the church and moving up here?" I asked. "Gramps said that his heart attack had you reevaluating some stuff."

"Yes, sort of. After I helped him and went back home, your mother wouldn't hear of it. The church has always been her baby, her dream. We couldn't just leave the flock, that's what she said. And even though I had misgivings about continuing to pastor, your mother can be very convincing. I wasn't about to split up with her. You kids were young, and marriage is all about compromise. So, I stayed and plugged away at the church."

"And now?"

Dad shrugged and kept playing with the frozen peas' bag.

"Your heart's not in it, is it?"

"It's more than that, even though that's a part of it. Meg and I are…struggling. We have been for a couple years. We don't see things the same way, and she won't go to therapy."

"Why not? Bob and Cecile are wonderful marriage counselors, or at least that's what you've always announced from the pulpit."

Dad smiled wryly. "They are, but according to your mother, therapy is for the common people, not for ministry. We're supposed to somehow figure it out on our own." He sighed again. "I think it's probably embarrassing for her to admit anything's wrong. Plus, going to therapy might open up some secrets that she'd rather keep hidden."

"Like what?"

"Oh, I don't know," he said, not quite looking at me. "Hidden secrets of the heart. You know…"

"Is that why you're here?"

"I'm here for you," he said simply. "It was at her suggestion to come talk to you about…well, you know. And I took care of it." Dad lifted up his swollen fist. "Anyway, don't concern yourself about me or your mom. We'll figure it out. Until then, let's get ready for the service. Gramps said you're going to sing."

"No one's asked me."

"Yes," Derek said from behind me. "She's singing."

I turned around and saw him standing there in a black suit and tie. He gave a hesitant smile.

"Is Lillian upstairs?" he asked, breaking the awkward pause.

I nodded, then turned around to face Dad again.

"You clean up nice," Dad said. "I'm glad you decided to come to the service."

"Macy talked some sense into me," he said. "If you'll excuse me, I need to talk to my daughter."

Dad studied me for a moment. "You're so much like your mother," he said quietly.

I tried not to twist my face in disgust. "No, I'm not. Mom and I are polar opposites."

"Not that mother…" Dad stopped himself. "And you shouldn't talk that way about her. She has a lot of good points."

I tried not to roll my eyes.

"Besides, I meant your grandmother. She's always giving of herself. That's you. Helping all of these people. I feel like we tucked you in a corner downstate. Here, you're thriving."

"Yeah, I am," I said. "Everything was always a competition with Hannah, and I learned early on that I couldn't win. So, I stayed quiet and kept to myself. But that got me in trouble too. I really ruined it with Hannah."

"Hopefully over time, she'll come to forgive you. Even though she might need to be honest with herself, as well. She pushed you to act out. Bullying you, embarrassing you in front of the youth group. Hannah needs to come to terms with her own culpability."

"And Jake completely took advantage of our sisterly feud," I said, realizing the truth of it.

"That he did," Dad agreed, scowling. "And to think I let him in my house every day. I let him infiltrate my family. Now I have two broken daughters, and a possible broken marriage because of it."

"I might have been broken," I admitted. "But I'd like to think the pieces are coming back together again. I might not be whole just yet, but I'm getting there."

Gram came into the kitchen in a midnight blue dress and hat combo. "What are you two doing sitting there? We've got to go. And what did you do to your hand? You know what? I can't worry about it."

"I was waiting for you to get done, so I could jump into your guys' shower," Dad said. "That way, Macy could have her privacy upstairs."

"Privacy?" I snorted. "Privacy means nothing to me anymore. I have a five year old who's taken over my room."

"Go, go, go," Gram shooed us out the kitchen.

I ran upstairs only to slow at the top. I hadn't heard Derek or Lillian leave yet. I found them sitting on my bed. Lillian actually sat in Derek's lap, crying. My heart broke. I didn't know what to do. My clothes were in the room, but I didn't want to interrupt. I tip-toed to the closet and pulled out a gray sleeveless dress with a thin, black cardigan to wear over the shoulders. Then I tip-toed to my top drawer and pulled out a pair of clean undies only to grab a pair of Lillian's by accident. When did she start putting her clothes in my dresser?

I heard the giggling behind me. Looking over my shoulder I saw Derek and Lillian watching me. "You grabbed my flower underpants," she giggled, wiping at her eyes.

"Yeah, and I don't think they'll fit," I said, putting them back in the drawer. I grabbed until I found one of my own. "I didn't mean to interrupt. Pretend I'm not here." I left the room and shut the door to the bathroom. I used the facilities, then hopped in the shower, scrubbing and shampooing quickly. Gram needed my help with one of the roasters full of baked ziti, and I wanted to practice on the piano before the memorial service started. Stepping out of the shower, I began humming to myself a variety of songs I could sing. I dried off and got dressed, still singing. Once decent, I opened the door.

And Derek stood right outside of it, holding my large sketchbook. "Did you do this?" he asked, showing me the drawing of him and Lillian and Lindsey. Thankfully, I had finally gotten her face right.

"It was supposed to be a gift for you and Lillian. I'm going to have it framed." I went to take it from him, but he wouldn't let go. "Why did you go through my stuff?" I hadn't hid my sketchbooks since mother left.

"It was right on the dresser, and I was curious. Macy, this is incredible. You drew this?"

"Yes," I said, suddenly feeling shy. "Let me frame it," I said.

Derek kept staring at the picture.

"How did Lillian handle the news?" I asked, needing to talk about something other than my art.

"I'm not sure she quite understands. I told her that her momma couldn't ever wake up, but I didn't know how to tell her about the cremation."

"Tell her about heaven," I said. "Tell her that her mother is in a better place where there is no pain and that one day she'll see her again."

"I'm not going to lie to her." He shut the sketchbook.

I blinked in surprise. "Lie? About what? You can't just leave it with she's not waking up either."

"Okay, but I don't believe in heaven or afterlife or any of that garbage."

"Why not?" I asked, trying to wrap my head around the idea of not believing in heaven. I might have a ton of questions and doubts, but heaven was kind of like a staple to the whole belief system. "What a miserable existence to think that there's nothing else. How do you explain that to a child?"

"Miserable existence? So, now you're insulting me?"

"No...yes...maybe...these last couple days you've been completely beside yourself, now I know why. You don't think you're ever going to see her again."

"I'm not."

"Maybe not in this life, but in eternity..."

"Stop," Derek said, shaking his head. "Thank you, Little Miss Churchgirl, but I will handle my grief in my own way."

"Well, then, you better think of something else to tell Lillian other than she's sleeping forever. That reasoning isn't going to work for long." I snatched my book and went into my room. Lillian had already left. Poor thing. I couldn't imagine there not being anything outside of this life. It made me depressed just thinking about it. I brushed through my long hair, then slipped into my shoes.

As I left the room, Derek still stood in the same spot. I went to move past him. "Macy," he said, reaching for me.

"I need to practice before the service starts," I said, trying to go down the steps.

"Please," he said. "Don't be angry with me. Not today."

"I'm not angry with you," I said. "I'm sad. I'm sad just thinking about how lonely you must feel."

Derek's eyes welled up with tears, but he tried to blink them back. "I have reasons for who I am and for what I believe or don't believe. Don't judge that, okay?"

"I'm trying hard not to judge, but I don't understand. It's not like I don't have a million questions, and a ton of doubts, because I do. I don't get why there's suffering. And I don't get why Lillian had to lose her mother. But…" I paused, not knowing how to put it into words. "Then there are people like my grandparents who remind me of what it's all about, and I see how peaceful and happy and content they are, and I want that. And I want Lillian to have that."

"Peanut," Dad called from the kitchen. "Are you helping with the roaster? My hands are full."

"Yeah, Dad," I called down. To Derek, I asked, "By the way, where's Lillian?"

"The Garrett's stopped over while you were in the shower and offered to walk her over to the church."

I smiled. "Good."

Derek shrugged. "Your grandfather was with them, so I knew she'd be fine. But I haven't told her yet that they're her grandparents. Sometime today, I will. Want help with that roaster?"

"If you don't mind," I said, walking down the stairs with him.

Dad did have his hands full. "Could you get the door for me?" he asked.

"Sure," I said, holding it open. As I held the door open for Dad to walk through, a police car pulled into the driveway. "What are they doing here?"

"Oh no," Dad said, watching the two officers step out of the car. "I forgot to tell you that Jake said he went to the cops to report Pedro, then he said he was going back to report me."

Any smile on my lips vanished. "Pedro," I whispered, my gut falling to the ground. "Oh my God, he can't..."

"Excuse me," the one officer said, as he approached. "We're looking for Macy Elmsworth. We have a few questions we'd like to ask her."

I couldn't help it. I looked across the street to the motel, hoping that Pedro's cart wasn't there, hoping that maybe he got sick or something. But no. I spotted him and his cart immediately.

"This is Macy," my father said, indicating me. "However, we're about to go to a memorial service. She's the musician. Could this wait? The service shouldn't be more than a half hour."

I gave a tight-lipped smile to the officers. "I can answer questions as soon as the service is over."

"Of course," the one said. "We'll sniff around outside while we wait."

Dad, Derek, and I stepped off the porch and began moving toward the church.

"One quick and painless question before you go inside?" The officer asked while walking beside me.

"Of course," I tried not to grimace.

"Do you know of a Jake Steward?"

"Yes, he's my sister's fiancé. Or, he was. He's not now."

"Is your sister up here with you?"

"No, I've been staying at my grandparents for about a month and a half."

"Who'd he come to visit?"

"I thought you said one question? That was like five."

"It was only three. We're just trying to put the pieces together. It doesn't make sense for Jake to be up here by himself and visiting you if he's getting married to your sister."

We were nearly at the church. I paused, choosing my words carefully. "Jake came to my grandparents' front door because he wanted me to choose him. He left my sister and came up here. I told him to get lost. That's it."

"One more thing, I promise. We are looking for a suspect in these parts. A young man who could possibly have been involved in an altercation last night with Jake Steward. Mr. Steward said the young man was Hispanic with several earrings, and that he was on your porch. Does that ring a bell?"

I knew I'd have to lie.

"We're at the church now. May we continue this later?" Dad intervened.

Just then, on the other side of the motel strip, Pedro looked up, and we made eye contact. His smile fell as he saw who stood beside me. His sudden grim facial expression told me everything I needed to know.

I couldn't help but wonder as I entered the church if I would ever see him again. I paused, wanting to run to him. We were only beginning to learn about each other.

"What about our date?" I asked out loud.

"Come on, Macy," Gram rushed to me. "We're ready to begin."

"Gram, there is something I have to do. I'll be right back."

"You're starting the service."

My heart was torn, but Gram was pulling on my arm. Not knowing what else to do, I followed her to the front of the church.

Chapter 22~

Missing Persons

The entire memorial service I struggled with concentrating. I knew who waited for me outside, but I didn't know what would transpire because of it. What could I say that wouldn't incriminate Pedro?

The more I thought about it, the more I wished he hadn't told me his first name. If they tied me up and made me take a lie detector test, I would fail. Then I would be an accomplice. Then again, he would have never told me if I hadn't been acting all weird about his past.

I shifted positions in the church pew and eyed the door, desperately wanting to go find Pedro. I wanted to warn him. I wanted to apologize. I wanted to let him know that he wasn't alone.

"Stop worrying," Dad whispered in my ear. "We'll fix it. Let's focus on one issue at a time."

"You don't even like him," I whispered back. "Don't act like you're not secretly glad."

Dad kept his gaze straight forward and nodded his head at Gramps like he absolutely agreed with whatever Gramps said. In all honesty, I hadn't paid attention to one second of the memorial service. I glanced over at the front of the church where Derek sat with Lillian and the Garrett's. Other than a spattering of Derek's work friends, some young woman who was close to Lindsey, and a handful of old church folk, the church felt too empty. And I felt completely torn. Stay in the service? Or go make sure Pedro was okay?

I replayed our moments at the lighthouse, and the way Pedro would stare out at the horizon longingly. And when I had no one to turn to, Pedro was there for me. I suddenly felt very guilty. If I hadn't messed around with Jake, then Jake would have never came up north. Pedro would have never punched him, and his life would be fine.

Dad placed his arm around my shoulders and squeezed. "Take a deep breath. Trust that God will work it all out."

"I'm not too sure about that."

Gram turned around from the pew in front of us and gave us a stern look.

No longer able to take the worry, I slipped out of the pew and headed to the vestibule. I shut the sanctuary door, so not to bother anyone, then began checking the windows. The police car was gone from our driveway. They must have found Pedro! I ran outside and down the steps, not knowing where to check first. I decided on the motel. Moving in that direction, I found his cart abandoned outside a room.

Lorette approached. "He's gone. Went with the cops."

My heart fell like a sack of flour. "No."

"He walked right over to them. Shook their hands. Then they took him. Crazy."

"But he's innocent."

"They didn't cuff him. It seemed all right. The truth always reveals itself." She reached in her pocket and pulled out a folded piece of paper. "Here. He said to give this to you. I read it. Hope you don't mind. I'm curious like that."

I unfolded the piece of paper with the motel's emblem on it. Pedro had scrawled:

Dear Macy,

Living on the run isn't living. That's why I got to turn myself in. I'm sorry about my past, and I'm sorry I kept it from you for so long. I'm embarrassed of it.

If my brothers want any hope of a decent life outside that trailer, then this is what's got to be done. I'm not sure how long I'll be gone, but I didn't do the crime this time, so hopefully, I can get out of here fast.

Thanks for giving me hope. Maybe one day I can take you on that date. Take care of our spot at the lighthouse.

Love,

Pedro (Ricky)

"I can't believe this is happening," I said, choking back the emotion. Just like that Pedro was gone. "I didn't even get to say good-bye. Can I go see him at the police station?"

"Sure. I don't think there'd be a problem," Lorette said. "Are you two a thing?"

I looked down at the note again. "I think so. Yes."

"If you wait for the perfect time to fall in love, then it'll never happen."

"Excuse me?" another voice called out.

I glanced up to see one of the motel's guests approaching me and Lorette. "Yes?"

"Do you know when someone will be in the office? We scheduled an early check-in today."

"There should be a receptionist there," I said, thinking of Pedro's mother. I hoped she didn't take off too. But I started walking over to the office, already knowing the answer. She was the guilty one. Knowing her, she took one look at the police and ran. I thought of Pedro's brothers and the sadness deepened. "This is ridiculous," I said.

"Tell me about it," the customer said. "But all the hotels in town are booked solid. I tried calling the number on the phone that's set up, but no one's answering."

I didn't have time to speak highly of Gramps' motel because as soon as I opened the door to the office, I saw that no one sat behind the desk and about seven different sets of customers were waiting for help...and quite impatiently. All turned my way and glared. Some crossed their arms and glowered. Great.

Forget the thin-lipped smile, I threw on my thousand-watt one. "My apologies," I said, smiling like a fool as I made my way behind the desk. I never worked the desk before, but I didn't show that to the customers. I had observed Gramps enough that I could figure it out. "We are short-staffed this Saturday afternoon."

I did the best I could, writing down everything, in order for Gramps to fix it if I did it wrong. In less than a half hour, I had everyone checked in. Unfortunately, rooms weren't even close to being done. "Rooms will be available in about an hour."

There was some grumbling, but I encouraged everyone to try the local restaurant just down the road, and I even stashed suitcases behind the counter, promising to deliver them to the right rooms when the rooms were ready. Then I placed my phone number next to the available phone Gramps had set up to call him, and ran outside to help Lorette with the rooms.

"Most of these are done," she said, wiping at her brow. Today was full sun and 70 degrees.

"I'll get the next set," I said. "Thank you so much, Lorette. I know my Gramps appreciates it."

"No problem. You gonna clean in that?"

I glanced down at my gray dress and heels. "I don't have time to change. It'll be fine."

Grabbing Pedro's cart, I pushed it the last set of rooms he had yet to do. Then I took off my heels and got to work. By the time one room was done, my hair had been pulled back with a rubber band and my antiperspirant was working in overdrive.

In the second room, my phone rang. "Oh God, not now!" I said, thinking a customer waited at the office. Instead I saw it was Mom's number. "Hello?" I asked, surprised she would call me.

"Macy, have you seen your father? I'm trying to get ahold of him."

"He's at a memorial service. I think the service should be done soon."

"He's not answering. I even had Adrianne and Lucas try to call."

"As soon as I'm done, I'll run over to the church and have him call you."

"You wouldn't have happened to have heard from Hannah, have you?"

"Um, how recently? The other night I texted her and told her I was sorry, but that's about it."

"And she replied?"

"Yes."

"She's not answering any of my calls, and no one has seen her since the day after Jake left town."

I heard the concern in Mom's voice. A genuine concern about her daughter. I pushed past the jealousy. I was done competing and comparing. "Maybe she's crashing at Sarah's."

"No, I've checked all those places."

"Okay, well, I can try to call her again or text her. She replied really fast to me."

Mom sounded close to tears. "I feel like my family's falling apart."

"Everyone's okay," I said, trying to reassure her. "Like Dad told me today, 'God's going to work it all out.'"

I heard her sniffle. "Okay, just have your father call me."

"I'll let Dad know," I said. "And I'll try to get in touch with Hannah." My phone rang again. "Dear Jesus!" I cried before accepting the call. "What?"

"Um, hello, is this the number of the motel's front desk person? There's a note here."

"Yes, I'll be right there." I ended the call then groaned as loud as I could, then I muttered the entire way to the front office that Gramps better hire more help or else.

As soon as I finished checking in another grouping of customers, Gramps and Dad came into the front office. "About time!" I said. "What took so long?"

"Your Gramps was long-winded. Plus we were hungry."

"No, I wasn't. We couldn't leave without eating with the family downstairs. It would have been rude."

"That's great. I'm glad you all enjoyed a lovely lunch spread." I slammed a stapler down. "Gramps, you need to hire someone reliable to work the desk. Pedro's mother is about as flighty as they come! And you're too busy with other duties to be here effectively. And Dad, your wife and other children have been trying to get ahold of you, so turn on your phone! And there's a stack of suitcases over here. Most of them can be delivered to their rooms. It'd be great to have a little help! Now if you'll excuse me, I've got two more rooms to finish! Then I've got to call Hannah, and then go check on Pedro's brothers, and then go see if the police will let me check on Pedro!"

Dad and Gramps blinked at me in surprise. I marched past them to the last two rooms on Pedro's list. Halfway through changing sheets, Dad showed up with two suitcases and a carry-on. "These go here," he said.

"That's fine. Leave them in the corner. This room wasn't that bad. As soon as I make the beds, it'll be mostly done."

Dad set the suitcases down in the small closet. "Hannah's missing," he said, acting concerned.

"I know. I'm going to call her in a minute." I fluffed the pillows and placed them in position. Dad leaned against the wall, worry on his countenance. "She's fine, Dad. She's got a lot to be upset about. Maybe she's trying to clear her head."

"You don't think Jake would have done anything, do you?"

"No. He's a jerk and stupid, but I don't think he's sinister like that."

"You're mother's really worried. She and Hannah are close."

"Yes, I know that." I started making the second bed.

"Macy, don't be like that."

"I'm not," I said, stopping long enough to seriously look at him. "I'm stating the obvious truth. She is really close with Hannah. But that might be the problem."

"What do you mean?"

"When I came up here, at first I was all hurt and upset, but I quickly found it liberating. Mom can be stifling. Hannah's never really had a break from that. And Jake was practically shoved at Hannah because Mom thought he'd be the perfect husband."

"So, what are you saying? Hannah didn't want to marry Jake?"

"No, I'm not saying that. She bought into his whole package easily enough. I'm saying that Hannah might want a break from Mom."

Dad rubbed his face. "So much of this is my fault."

"There's blame to go around," I said simply. "Some of it is my fault. I should have never allowed him in my room. And I should have told you or someone…anyone…who would listen. Some of it is your fault. You could have been more understanding of the situation. You could have handled the sketchbook incident better. Then there's Mom and Hannah. Mom took something that wasn't hers and used it against me. Hannah publically made fun of me. Jake would have never known about my crush if Mom and Hannah hadn't done what they did." I took a breath and continued, "But I can't change the past. None of us can. All I can do is be better now and in the future. And I'm trying, so that's got to count for something, right?"

Dad acted like he wanted to say something. "You make me proud," he finally said. "Helping your grandparents up here. Taking charge. Being kind. I'm just sorry that your mother and I were so stifling in the first place. I'm sorry your own family humiliated you, and that you didn't feel safe enough confiding in me about Jake."

I finished up the beds. "Dad, don't worry about it. I'm up to my ears in other people's problems, so I don't have time being bitter about my own life."

Dad gave a half-laugh as he walked to the door. "I'm not really sure how to respond to that."

After he left, I wiped down the mirrors and sink. I stepped outside, shutting the door behind me. I started to push the cart to the laundry room when I noticed Derek and the Garrett's standing outside the church arguing. I didn't see Lillian. Trepidation tickled my stomach. After a day like today, I wasn't about to take any chances.

I hurriedly dumped the cart in the laundry room then ran over to Derek, which was hard to do now that my heels were back on. "Hey," I said, smiling at him and the Garrett's. "Forgive me for interrupting, but I was going to take Lillian back to the house."

"She's with your grandmother," Derek said.

"Oh, okay. Are they still in the church or over at the house?"

"At the house. I think Ms. Elmsworth was going to see if they could both take a nap."

"Got it," I said, exhaling in relief. "So, how are you holding up?"

"I'd be doing better if the Garrett's could actually wait a few days before trying to take my daughter away from me."

"Be reasonable," Mr. Garrett said. "She's our granddaughter."

Derek ran his hands through his hair and pressed his lips together. I could see he was trying to behave. "You're not taking my daughter. It's that simple. And if you threaten anything more, you won't ever see her either."

"She lives in a dingy motel," Mrs. Garrett said. "I'm sure the courts will see it our way."

I studied them, then Derek. I thought of me and my father. Situations might be difficult with him at times, but I couldn't imagine my life without him. Suddenly, I wanted—needed—Derek to know that he wasn't alone. So, I turned to the Garrett's and, with a courage I didn't know I had, said, "How dare you."

"Excuse me?" Mrs. Garrett asked.

Derek glanced up at me, apparently surprised by the anger in my tone.

"You have no idea what kind of father he is because you haven't been around. You don't know what he's been through these last months, working two jobs, providing for his daughter while at the same time paying for enormous medical bills on a hope and a pray that his wife may recover."

"We haven't been around because there's been no communication."

"And whose fault is that? You cut her off." Both of them acted pained at my comment. I softened my tone and added, "Listen, everyone makes mistakes. So, it's not fair or right to judge Derek when you two have made plenty of your own mistakes."

"But you saw how drunk he was the other night!" Mrs. Garrett stepped forward, staring me down. "Lillian could have been seriously injured! It's probably what happened to Lindsey!"

"It was an accident. And it wouldn't have ever happened if Derek hadn't been threatened by your sudden--and uninvited--arrival! Do you think that you can just show up after years of disowning your daughter and take Lillian away? Well, you can't!"

"Fine. We'll talk about this later. You're making a scene," Mr. Garrett said to me.

"No, I don't think so. You don't get to put this on me," I said. "I'm not the one threatening Derek. If you truly cared about Lillian, you would care about her father. Because to her, Derek is her world. And what would Lindsey say if she were here right now? Would she want you trying to take her daughter from Derek, or would she want you forgiving each other so that Lillian can have a father *and* grandparents? Because I tell you what, I need my Dad, and I need my Gram and Gramps. It'd be a shame if Lillian didn't get to experience that."

I left the three of them and walked across the street and up the driveway. Okay, maybe I should have minded my own business, but

Lillian would be heartbroken without Derek. Maybe it had something to do with Derek's and my earlier conversation. Even with him acting like a complete jerk these last few days, I didn't have the heart to see him get emotionally beat up anymore.

Once inside, I took off the heels and ran upstairs to change. Lillian lay on my bed, fast asleep. I found myself tip-toeing again, changing from my dress to a pretty shirt and leggings. I wanted to look nice and professional when I entered the police station, but I didn't want to wear heels. First, I would stop by Pedro's trailer and see if the boys were there. But I needed to check with Gram to make sure they could come with me if they were by themselves.

As I made my way down the stairs, Mr. and Mrs. Garrett were opening the front door and walking inside. What ever happened to knocking? I realized Gram and Gramps could be very inviting and warm with anyone they met, but I still found it unnerving that they would walk right in.

We made eye contact. "Where's Derek?" I asked.

"He's changing. He said he'll be over here in a minute."

"Okay, well, Gram is resting and Gramps is at work, so…"

"We only wanted to say good-bye to Lillian before we head back to the hotel."

"She's sleeping upstairs. I don't really want to wake her."

"Not a problem," Mrs. Garrett said. "We can wait until she wakes up."

They continued standing in the foyer. The lack of conversation extended too long, but I didn't know what to say.

Dad burst through the door, saving the situation. He'd know what to do. "Has she responded back to you?" he asked.

"Oh, I haven't texted," I said, pulling out my phone. I typed fast. *Where r u? Everyone's worried.*

When I looked back up, Dad had already invited the Garrett's in for coffee. I took Gram's keys from the hall table. Walking to the car, I spotted Derek coming up the driveway.

"Where're you headed?" he asked.

"Got to check on Pedro's brothers. He was picked up today."

Derek exhaled loudly. "I wondered if that might happen."

"He turned himself in. Said he was tired of running." I opened the car door. "Lillian's in my room. Sleeping. I'll be back in a few."

"How long has she been out?"

"Not long. The Garretts are inside with my dad. It was weird. They walked in through the front door without even knocking."

"I come in sometimes without knocking."

"I realize that, but we know who you are. Oh well, it's no big deal. I've watched too many murder mysteries on the Hallmark channel."

"They probably wouldn't do anything like that. They're annoying and self-righteous, but they're also very smart. They're not going to do anything that would jeopardize their reputation."

"So, they're calculating."

"Of course. Which means that they'll probably make my life miserable for the next little bit, but hey, at least Lillian knows she has grandparents."

"Easy on the sarcasm," I teased.

"Can't help it," he said, coming closer. "I took your advice and told Lillian, and now the Garrett's want at least partial custody if not complete custody. So, thanks, but not really."

"Don't turn this around on me," I acted insulted.

"If I blame you, I don't have to blame myself."

I opened my mouth to respond, then saw him grinning. "Right. You know you've already said some pretty horrible stuff to me, so let's ease up." I rolled my eyes and went to slip into the car. Derek stopped me.

"I'm sorry for acting so poorly and saying really horrible things. I don't remember much about the events, but I do remember saying some mean things to you. Which was dumb. You've been a big help." He paused, then added, "I don't know what I would have done without you or your grandparents."

"Yeah," I admitted. "You said some mean things. Well, I got to go. I want to check on Pedro."

"Want company?"

I wasn't sure how to answer that. "Uh..."

He had already went over to the passenger side. "If Lillian is sleeping, I don't want to be near the Garrett's," he said. "I'm trying not to drink. So, keep me occupied." Then, he slid into the other side of the car.

I took a deep breath before getting in. "All right, let's go see Pedro."

Chapter 23~

Vent Session

I put the car in reverse and backed up down the driveway and into the street, and began to laugh.

"What's so funny?" Derek asked.

"Nothing. Just laughing at myself. And the craziness of everything." As we drove to Pedro's trailer, I purposefully told him about everything that happened while the memorial service and luncheon were taking place.

"It doesn't surprise me that Victoria took off. She's been throwing Pedro under the bus for a long time."

"How?"

"I think that she pins a lot of her problems on him. It was her idea for them to hide out up here and to change names. All she has to do is say that his brothers are going to get taken away, and he does what she says. I told him he didn't have to be afraid of going to the police. But she convinced him otherwise."

"Wow."

"I personally think she's hiding something. Just a gut feeling I have."

"What a mess," I said, thinking of what Pedro told me. "Do you know how they got this trailer in the first place?"

"They're renting from one of Victoria's boyfriends. It's his hunting cabin."

We drove through the woods and made it to the trailer. I parked the car, turned off the engine, and sat back in the seat. "He deserves better."

"Macy, you are from a different world. And I know that you two are a thing, but someone like Pedro wouldn't be able to give you a future. A guy like Pedro can't change his past, and even if he tries to forget it, it never really goes far."

"Don't be like everyone else," I said.

"How am I like everyone else?"

"You're judging him."

"I'm stating facts."

"No, you are using his past to determine his future. And that's not right. Everyone deserves second chances."

"I'm not saying that. I'm only being real. You two are…"

"Different? Yes, we are. So?" I got out of the car and shut the door. I didn't want to say anything more. Maybe Derek was trying to protect me, but I'd dealt with enough overbearing people in my life that I didn't want one more. And the truth was that I liked Pedro…a lot. And whatever he did in his past, didn't match up with who he was now.

As I approached the trailer, the first thing I noticed was that the bikes were gone from outside. I went up and knocked on the door. "Filipe? Pablo?"

"They're gone," Derek said from behind me.

I tried the door, and it opened. "Hello?"

The inside still had the worn couch, the table with mismatched chairs, but nothing personal. I walked down the hall to Pedro's room, all the stuff from the top of the dresser was gone. I pushed past Derek and went back outside. I sucked in a breath and wiped at the tears that started. The idea that those two boys were out there with no place to live was killing me. "That's it?" I asked Derek as he approached me. "Those kids…" I covered my mouth and closed my eyes, turning from him. He'd probably think I was a sap, and I didn't want to hear his criticism.

"We could contact local authorities."

"No, Pedro wouldn't want that. They might separate his brothers."

"Then we're out of options. I have no idea where she'd take them."

I studied the trees, not really knowing what I was looking for. "Do you know what I admire about Pedro?" I asked, turning around to face Derek. "I admire his commitment to family. His mother is a mess, and he still looks after her. He looks after his brothers, even when Victoria takes off for months. He could leave all of them, and his life would be easier, but he doesn't."

Derek came over to me. "Deep down, he's got a good heart."

I nodded. "See. Was that so hard?"

"Hey, I like Pedro. We're friends. I want him to be okay."

"Well, you're kind of harsh on him."

"Only when it comes to you," he said quietly. "I'm trying to protect you from guys like us. Bad boys break good girls' hearts. Or get them killed. I don't want anything bad to happen to you."

The tears had dried up, and I now had a big lump lodged in my throat. "You just said he has a good heart."

"A lot of bad boys have good hearts and good intentions. Shoot, I did. But at the end of the day, if we don't find trouble, it finds us."

We studied each other for a little too long. I wanted to say something, but I didn't know what. I knew the guilt had to be eating away at Derek, but I already told him several times that the motorcycle crash was an accident. Then again, how many people told me that what happened with Hannah wasn't entirely my fault? "Let's go see if Pedro's okay," I finally said, breaking eye contact, and getting into the car.

As I turned the key, Derek slid in next to me. "Macy," he said.

"What?" I barely breathed.

"What are your intentions with him?"

"I like him. He gets me."

"So, you two are a thing?"

I thought of our kiss and how nice it had felt, but that seemed long ago. "Maybe, I hope so."

"So, what are your future plans? And do they involve a boyfriend in prison?"

"He's not going to prison. He didn't do anything wrong."

Derek went to say something, but I stopped him. "No, please stop. Stop trying to get me to see the bad. For years, that's all I focused on about myself. The negative. And do you know who was the first to truly see me? To see me, mistakes and all? Pedro. I'm not going to judge his past." I thought of Pedro's words and smiled. "I'm going to be hopeful. With him, I'm hopeful."

"What about college? You two going to clean motel rooms for the rest of your lives?"

"Why do I have to have all the answers? I don't know. My first plan is to get through today. I'll figure out the rest later."

"You should go to college and major in the arts."

"That's a wasted degree," I said, quoting my mother.

"How?"

"It doesn't pay the bills. Anyway, Gramps needs me here, so I'll probably hang out for a while."

"You're killing me," Derek said. Now he took my hand in both of his. He had calloused, rough hands that were warm. "Macy, do not throw away your talents. Don't do it! Not for your uptight family or for Pedro. If you want to pursue art in any capacity, you should go for it. All the way. And that means cutting the ties that bind."

"All right," I said, still staring at our hands. "I'll think about it." I pulled my hand from his and put the car in reverse. As I turned it around and headed down the two-track path, the air hung thickly in the vehicle. Needing to break the tension, I teased, "You know you're giving me a complex by pushing me to leave. It's almost as if you want me to go away. Far, far away."

"Then who would I get to babysit for free?" he teased me back. "Trust me, if I was acting selfishly, I'd tell you to never leave. You know how much Lillian adores you."

"Yeah, she's pretty special."

"Hopefully, in the next month or so, we'll be able to move into a little two bedroom house, one of my coworkers was telling me about."

"That's wonderful!" I said. "What about the hospital bills?"

"I filed bankruptcy a couple days ago," he said, acting embarrassed. "I didn't want to do it, but there's no way I could ever pay any of that back. Then we both had a small life insurance plan. It's not much, but it's $10 thousand."

"Can the bill collectors take it?"

"I'm not sure. Your grandfather's helping me navigate a lot of this. Which is great. I don't know what I'd do without him. He's like the dad I never had."

"Yeah, he's pretty special."

"Is your father they're only kid?"

"No, they had a daughter. My Aunt Tessa, but she died a long time ago. She was their wild child. Overdosed on pain meds, I think. No one really talks about her much anymore."

"Really?" Derek's voice didn't mask the surprise.

"Yep. She was a cautionary tale, growing up. She and Mom used to be really close, if you can believe that. Went to Bible College together. Aunt Tessa introduced Mom to Dad. Weird."

"From Bible College to drug overdose? How in the world did that happen?"

"From what Mom told us kids, Aunt Tessa never wanted to go to Bible College. She was really rebellious and did crazy stuff. Like bring alcohol back to the dorms and making out with all the guys. I don't know. Stuff like that. Then she got kicked out of the college and kind of spiraled downhill after that."

"Why'd she get kicked out?"

"She was caught with the pastor's son."

Derek started laughing. "I'm sorry. I don't mean to laugh at your family's pain, but wow. They say every family has a skeleton in the closet. You would never think it, encountering Mr. and Mrs. Elmsworth."

"I wonder if that's why they're so good and kind. Maybe losing Tessa altered their views on things."

"Maybe. Sorry again. I shouldn't have laughed at their pain. I'm never good at awkward situations. I laugh at the most inopportune times."

"I've figured that out."

"During your grandfather's ending prayer today, I started laughing."

"You didn't!"

"I did. Everything seemed so final. And the Garrett's were crying, and Lillian was hugging my neck, and all I could think was what I would do for a straight shot of whiskey, and that was it. Commence laughter."

"You're horrible," I said.

"Tell me about it. But I stopped laughing quickly. As soon as I remembered that I vowed to give it all up. I stopped laughing real quick."

That got me giggling. Soon we were both laughing.

I stopped and turned down a street that supposedly led to the Manistee police department. "Google maps says it's down here."

"Yeah, it's that ugly brown building to the right."

Once parked at the police station, I said, "Maybe I should go in by myself." I shut the door before I could hear his response. I walked inside the police station and approached the front desk. "I'm here to see Pedro—I mean Ricky—I don't know his exact name. But he's Hispanic, a little taller than me, with piercings and tattoos."

"Sorry, I can't help you," a woman behind the counter said. "If he's not out here, then he's back in one of the rooms. I don't have any information, other than if he's detained, he'll get a phone call."

"He's not going to be detained. He hasn't done anything wrong."

"Just be patient," she said. "If he's just answering questions, they'll release him. There's nothing more I can say."

I would have walked out of the building, but I spotted Jake coming down one of the hallways. His nose looked blue and swollen, his mouth was cut and swollen, and his left eye had turned greyish blue. I kept myself from smiling. I was too irked to see him here. "Ratting someone out?" I accused, closing the gap between us.

"Come to find out that guy who shoved me off the porch is a criminal. Who knew?"

"Well, since I'm here, maybe I'll file a report about a youth pastor sneaking into my room without permission, then coercing me into inappropriate activities." I made sure to have enough bite to my words to sound menacing.

"It doesn't matter if your door was locked or not. You wanted it," he said the words with pride "All I'd have to do is show them the sketchbook of your obsession, and then we'd see who they'd side with. Besides it's not like you were an innocent, little girl."

312 | Janice Broyles

I stepped back, knowing he was right. The authorities would never believe me.

"If she had a witness, which she does, attesting to the fact that you broke into her room uninvited and kept doing so, then you'd be charged and arrested," Derek said from behind me.

I couldn't hide my smile this time. Perfect timing, Derek!

"She doesn't have a witness," Jake scoffed.

"Yes, she does. I heard you confess to breaking in her room uninvited and coercing her into inappropriate activities because you thought she'd like it. Come on, Macy, let's report this."

"That's not true!" Jake said, getting worked up.

"Yes, it is," Derek said, completely unruffled.

Jake started sputtering.

"The only thing that will keep my mouth shut," Derek said, stepping closer to Jake. Both of them were tall, but Jake shrank back. "Is if you drop the charges against the guy who threw you from the porch. If you do that, I won't tell a soul about your dirty secrets. If you don't drop the charges, Macy and I will file a report against you, and we will write a letter to all of the churches in your organization, explaining how you took advantage of an innocent girl in the youth group you were pastoring. Your call, buddy."

Jake looked over at me. "Who are these guys you're hanging with? Are they all a part of a gang?"

I grinned. "They're my friends."

"And we don't like seeing punks like you mistreating good girls like Macy. So, what's your decision? I don't have all day."

As if heaven itself smiled down on us, a young police officer approached us. "Derek? How's it going?"

"Hey Jason," Derek said as they shook hands and leaned in for a quick hug. "Things have been better."

"Yeah, man, I'm sorry about Lindsey. That's rough."

"Her memorial service was today."

"No way. Aw, man, that's terrible. Well, anytime Lillian wants to play with Brittany, let me know. Tracy won't mind."

"Great. I'd appreciate that."

"So, what brings you here?"

"This guy right here," Derek said, turning a steely glare toward Jake. "He needs to drop some charges. Isn't that right?"

Jake nodded. "I'm not going to press charges against the two men who attacked me," he said. "It was all a misunderstanding."

"Two men?" I asked. Then I remembered Dad's hand. "You were charging my dad?"

Jake glanced over nervously at Derek. "I'll take care of it."

"Once you're done dropping the charges, make sure to go back to where you came from. You're not wanted up here." It seemed like Derek made sure to stare at Jake a little too long to get the point across.

The police officer—Jason—chuckled. "Okay, I'll take care of this guy. See you later, Derek."

Derek took my hand and led me out the door and to the car. When we got to the driver's side, he turned to me and shook his head. "That's the guy who hurt you?"

"Yes. I can't believe he was pressing charges against my dad."

"You okay?"

I stopped thinking about Jake after hearing the concern in Derek's voice. "I'm fine. Thanks for being there. You spooked him."

"Good. It'll go easier on Pedro if this isn't hanging over him." Derek opened the door for me, then shut it once I was inside. Once he had walked around and got in himself, he kept going, "So, they wouldn't let you talk to him?"

"No, he's being questioned, I guess."

Just then, my cell phone buzzed. It was Mom. "Hello?"

"Have you heard anything?" she asked, clearly distraught.

"No, I haven't," I said. "I texted her, but no reply."

"She packed," Mom said in tears. "I can tell. Some of her favorite things, such as outfits and perfume and shoes, are missing, and so are two of the suitcases."

"That's good, isn't it? If her stuff is still at the house, then she'll come back."

"Where would she go without me? Without even telling me? This is so unlike her."

"I know. I'm sorry."

"If she wouldn't have been dumped by Jake, this would have never happened," Mom said. I could hear her tone change from sadness to anger.

"I am sorry that all of this happened. I've tried to apologize, but she won't hear it."

"Do you blame her?"

"No, I don't, but I don't know what more I can do."

"You've done plenty!" Then she hung up.

"Family problems?" Derek asked.

I started up the car and put it in reverse. "I'm realizing that families are crazy. I mean, there's my micromanaging, in-your-face parents who pretend to be all put-together only to be separated. Then there's your family issues. What kind of parents disown their daughter? Who does that? Then, there's Pedro and his family, living in a trailer in the middle of nowhere, hiding and barely surviving. Crazy. That's all I've got to say."

"I firmly believe that sometimes your closest family are people who aren't even your blood," Derek said. "Your grandparents, for example. And you. I've only known you for like what? A month or two? And I know that I could ask you anything, and if it was feasible, you'd do it."

I had already started driving down the road toward the house and was glad that I had to face forward. "So much has changed," I said more to myself. "How is it that the end of March I was in a hospital, enduring a psychiatric evaluation, and now it's not even June 1, and I couldn't imagine going back."

"You already had your wings," he said. "Moving up here finally allowed you to open them up. But they were always there."

"That's why Pedro means so much to me," I said, finally seeing it. "He helped me truly see myself for the person I was, not what others saw or wanted me to be." I remembered his words the night he first took me to the lighthouse. "He's the first person who truly saw me."

I pulled into Gram and Gramps driveway and shut off the

engine. We stayed seated for a few moments, both lost in our thoughts.

"Maybe it'll work for the two of you," Derek said before slipping out of the car. "I'll try not to be such a downer about it."

"I'm hopeful," I said to myself as the weight of all our life's circumstances fell heavily on my shoulders.

I unfolded Pedro's note and read the words again and again. Then I remembered our bike ride together, and how he saved me from drinking anymore of that liquor. I remembered our kiss, and how hesitant he had been at first. I remembered the lighthouse, and his expression as he stared off into the sky. And my heart broke for him.

Closing my eyes, I took a deep breath and for the first time in a long time, I prayed. I prayed that Pedro would get another chance. That he wouldn't have to get in trouble for a crime he didn't commit. And I prayed for his brothers. I felt like there was so much more I needed to say, so I rested my head against the steering wheel and dumped all my worries out and into the air. If God was truly there, and I was pretty sure He was, then hopefully he wouldn't be too upset about the vent session.

Chapter 24~

Stolen Bottles of Liquor

I watched as the pool company filled the motel's swimming pool with water. I'd be lying if I said I wasn't excited. Lillian stood beside me jumping up and down and squealing with glee. I couldn't blame her. I'd be doing the same thing if we didn't have a crowd of motel guests in the area. Normally Gramps waited until mid-June to get the pool ready, but it had been such a warm May that I convinced him to have it ready by Memorial Day. And since my birthday was next week, he obliged.

"Next week, I'm having a poolside birthday bash," I announced to Gram earlier this morning.

"Oh wonderful," she said. "Is the whole family coming?"

I made a face that demonstrated my lack of enthusiasm. Dad had left last week to go back home. After Mom threatened to get the police involved, Hannah eventually sent Mom a cryptic text along the lines of *I'm fine. Leave me alone.* Because of Mom's emotional state, Dad decided to go back and make amends. "Yeah, but the person I want to come won't be there."

"Your grandfather's heard good things," Gram said, patting my hand. "It looks like Pedro gave them the whole story about the guys looking for him."

"That's a miracle," I said. To think that Pedro's testimony would help hold those guys accountable blew my mind. This whole time he had stayed worried, instead of going to the police in the first place. Unfortunately, there was still no word from Pedro, his mother, or the boys.

And I missed him.

"Is free swimming an employee perk?" Lorette said, coming up behind me.

"For sure," I grinned. "Hey, next Friday, I'm having a birthday bash right here. You're more than welcome to come."

"It's your birthday? I wouldn't miss that. Do I need to bring anything?"

"A present for Macy!" Lillian said, jumping up and down again. She was more excited about my birthday than I was.

"Just your drinks. We'll be grilling."

"Will the pool be ready?"

"I'm going with yes. Technically, I'm not sure how warm it'll be, but Gramps bought a new high-tech heater thing in honor of my birthday, so I'll probably be jumping in at some point."

"Sounds fun. Well, I'm finished for the afternoon, so I'll put the cart away and get going."

"Thanks!" I said, waving good-bye. Even though Lorette was an excellent co-worker, it didn't feel right without Pedro. Gramps gave me permission to put an ad in the paper for more help, but it felt like I was trying to replace someone who was irreplaceable.

Derek pulled up, parking in front of their room. Lillian ran over to him, but I stayed put. With Lillian gone, I opened the gate and started cleaning the poolside tables and chairs. They had been chained to the fence all winter long, and it showed. Taking a spray bottle, a bucket of warm water, and a couple rags, I got to work.

I had just finished scrubbing a table when I saw Derek approach. He was holding the framed picture I had wrapped and laid on their dresser. My heart started racing.

"I don't know what to say," he said.

"Then don't say anything. It's only that picture you already saw. I finally got around to framing it."

"It looks different than before."

"It's colored in some, and of course the lighting has changed. That's all."

"It's great. You're great."

"No problem." I focused my attention on a lounger and got cleaning.

"Macy…"

"Hmm?" I asked, still cleaning.

"Macy…"

Sighing, I looked over at him. "What?"

He acted like he wanted to say something, like his face got flushed and his brows furrowed, and his mouth set into a confused frown. I told my mind to remember that look because I wanted to draw it. "Don't waste any more of your time at this motel," he blurted. "With this talent, there is so much you could do. Maybe even work for Disney or something." He turned the frame around to show me my artwork. "This is incredible. And you're wasting the talent, cleaning up after people here."

"I've thought about applying at a couple different places this week. The Art Institute in Chicago would be sweet."

"Yes, definitely," he said smiling. But the smile didn't reach his eyes.

"Chicago's not that far. I'd come back on the weekends."

"That doesn't matter. Besides once you get in the college life, you'll forget about all this."

"No, I won't. And it matters to me. Lillian and I are buds. I can't just leave her. Especially with Lindsey being gone."

"Lillian will be fine."

"Maybe I'm not coming back for her, maybe I'm coming back for me."

"It'll change once you're there."

"First of all, I haven't applied yet. I'm past the deadline, so it might not happen this fall. Second, are you trying to push me away? If I want to come back, I'll come back."

"I just don't want you to have any regrets." He turned and left me in the pool area.

"Are you coming to my party?" I yelled after him.

He looked over his shoulder at me. "Duh. Of course I am."

I laughed to myself and continued scrubbing the pool furniture. I kept working into the evening. It was absolutely gorgeous out, plus it was still daylight at 8:30 p.m., so I was in no rush. Even when I finished the cleaning and put the supplies away, I lay across a lounger and chilled. The pool maintenance crew had long gone, and I was so tempted to stick my foot in. But they warned me about the chemical cocktail of chlorine and other pool stabilizers in the water right now, so I left it alone.

My phone buzzed. It was Gram. "Hey, I'm by the pool."

"I know. I can see you. Wanted you to know that dinner is on a plate, warming in the oven."

"Thanks, Gram. I appreciate it."

"I see you have all the pool furniture out."

"Yes, ma'am, and it's clean too."

"Adrianne is so excited. Did she get ahold of you?"

"Only a hundred times," I teased. "Are you sure you're okay with the both of us up here?"

"Don't you dare ask me that question," she said, acting insulted. "I used to have all four of you up here for most of the summer. It's been a while since that's happened. I'm excited myself."

"All right. I was only asking because I don't want to stress you out. There's been so much going on."

"This is what life's about!" she exclaimed. "It's boring when your grandfather and I are by ourselves with nothing to do."

It hadn't escaped my notice that Gram had been taking more and more naps lately. Gramps told me not to worry, that she'd always been a nap-taker, but I still did. I told her to stop making dinner for me that I was fine with sandwiches, or that I could make them dinner for a change. Nope. She wouldn't hear of it.

My phone buzzed through with another call. "Got to go, Gram.

Mom's calling." I ended the one call and answered the other. "Hello?"

"Macy, dear, would you be terribly offended if I stayed back from your party?"

"Of course not." Even though it'd be better without her here, it still stung that she didn't want to celebrate my birthday. "I'm not a little kid anymore. I'll be fine."

"Good," she said, sighing in relief. "Your father has been on my case about going, but with Hannah being gone and not talking, it's really put me down in the dumps. I'd rather stay put, in case she comes home."

I didn't say anything because I didn't know what to say to fix the situation.

"Oh, and don't be upset, but Adrianne can only stay up north for as long as your Dad and Lucas are there."

"What?" I yelled, sitting upright. "She's spending the summer with me and Gram and Gramps. It's already been decided."

"Well, I changed my mind. I don't want to have my last daughter not here. Besides, there're some sketchy people up there with you all. She still impressionable."

"You can't do this," I tried. "Adrianne and I are both looking forward to it. I won't do anything bad. I promise. Plus, Gram and Gramps will be here. The pool's ready for swimming. You know she'll have a great time."

"You might have gotten Ahmad to drop charges, but it was only two months ago that you were caught with stolen liquor and nearly dead."

"When are you going to let it go?"

"Hear me out," she said. "I know you've been working hard, and I'm glad you are doing well up there. But you can't get upset that I'm being cautious."

"And you're telling me this now? The week before my birthday?"

"I didn't say she wasn't coming up there, only that she would be coming back with your Dad. Stop being so dramatic."

I ended the call before I would say anything more. It was pointless. Mom was mom. Nothing I could do to change her or her decision. But I was still so disappointed. I might have enjoyed my freedom up here, but I missed Adrianne. We talked almost every evening about our plans for the summer. Furious, I texted Dad: *Did u know about lima bean not staying summer? If so, gr8 bday present.* ☹

Suddenly a scent wafted through the air. A familiar scent. But it was light and the breeze carried it away. Chills erupted along my spine. I stood up suddenly and checked the surroundings. I immediately thought of Pedro's mother and the boys. Maybe they were here and trying to get my attention.

That's when I spotted the familiar car in the motel's parking lot. Of course.

Hannah.

I walked to the car and looked inside. She wasn't in it. What I did see was the passenger side littered with liquor bottles. "Oh God," I whispered, searching the parking lot. Where would she have gone? As if answering my question, I heard the pool gate open and shut.

Hannah walked slowly to the pool, a bit wobbly, holding a bottle in her hand.

"Hannah!" I yelled, running to the pool gate and entering the enclosed area.

She stood across from me at the edge of the deep end, looking just as lovely as ever. She lifted the bottle and took a swig.

"Hey, sis," I said, going to walk over to her.

"Don't," she warned. "I don't want you anywhere near me."

"Everyone's been worried," I tried.

"Pfft," she made a noise of disbelief. "I had to get away from her."

"I understand."

Hannah narrowed her eyes at me. "Right. Poor little Macy, the wallflower. Be nice to Macy!" She started to mimic Mom and Dad. "She's so sensitive! Why can't you be more like Macy? Why can't you sing that effortlessly? Why can't you play the piano like her?"

"What are you talking about?" I asked, confused. "I was the one who was scolded for playing or singing. I could never measure up to you. So, I learned to be quiet."

"Oh my word, you don't know anything. Living in la-la-land. Mom was a slave driver, and *you* were the measuring stick! *Why can't you play like Macy? Practice harder! Sing louder!* And then, I met Jake, and I had hope that I would get out of the house and be free. But guess how that turned out?"

My mind reeled with the information she hurled at me. *I was the measuring stick?* That didn't make any sense. Not knowing what else to say, I decided I would apologize until it got through. "I'm sorry. If I could take it back, I would. I was young and stupid and insanely jealous."

"Why are you acting like it's been years since it happened? It happened not even three months ago."

The words stung, but they were true.

"Everyone knew what a crush you had on Jake. Especially after that sketchbook gave you away."

"That was private."

"Boo-hoo," Hannah said, scrunching up her face. "So was my relationship with Jake until you decided to seduce him."

"No, I didn't," I said. "After you showed him and everyone else my sketchbook, I basically had to hide in my room. He came to my door uninvited. And I told him to leave!"

"How'd that work out?" she tilted her head. "Did he tell you the same things he whispered in my ear? He must have said something for you to keep your door unlocked."

"I don't know. Probably. I was impressionable. I had never had a real boyfriend, so I fell for it. *I'm sorry*. I don't know what else to say. I know I can never take back what I did. That's why I'm up here."

"Yep. You're up here with Gram and Gramps. I bet they're thrilled. You get a fresh start while I get a broken heart. That's great. So glad it's working out for you." She took another swig from the bottle.

"What can I do to fix this?" I asked, getting choked up. "Tell me, and I'll do it."

She gave me a cold, hard stare. "Nothing. We're broken. That's it."

"No," I said, shaking my head. "I love you, Hannah, and I'm willing to do what it takes to fix what I broke. So, tell me what to do."

"You love me?" She spit out the alcohol. "You're full of it! Love doesn't steal boyfriends! Love doesn't ruin your sister's life!"

"Yeah? Well, you ruined my life too!" I yelled, sick of the accusations. "You bullied me for years! I could never have any friends because you stole them from me. And you always picked at me over my singing. And what you did with the sketchbook was hurtful! If you would have never shown Jake, he would have never known how I felt!"

"Everyone knew how you felt!"

"That's not true. Jake told me that he thought I hated him until he saw my drawings. If you wouldn't have been so intent on embarrassing me, maybe you'd still be engaged to that...that...jerk."

"So, it's my fault? I knew you weren't really sorry."

"Oh, shut up!" I yelled. "I can't say anything right now without you turning it around and spinning it to fit your *victim* card. I am sorry, but it is partly your fault. If we weren't always at each other's throats, then a lot of things would have been different."

The pool's gate opened, and Derek entered. He glanced over at Hannah, then looked at me and raised his eyebrows. "You two are really loud."

"Sorry," I said.

"You okay?" he asked me.

I shrugged. "No, but we're working things out."

"No, we're not," Hannah said, looking from me to Derek. Then she shook her head. "I can't believe you. You're already onto the next?"

"What? No!" I sighed. "Derek is a friend. I babysit his daughter."

"Yeah, she babysits my kid, and we hang out. Not that it's any of your business."

"Let's go to Gram and Gramps. They'll want to see you."

"Not as long as you're there."

"Then I'll go somewhere else," I said.

"Where? His bed?" She pointed to Derek.

"Will you stop?" I said again.

"She's a piece of work," Derek said to me before leaving the pool area.

"How do you get all the guys?" Hannah asked. "I mean, look at you. You're chubby."

"Yes, thanks Hannah, for telling me what I already know. And I don't get all the guys. I've never been on a date before. Well, I take that back. Pedro and I sort of went on a date, but still."

"Who's Pedro?"

"Never mind." I started to walk around the pool to her. "Let's get out of here. You visit Gram and Gramps without me there."

"No, I'm going to get going."

"Not drunk, you're not. And why did you come in the first place if you're going to turn around and leave?"

"Because I only came up here to do to you what you've done to me. It's time for you to hurt just as much as I have."

"I don't understand. You want to fight? I've got like twenty pounds on you. Chances are high you'll get hurt."

Hannah nearly cracked a smile, but there was too much hurt and anger behind her eyes for it to last. "Everything you think you know is a lie. And I wanted to be the one to tell you. I wanted to be the one who sees the look of betrayal on your face when you first hear the news."

"Well, I'm clueless, so okay. What've you got?"

Now she smiled. Cruelly. "It's actually good news for me."

"Okay…still clueless."

"You're not my sister."

"You can disown me all you want, but we'll always be sisters."

"No, you don't get it. You are seriously not my sister."

I blinked, not fully understanding. "Yes, we are. What are you talking about?"

"Mom and Dad aren't your parents!" she shouted. "Mom told me after Jake dumped me. I don't know why she told me, maybe to make me feel better, but it's true. It makes perfect sense. You've never fit in with us, and now I understand why."

"Stop," I said, feeling confused, worried, and a bit upset. "I don't like you saying that."

"It's true. Ask Gram and Gramps. Ask them whose daughter you are."

It couldn't be true. Hannah must be determined to rile me up. Mom and Dad had a ton of my baby pictures. And they were in most of them. I shook my head. "I don't know what you're trying to accomplish, but I'm not dumb."

Hannah took out her phone and called someone, then put it on speaker. The ringing seemed to bounce across one end of the pool to the other.

My skin suddenly began to crawl. "Stop it," I repeated.

"Hannah, is that you?" Mom said, through the speaker.

"Hey mom," Hannah said. "Sorry I've worried you."

"Oh hon, please come back home. I miss you. We can talk about whatever it is you want to talk about."

"Macy," Hannah said. "I want to talk about Macy."

There was a pause. "Okay…why do you want to talk about her? You need to let all of this go. You don't need Jake, and you don't need Macy."

My stomach rolled, and I wondered if I would be sick.

"I still can't believe it," Hannah said, her eyes never leaving mine. "What you told me."

"Hannah, hon, I told you not to bring it up. Your father can't find out about you knowing. Just come home. We'll put all this behind us."

"How can I pretend that she's my sister when she's not?" Hannah asked.

"She's been your sister for eighteen years. Well, nineteen years next week. You shouldn't look at her differently."

I couldn't hear anymore. I left Hannah at the pool. I told myself not to get upset. There was a perfectly good explanation. My parents would not keep something like this a secret. *My parents.* Dad was my dad, *right?* I ran across the street and up the driveway. When I stepped inside, I heard the television going. I entered the living room where Gram and Gramps watched another Hallmark movie. "Mom and Dad are my parents, right?"

Both of them looked over at me, and I saw the answer in their eyes. How had I never seen that before? "Why wouldn't they be?"

Gramps asked.

"Yes or no. Are Mom and Dad my biological parents?"

"They're your parents," Gramps answered. "They raised you, took care of you. You're their daughter."

"Why are you evading the question? Did Meg birth me?"

"Maybe you should call your dad," Gram said, her voice shaky. "He can explain it."

"Explain what?" I demanded. "Did I come out of my mother's womb or didn't I?"

"Don't upset your grandmother," Gramps said. "Go use the phone in my office."

"No need," I said, a hard knot stuck right in the pit of my stomach. I took my phone out and dialed Dad's number. He picked up on the first ring. "Am I your biological daughter?" I asked without greeting.

"Wh-Wh-What?" Dad stammered. "Repeat the question."

"You heard me. Yes or no? Hannah's here, and she's telling me that you're not my dad."

"Hannah's there?"

"Answer the question!"

"Of course I'm your father. Lower your voice. Now, what's up with Hannah, and why are you asking ridiculous questions?"

"So, you are my biological father? I heard Mom talking with Hannah on the phone. She said I wasn't Hannah's sister."

Dad stayed quiet.

"Dad?" I pleaded. "Please tell me what's going on."

"I've always been your dad," he said. "And you've always been my peanut."

I ended the call, sick with what wasn't being spoken. How could it be possible? Yet, my eyes were opened to the very real possibility. To Gram and Gramps, I simply said, "Listen, I'm an adult. If I've been living a lie my whole life, I think I have a right to know. I'm not a little child that needs protecting. But I am a young woman who's asking for answers."

"Here is the God's-honest-truth," Gram said. "You are my real, biological granddaughter."

"Then why would Hannah say that I wasn't?"

"I didn't say that." Hannah came through the front door and entered the room. "Hello, Gram and Gramps."

"Oh dear," Gram said, getting up. "Hannah, you should sit down. You look wobbly."

Hannah began to laugh. "I am wobbly. Then again, I can't remember how much booze I drank. I started downstate, stealing from the same 7-11 you stole from, and I've worked my way up here. And guess what? I didn't get caught at any of them. At least that's one thing I'm better at than you. I can steal and not get caught. And I can hold my liquor. I haven't gotten sick once."

"You're telling me you stole all that liquor in your car?" I asked. I didn't know if I should be worried or impressed.

"Yep."

"I would have bought mine if I hadn't been underage. But you're over twenty-one, so what's the point?"

Gramps walked over to Hannah and steered her toward a chair. "Sit down, young lady."

Hannah did as she was told. Gram came in with a cool washcloth for Hannah's forehead. "This will feel good," Gram said. "You're a little flushed."

"Oh no," Hannah said. "I shouldn't have sat down." She pushed herself up and ran out the front door, nearly tripping.

"I guess she can't hold the liquor like she thought she could," I said to Gram and Gramps.

"Shh," Gram scolded. "Don't tease."

"You should have seen all the empty bottles in her car. I'm still impressed she kept it down as long as she did."

"I feel bad for her," Gram said. "One minute she's getting married, and the next…"

Guilt hit me hard. "And the next minute her fiancé breaks up with her for her sister. The same sister who'd been sneaking around with him at night for almost a year."

"You have a decision here," Gramps said. "Hannah came up here for revenge. To get back at you. You can either let that happen, or you can try to restore what's been broken."

"That's a lot to put on my shoulders. Obviously there's some big secret, and I've been living a lie."

"What lie have you been living?" Gramps asked. "So, your parents have a secret. Whatever they decided eighteen years ago they did so out of love. Because you are a part of this family. Like I said, you have a decision to make. And yes, it rests on your shoulders."

"In order to fix anything, don't I need answers?"

"You'll get answers, and none of those answers are going to change the life you've lived. You had two parents who raised you to the best of their ability. Were they perfect? No. But were you? No. What matters is that you have always been loved."

"So, I'm adopted." I said it with finality. There. The truth.

"But you're still blood," Gramps said.

The answer dawned on me slowly, as if revealing itself in layers. "Aunt Tessa."

Gram wiped at her eyes and nodded. "Every time I see you, I see my daughter."

"Why keep this a secret? Why not tell me?"

"Because it was decided that there would be nothing to tell. You would be their daughter," Gramps said. "They were struggling with second child infertility, and you were the most beautiful gift. A sister for Hannah. We knew that Tessa wouldn't want it any other way. So, the only ones who knew were us and your parents."

"Did Aunt Tessa know?"

"She passed away with you in the crib in the other room. She was suffering from postpartum depression severely. I had just got on the plane to come back to Michigan," Gram said. "We had decided that she would move back in with us until she got on her feet again. We were going to drive all the way out to California to get her things. She was dead before my plane landed in Michigan." Gram squeezed my hands.

I envisioned Aunt Tessa—my mother—and how she would have looked holding me as a baby.

"You've always been a star that has shone brightly. Sometimes people don't know how to handle it," Gramps said. "I'm not making excuses for anyone, but please try to stay strong through this. What matters is that you are loved. More than you'll ever realize."

I heard Hannah retching outside again. "I've got to process all of this," I said, heading to the door. "For now, I'll be outside helping Hannah clear her system from all those stolen bottles of liquor."

Chapter 25~

My Sister's Keeper

I sketched frantically, as if my feelings would create large droplets onto the page if I didn't draw fast enough. I didn't take time to examine the contents or to redo any mistake. Instead I let my hand communicate what my heart was feeling. Page after page. Past midnight. I guess my heart had a lot to say.

Hannah slept on the futon across the hall. After she finished getting sick, I helped her to the bathroom where she showered. Then I helped her to the futon. The entire time she had snide remarks and hurtful words, but I let her say them. As soon as her head hit the pillow, she started snoring, and she'd been out ever since.

At some point in the middle of the night, I ran out of paper. I checked my dresser drawers for a clean sketchbook. I never ran out. Keeping extra sketchbooks on hand was a must for an artist. When I moved up here I had three clean ones, never touched. But there they lay across my bed. Full with my feelings. "Wow," I whispered to myself as I flipped through pages. I must have done a lot of venting.

But not really. Some pages were doodles and a myriad of colors, some were setting pieces like a drawing of the church or Gram's front

336 | Janice Broyles

porch or the pileated woodpecker that always visited Gram's birdfeeder. Most though were people. My people. Lillian laughing at the dinner table. Pedro at the lighthouse. Gram's sweet smile while holding a cup of coffee. And a newer one of Derek sitting on the front pew at church.

I picked up the one sketchbook I just finished and studied the artwork I sketched tonight. I tried drawing what I remember of Aunt Tessa. Another drawing was a baby in the crib alone. But then I stopped flipping through the pages when I saw the one I sketched of two girls swinging on the bell's rope in a church vestibule. "Hannah," I whispered, running my hand over the page. Like a wave of sorrow, I suddenly felt the deepness of her pain. A girl in love, ready to get married. And it had been ripped from her.

By me.

I set the book down and tried to even out my breathing. Yes, I knew that I wasn't entirely responsible. I could argue that she should have never showed the sketchbook to Jake in the first place. That if she wouldn't have been so mean, none of this would have happened. But why would I draw an entire sketchbook completely devoted to Jake? What would make me think it was okay to let him in my room, time-and-time again? Why would I take her car to steal liquor only to purposefully drink and puke in it? Why shouldn't Hannah hate me?

And even though I was still in shock over the big family secret, it surprisingly didn't concern me as much as repairing my sister. I needed to make it right. Somehow.

"Please God," I prayed. "Please help me fix this."

As soon as the words left my mouth, I heard a thud and then

footsteps heading to the bathroom. Suddenly Hannah was moaning.

"Do you need anything?" I asked, peeking inside.

"Nothing from you," she said. She sat on the toilet, her head in her hands, moaning. "My head hurts so badly."

I opened the medicine cabinet and took out the aspirin bottle. "Can your stomach handle a couple aspirin?"

Hannah made a disgusted face. "No. Nothing. I feel like there's poison in there eating away at my stomach."

"Need help back to the room?"

"Just go away."

I set the aspirin bottle on the counter. "Here's medicine if you decide to take some."

I left her in the bathroom and shut the door to my room. I leaned against the door, my heart heavy. Checking my phone, I saw it was past four in the morning. But sleep wasn't an option. Too much was going on in my brain. Making a quick decision, I grabbed my Converse, put them on, and laced them up.

As I threw on a sweatshirt, I heard the sobs. I stopped and listened. They weren't loud and obnoxious, but stifled and heartbreaking. I went out of the room and opened the bathroom door just a tiny bit. "Hannah?"

"I told you to go away."

"I...can't."

I heard movement. Hannah blew her nose, then flushed the toilet. The water from the faucet ran, and the pill bottle opened. Suddenly the door flew open. Her eyes were bloodshot and puffy, her nose was red, her skin blotchy, and she still was pretty. "What will it take for you to leave me alone?"

"I don't know. I'm worried about you."

"Don't be. You weren't worried a few months ago." She pushed past me to the other bedroom.

Sighing, I said, "I'll be back in a few. In case anyone's wondering." I moved toward the steps.

"Where are you going?"

"There's a place I go when I want to think. I tried to sketch, but I'm all out of paper. I'll be back."

"Where is it? It's in the middle of the night, it's not like you can just leave the house."

"Why not? I've done it before." I took the first step, then stopped and turned around. "Come with me."

"Are you out of your mind? I can think of a million other things I'd rather do then go with you."

"I thought I'd give it a shot." I took the rest of the steps down. I had no idea why I had invited her. The invitation sort of came out without any thought. Luckily she saw the disaster that it would be.

"Wait," she said from the top of the steps. "I'll go, but only because I want to see where you are sneaking off to at four in the morning. And to make sure you don't take my car like last time."

"Uh, o-kay," I said in surprise, silently kicking myself. "Aren't you still sick?"

"I feel like garbage," she said. "But I took an aspirin, and I'm still going."

"All right. Dress warmly. Wear tennis shoes."

I took Gram's keys on the hallway table and went to wait in the car. The night smelled fresh and clean, and the clear sky looked like an explosion of stars. But an owl hooted and some critter scurried along the side of the house, which was enough to get me in the car.

Hannah eventually came outside, scowling at me. "Why did you ask her to go?" I asked myself.

She slid in beside me. "Is it a bar?" she asked. "Do you seriously sneak out of our grandparents' house to booze it up?"

"At four in the morning? Are bars open that late?"

"Don't ask me. You're the drinker."

"Coming from the girl who's got about twelve liquor bottles on the floor of her car and just puked her guts out on Gram's front yard."

"You started it. It's not my fault you're a bad influence. But now that we know who your mother is, it sort of makes sense, doesn't it?"

I was backing out of the driveway, but I slammed the brakes. "Listen, I get it. You don't like me. I've done bad things. I don't even blame you. But if you're going to come with me, ease up on the attitude!"

"So, I'm getting under your skin?" she said with a smirk. "Good."

Against better judgment, I put the car in drive and headed to the beach. Hannah stayed quiet, staring out the window. Until we drove through downtown. "See?" she said. "That bar's open."

"I'm not going to a bar," I said.

"So you confine your drinking to cars?"

"I haven't really drank since I've been up here. I did one time, but I don't know, a friend helped me to see that I didn't really need it."

"Friend? That guy who showed up at the pool?"

"Derek is my friend, but I was talking about someone else."

"Who?"

"Pedro. You haven't met him, and I doubt you will."

"There's a Derek *and* a Pedro?" Hannah raised her eyebrows. "If I didn't hate you so much, I'd be impressed."

"There isn't anything to be impressed about. Pedro was the other housekeeper at the motel, and Derek and his daughter live at the motel."

"Oh okay, now I understand. They don't have a lot of options."

I bit my tongue. No use arguing with her.

I pulled up to the beach and parked the car. Hannah had already opened her door and had begun walking to the shore. I quickly followed.

At the shoreline, we both sat on the sand and stared out at the dark water and the light of the moon bouncing off of it. We didn't speak for a long time. Something about the lake was so peaceful. I yawned. Laying back against the sand, I stared up at the stars. But sleepiness took hold and before I knew it, I was out.

***

The vibrating in my pocket woke me up. I fumbled to find it, not quite ready to wake up. "Hello?" I croaked.

"Where are you?" Gram asked, panicked.

"At the beach. With Hannah."

I opened my eyes to see Hannah sound asleep beside me.

"Oh, thank God," Gram said. "By the way, I think your parents may be coming up."

"We'll be back in a little bit."

I turned the phone off and saw Hannah now watching me. "I guess our parents are coming up. Or, your parents."

Hannah sighed and rolled her eyes. "Let me guess. They expect us to get back right away."

"Feeling better?"

"A little. I still feel like death warmed over, and I have sand everywhere, but my head isn't pounding as badly."

I sat up and stretched. "Wow, it's past nine. And I didn't even get to take you to my spot."

"This wasn't it?"

"Nope. It's the lighthouse." I pointed out to it.

"You walk all the way to it?"

"Yeah, want to see?"

"I'm in major need of a shower. I have sand in my underwear." She paused, "Then again, I'm not about to drop everything and head back to our parents just because they tell us to. Come on, show me the lighthouse."

I didn't correct her when she said our parents. Truth to be told, I didn't know what else they were to me. With the whole Hannah situation, the Aunt Tessa situation had been put on the backburner. And I knew why. I wasn't ready to address it. Not yet. I couldn't wrap my brain around Mom and Dad not being my Mom and Dad.

Hannah and I took the walkway all the way up to the lighthouse. "Wow," she said, looking around.

"Just wait until you get up there. You go first. Lean and grab the ladder."

She didn't act scared or anything. Hannah reached for the ladder and climbed up without hesitation. "Impressive," I said.

I moved to climb the ladder while Hannah had already left me to walk the perimeter of the lighthouse. I still had a little cold knot of fear every time I climbed the ladder. But I made it.

"This is where you go," she said simply.

"Yep. See? It's not a bar."

She stared out across the horizon. For whatever reason, I wanted her to approve. We stayed there, both not speaking. Eventually, she said, "I never wanted to be a pastor's wife. That's what Dad and Mom were grooming me and Jake for. To be assistant pastors, then to take over for them." Hannah turned to me. "I'm not cut out to be a minister's wife. I don't even like people."

"You...love people. You have so many friends."

"Everyone annoys me. And it all feels so fake. I hated smiling all the time. And being so busy. There was always something going on. Some event or church special." She stared out at the water. "I never wanted it. I just wanted to be left alone."

"One thing I've learned while living up here, is how freeing it is to be away from...Mom."

"You were always Dad's favorite," she said, still not looking at me. "He was always telling me to include you, or to be nice. It was annoying. Mom in one ear ordering me to beat you, and Dad in the other ear telling me to be kind."

"Dad loves all of us. He fights for you too. He told me that himself after he…," I paused, realizing that she probably didn't know about Jake coming up here.

"What Dad do?"

"He punched Jake in the face," I admitted, not wanting to lie anymore.

"When was that?" Hannah's tone had shifted. She must have noticed my hesitation. "When was that, Macy?"

"Jake came up north to confront me," I said. "Pedro pushed him off Gram and Gramp's porch, and then the next morning, Dad went to his hotel room, knocked on the door and punched him in the face. So Jake went to the police to press charges."

"He came up here?" her face crumpled. "To be with you?"

"N…N…No…"

"Don't LIE to me! He broke up with me because he had feelings for you! He said that he had tried to deny them for months, but with you gone, he realized how much he wanted YOU! Not me!"

"Hannah, I told him no. I told him to get out of my life. I didn't want him up here."

"But you had already done the damage, Macy! Don't you get it?"

"I do! I get it, and I'm sorry. If I could take it back, I would."

"But you can't." Hannah's expression turned to stone. Only her quivering chin gave away her heartbreak. "You get to move up north, and of course, our grandparents are more than thrilled to have Tessa's daughter living with them. And you get to start fresh. With Derek. With Pedro. Whatever other guy you have up your sleeve. You just get to have everything, don't you?"

"I don't have everything," I said. But Hannah had already turned to go down the ladder. "Be careful!" I said, but she lithely jumped to the walkway without any pause. I clamored down, calling, "WAIT!" I was a bit slower than she had been. Once I got on the walkway, I moved fast. "Hannah, wait!" It wasn't until she had nearly reached the street that I caught up with her. "Will you wait a second?!" I yelled, grabbing her arm.

She whirled around. "Don't touch me."

"At least let me explain."

"Explain what?"

"I don't know. Let me drive you back to the house."

"No. I want nothing to do with you. I'm going to go to my car, and I'm going to leave. And we're never to see each other again. The end."

"Hannah, don't do this," I said, reaching for her again. "I did the right thing this time. Can't you see that Jake is bad? That you can do so much better than him?"

She ran a shaky hand through her tangled hair, only to stop. Then she began to sob.

"What kind of guy sneaks into a girl's room who happens to be his girlfriend's sister? And he took advantage of both of us. I was so socially awkward and jealous of you, and he *knew* that and played me. I'm not saying that I'm innocent because I know I'm not. But Hannah, you deserve better than him."

"But he was the one I wanted," she said through the tears.

"I know. I wish he was the type of man you deserve. Shoot, I wish I was the sister you deserve. Because you deserve good things. And I'm sorry I never noticed that before." Tears poured down her face, so I kept going. I said what needed to be said, "I have been so jealous of you, and I ruined our sisterhood and any hope of friendship we may ever have. And I'm going to have to live with that. But please don't mourn over that jerk. Because there are a billion guys who would treat you like a queen if given the chance."

She wiped at her eyes and blew out a breath. "I don't know what to do. I'm such a mess. I quit college to focus on the wedding, and now it's like our family is falling apart with Mom and Dad fighting. Over you, of course. But there's other things, like Dad wanting to step down and Mom not wanting him to. And I'm just like in the middle of everything with the rug pulled out from under me, and I feel like I can't even breathe."

"Start again," I said. "That's what I did up here. You're right. Coming up here was good for me. It's been hard work, but I've made friends, and I have a job, and I help Gram and Gramps at the church. It feels good. Maybe do the same thing."

Hannah stared at her hands. "Not everyone can do things as easily as you, Macy."

"What are you talking about? You're the most talented person I know."

"I have to *work* at singing and playing the piano. It comes naturally to you. You've never had to practice. I had to clunk on the piano over and over again to make it sound remotely close to your melodies."

"I never knew that." Memories of the two of us at the piano came flooding back. All I remembered was Mom telling me to stop hogging the piano and let Hannah have a turn.

"Let's get back. I need to shower, and so do you."

I sniffed my armpit. "I'm not that bad."

"Stop doing that. It's unladylike." Hannah headed to the car.

"You sound like Mom."

We slid into our seats, and I started the engine. I reversed the car, then put it in drive. Hannah didn't say a word until we were almost to the house. "Drop me off at my car."

"Oh, do you need to get your things?"

"No, I'm going to take off."

I pulled into the motel and stopped the car. "What about Mom and Dad coming up? They'll want to see you."

Hannah didn't respond at first. Instead, she rested her hand on the door handle. She didn't say anything at first. As if deciding on the words, she said, "Macy, I knew the moment I found your sketchbook that I shouldn't show Jake."

"You found it? Not Mom?"

"She asked me to set a laundry basket on your bed, and I snooped around. When I found all those drawings, I wanted to put you in your place once and for all. That didn't happen. I saw it in Jake's eyes when he saw the pics. He started looking at you differently. So, I know that he is largely responsible for this huge mess, and so am I. And I've got to deal with that." Without looking me in the eye, she added, "But you could have said no. He came to you, but from what he admitted to me, you didn't turn him away. I get that Jake played you. But he was *my* fiancé, and you did things with him that were meant for me."

"I know," I whispered, feeling the guilt weigh heavily on my shoulders. "With him, I felt wanted. Even though we had to hide. That was how I validated it. But there's no getting around it. I'm the villain in this story. And I don't know how to make it right."

"Time," she said simply. "I can't pretend it didn't happen. I'm not saying that I'll never forgive you. And I'm not saying that I don't love you. But I can't forget just yet. The emotions are still raw. You've got to give me time."

"Where are you going to go?"

"I've been staying at different hotels, driving around, spending all my savings. Trying to find myself." She opened the door. "And I'm sorry I spilled the beans about Aunt Tessa. It shouldn't have come from me."

"I'm glad someone finally told me, but I haven't even begun to process it yet. One dilemma at a time, you know? Look on the bright side. At least you don't have a wild, rebellious sister."

"Oh Macy," she said with a slight grin. "There's a lot about me you don't know. You've got nothing on me. The only difference between us is that I never got caught for any of my indiscretions."

She opened the door and got out, and then slipped into her car. I wanted to stop her. To convince her to stay. But I understood the need to get out from Mom. And to get away from me. I hoped against all hope that time would heal the wound I helped create.

Not knowing what else to do, I drove the car over to Gram and

Gramps, parked it, and hoped I could escape to my room without any drama.

"I'm going to go take a shower," I said to Gram, as I walked inside.

"Where's Hannah?"

"I don't know. She said she was going to go figure things out and find herself."

"She'll be fine," Gram said. "Hannah is a strong girl. She'll come back ready to take over the world."

I couldn't get into the hot water fast enough. Once it poured onto me, I realized that my insides felt numb. I couldn't think about the truth staring me in the face. My brain didn't want to go there. So, as I lathered and rinsed, I gave myself permission not to go there. Not today.

Chapter 26~

A Prince and a Peanut

Someone knocked on the bedroom door. "Sleeping," I called out. I turned over, threw the blanket over my head and started to doze again.

The door opened. "Hey peanut," Dad said.

"I'm trying to sleep," I said into the pillow, without looking over at him.

So, the family had arrived?

Knowing my nap was over, I stretched and sat up. "Hey," I said. An awkward pause hung between us. Needing to fill the silence, I said, "I was trying to take a nap because I didn't sleep real well last night."

"I bet," he said and came over to sit on the edge of the bed. "Gram said that you and Hannah spent some time together before she left."

A snarky remark nearly left my mouth, but instead, I answered, "I took her up to my spot. At the lighthouse."

"I've yet to go up there with you."

"You should sometime. It's pretty sweet."

Our conversation paused again.

This time Dad interrupted the silence. "So, I guess the cat's out of the bag."

"I guess so." I began to fiddle with the edge of the blanket.

"I'm sure you have questions."

"I haven't had time to really think about things," I said. "With Hannah stopping up here, I've been distracted. There is one question that keeps replaying in my head."

"What is it?"

"Why keep it a secret?"

"You weren't supposed to ever find out. We made a pact, your mom and me."

"She's not my mother."

"Yes, she is, as much as I'm your father."

"But has she ever loved me?"

"Of course."

"Then where is she? Why wouldn't you two come and talk with me together?"

"She doesn't know I'm upstairs. The last I checked, she was with your grandmother planning your birthday present. But she does love you."

"Not the way she's loved her three children," I said with sadness. But now that the words were out, my feelings flowed like a river. "And please don't justify her actions. Love doesn't make someone question their worth. Love isn't critical ALL the time. It doesn't constantly look for the bad. It doesn't gloat, and it certainly doesn't favor one child over another. And what bothers me even more than knowing that she did those things—because to her I was never her child—was that you allowed her to behave that way because in your eyes I was nothing more than Aunt Tessa's abandoned baby."

"When you have children of your own, you'll understand. You'll understand that you can give and give and give and still be imperfect. Your Mom and I have been tough on you and the others. Being pastor's kids is a difficult position to be in, and we probably made it more difficult. But we tried. We worked hard to have a nice home where all of your needs were met. But we're not perfect, Macy. And that has nothing to do with the other kids or Tessa or anything. I'm not going to say you don't have a right to feel that way because yes, I can see why you think that about your mother. She can be critical, but trust me, she's that way with the whole lot of us. Why do you think Hannah took off? I'd venture it had something to do with Meg. I told your mother to lay off, but she is just that way." Dad paused, then added, "For what it's worth, I'm sorry you found out this way. We were going to take it to the grave with us because we never wanted you to feel different."

"I've felt different my whole life."

"Because you are different. And not because we have this family secret about you, but you're different, Macy, in so many beautiful ways. You hold more talent in one finger than most people do in their whole bodies! Have you ever thought that might have something to do with it?"

"Then why didn't you let me pursue it? I never sang or played the piano at church. And you wouldn't let me apply for art school!"

"You chose not to sing and play, but it wasn't because of us. We wanted you to get up front, but you were content sitting in the back with a sketchbook. How many times did Hannah ask you to sing a duet? You told her no so many times that she stopped asking. And we didn't say no to art school. We said go to a community college for a couple years and get all your general classes out of the way. College is expensive, but doing community college would save us some money." Dad exhaled slowly, then walked to the door. "We did the best we could. We love you, peanut. If I could change certain things, I would."

"Me too," I admitted. "I would have never drawn all those sketches of Jake. Why would I even do that? It sort of started a lot of problems."

"Our family needs to come together and sit down and talk. Having a therapist for all of us will help communication without yelling or anger."

"What will the church say?"

"Part of being a good pastor is being a good husband and a good father. That means that my family needs to heal. Therapy shouldn't be so stigmatized."

"I agree," I said.

"So, you'd be willing to some group sessions?"

I swallowed hard. Going to therapy meant opening up old wounds. It meant confronting Mom on past hurts. But how long was I willing to hold on to resentment? "Yes, I'll go."

Dad outstretched his arms. I got up from the bed and went to him, allowing him to wrap his arms around me.

"By the way," I said, still hugging him. "If Aunt Tessa's my biological mother, who's my father?"

"That's a good question. I don't know for sure. The guy she went to California with didn't stick around long. But the courts might know. By the way, I forgot that I came up here because you have a visitor waiting for you on the porch. It's that guy with the tattoos and piercings."

"Pedro!" I flew past my father and down the stairs. As soon as I stepped outside and saw him, I threw my arms around him. "You're okay!"

He wrapped his arms around me and hugged me just as tight. At that moment I didn't care about his past. I felt safe. Pedro said that he could see me, really see me, and I realized now how much that meant. "No more running," he said in my ear.

"Really? Is everything good?"

Neither of us had let go. But when Pedro didn't answer, I pulled away. "Is everything all right now?"

"Let's not talk about me first. Let's talk about your birthday. I know it's early yet, but I got you something."

I knew there was something he wasn't saying, but I also knew him enough to know that he'd tell me when he was ready. "You didn't have to get me anything."

"Of course I did." He reached down and handed me a gift wrapped in newspaper. "I didn't have birthday wrapping paper. So I improvised."

"It's great. Very creative. Want me to wait until next week? I think they're planning on some birthday bash."

Pedro shook his head slightly. I saw the sadness in his eyes. "I want you to open it now."

"Don't tell me you have to go," I whispered. "My life is crazy right now. I need you here."

"Just for a while."

"How long?"

"I have to witness for my mother. She's being tried in Chicago, where we were at. Stolen goods and a list of other things. This whole time she's made me believe those men were after me when really she was the one on the run." He rubbed the back of his neck. "It doesn't look too good for her, but I have to try."

"You're going back to Chicago?" My heart fell at my feet.

"Only until I go to court and testify." He took my hand. "I promise I'll come back. If you're still here, we will do that date."

"What about your brothers?"

"They were taken into custody." I watched as Pedro blinked back tears. I hugged him again. "Once I get a place, they'll come back to me. This is only temporary."

"Then that's what we'll do," I said, looking into his eyes. "We'll have hope."

He nodded. "I'm going to get them back. I promised them. But first, I've got to do what I can to save my mom. If that's even possible."

"Are the boys going to be in foster care up here or down in Chicago?"

"Up here. We've built a life here, and I want to come back."

We made eye contact, and I felt the butterflies explode inside me. "I'll count down the days."

"Open your present."

I tore off the newspaper and smiled at the new sketchbook. "Perfect."

"It's the right kind? Your grandfather helped me order it off of the internet. There were a lot to choose from."

"This is perfect," I repeated. "Thank you." Without talking myself out of it, I leaned in and kissed him.

Someone coughed at the bottom of the porch steps. I reluctantly released Pedro, only to see Derek watching us. "Didn't mean to interrupt," he said, not looking at me. "Good to see you, man."

"You too," Pedro said.

Neither said anything more.

"I'm only here for Lillian…" Derek said.

Mom's SUV pulled into the driveway at that moment. Adrianne and Lillian stepped out of the vehicle and clamored toward me.

"We're planning the best party!" Adrianne gushed.

"There's going to be cake and presents, and we get to swim at the pool!" Lillian jumped up and down.

"Where's my hug?" Derek teased his daughter. "You run straight to Macy, huh?"

Lillian released her hold around my waist and ran to Derek. "Daddy, can we go to Macy's party?"

Dad stepped outside, nodded at Pedro, then stepped off the porch to help Mom and Gram with the groceries.

As Mom approached, she paused and smiled at Derek and

Pedro. "Hello, you two must be Macy's friends."

"Nice to meet you," Pedro said, reaching for the two grocery bags. "Allow me to help you."

With Mom's arms free, she walked up the steps and over to me. "Hello," she said, giving me a brief hug. "How's everything?"

There was a lot of meaning behind the question, but after my conversation with Dad, I decided that it was time to take the high road. "It's good. Everything's good."

"I'm glad," she said quietly. "And…Hannah? You saw her?"

"Yes, and she's okay. I think she just needed time to get over everything that happened."

Derek interrupted us to say good-bye. Pedro stepped back outside after dropping off the groceries and mentioned he needed to go, too.

"Your friends are here," Mom said, and gave Pedro her thousand-watt smile. "We can talk later."

Pedro and I watched as she and Adrianne went inside, then waiting until Dad and Lucas carried the rest of the groceries in. Gram was the last to go in, and she winked at both of us. "Behave," she teased.

Pedro took my hand. "I wish I could stay a little longer, but I've got to get going. I'm taking the bus down to Illinois."

"How'd you get here?" I then noticed the bike. "You rode the bike here from the police station?"

"It's not that far," Pedro laughed. "But I'm not going to lie. I'm looking forward to the day I have a better set of wheels."

"I'm going to miss you," I admitted. "Cleaning those motel

rooms is not going to be the same."

"I'll be here before you know it. I promise. For you. For my brothers."

We hugged again, and this time the contact felt different. As if we knew it'd be a long time before we saw each other. I breathed him in and let out a shaky breath. "You helped me so much," I whispered. "I always felt that with you I had someone who truly understood me."

Pedro let me go and quickly moved toward the steps. "My new phone number in Chicago is inside the sketchbook."

I nodded, not ready for him to leave, but knowing he couldn't stay.

"Whatever happens," he paused, briefly glanced at the front door, then back to me, "I'm here for you. Even if I'm in another state."

I nodded again, a wave of turmoil nearly taking me under. At that moment, it all hit. All of it. The pain I caused. Hannah's departure. The family secret. All the years of isolation and loneliness. And now Pedro would be gone. I tried to keep it together, but all of the emotion came flooding out at once. I covered my face and tried to contain it, but Pedro was back up the steps in seconds.

"What is it?" he whispered, rubbing my arms and shoulders.

But how could I unload on him? He had enough to deal with. He had his own demons to face, and his own family secrets to bear. "I'm going to miss you," I choked out. I wiped at the tears and took a shaky breath.

"I'm a phone call away, and as soon as I can, I'll be back here, giving you grief."

I watched him leave, then sank onto the top porch step. I leaned my head against the railing and focused on keeping my emotions in check. The last thing I needed was questions, and the minute I walked through that front door, there'd be questions. I could hear the conversation and laughter in the kitchen. Good. Glad someone was happy.

Suddenly the screen door opened, and Adrianne came out.

"We wrapped your presents!" Adrianne said, squeezing my neck.

"You did?" I said, forcing myself to act like she felt. "Are they big or little?"

"There's FIVE presents!"

"I already got a present," I said, showing her the new sketchbook.

"Is Pedro your boyfriend?" Adrianne asked, giggling.

My heart tugged, "Maybe."

"He's not a prince," Adrianne said. "And Lillian told me that we're all going to marry princes."

"He's a prince to me," I said.

Chapter 27~

Best Birthday Surprise

I entered the dining room and saw the enormous pancakes. "Gram, you outdid yourself!"

"It wasn't me," Gram said, kissing my cheek.

"Happy birthday!" Adrianne jumped up from her chair. "Mom made us chocolate chip pancakes with whipped cream."

"Mom?" I asked in disbelief.

"Yes, everyone deserves carbs on their birthday." Mom came into the dining room from the kitchen and set a plate of bacon on the table. "And bacon, of course."

"Wow," was all I could say.

"Happy birthday," Mom said, before busying herself with something on the stove. "Eat," she ordered. "Before it gets cold."

I looked over at Gram who shrugged her shoulders. "Let's eat some carbs and bacon," she said. "Come on, birthday girl. It's not every day we get chocolate chip pancakes."

The dining room quickly filled with Dad and Lucas giving me a birthday bear hug. Gramps couldn't leave the motel office for breakfast, but left me a note on the table.

The last couple days had been relatively drama-free. Mom had yet to broach the subject of adoption with me, but I did notice Dad and her spending more time together, and she seemed to really focus on not being critical.

"So, what do you think of the lighthouse?" I asked Dad. Just yesterday the family went to the beach. Dad wouldn't let Adrianne or Lucas climb to the ledge of the lighthouse, but it had been a warm, fun, relaxing day.

The only person missing was Hannah.

I overheard Mom talking to her on the phone, which helped relieve some of Mom's anxiety about the situation. But it still felt as if this one piece to the puzzle was missing.

"It's dangerous," Dad said. "I nearly had a heart attack."

"It's not that dangerous," I said, biting into a warm pancake. "Plus, it's a great view."

"Yes, it is a great view. But it's dangerous."

Mom sat down at the table. "Hannah just texted me. She said to tell you, 'Happy birthday.'"

"Thank you," I said, and kept eating. The whole situation felt so awkward, but I didn't know what else to do.

"When should Macy open her presents?" Adrianne asked.

"Tonight at the party," Dad answered.

Lucas looked up from his tablet. "Do I have to stay long tonight? I'm supposed to go online with some friends." To me, he added, "No offense."

"None taken."

There was a knock at the front door.

"Come in," Gram said from the table.

The screen door opened, and Lillian came running into the dining room. "It's your BIRTHDAY!" she yelled, running over and throwing her arms around my neck.

"Sorry to interrupt," Derek said. "But she would not stop pestering me."

"Want some pancakes?" I asked them, but Lillian had already pulled up a chair while Gram filled her plate.

Derek glanced over in my direction. "Can I borrow you for a second?"

"Sure," I said, finishing the last bite of bacon. "Thanks for breakfast."

Mom was playing a game on her phone, but she waved at me.

I followed Derek outside. "What's up?"

"How's it going?" he asked. "Everyone seems to be trying too hard to act like everything's fine."

"I know, right?" I leaned my head against the railing. "Thanks for giving me a reprieve."

"I only wanted to show you something. Are you up for a little road trip?"

"Road trip? Sure. How far are we going?"

"Into town."

"Wow, we're such rebels." We headed to Derek's car.

"Have you heard from your boyfriend?" Derek teased.

"Yes, I have. And we're doing great, thank you. Speaking of other people, what did the Garrett's decide to do, anyway?"

"They want to work out some kind of custody agreement. Like a couple weeks in the summer, maybe a weekend a month, I don't know. They did decide to avoid court. I think what you said got to them. Thanks for that."

"I think it's great for both of you. Lillian will enjoy getting to know her grandparents. And they'll enjoy her." I thought of Gram and Gramps, and how much they had enjoyed me being up here.

Derek started the car and pulled out of the motel's parking lot. "It's okay to grieve," he said quietly. "I learned that the hard way. Just make sure to come up for air. And I'm talking about you too."

"Grief? I'm not too sure I'm grieving. Guilt? Yes. Anger and hurt. Definitely. Confusion? For sure."

"And more than any of that, you're grieving. You're grieving the loss of your past because from this point forward, everything changes. You're grieving your sister and your parents. But you don't have to let all of these emotions overtake you. Trust me, I hurt Lillian because I couldn't get a handle on my feelings."

"My Dad mentioned therapy. I think that's a good idea. For all of us."

"I've watched you and your family. And yeah, there's a lot of family drama. *A lot.* But there is a lot of love. Your Dad cherishes you. It's so easy to see. I was helping him set up for the party, and he kept asking your grandfather, 'Are you sure she'll forgive me...I don't know what to do...' And Adrianne? She and Lillian look at you the same way. With absolute adoration. And your Gram and Gramps?" he smiled at the term of endearment. "They would do anything for you. Anything. I wish I had that kind of family growing up."

"And my mother? Meg?"

"Let it go. She was tough and mean, but you've risen above it. No harm, no foul. Be the better person. All that jazz."

"No harm, no foul? Our family's kind of a mess right now, and she's got a lot of the blame. Not that she'd own it."

"Don't wait for an apology that may never come. You turned out all right, all things considered. What didn't kill you, made you stronger. Give yourself permission to move on. Once everyone sees you're at peace, then everyone else will be too."

"Look at you, Mr. Motivational Speaker."

"I don't know about that. I basically rehashed a lot of what you told me...and a lot of Rocky Balboa."

We drove into town, neither one of us speaking. I appreciated that Derek didn't feel the need to the fill the silence. I had a lot going through my mind, but what Derek said made sense. I didn't have to let the craziness rule my emotions. I could rise above and be better than that. "I think what bothers me the most is that I want to fix things," I said. "I broke some things too. I'm more upset about that than I am about the adoption."

"Your sister was pretty upset. But time has a way of taking care of things."

"Yeah, she said to give her time. She also told me she didn't hate me, so there's that."

"See? Progress."

I laughed.

"We're nearly there," Derek said, maneuvering down a side street. "I still need to give you your birthday present. And I'd like to do it before your wild and crazy pool party."

"Are you mocking me?" I asked.

He pulled me up to a stoplight. "Well, let's just say, I'm not expecting some huge, sordid, alcohol-loaded, up-all-night, wake-up-next-to-someone-I-don't-know kind of party. I mean, you are, after all, a church girl."

"Then stay home, big shot. You don't have to come to my lame party."

"I never said what kind of party I liked."

"Yeah, well, what kind of party does Derek Blackstone like?"

"Your 19th birthday party. I heard it'll be great fun."

"You're just saying that to be nice."

"Sort of." He pulled into a parking spot in the middle of downtown. "Come on, I want to show you your present."

"Do I get any hints?"

"Um, I hope you don't get mad at me."

"Really? That's the hint?"

"Yes." Still, he wiggled his eyebrows at me in excitement, and I could see that he really wanted me to like it.

"See that four-storied building, right at the end of Third Street? That's where I'm a security guard on the weekends."

"Cool," I said, as we headed in that direction. "Is that where we're going?"

"Not quite," he said. "Every time I head to work, I pass by this one shop. Really high-brow, so I've never took notice before. But after meeting you, I started to check it out, and well, you'll see."

Okay, he had definitely peeked my interest.

"This is the ritzy area of town," he said, as we crossed the street.

I noticed the art and design gallery immediately. The excitement started to bubble, but I didn't say anything in case he was taking me somewhere else. When he led me inside, I let out a sigh of pleasure. "Oh my," I breathed, taking in the various art pieces on the walls and in display cases.

We were immediately welcomed with a brochure and ushered in.

"This is fantastic," I whispered. "Thank you."

"I can't believe how busy it is," he said. "But that's great. More people to see your work and vote on it."

I had been staring at a lush garden piece created with watercolor when his words hit me. "What?"

But he wasn't looking at me, he was searching the gallery. "Follow me for a sec. I promise we'll come back to the others."

Derek led me to a display case where a soft light illuminated the framed picture I had sketched of Derek, Lillian, and Lindsey. Several people stood around it, studying it and talking amongst themselves. Derek watched me now, trying to gauge my response.

But all I could do was stare at the vivid picture, reviewing the lines, remembering the contours of the facial features. Whoever displayed the picture knew how to light it appropriately because its soft touch added a beautiful, hazy glow. Like a scene from a not-so-distant memory. Hanging from the frame was the small tag with artist name and title. *Macy Elmsworth: Gone but Not Forgotten.* Underneath the title was one, underlined word: *finalist.*

"Say something," he whispered. "I had to come up with a title because I didn't want you to know I had entered the picture into the contest. That's about as creative as I get. Did I do good? Bad? I can't tell from your facial expression."

I opened my mouth to say something, only to close it. My artwork stood in front of me, displayed in a trendy art gallery. Patrons of the gallery were admiring my work. I overheard the compliments. I saw some writing notes onto small pads of paper. And my heart nearly burst right there. From pride, from surprise, from joy. For so long, I had hidden my work. It had been more a source of venting and shame. I breathed in a shaky breath, realizing that tears were sliding down my face.

"I know," an older woman said, approaching me. "This piece does it to me too."

"This is her piece," Derek said proudly. "This is Macy Elmsworth."

The woman's eyes widened. "Really? You're so young!"

"Nineteen, today," Derek said.

"Do you have any formal training?"

"No," I said, trying to pull myself together.

"Astounding." She studied my art work, even leaning forward to squint at it. "Your attention to detail in the minute features is so precise."

"Thank you," I said, noticing Derek beam with pleasure. I couldn't think of a time when I saw Derek this happy, and it made my heart swell about a hundred times bigger than it already was.

"Do you have any other completed pieces?"

"Books of them," I finally said, wiping at my eyes. "None that are worthy of this gallery."

"I might disagree," she said. "Especially if they're of this caliber. Bring a few in and let me assess them. I've already had two of my regulars ask if this artist has a collection. Whether or not you win the contest, it'd be nice to have a few on display. We always like to feature local talent."

I nodded. "It would be an honor for you to look at them."

"Well, good luck with this one. Our finalists this year are all so magnificent."

Once she had slipped through the crowd, I turned and moved toward the door. It was so overwhelming, everything I was feeling, that I started to feel claustrophobic. Outside, I didn't stop. I just kept walking. My stomach was a pit of nerves. My work! On display! And it didn't look like anyone hated it.

I found a small city garden that connected one street to another. I stopped in there, leaning against a tree, trying to catch my breath. I noticed Derek approach me tentatively. As if still unsure of my reaction. "You did that?" I asked him. "Turned my work in to the gallery?"

"The idea actually came from Pedro. We were talking one day about how good your artwork was. One night at work I was bored, so I started flipping through the newspaper. There was an article with that woman in it. I forget her name, but the one you were just talking to. The article was about this annual art contest, and how impressed she was with all the entries. The next day, you left the framed picture in the motel room. I took your drawing to her and asked if I could enter that piece in the competition. She said that the deadline was weeks ago, but then she studied your sketch and commented on how good it was. She said if I paid the late registration fee that she'd put it in with the others. Yesterday, I saw it displayed in the front window of the gallery!"

"There was a registration fee?"

"I took care of it."

"How?"

"Don't worry about it. I knew you'd be in the running for the grand prize. You're *that* good."

"It's the nicest thing anyone has ever done," I said. "I don't know how to thank you."

"If you win the grand prize, you can take me and Lillian out to dinner. How's that sound?"

I laughed through the few tears that had escaped. "Sure. Depending on how much the prize money is, it might just be McDonald's."

"Considering the grand prize is ten thousand dollars, I'm going to expect a nicer place than McDonald's. Maybe Red Lobster."

"Shut up!" I said in shock. "Ten thousand?"

Derek grinned like a kid on Christmas. "That's what I've been wanting to tell you. It has been so hard keeping this secret for the last couple days! There are seven finalists, all of whom receive a hundred dollars, then the top three art pieces will be paid three thousand, five thousand, and then ten thousand!"

"Shut up!" I laughed. "As it stands, I'm already going to get a hundred bucks!"

"Plus she wants to look at more or your work. That sounds promising."

"Yes, it does." I couldn't stop smiling.

"So, I did good?"

"You did very good," I said. "I can't wait to tell Pedro."

"I know you're going to go on and do amazing things," he said. "No one should hold you back."

"No one is going to hold me back," I promised. "But what you did for me today, I'm...I'm overwhelmed."

"You have helped me and Lillian so much. I can never repay you. It takes a lot to restore an angry, grieving man's faith," Derek stopped and looked down at his feet. "But somehow you and your grandparents did just that."

"Are you saying...?" I remembered our conversation about telling Lillian about heaven. Derek had been so angry.

"I don't know what I'm saying, other than thank you. Oh, and if Pedro ever hurts you, let me know. I'll take care of it." Derek made a fist and wagged it.

I could see he was teasing, so I rolled my eyes. "Easy, killer."

Derek laughed. "The party will be starting in a couple hours. We should probably get going."

"We can get going *after* we vote." Then, with my head held high, I walked back to the art gallery.

Best birthday surprise ever.

Chapter 28~

When It's All Said and Done

I stared at my reflection in the mirror and seriously reconsidered wearing the swimsuit. "Girl, you have let yourself go," I said, throwing my deep purple cover over the pretty polka-dotted swimsuit. I had ordered it online, but this had been the first time I tried it on. I zipped up the cover, then opted for a short jean skirt to cover my legs. There. Everything had been effectively camouflaged.

Someone knocked on the door.

"It's open."

Gram stepped inside the bedroom. "Don't you look cute?"

"Fat. I feel and look fat. I think I've put on ten pounds. Look at my butt!"

"Nonsense. You're still too skinny. You don't think I see you checking your wrists, but I do."

"It's a hard habit to break," I said.

"You barely eat breakfast or lunch when you're working, and you're working nearly every day."

"The cover and skirt at least hide my large derriere. Is everybody down at the pool?"

"Yes, and the kids are going crazy, waiting for you. Your father had the idea that you were to be the first one in the pool since it's your birthday. So, let's get down there, so you can jump in."

"How warm's the water?"

"Not at all. It's cold."

"What about the heater?"

"It's swimmable, but to this woman's old bones, it's cold."

"Oh, just let the kids swim then."

"You know that at some point tonight you're going to be shoved into that pool. You know it. Everyone knows it. Might as well jump in and get it over with."

I gave a half-laugh. "Good thing it's warm outside."

"Yes, the sun is warm, and the barbeque is smelling really good. All we need now is the birthday girl."

I hugged Gram. "Thanks for everything. I know I kind of made your life crazy these last couple months."

"I wouldn't have had it any other way."

I took in a breath then nodded. "All right, let's go have a party."

The two of us headed down the stairs and out the front door.

"Did Derek tell you what he did?"

"No. What he do?"

"He turned my drawing into the art gallery downtown, and I'm actually being showcased as a finalist!"

Gram stopped walking, her mouth open in surprise. "Macy May, that's incredible!"

"What's incredible?" Dad said, coming over to us. He smelled like charcoal, smoke and barbeque sauce.

"Macy's art is being showcased at the art gallery," Gram said, grinning from ear to ear. "Does that mean you're famous?"

"Not really, but if I win first place, I'll win ten thousand dollars!"

Dad wrapped his arms around me in a bear hug and let out a whoop. "That IS incredible!"

"We have to tell everyone," Gram said, pulling at me.

"Yeah, because I need as many people as I can to get over there tomorrow and vote."

"It's as good as done," Dad said. "I'll fill buses."

As soon as we made it to the pool, the kids started cheering. "It's about time!" Lucas said. "Jump in the water before I throw you in!"

"Okay, okay, hold your horses," I teased. Adrianne and Lillian pulled at me, one at each arm. I waved at Derek who was helping Gramps at the grill. He smiled but turned his attention to the grill.

My cell phone buzzed, and I saw Pedro's name flash on the screen. We decided that I would forever call him Pedro. "Hey there," I said.

"How's the birthday girl? Did Derek show you his present?"

"Yes! And he said you helped him make it happen! Thank you."

"He did all the work. I was supposed to help, but things got busy. He told me it's a finalist. You'll win. I know it."

"Thanks for the vote of confidence."

"Attention, everyone!" Dad said in his booming preacher voice.

I waved at Lorette and her family. Even Mom was taking pictures of everyone. "I've got to go," I said to Pedro. "The party's starting."

"Okay, I just wanted to wish you a happy birthday. I'm coming up next weekend to visit my brothers. Maybe we could try for that date?"

"That's a definite yes," I said.

Dad took my phone. "Pedro, she'll call you back." Then to the small crowd, he announced, "Our very own Macy is a finalist at the art gallery here in town!"

The dozen or so people clapped and cheered, and I felt my face redden from embarrassment and pride.

"This is indeed a tremendous birthday for our girl." Dad wrapped his one arm around me. "You'll always be our girl," he said in my ear, kissing my forehead.

"Stop it, Dad," I said, blinking back the tears. "I vowed not to get choked up at the party. Let's just have a good time."

"Sounds like a plan."

The pool gate opened and slammed shut. "Congratulations."

I turned to see Hannah standing at the gate, looking just as she had when she left. She still wore the same clothes from last week, and her hair and make-up were disheveled. But at least she didn't have a bottle of alcohol in her hand. Not that any of that mattered. "You came back."

"Hannah," Dad breathed a sigh of relief.

Mom squealed from around the pool. I could hear her heels clicking toward us.

Hannah put up her hand to Mom and Dad, her eyes completely on me.

"I'm glad you could make it," I said, trying to smile.

She didn't say anything at first. Then taking a deep breath, she stepped closer to me. "I forgot to say happy birthday, so I thought I should come back…If you'd let me…"

"Of course," I said. "It's not complete without you. It never has been."

Hannah walked until we stood facing each other. She smelled faintly of stale liquor, but her eyes were crystal clear. "I drove around for a couple days. But I couldn't rest because I knew I had to tell you something. It's been eating at me, and I knew that I wouldn't be able to move on with my life if I didn't tell you what you needed to hear."

A part of me didn't want to hear it. Not another bombshell. Not at my birthday party. But Hannah was here. In front of me. And what I wanted more than anything—even that art prize—was to fix this. To fix the broken pieces of our relationship. "Tell me."

"I…I…I have always been jealous of you, Macy. Always. But now. Driving around, I realized that I think I miss you more than I'm mad. I mean, I'm still so angry, but I feel like with Jake out of the picture, I don't know, like I can have my sister back."

Hearing her say the words "my sister" had me choked up. "I have missed you for years," I admitted.

"One more thing," she said with a shaky voice. "You are my sister. Always have been. That's not about to change now. For better or worse, we're stuck with each other. I shouldn't have said what I said. It wasn't my secret to tell."

"You know, I thought it'd upset me more than it has, but if

anything, it made sense. And really, what can I do about it now? Aunt Tessa is gone, and I'm here. As a friend told me earlier today, 'No harm, no foul.'"

"Then you're telling me that my vicious plan of revenge didn't really work anyway?" Hannah acted slighted.

"You telling me you hated me was enough revenge, trust me. Not that I blame you. I'd hate me, too."

"I might have strong, negative feelings, and I'm still trying to deal with a lot of what happened, but I don't want to be alone right now. Maybe tomorrow. But for tonight, I wanted to be with people who love me. So, I can go drive around and lick my wounds, or I can come to where my family's at and not be alone."

"I'm glad you came back," I said. "The party would have been missing an important piece."

Suddenly, Hannah threw her arms around my neck and began to cry. "Oh Macy, I've been so ugly to you."

I hugged her back fiercely. This. This was what I wanted. The tears came, and I let them flow. "I'll live with regrets the rest of my life."

"There's enough regrets to go around for the both of us," she said in my ear.

When we finally released, I said, "You have given me the one present I wanted more than anything else."

"Please," she said, laughing and wiping her face. "Not even that art contest?"

"Not even that art contest compares to knowing that my sister is here. With me."

Cheers erupted as Adrianne and Lucas and Mom and Dad threw their arms around Hannah. I watched, my heart full. "Hey," Hannah said. "We're missing one."

Dad grabbed me and pulled me to the pile-up. "Come now, family. I think Macy needs her birthday dunking."

"Oh no!" I said, trying to escape.

But Dad had picked me up by the waist and Hannah and Lucas had grabbed hold of my legs. My screams only fueled the cheers from the onlookers. At this point it looked like every motel guest had come outside to join the party.

"On the count of three!" Hannah shouted.

"ONE!" They began to swing me. "TWO! THREE!"

I flew in the air, gave one last scream, and sank into the cool waters.

And as the waters baptized me, I realized that I had never been happier.

The End

Coming Soon! Book Two

Broken: Hannah's Story

CPSIA information can be obtained
at www.ICGtesting.com
Printed in the USA
LVHW092335070420
652594LV00003B/1043